Stolen Hearts

Leslie Ann

Editing by: Nina Fiegl

Cover Design by: Echo at Wildheart Graphics

Formatting by: Leslie Ann via Atticus

Stolen Hearts

Playlist

Music plays a huge roll in my writing.
These songs helped me bring Stolen Hearts to life.
I hope you enjoy the tunes.

Paradise—Bazzi
Love at First Sight—Kylie Minogue
Falling—Trevor Daniel
Alone Together—Dan + Shay
Butterflies—Kacey Musgraves
All To Myself—Dan + Shay
King Of My Heart—Taylor Swift
Angel Baby—Troy Sivan
Electric Love—BØRNS
Say You Love Me—Jessie Ware
Only Love Can Hurt Like This—Paloma Faith
Bad Timing—Rhys Lewis
This is What Losing Someone Feels Like—JVKE
I Should Have Married You—Old Dominion
Still—Niall Horan
Charlie Be Quiet—Charlie Puth
Still—Luke Combs

Love Again—Dua Lipa
All 4 Nothing—Lauv
Love Me Low—Ai Bendr
Death Bed (Coffee For Your Head)—Powfu, Beabadoobee
Something in the Orange—Zach Bryan
Be Good to Her—BEXAR
Always You—Ava Bryant
All Love Everything—Aloe Blacc
Me—Forest Black
I Can't Wait to Meet You—Niko Moon, Anna Moon

You can find the full Spotify Playlist on my website at ...
www.lawritesromance.com

Dedication

To the girl who always had big dreams.
You made this one come true.

Part One

There are unknown forces in the universe that work
in tandem to bring two people together.
Even if only for a moment.

CHAPTER ONE

Rylann

How could I let this happen?

Thump, thump, thump.

Hitting my forehead against the front door of my bungalow smarts. Maybe if I hit my head hard enough, the door can at the least knock some sense into me. I can't believe I let Sam freaking break up with me.

Again.

My chest tightens, and I know without a doubt I need a drink and my bestie. Reaching into my pocket, I look for my cell and come up empty. I groan. *Crap. It's still in my bedroom where I left it.*

"Can't something go my way?" I knock my head against the door once more, knocking my tears to the floor in large drops.

Turning my sorry butt around, I grab the tissue box off the coffee table, wipe my face, and blow my nose before trudging back to my room. I pick up my cell, plop myself on my bed, and call Scarlett.

The line only rings once before she answers. "Hey, hoochie! I'm almost done packing. Look out, Hawaii. Here we come!"

I pull the phone away as she shouts in my ear.

The last thing I want to do is ruin her good mood—this is supposed to be a happy occasion. We are leaving in a few hours for her destination wedding, for crying out loud.

I never should have opened my door last night. *What was I thinking?*

"Hey." I choke back a sob, pinching my eyes tight. Hot tears that haven't stopped since Sam walked out the door leak out the corners of my eyes.

Scarlett's worried voice comes through the line. "What's wrong? Why are you crying?"

Of course, she knows I'm crying. She doesn't miss a thing; she knows me better than anyone. As she should. We've been best friends since ten years old. We do everything together and always will. She's my ride-or-die. My sister from another mister.

And, boy, is she going to be pissed at me.

Swallowing down the lump in my throat, I answer, "I fucked up, Scar."

"Is this a 'bring a bottle of tequila' or 'a shovel' type of situation? I can be ready in five either way."

I bark out a laugh, my tears forgotten. "First one. Sam broke up with me." I sniffle.

"I know."

"Again."

"Again? What the fuck do you mean *again*?!" she yells into the phone.

"He came over last night. Showed up at my door with these sad, puppy dog eyes. And ..." I can't even finish the sentence. My gut churns. I'm so fucking stupid. Him and those damn baby blues of his sucked me in again. I'm more mad at myself than him at this point.

Fucking Sam.

Scarlett gasps. "Did you sleep with him? Ry, please tell me you didn't fucking sleep with him."

"Umm ... Kind of?"

"Kind of? Are you serious right now?" She groans at me in frustration. "What the fuck were you thinking, Rice Cakes?"

"I wasn't."

"Well, that's fucking obvious," she grouses.

"You said 'fuck'. A lot," I tease, making us both chuckle.

Unlike me, Scarlett doesn't swear. She refuses to have the sailor-level potty mouth her grandmother had. Grams, as everyone called her, loved to let the F-bombs fly.

"Kind of necessary right now."

"Ain't that the fucking truth?" I sigh.

How did I let myself get back to this place?

After wallowing for a respectable two weeks, I had finally pushed Sam and the breakup out of my head. I was geared up and ready to go and have fun on vacation with my friend for her wedding.

Now, I'm ... confused. Hurt? Pissed?

"Can we meet at the airport bar, like, now? I need alcohol. Stat."

I look at my watch. Our flight is in four hours, giving us plenty of time to get a cocktail—or, in my case, two—before our flight. "Think you and Levi can leave early and meet me there? I need you." My voice cracks.

"Of course, Ry. You know I'm here for you. Always," she says supportively, her voice soft.

I'm lucky to have her in my life. I hate that it took losing her parents for me to gain a sister.

"Short Stack! Get your cute ass out here!" Scarlett's fiancé, Levi, yells from the background. He recently moved to Portland to live with her, and he's still learning her crazy.

Their whirlwind romance began seven months ago when they met in Mexico. We were on a girls' vacation and he was on a guys' trip. They've been inseparable ever since. I dream about someday having what they do.

Levi shouts something else that I can't make out. I have no doubt he's either complaining about how much stuff she's trying to pack or trying to get into her pants. It's fifty-fifty at this point. I hope it's about the packing. He doesn't yet know the chaos that is traveling with Scarlett Collins like I do. It's only hilarious since I don't have to deal with her insane amounts of luggage anymore. That's his problem now.

"Ignore him. I'm ready to go. Levi is trying to convince me I need less stuff." Her voice lowers. "Like that's gonna happen. But now, I have a real excuse to ... Please hold." Her voice cuts out, leaving me on hold. "Okay, sorry about that. We'll leave soon." She huffs in frustration. Levi shouts again in the background. "Deal with it. I'm getting married. I need it all!" I can't help but chuckle at how stubborn she's being, which she doesn't miss. "Hush, you."

"Sorry. Try not to be too hard on Lee." Levi is honestly one of the coolest guys I've ever met and has become a fast friend as well.

"Don't defend him. He needs to learn. Text me when you get there." She pauses for a second. "It's gonna be okay, Rice Cakes."

"I know."

"Love you, babes."

"Love you too." I end the call. With a deep breath, I drag myself out of bed and finish getting ready.

I'm too sad and annoyed with myself to put on anything other than a white tee and my favorite neon-yellow leggings that make my ass look good—a much-needed self-esteem booster. Bringing up the Rideshare app on my phone, I order a car and pack the last of my stuff.

Fifteen minutes later, I'm in the car headed to the airport. I stare out the window and replay the last few weeks in my head.

I loved Sam before he ripped my heart in two. Our initial breakup felt like it had come out of left field. To make it worse, he did it on the same day I needed to meet Scarlett at the bridal shop for our final dress fittings. When I showed up to her appointment heartbroken, she tried on her dress as quickly as possible, rushed the seamstress, and then walked me to the first open bar. She proceeded to ply me with shots of tequila until I told her everything. Levi had to pick up our drunk asses and take us home.

Merely thinking about that day makes my gut churn. Not only for the heartache I endured but also for the hangover that followed it. I don't think I've ever drank that much before. It's possible I puked up a boot.

I shudder at the memory.

I've replayed our relationship over and over, and I still can't figure out what changed. Nothing makes sense. There wasn't any specific event I can pinpoint that would have Sam breaking up with me. I thought we were on the same page.

My mind drifts back to the day I met Sam.

I literally bumped into him on my way out the door from a business meeting. Scarlett, who is also my business partner, and I had just been hired by another company in the same building he worked in. Walking into Sam brought me down to earth and put the cherry on top of my happy sundae.

He was handsome, taking the blame for stumbling into me when we both knew it had been completely my fault, but he was charming as hell. His whole presence screamed smart, sophisticated, and safe. Deep in my bones, I sensed he was the kind of man that would go out of his way to take care of me, and when he smiled at me, it reached his eyes and made them crinkle at the edges. Those crinkles absolutely did it for me. The more, the sexier the man in my opinion. He looked a little older, which was a plus. *I like my men that way.* He had me smitten on the spot.

"We're here, miss," the driver says, pulling me out of the past. He's already parked along the curb at the airport.

I grab my purse and reach for my wallet.

"Need help with your bag?"

"Nah, I'm good. Thanks, though. You can just pop the trunk."

Before sliding out of the car, I hand the driver a tip and throw my carry-on over my shoulder. Grabbing my suitcase, I slam the trunk shut and head into the airport to check in for my fight.

After making it through security, I park myself on a stool at the bar and text Scarlett.

Rylann: Here

When she doesn't text back, I order a margarita. If I know Scarlett and Levi, I have a while to wait; those two love birds can't keep their hands off each other and have no self-control. Scarlett is late for everything these days. It used to bug me, but I've gotten over it. At the end of the day, I'm super happy my friend has found her person.

She's lost a lot in her life. First her grandfather, then her parents, and last year her grandmother. Levi is perfect for her. He makes her incredibly happy, and she deserves it. He fits into our world and has quickly become one of my best friends as well.

I thought Sam was perfect too.

At first he was, but looking back, all the signs were there. He didn't like to talk about the future, and when Scarlett got engaged, he started to pull back and put up walls between us. When he came at me with the *I think we should break up* talk, I shouldn't have been shocked, but I was, and his reasons took me even more by surprise. It was obvious he'd practiced his, "*It's not you, it's me.*"

Such a crock of shit.

Something tells me there is more to the story, but since he's the one that decided to break us up instead of talking to me, I'm not going to fight him. At least, not anymore. I'm done.

Taking another sip of my margarita, I focus on the mix of sweet and sour, and not the bitter taste of my breakup lingering in my mouth.

CHAPTER TWO

Rylann

I'm lost in thought and only halfway through my drink when Scarlett surprises me by plopping down in the seat next to me at the bar.

Wow.

She totally skipped the panty-dropping to be here for me. She's such a good friend.

"Mind if I sit here, pretty lady?" Freaking Scar is using her dudebro voice.

She loves playing this game because it makes me laugh. It started in college when we used to work at the coffee shop close to campus and all the frat bros would hit on us. We had fun ragging on those douche canoes.

I shake my head to try and hide my smile. "God, you're such an idiot."

"Come on, play along," she whines.

"Okay, fine." Clearing my throat, I channel my sexy voice. "No, I don't mind at all, handsome. As long as you are interested in getting a little tipsy with me."

"I can do more than get a little tipsy with you, pretty lady. I'm looking to get you drunk and in my bed. I can do this thing with my tongue—"

"No! Do not finish that line," I warn, throwing my hand over her mouth. Lately, my bestie's jokes have been a little bit pervy. It's all the lovin' she's been getting from Levi.

She licks my hand. I yank it away, wiping it on her shirt. "Fuck, you're gross sometimes."

She blows me a kiss and hugs me. "I'm not gross. I just like a little dirty talk every now and then."

"Ugh. Lee has really corrupted you, Scarface." Yes, Scarface.

When we were thirteen, we snuck out of her room at her grandma's house to watch the old Al Pacino movie. We had to see what all the hype was about. To say we weren't impressed is putting it mildly. The best thing to come out of that movie was Scarlett's nickname. It goes with the feisty little personality she reserves for me, and now Levi.

She used to be shy when we were younger. Between Grams and me, we coaxed the crazy out of her. She never showed that side in public, always keeping parts of herself hidden away—until Levi.

Since they've been in a relationship, she's really blossomed. He has given her the support she needs to grow into a strong, confident, and completely filter-free woman. Before him, not one of the guys she dated looked beyond her beautiful face to appreciate how smart and sassy she is. I owe Levi for making my sister so happy and a little more funny. I could, however, do without some of the perviness.

Actually, no. I wouldn't change a thing ... But she doesn't need to know that piece of info.

With that thought, I know I can't let my breakup with Sam affect my mood. Scarlett's destination wedding has to be perfect. I'd rather suck it up—and suck down a gallon of margaritas—to get through this trip for her. Fake it till you make it and all that.

"So, how are we doing this? The usual?" With a knowing look, she calls over the bartender.

He's an older gentleman with light brown hair that's graying at his temples and a muscular body, and is extremely good-looking. I'd guess he's in his early forties, and he makes it look good. "What can I get you ladies?"

Damn, even his voice is sexy as fuck. Rich and smooth like the drink he no doubt pours.

"We will have four shots of Patrón with lime, a margarita with no salt for me, and a fresh margarita with salt for this fine and spicy Latina." Scarlett thumbs my way and flashes him a beaming white smile, all while shimming her shoulders.

"Coming right up." He gives her a wink, and his returning smile is a little too friendly. Fortunately, he slaps the bar and turns away to get our drink order, leaving us alone.

I shove her shoulder and she laughs, sticking her tongue out at me. She knows I want to give her shit for her antics—I won't. It's not her fault another one bites the dust. She is that beautiful, with the tall, blonde, blue-eyed thing she's got going on. I swear, she could be Margot Robbie's double.

The bartender places our shots and fresh margaritas in front of us and walks away without lingering. A flirt but not a perv. What a relief. I'd hate for Levi to come over here, wanting to kick the hot bartender's ass for flirting with his girl.

We pick up our shots at the same time and Scarlett turns to me, waiting for me to toast first. I clear my throat and the toast from *The Wedding Date* tumbles out of me.

We clink glasses and simultaneously throw back our shots before biting into the limes. *No salt-licking required, folks. That stuff's for amateurs.* The tang of the lime has me puckering as the liquor burns my throat, before hitting my stomach, warming it up.

"Really? *The Wedding Date*?" she deadpans, her side eye on point.

"What can I say? It seemed appropriate." Lies. I had no idea what to say. I shrug her off. "I feel like Kate right now. Totally dumped and in need of a date to this wedding I've been forced to attend in Hawaii. Think I could find a replacement?" Putting my hands to my eyes like fake binoculars, I pretend to look around the busy airport.

"The bartender's a hottie. I'm sure he'd be interested." She slips her finger through the circle she's made with her other hand, making me laugh.

"Doubtful. Besides, I'm pretty sure he's into the whole beach Barbie vibe you got going right now." I huff, waving my hand over her whole area. She's wearing a tropical print maxi dress and flip-flops, looking beach-ready, not for flying on an airplane for six hours.

"Asshole," she mutters into her drink, pretending to hate when I call her Barbie though I know she secretly loves it. Case in point, the smile lilting her lips. "Also, I hate to tell you this ... but we don't have time to hire you a sexual surrogate on such short notice," she quips, making me chuckle. "Cheers, sis."

Scarlett clinks her glass to mine. Then, using her other hand, she lifts my margarita up, bringing the straw to my lips and forcing me to take a deep drink. The cool liquid hits my tongue, and I close my eyes in reverence.

What the hell am I gonna do now?

Instead of thinking, I finish my margarita and start the second that's sitting next to the empty shot glasses. I'm surprised Scarlett has let me drink in peace instead of forcing me to spill my guts.

On my second sigh, she's had enough. "Normally, I would say I can wait all day, but we only have about another hour before we board our flight."

"Ugh, don't remind me," I grumble.

"It's going to be fine. We are going to have so much fun. Now, start talking."

I nurse the sip of my second margarita.

She sits there with her arms crossed over her chest, her leg over her knee, watching me. Waiting. When I slurp the last dregs of my drink, she grabs it and slams it on the bar top.

"Okay, you had your two drinks. The time has come for yee to spill it, ya wench."

"Wow. One drink in, and you're already switching to the pirate accent?" She hits me with that side eye again. Time to rip off the Band-Aid. "Shit. Fine!" I growl and proceed to tell her everything.

How Sam showed up at my door with those sad puppy eyes, telling me how much he missed me. How he kissed me stupid, making me forget all about hurting me. How we ended up in bed, and I woke up to him breaking up with me all over again, using the same excuses as before.

Scarlett sits there, sipping her drink, unnervingly quiet. That's not like her, and it's freaking me out. "Just say it."

"Say what? For once, I don't have anything to say." Figures. I have no words either. "I'm with you on this. Sam's keeping something from you. Before your break up—the first one—you two seemed ... happy. Smitten kittens."

"Yup," I lament, popping my P. I drop my head onto my crossed arms on the bar, feeling like I did something wrong.

"You know what?" Scarlett blurts out, making me jump.

The bartender turns his attention our way and cocks his perfectly groomed eyebrow in question. I wave him off, and he returns to his job of wiping down the counter.

Scarlett sits beside me, tapping her chin with her index finger. Her eyes are a little glossy, and it looks like she's thinking harder than usual. I gotta make sure she paces herself—her tequila tolerance is not as high as she thinks it is.

"Let's make a deal. A promise. A new mission. Whatever you want to call it." She turns to me with a devious smile on her face.

Oh, no.

"O-kay ... Elaborate, please?" My palms start to sweat at the way she's smiling at me.

"I think you need to put Sam and this whole fuck-tacular breakup behind you," she says excitedly.

"Oh my god, you said 'fuck' again." I grin, interrupting her train of thought. I'm pretty sure I know where this is going, and I'm out.

"Shut up, assface. As I was saying … Sam let you go. You're a single woman. A *hot* single woman, and I think you need to mingle. Forget sucky Sammy. His loss, babes. It's time to make someone else's lips the last ones to touch yours, to wipe the memory of last night away."

"Scar, I don't like where you're going with this."

"I'm not saying you need to find the love of your life like I did with Levi. All I'm trying to say is be open. Get your flirt on. Throw caution to the wind." She winks at me, purring and giving me an air cat claw. "A little smooch with a hottie could be good for you. Or a fling?" She bounces up and down in her chair, excited by her idea. "Yes. A fling. You should totally sex up some hot guy. Get flung, Ry!" she yells, throwing her arms out wide and drawing the attention of everyone at the bar.

I adamantly shake my head at her. But …

Something twinges in my gut, and suddenly her crazy idea isn't the worst one she's had. Twisting my head side to side, I mull it over. My ego could definitely use a boost after being dumped. *Twice.*

"You know what? Fuck it! Not the whole fling thing, but to at least get my flirt on. Maybe dancing with a hot stranger."

"Yes! Operation Kiss New Lips is on." Scarlett blows kisses.

"No! No kissing. Knock it off." I shove her, making her fall off the stool.

"Fine. Spoilsport." She climbs back in her seat and rolls her eyes at me.

"Here's to Hawaii," I amend, lifting my second shot in the air.

"You can drink to Hawaii while I drink to you getting royally flung in paradise," she quips.

Now, it's my turn to roll my eyes at her.

We tap our glasses and gulp them down. When I'm done, the sparkle in Scarlett's eye has me feeling uneasy. Like she knows something I don't. I shake it off. Maybe two shots weren't such a good idea.

Levi is going to kill me.

"Where's Levi?" I'm only just realizing he's been MIA the entire time we've been at the bar drinking. He's usually attached at her hip, turning all the ladies' heads with his sandy blond hair, blue eyes, and killer smile. Barbie and her Ken, folks. They even make me swoon.

"At the gate. He said he would come and get us when they started boarding. Give us some girl time, ya know?"

"Good man. A total keeper," I confirm, slamming my hand on the bar.

Maybe the tequila is starting to get to me too.

"Yeah, he is. Hella sexy too." She gets a dreamy, faraway look in her eyes.

Aw, shit. This is going to be one long flight, leading up to the longest week of my life as the third wheel in their relationship. I cringe, thinking about all the PDA I'm about to witness.

Fuck my life.

"One more before the flight?" I'm pushing her limit, but I need to get a little more drunk if I'm going to endure her and Levi for the next eight hours.

"You know it! Mr. Bartender, one more margarita for the road, please!" She raises her hand and waves at the bartender, who flashes us a huge smile and starts making us another round of drinks.

Just like that, I feel a hundred pounds lighter. While getting sauced before our flight might not be the best idea, I'll let future Rylann deal with the fallout.

Right now, this bitch needs a drink.

CHAPTER THREE

Rylann

"Ugh, I really hate you, Rylann 'Bitch Face' Price." Scarlett groans.

She's hunched over the front desk, waiting for the concierge to check us into our suites. I'm pretty sure she has a hangover after all the shots and margaritas at the airport, *and* the tequila sunrises on the plane.

Poor Levi is going to have his hands full unless she takes a nap and he gets some food in her. She can get pretty "hangry" when she's drunk or hungover.

"Not my middle name, Scarlett 'Can't Hold Her Liquor' Collins," I tease.

The concierge bites her lips, trying to hide her smile as she finishes checking us in. She hands over the keys for the honeymoon suite to Levi and a key to me for a suite on the tenth floor. It's way too big for one.

Stupid Sam.

No. I will not think about him.

I've never been to Hawaii before, and I refuse to let myself be sad during what is to be the best time of my best friend's life. I have hoped and prayed to the universe for her to meet someone awesome and worthy of her. Scarlett deserves to be happy.

I deserve to be happy and have fun.

You know what? Fuck it.

Maybe I *will* let someone else put their lips on mine.

Oh, yeah. I've had *way* too much to drink today.

Shaking my head out of my thoughts, I grab my key card and my bags. Next stop: bath and nap before our early dinner.

Then, we'll see about some possible lip action.

I roll my eyes at myself. I blame Scarlett for putting this idea in my head.

"Good one, Ry." Levi chuckles. "Come on, Short Stack. Let's get you a snack and a nap and some vitamin D," he half-ass whispers into Scarlett's ear.

"Dude, Lee. I can hear you. Everyone can hear you. You're not as quiet as you think."

Levi busts up laughing and shrugs. "Sorry, Ry, but you know as well as I do that the D, some food, and a nap will in fact make her better and ready for dinner."

"TMI, Levi. T.M.I." Giving him a faux glare while trying to hide my smile, I shove his shoulder as we all head to the elevator.

He's right, though. She is more fun and amenable when she's getting some. Ever since they met, these two jackrabbits have been all over each other, and my friend has never been happier.

But I'm sure as heck not about to admit that to him. I've had the displeasure of walking in on them in way too many compromising positions. This is a little bit of payback for me. A rebalancing of the scales, if you will.

"My head is killing me." Scarlett groans.

I burst out laughing, and she swats at me but misses, and Levi laughs. She swats at me again, hitting her mark.

"Sorry, Scar. Please don't hurt me." I wince at the swat she landed on my arm like a mean old cat with claws. I'm surprised she didn't hiss at me too. "I shouldn't have let you have those last few drinks on the plane. But it's not my fault that tequila is like water to my Mexican side. You can blame Rita for my high tolerance."

Rita—short for Margarita—is my momma and the name of her favorite drink. And mine. She likes to tease me and call me her mini-me. I hate it, even though she's not wrong. I look exactly like her. She's short, big-breasted, curvy, with dark brown hair and eyes to match. Not a trace of my dad's dirty blond hair or light brown eyes here. I smile to myself, thinking about my mom.

"Yeah, yeah. Totally Momma Rita's fault. Are we there yet, babe?"

Levi pushes the button, calling the elevator.

"Almost there, baby." He kisses the crown of her head, and my heart warms.

"What's the plan again? Rest and then—"

I'm in the middle of trying to distract Scarlett from her still half-drunk groaning and complaining when a voice so warm and deep cuts me off.

"Hey there, love birds!"

The husky sound settles low in my belly, making it sizzle like a shot of reposado tequila. My breath escapes me in a whoosh, and all the hairs on my arm and neck stand on end.

Oh, my goddess in heaven.

That voice makes my insides lurch in all the right ways. Trying to catch a glimpse of the owner of the voice that sends shivers down my spine, I turn around and stop dead in my tracks.

A tall man approaches Scarlett and Levi, rocking a pair of aviator sunglasses and a megawatt, panty-melting smile. Seriously, this giant of a man has the most beautiful smile I've ever seen. He has perfectly straight teeth and plump lips. Lips worth kissing.

I stand frozen and watch as he gives each of my friends a hug. My eyes scan his broad back and fall to his ass, which I shamelessly stare at.

Yum. I wonder what that bubble butt looks like without clothes blocking my view.

What the hell is wrong with me? I push those thoughts away, wondering who this guy is. If only I could see his whole face. Although, what I can see, I definitely like.

He towers over my 5'4" stature and has an inch or two on Levi, with muscles galore. Not those gross, meathead kinds of muscles either. This man has the deliciously sexy kind that come with playing sports. His waist is trim, and he has strong thick thighs. The muscle shirt he's wearing accentuates his broad shoulders and chest, bulging biceps, and gives a peek-a-boo shot of his side abs. His brown hair with caramel highlights looks like it's been regularly kissed by the sun. My fingers itch to run through those thick locks.

"Jay, my man! Good to see you." Levi and the hottie do that bro-hug handshake.

The lust fog currently impeding the neurons in my brain from functioning lifts, and everything clicks into place.

The Adonis is Jace. Levi's childhood best friend.

I've heard a lot about him, but we've yet to meet. He was MIA when Scarlett and I met Levi in Mexico. I did have the pleasure of meeting Jace's younger brothers, and let me tell you, those guys are a good time and ridiculously good-looking.

My curiosity piqued, I give Jace another casual once-over, looking for the resemblance, which I find in the hair and the build of his body. The clincher would be the eyes; if I'm not mistaken, the Miller boys each have very distinctly colored hazel eyes.

"Did you check in?" His sexy voice pulls me from my ogling.

"Yeah. We are on our way to the room. I need to get Short Stack here upstairs for a nap before tonight's dinner and shenanigans." Levi kisses the top of Scarlett's head.

"What happened, Little S?" Jace's gravelly voice skates across my skin like warm syrup.

"She had too much to drink on the plane," Levi explains for Scarlett.

"Great minds think alike." Jace lifts his shades onto his head and points two fingers to his temple, swishing them back and forth between himself and Scarlett like they're on the same wavelength.

"You're already sauced this early in the day too?" Levi's forehead crinkles as he tilts it to the side, staring at his friend like a long math problem he's trying to solve. Levi does that a lot. Must be a lawyer thing.

"Maybe a little." Jace shrugs, gesturing with his thumb and forefinger to indicate a small amount. The gesture makes him look cute in an embarrassed, boyish kind of way.

"Alina isn't here?"

"Nope. We broke up. For good this time."

"How are you feeling about it?" Levi asks with genuine concern in his voice.

If I wasn't so intrigued with the tall stranger in front of me, I'd have excused myself a long time ago. This conversation is too personal for me to be listening in on. Having just ended a relationship myself, talking about it isn't something I'd want to do in the middle of a hotel.

"Fine. Actually, I'm great." Jace smiles, and even though I'm still staring at the back of his head, I can tell that his smile reaches his eyes. "I brought Eli with me, and we are ready to celebrate."

"That's great. We have a lot of stuff planned for everyone to do together before the big day," Levi tells him.

"Cool. So, what did you do to make the wifey-to-be here want to drink away her problems? Need me to kick his ass, Little S?"

"Oh, no. Not Levi." Scarlett smarts, pointing an accusing finger at me, an evil glint in her eye. "She did it. She got me drunk. Let me introduce you to the little she-devil herself. Jay, this is my bestie, Rylann. Ry, this is Jace."

It happens in slow motion. Jace looks over his shoulder, and our eyes lock. I'm trapped in a tractor beam, being sucked into light by two of the dreamiest hazel eyes imaginable. Mossy green, like lush evergreen trees. Like home. The color around his pupils is the lightest brown in existence. The golden color greets me like warm honey, the depths of which tempt me to swim in forever.

Holy fuckballs.

Jace is hot as hell.

I think my panties melted right off because I'm feeling uncomfortably wet between my legs. I should feel bad for objectifying him, but he looks like he walked straight off the cover of a magazine—the women's version of the swimsuit edition.

What have I gotten myself into here?

"Nice to meet you, Rylann. I've heard a lot about you." Jace offers me his huge hand.

I glance at it, and I swear my heart skips a beat. I'm scared to touch this gorgeous man. If one look can throw me off balance, what will touching him do?

It doesn't help that he's so freaking handsome, it's a little intimidating.

My eyes find his, and an inexplicable energy bounces between us. It's exhilarating and soothing at the same time. Like he's the part of me I never knew I was missing.

My eyes widen at the direction my thoughts are going.

Get a hold of yourself, woman.

Jace must read the reaction on my face because the corners of his lips pull up in a cheeky little grin.

What would you expect from a lawyer? They are practiced in reading facial expressions and body language.

In an instant, I pull myself together. Shoulders back and huge flirty grin in place, I put my small hand in his and give it a shake.

Big mistake.

When our skin touches, an electrical shock rushes from my palm, up my arm, and straight to my chest. I can't stop the small gasp that passes my lips as my heart leaps behind my ribs.

What the hell was that, and why is my body reacting to this stranger?

"Hi," I say, all breathy. For fucks sake, could I sound more obvious about his effect on me? I clear my throat and gather my wits. "It's nice to finally meet Levi's better half."

Releasing his hand, I find myself missing his warmth immediately. The world comes fading back with the laughs my joke solicits. The rich, crackling heat in the air swirls and reduces to a simmer.

"If he's my better half, then you, my dear, are Scarlett's worse half," Levi accuses, pointing at me playfully.

"She-devil. I told you that already," Scarlett teases, blowing me a kiss.

I return her kiss with a dimple-popping grin. We exchange a look because we both know something Levi doesn't.

While he is right to some degree, Scarlett is also my worst half. I can't fully explain it, but we somehow switch back and forth. When I'm being a she-devil, she's being an angel, and vice versa. It works for us. If I wasn't her personal little she-devil sometimes, she would overthink everything, and then maybe things like Mexico wouldn't have played out the way it did. Levi still has a lot to learn about our little family.

"So, what you're saying is that the she-devil made you do it? She got you drunk?" Jace's eyes roam over my body, from head to toe, the wake of his golden flecks setting my skin on fire.

"Drunk as a skank! Wait …"

Jace tips his head back and laughs at Scarlett's mix-up. He laughs with his entire body, loud and carefree, and it is downright sexy. The rich sound makes my insides sizzle.

Damn! I wonder what else he can make sizzle.

Uh oh, I think I'm in trouble.

This is Levi's best friend, for crying out loud. I can't go there; talk about don't shit where you eat. Plus, we both recently got out of relationships. This has red flags all over it. Rebounds are bad. Right?

Right.

I admire Jace one more time before looking away to avoid getting caught. He is way too good-looking. For my own good, I need to get out of here before he laughs again. I don't think my head would win the battle it's having with my raging hormones.

"And that's our cue. Come on, Short Stack. Let's get some rest before the wedding weekend commences." *Levi for the save!*

"Later, you two." Levi wraps an arm around Scarlett's waist and grabs the luggage cart, forgetting all about me.

"See you, Jace. Bye, Ry. I'll text you later, my MOH-fo biotch," she says over her shoulder with a sly finger wave. Then she hops onto the elevator with Levi, leaving me behind.

"Mo-fo?" Jace turns back to me with an arch in his brow, making me chuckle.

"Not mo-fo, like ... you know ..." I look around and lower my voice. "Mother fucker. MOH is for maid of honor. I wish I could blame the tequila for that cheesy joke, but that's all Scarlett."

"Yeah, she's great." He rolls back onto his heels and runs a hand through his hair. "You know, it feels like I know you when I really don't. Scarlett did nothing but talk about you when she came to L.A. with Levi for a visit. It really is great to finally meet you."

"Thanks. I feel the same way. There isn't a story that Levi doesn't start with, 'So, Jace and I were yada yada yada.'"

We both laugh, the awkward tension between us loosening.

"Makes sense. Mine sound the same," he says with a smile.

Gah. His smile is breathtaking, with the way it reaches all the way up to his eyes. Oh, goddess of the universe, help me. He has little crinkles in the corner of his eyes because, you know, the guy smiles a lot.

My kryptonite.

The urge to rub my thumbs over his lips before kissing them falls over me. I really need to get out of here. Stat.

He runs his long thick fingers through his hair again, and my eyes follow the action. I can't help staring at the corded biceps and forearms ripple and flex.

"It was nice to meet you," I croak out. *Girl, pick up your jaw.*

"Same. I'll see you at dinner then?" His lips quirk up at the end. He knows I'm going to see him again.

I bite my lip with a smile and nod. "Yup, see you at dinner."

I hope I'm not reading this wrong, but I think he might be feeling this too.

Grabbing the handle of my suitcase, I walk away. The hair on the back of my neck prickles like I'm being watched. A part of me wants him to be watching me walk away.

Don't look back. Be cool. I'm so not cool.

I glance over my shoulder and, sure enough, Jace is staring at my ass. The grin on my face can't be contained. He lifts those glowing hazel eyes to mine, and I swear he almost blushes. Almost. If the proud smirk on his face is anything to go by, he is not in the least bit ashamed at the obvious check-out of my curvy butt. He definitely enjoyed the view.

Offering him a coquettish smile, I walk away.

I also make sure to add some more sway into my hips. What's a little harmless flirting with an Adonis going to do?

Maybe Hawaii is going to be fun after all.

CHAPTER FOUR

Jace

Rylann totally busted me checking out her ass in those skin-tight neon yellow yoga pants she had on.

I *should* feel bad for staring but ... I don't.

Not in the least bit. That is one ass worth staring at. In fact, it should be worshiped.

She is nothing like I pictured her to be in my head. Based on Scarlett's stories, I was expecting to meet someone who looked more like her. I was wrong—Rylann is Scarlett's total opposite. In all the best ways. She's a bombshell.

When our eyes locked, only minutes ago, I felt the earth shift under my feet. Her hesitancy in shaking my hand made me suspicious as to whether she felt it too. The smug smile that lifted my lips had her straightening her spine and flashing me a smile so bright, it did something inside my chest. A scorching heat washed over me that simultaneously soothed my soul and boiled my blood. The zap of electricity that buzzed between us surprised the hell out of me. I wasn't expecting the shock that traveled up my arm and sent my heart into overdrive when our hands touched.

I rub my fist over my chest, still feeling my heart pound like a jackhammer below.

What the fuck was that?

Did she feel it too? She had to, with the way she got tripped up and her words caught in her throat. Thinking about the way her lips parted in surprise puts a smile on my face. I've never experienced a visceral reaction like that with another woman. Not even with my ex, and we were together for years.

I wonder if that's how Levi felt meeting Scarlett.

I push that thought away.

I can't stop thinking about Rylann as I head towards the pool. How her dark brown hair framed her face, draping over her shoulders and falling down her back. How her big brown eyes pulled me into their coffee-colored depths, almost drowning me.

Mental images of me pulling her hair as I make her mine flood my brain.

Where did that come from?

I don't even know this woman. And yet, after all I've heard about her, I feel like I've known her forever.

Shaking my head and my wayward thoughts away, I head towards Eli at the pool. We got in early and planned on a swim and drinks before getting ready for dinner. He left before me while I took a quick work call. Catching Levi in the lobby was pure luck. Now, all I can think about is Rylann.

For some unknown reason, I look forward to seeing her later. Not only does my best friend think the world of her, but there is something about her that has me intrigued. Her looks alone have me hypnotized.

Without a doubt, she's fucking gorgeous. She comes up to about my chest—and that puts her at 5'5" at best—has caramel skin, the cutest heart-shaped lips perfect for kissing, and curves in all the right places.

"Jace, dude, over here!" Eli shouts, waving me over to where he is lying in a lounge chair, a beer in his hand. Pulling his glasses down, he gives me a once-over. "What took you so long?" he asks, handing me a beer.

He is determined to get me drunk all week to help keep my mind off Alina. I don't think he has anything to worry about anymore. She's not who I'm thinking about now.

Excitement courses through my veins. Getting to know Rylann is all I want to do now that I've met her.

Collapsing into the sun chair next to him, I lay back and pull my shades down over my eyes. Before I answer, I take a long swig of the cold beer and run my hand through my hair. It's a habit I tend to do often. It's my tell and the reason I always lose at poker with my shithead brothers.

"Ran into Levi and Scarlett in the lobby," I explain.

"Cool. I take it they just got here?"

"Yeah. They were headed up to their room." Clearing my throat, I take another drag of my beer. "Apparently, she got wasted on the flight here and needs a nap. I also, uh, got to meet Scarlett's friend, Rylann."

His head snaps in my direction. "Oh, did you now? She's fucking hot. Am I right?" He hums like he's thinking about her.

Rylann is hot, but for some reason, I don't like the idea of him thinking about her like that. Like he wants her. A possessive feeling I've never experienced washes over me, and I suddenly want to punch my brother in the dick.

I take a deep breath, forcing that urge down. What is wrong with me? I know my brothers already met Rylann during their trip to Mexico for my little brother Cameron's birthday. A trip I should have been on but ended up bailing at the last minute. Alina and I were on the rocks at the time, and she was against a guys' trip. She suggested we go away together to focus on our relationship. It only ended up pushing us further apart until we finally called it quits a couple of weeks ago.

"She's something, that's for sure."

"Something? Yeah, no. That chick is smokin' hot and funny. I'd make a play for her if I could. Too bad she has a boyfriend."

Boyfriend? I'm pretty sure she was by herself. Still, I backhand Eli in the chest right as he is about to take a drink of his beer, making it spill across his chest instead.

"Dude. No making moves on Scarlett's friend. We are here to relax and have fun. Keep it in your pants for once." I have to force the growl out of my voice.

He wipes his chest with his towel. "Hmm, interesting. Why can't I make a move, huh?"

"Because you shouldn't shit where you eat. And Levi will kill you."

"Levi or you?" Eli scratches his short beard and looks at me again. He sees right through me. "You like her!"

"Like her? I don't even know her."

He shrugs, sipping his beer. "Well, she's awesome. And fucking hot. What's not to like?"

I glare at him through my sunglasses, and he raises both hands in surrender. Jealousy tears through me at the thought of my brother liking her, hitting on her, and touching her. There is no way in hell I will let that happen. Over my dead body.

"Got it. No moves on Rylann," he says with a huge shit-eating grin.

I know what he's doing. He's stirring the damn pot.

I need to change the subject. If I keep thinking about how hot she is, I might give the people at the pool a view of my dick. It's bad enough that I feel like I've been sporting a semi since I laid my eyes on her.

"Time for a swim," I mumble and jump into the pool. I need to cool off my dick and the irrational feelings of jealousy coursing through me.

Instead, all I think about is Rylann. The way she looked at me. The bolt of electricity that shot through me when her hand was in mine. The way we stared into each other's eyes after as if nothing else existed except for us.

There is no way she has a boyfriend. If what Levi says is true, she never would have looked at me the way she did. Not if there was someone waiting for her back home.

That smirk on her lips when she busted me staring at her ass and the extra sway she put into her hips as she walked away?

Definitely no boyfriend. That show was all for me.

CHAPTER FIVE

Rylann

Scarface: Hey, biotch! Are you ready or what?

Rice Cakes: Finishing my makeup. How are you feeling?

Scarface: Better now. No thanks to you my little **Devil emoji**

Rice Cakes: Don't blame me for your weak-assness. Learn how to hold your liquor.

Scarface: **Middle finger emoji**

Rice Cakes: LOL **Laughing tears emoji**

Scarface: Tell me ... What do you think of Jace? Hot, right?

Rice Cakes: **Eye roll emoji** He's good-looking.

Scarface: *You liar! I know you, Ry. You think he's hot. Plus, I saw you eye-fuck him. I think you two will have fun hanging out. **Wink emoji***

Rice Cakes: Fine! He's hot. And I did NOT eye-fuck him. I was shocked. You never said how hot he was.

Scarface: *Well, you did meet his brothers, and they are hotties. FYI, NO ONE is hotter than Levi.*

Rice Cakes: Yeah yeah, you love your man. I get it.

Scarface: *Well, I saw something between you. I think you should have some fun with him.*

Rice Cakes: I just broke up with Sam. I'm not going to have any fun with him.

Scarface: *You dirty girl. I didn't mean that kind of fun. I meant fun like hanging out while we party. But I see where your mind's at **Eggplant emoji* **Water emoji***

Rice Cakes: Fuck off! Are we meeting up or what? And you better not do that thing you do at dinner.

Scarface: **GASP* holds hand to chest*
Scarface: *Whatever do you mean?*

Rice Cakes: You know what I'm talking about. When you try to act all cute and flirt for me.
Rice Cakes: Or when you can't help but make everything a sexual innuendo. Worst wing woman moves, BTW.

Scarface: *I would NEVER (fingers crossed behind my back)*

Rice Cakes: You suck. Fine. Do whatever. My room or yours?

Scarface: Yours. I'm ready. I'll be down in a minute. Levi is going to head down and meet up with everyone else.

Rice Cakes: **thumbs up emoji**

I head back into the bathroom, apply my mascara, and take one last look in the mirror. I run my hands down the summer dress I chose. It falls mid-thigh and is my favorite shade of pale yellow. With the warm weather, I should be comfortable through both dinner and cocktails at the karaoke lounge.

A knock on the door sounds as I slide on my nude wedges. Grabbing my clutch, I double-check that I have my cards and phone on me. Opening the door, I find my bestie in a matching baby blue summer dress.

"Girl, great minds think alike." I wave my hands over my dress *à la Deal or No Deal* model.

"Don't we always?" She is full-on glowing as she grabs my hand and pulls me out of the room. "So, tell me. Are you ready to meet the parents?"

"Scar, these are your soon-to-be in-laws, not mine."

She links her arms through mine as we walk down the hallway. "I know. I want you to love them as much as I do. I want them to love you too."

"I mean, who doesn't love me?" I joke as we step onto the arriving elevator. "As for me loving them … They made Levi, and he's pretty awesome. How can I not love him? I just wish Mom and Dad could have made it too."

My parents are like Scarlett's surrogate parents; they love her like a daughter. Unfortunately, my dad, Ryan, had knee surgery a couple of weeks ago. He plays basketball every Sunday with his friends and ended up hurting himself during one of his pick-up games. Although Dad is recovering, he's not well enough to fly to Hawaii for the wedding.

"Me too. I'm glad we booked a wonderful photographer for the wedding day and will have plenty of pictures to show them."

The elevator dings our arrival to the lobby. Scarlett and I head towards the hotel's restaurant but are stopped in the lobby by the delicious deep voice and laugh. It hits my ears and sends butterflies soaring in my stomach.

Jace.

I'm anxious to see him. I know I shouldn't be—I'm not ready to get into something with someone else. No matter how hot he is. I especially can't have that with Levi's best friend.

Yeah. Keep telling yourself that.

"There she is!" Levi's mom rushes over and scoops Scarlett up into a giant hug. "I am so excited for this weekend."

"Me too, Julie!" Scarlett squeals, hugging her back. They break apart, still smiling. "Ugh, where are my manners? Julie, this is Rylann. My best friend and maid of honor."

"It's wonderful to meet you, Rylann. Scarlett has told us so much about you," Julie greets me. Attempting to shake her hand, I reach out, but she pushes my hand down and wraps me up in a warm hug too. "We will have none of that. We give hugs around here."

No wonder Scarlett loves her. She's so sweet and motherly.

"It's so nice to meet you too, Julie." I release her from our impromptu hug fest.

Scarlett finishes introductions. "Rylann, that's Levi's dad, Bob. That's Laci and Lexi, Levi's sisters. Jace, the best man. And, of course, you've already met Eli."

Eli comes over and gives me a hug. "Hey, beautiful. I see you're still as gorgeous as ever and looking extra sexy tonight," he says wolfishly.

I roll my eyes at him. "Hey, Eli. Still a big flirt, huh?"

This gets a laugh from him and the rest of the group.

Still grinning, I glance at Jace, who seems to be clenching his jaw and looking rather irritated.

"She got your number, Eli," Julie teases, patting his chest like only a mom could.

Forcing myself to pull my eyes away from Jace, I laugh at the dig. "So, what you're saying is that I'm not special, and he's a gigantic flirt with everyone then?"

"Yes!" the whole group answers, making us crack up.

"Yes, yes, I'm a flirt. Get over it." Eli turns his attention back to me. "Do we get to meet this boyfriend of yours this weekend?"

My chest pinches. It's the first time I've thought about him since we checked in. Someone else has been on my mind all day, making me feel incredibly guilty. It must show on my face because Eli sucks in a breath and everyone goes silent.

"Oh, shit. Sorry. I didn't realize, sweetheart."

"It's okay. We broke up. It's just me this week. His loss, right?" I shrug, not bothering to discuss the details. I put on a smile, which I know doesn't meet my eyes but I force it. I'm surprised Eli remembered about Sam. I guess I talked about him in Mexico more than I thought I did.

"Way to go, Eli." Levi smacks him in the back of the head.

"It's all good," I explain as Scarlett moves to my side and holds my hand.

She mouths, *Are you okay?*

I give her a nod. Until this moment, I hadn't thought about Sam since checking into the hotel. Not since I met Jace.

"Let's eat!" Levi shouts, pulling everyone's attention away from me. He shoots me a finger gun, making me chuckle, and leads everyone to our table. My soon-to-be brother from another mother for the save. He really is the best.

I look over to find Jace watching me with rapt attention. Eli sidles up next to him, whispering something in his ear. Jace nods, but his eyes never leave mine. My cheeks flush at his attention. He gives me a smoldering smile, making my insides heat up.

Holy moly. How can he make me melt with only a look?

Jace releases his hold on me. He turns to follow his brother and the rest of the group to our table, giving me the perfect opportunity to check him out for the first time tonight.

He's wearing an expensive yet casual-looking black t-shirt, dark jeans, and black ankle boots. His outfit is simple and sophisticated. It accentuates his hard muscular body, as do his perfectly sung jeans. There is that glorious-looking ass I've quickly come to appreciate.

He looks sexy and delicious tonight.

"I saw that," Scarlett sing-songs in my ear, making me jump in surprise. I forgot she was holding on to me.

"Saw what?" I challenge. Attempting to play dumb isn't smart when she caught me red-handed.

"That look. You checked out his ass."

"Did not!" I scoff. I did. *A lot.*

"He checked you out too. I think Jace likes you."

"You can't be serious. He doesn't even know me."

"Fine. He likes what he sees." There goes Scarlett and her stupid eyebrows. "Plus, you two did that whole eye-contact thing."

We totally did share a look back there. A look that made my stomach flutter and my body heat up from the inside out.

"Oh, please." I wave her off.

She gives me the "don't bullshit me" look and rolls her eyes. "Sure, you keep telling yourself that."

When we get to our table, Scarlett—the not-so-sneaky bitch—pulls the bride card and directs everyone to their seat. Of course, she conveniently places me across from Jace and Eli.

Dinner is a wonderful event. Bob and Julie share stories about Levi and Jace. Even some stories about Jace's brothers—the guys sound like a rambunctious bunch. It's foreign compared to how Scarlett and I grew up, but I'm so happy she gets to inherit these wonderful people as her own.

My only hope is that we get to raise our children together like Levi's and Jace's families did. It would be a dream come true. Being an only child was lonely until Scarlett came along. We bonded immediately and became sisters. I can't imagine life without her.

When Scarlett first met Levi, I was convinced she was going to move to Los Angeles to be with him. He told her that he would never make her leave Grams's home. I cried with relief after she told me he was moving here. Selfish, I know. But she's my girl. I'd sacrifice losing my roommate for a small place of my own any day to keep her in Pine Hills.

"Rylann! Hey!"

Shaking my thoughts free, I look up to see everyone staring at me. "Huh, what?"

"We were talking about Rita. I was telling Bob and Julie that Rita is the best cook," Scarlett shares.

My chest swells with pride, and a huge smile takes over my face at the mention of my momma. She really is the best cook. She's the best everything.

"Without a doubt the best cook. Levi can attest to that. I think he eats dinner with my parents more than I do."

"I never pass up a home-cooked meal," he says, patting his stomach.

Everyone laughs. We all know he's a bottomless pit. He's also the nicest guy, and my mom adores him.

Thinking about her makes me feel a little homesick all of a sudden. We haven't spoken since I landed at the airport. I haven't had the heart to tell her about what happened yesterday.

I grab my margarita and suck it down, hoping the alcohol will help me relax. When I look up, Jace is staring at me again.

"Your mom really that good of a cook?" he asks.

"Of course. She's the best. I'm surprised Levi hasn't gained 20 pounds since moving in next door."

"It will catch up with him one day," he retorts.

I wonder if that's true and try to picture Levi ten years from now. In my mind's eye, he looks like my dad with a little pot belly, which makes me laugh.

"What's so funny?" I turn to Scarlett, attempting to answer her, but when I peek at Levi eating next to her, I burst into giggles.

"Sorry. Jace said that one day all of Levi's Rita meals were gonna catch up with him. Then I pictured him with a little pot ..." I can't finish. I lose it, Jace joining me this time. We both laugh hard at Levi's expense.

"I think what she's trying to say is that she imagined Levi with a pot belly."

I point at Jace and tap my nose. I'm hysterically laughing as the words evade me. "Yes! Exactly! Like Dad!"

"Shut up! That can't happen. You hear that, Levi? No pot bellies allowed."

Levi looks at us like we're crazy, which sends Scarlett into a fit of giggles with us.

"Oh god, Ry. You know this pot belly might be possible if Momma Rita doesn't stop feeding him and sending over dessert and shit. You're gonna have to make her stop."

I sober up. "Yeah, no. *You* tell her that. I'm staying out of it. In fact, you stay out of it too or she'll cut us both off as punishment. And you know she can hold a grudge. I can't go without tamales."

"She's not the only one who can hold a grudge."

"Hey!" I shout, pushing her out of her chair.

"I'm kidding." She nudges my shoulder while I give her the evil eye.

Jace watches us with a smile on his lips. She turns her attention back to Levi's family, leaving Jace and me to stare at each other.

"You two really do act like sisters. I like it."

"Me too. I'm an only child, and not for the lack of my parents trying. It never worked out though. I think that's why my mom goes so crazy now that Levi's around—she has another person to feed and fuss over."

"I take it you're close with your mom?"

I tilt my head to the side, thinking about the best way to answer that. It's true, my mom and I are close. She has the biggest and most understanding heart. She's the best mom a girl could have. So I go with the truth.

"You can say that. And more," I confirm, pulling my bottom lip between my teeth. I won't elaborate further, but I hope the smile on my face conveys how much I love her.

Jace smiles back at me, and his eyes bounce to my mouth. I look away a little embarrassed but when I look back at him, he's still focused on me.

After a long pause, he gives me a flirty wink and what I'm starting to think is his signature charming smile.

The conversation continues to flow between Jace and me, with Scarlett and Eli joining in every once in a while. Jace is very easy to talk to, and I find myself having the best time chatting with him. Even though we are sitting at a table full of people, it feels like it's been the two of us the whole time.

Dinner ends with Bob toasting to the happy couple. It's sweet and heartfelt—totally not how Scarlett and I toast. We share a knowing look during the toast.

With the bill paid, we say our goodbyes to Levi's parents and, per Scarlett's itinerary, head to a karaoke bar.

I could use some musical relief and a shot of tequila to calm the butterflies I get in my stomach whenever Jace looks at me. It's equally unnerving and electrifying. I can't shake the feeling that when our eyes lock, he *sees* me. The real me.

The crazier part is that when I look him in the eye, I feel the same way.

There's no way around it—I am in so much trouble with this man.

CHAPTER SIX

Rylann

The group of us—Scarlett, Levi, Jace, Eli, Laci, and Lexi—walk the few blocks to the karaoke lounge. Everyone has broken up into groups, and I'm left beside Jace.

Since dinner, Jace and I have had this flirty vibe between us, but as we walk down the street, I'm starting to freak out. My nerves are frayed, and there's a ball of anxiety fluttering in my stomach. I'm like a teenage girl with her first crush. My skin prickles with awareness at his nearness, and I still haven't uttered a word. I've had crushes before. I've experienced the rush of anticipation when meeting a guy. But with Jace, it's next level.

There is this magnetism between us that has me gravitating towards him. He's beyond charming, and the more I learn about him, the more I like. His smile. His laugh. I like that he doesn't take himself too seriously. He's confident without being cocky. The weirdest part of all this is that I feel like I've known him forever. We naturally click. He makes me nervous, excited, and turned on, all at the same time.

I'm pulled from my thoughts when I'm knocked from the side. Teetering on the edge of my heels, I find myself about to eat concrete. I close my eyes, waiting for the inevitable fall that never comes. Instead, I'm lifted off my feet and flown across the sidewalk.

"Ah!" I yelp, my eyes flying open in shock. With my hand on my chest, I attempt to calm my racing heart.

Looking up, I find Jace hovering over me, concern etched across his brow. He's so tall that I have to tilt my head back to look up into his eyes. A beautiful shade of green and gold takes my breath away.

"Are you okay?" he asks, pulling me out of my daze. He looks back at a group of guys passing us by.

Ah.

"Uh ... Yeah. I guess my mind was elsewhere for a minute. Thanks for saving me from falling over."

He places his large hands on my shoulders and searches me over, looking for any injury—there isn't one. Running his hands down my arms, he pulls me into his embrace. The scent of citrus and leather floods my senses; he smells incredible. I want to lick him. I want to know if he tastes as good as he smells.

When he finishes inspecting me, he releases my arms and places his hand on my lower back, leading me to catch up with our group. My skin breaks out in goosebumps, and my nipples pebble at the heat of his hand on my back.

"My pleasure. Want to talk about it?"

"Not much to say. I was just thinking I'm having a great time, and ... Well, it's surprising."

"I understand. I feel the same way." After a few minutes, he breaks the comfortable silence that's settled between us. "Are you ready to sing tonight?"

"Yeah. It will be fun. Scarlett's the one that's excited. But you should know ... I don't sing."

Jace's eyebrows shoot up. "What? You're Scarlett's best friend, and you don't sing?"

I shake my head, biting my lip to stop from chuckling at his accusation. My bestie is well-known for belting out a tune. She has a great voice. While I love music, I'm not much of a singer. Scarlett thinks I have a good voice, but she also thinks the sun shines out my ass. I can't trust her opinion. I mean, I certainly feel the same way about her.

"Nope. I rap," I say, popping my Ps.

"Hold up."

Tingles shoot up my arm when he grabs my wrist bringing us to a stop on the sidewalk. I fight back a shiver as I watch the biggest, most playful grin spread across his face. Gah, he's gorgeous.

"What's that smile for?"

He shakes his head like he can't believe what I just told him is real. "You rap? Rap what, exactly?"

"You will have to wait and see." My tone is way more flirty than intended. But damn, he has my feelings and hormones going wild. "What about you? What's your go-to for karaoke?"

We continue walking behind the group. Still holding my wrist, his thumb grazes over my skin, and I'm sure he can feel my thumping pulse below the surface.

"Nuh uh. I'll share … when you do. I will say that you have a little competition tonight."

"Is that right?"

"Yup." He pops his P like I did earlier and laughs, bumping my shoulder. He lifts his eyebrows suggestively, outright flirting with me.

The teen girl in me squeals in delight. "Well, I guess it's on then." I flirt back.

We come to a stop, and he rakes his eyes up and down my body, soaking in every inch of my skin. The air around us crackles with energy. I watch his tongue swipe across his bottom lip. Surprising me, he gives my hand a squeeze. I don't know how or when it happened, but his fingers are wound through mine.

"It's definitely on," he rumbles, his voice thick and gruff, making my knees wobble.

"Ooo, I heard that. I think we have ourselves a little battle to look forward to," Scarlett teases, breaking our bubble.

Jace drops my hand. I know it's for the best, but I miss his warm touch.

"Yes! This is gonna be awesome. I totally forgot that you both have a love affair with rap. You two are *so* going to battle," Levi says, opening the door to the lounge.

The men move aside, allowing us ladies to enter first.

As Scarlett walks by Jace, she pats his cheek. "Yes! The best man versus the maid of honor. The bride commands it!"

"Oh, I'm ready." Jace rubs his hands together, following behind.

"I don't know, Jace. I think you've met your match," Scarlett taunts, laying the match part on thick.

I shake my head and roll my eyes at her ridiculousness.

"We'll see about that. I can hold my own."

"Please, stop! You know what challenging Jay to anything does to him," Eli proclaims.

Levi throws his head back in laughter, making me wonder how competitive Jace is. "Oh, I'm counting on that. Since there isn't anything to hold him back tonight, I'm expecting him to bring his A-game," Levi retorts.

"I don't know, babe. My girl has real talent here. She can rhyme like a bad bitch."

The trash talk continues all the way to our table.

I lean into Jace, whispering, "It's like I have my own little Don King repping me right now. Put your dukes up, Jace. I'm coming for you." Bringing my fists to my chin, I do a little butterfly step and give him a one-two punch in the stomach. His very hard stomach. Now, I'm wondering what he's hiding beneath his shirt.

"Okay, Tyson." He feigns left and right, a perfect bob and weave to my jabs. He throws his arm over my shoulders, holding me close, where I fit perfectly at his side.

When we arrive at the table, he releases his hold on me and we all squeeze into a rounded booth in the middle of the bar facing the stage. Levi and Scarlett sit in the middle, leaving the guys on one side and the girls on the other, with Jace seated directly across from me.

At his distance, disappointment washes over me. Before I can pull on that thread, I remind myself that tonight is about Scarlett and Levi, not the best man.

The waitress arrives to take our drink order, and my bestie orders shots of tequila with limes for the table and, of course, margaritas for us.

"You're having fun, right?" she asks, giving my leg a squeeze.

I tilt my head, pretending to think about it. I don't need to think—I know. "Yes, I'm having fun. I didn't think I would be … but I am."

"I think there's a certain handsome man that's interested in having some fun with you. Are you in for some lip action with him?"

"What? No. Nuh uh." *Liar.*

Before she can heckle me more, our drinks arrive, ending our conversation. But thoughts of kissing Jace don't. Those linger.

Scarlett raises her voice over the singing, bringing her shot glass up in one hand and her lime in another. "Alright, everyone. Grab your shot. It's time to toast. I don't know if you know this, but Ry and I have a tradition where we toast every shot. Everyone here tonight will be forced to make one too. It can be borrowed or new. I will start it off, then Ry and Levi, so get yourself ready to take a turn." She clears her throat. "Raise your glasses up. Here's to this tequila—let's hope it doesn't give us amnesia!"

"Cheers!"

We shoot back the liquor, slam our shot glasses down, and bite our limes. Laci and Lexi, who recently turned twenty-one, copy us and cringe as the tequila hits their stomachs.

They are super excited to be out with us tonight instead of being stuck at the hotel with their parents. Talking to them has been a welcome distraction to avoid looking across the booth at Jace every chance I get.

When they get on stage to sing *Lady Marmalade,* I finally give in and peer across the table in Jace's direction. Mesmerized, I watch as he takes a gulp of his beer, his Adam's apple bobbing in his throat as he swallows. His tongue swipes across his plump bottom lip, catching a drop of liquid left behind.

A flash of me licking the little drop instead has me squirming in my seat.

When I look up, I find him watching me. His eyes bore into mine, and I swear he's reading my thoughts. Without breaking eye contact, I bite my bottom lip and witness the honey in his eyes glow in the dark room. Rolling his tongue over his lips, he continues to watch me watch him.

With a cocky smirk, he winks at me. My thighs clench, and my panties go from damp to soaked.

Eli asks Jace a question, breaking his spell on me. Glancing away, I feel my face flush.

What is wrong with me? Good thing it's dark in here and no one saw that.

"I saw that."

Shit. I was wrong. Scarlett doesn't miss a thing. She can also read me like no other, the blonde little witch.

"What? No. Nothing to see here. What song are you gonna sing?"

"Nice try. But the lady doth protest too much, eh?" she says, smugly. "But I will let you change the subject ... for now. I think I'm going with *Firework* to start off. What about you?"

She knows what song I'm gonna do first. It's always my first song, so why change it now?

"Same as always."

"Who is ready for round two?" Eli shouts and places a tray of shots and limes on the table. Looks like it's going to be a crazy night.

"Ry, you're up!" Scarlett shouts at me to raise it up.

"Here's to Scarlett and Levi." Raising my glass up and pointing to Levi, I say, "You may have found your missus, but I'll kill you if you diss us." Our group jeers Levi, who playfully puts his hands up in surrender. I turn and point to Scarlett. "And to you, my beautiful friend. You may have found your mister, but I will always be your sister. Cheers!"

The bride-to-be takes her shot, slams her glass, and with her lime in her mouth she wraps me up in a bear hug. When we pull apart, we point to each other and yell, "No crying!" It makes us both burst into giggles.

"Alright, you two, break it up. Baby, you're up. Go knock 'em dead." Levi smacks Scarlett's ass as she stands from the table. She lays a kiss on him, leaving him dazed, and then struts to the stage where she kills it.

Levi follows her performance with a cute rendition of *Hanging by a Moment* by Lifehouse. Between the performances and Eli's trip to the bar, we've all shuffled seats, finally leaving me next to Jace.

Our shoulders and legs touch, and I feel my body come alive. Electricity and anticipation run through my system.

He whispers in my ear, and I shiver at his deep resonating voice. "Are you ready for the battle to commence?"

He's so close, I can smell him. I don't know if it's him, his cologne, or both, but he smells divine. Like orange peels, spice, and leather. It's clean, expensive, and unbelievably intoxicating. Tilting my head back to look into his dreamy hazel eyes, my sassy comeback gets lost on my tongue.

Levi shouts, "Jay, the time has come for you to put your money where your mouth is. Get up on that stage right now, *best man*."

"Yeah, you're up, fucker!" Eli reaches across the table and punches him in the shoulder.

"Shot first!" Scarlett passes out shots to everyone.

Levi raises his glass and clears his throat. "To my bride-to-be, Scarlett. You are beautiful, smart, and full of class. I can't wait to tap that ass."

"Gross!" Laci and Lexi groan, making me laugh. I'm so used to his lewd toasts, but they are hilarious.

"Yes! Now, that's a toast! I got one now that I know how it works." Eli raises his glass and shouts, "To the lucky ladies that get to touch my dong. I promise I'll take care of what's under your thong!"

Everyone groans while Levi and I crack up laughing. Jace smacks his brother in the back of the head, making me laugh more.

"Don't encourage him." He gives me a teasing, bossy stare.

"I'm sorry, but that was a good one. Scar and I have been doing this a long time, and I haven't heard anything that clever before. Dirty, but clever." I yell, "Mad props, E."

I stand and lean across the table with my hand out for Eli to bump my knuckles. When I sit down, Jace's hand lands on my upper thigh and squeezes.

"You're gonna pay for that, Rylann," he whispers in my ear.

The air gets sucked out of my lungs at the gravel in his voice. I can't breathe and my body buzzes, and it's not the alcohol. How does he do this to me?

"Why?" I croak out, turning to face him. His face is only millimeters from mine, close enough that I could easily kiss him.

"You encouraged my brother and then leaned over the table putting your barely concealed sexy ass in my face. I don't know if I'll be able to keep being a gentleman if you do that again."

Oh. My. God. Did he really just say that to me?

My pussy throbs, and my clit pulses at his threat.

Yes, he did.

Biting my cheek, I stifle an audible groan. I never would have pegged Jace for a dirty-talking gentleman. I'm in deep with this man. Now, all I want is for him to say more inappropriate things to me.

Before I can respond, he gives me that sexy wink—the one that sets my panties on fire—and jumps up from the table.

"Time for me to win this battle." He rubs his hands together and points to me. "May the best rapper win."

I have no comeback. I watch his firm, denim-clad ass all the way to the stage.

Pulling me out of my Jace fog, Scarlett elbows me. "He is totally flirting with you."

He *was* totally flirting with me. It's harmless fun though, right? Well, not completely harmless. His dirty threat ruined my panties. This flirty thing we've got going on is thrilling. He's definitely captured all of my attention.

"I think you're right," I admit.

"Um, duh. I'm always right." Scarlett rests her head on my shoulder as the emcee introduces Jace to the stage.

"Au' rite. Next up is Jace. Show dem ya ting, bruddah."

The opening bars to *Ice, Ice Baby* begin to play, and for sure I'm toast. He is rapping one of my all-time favorite songs. Holy hotness, Batman ... Jace is the most perfect specimen of man there is.

"Oh fuck, Rice Cakes. You're so screwed. He's your perfect man," Scarlett whispers, reading my mind.

A smile spreads across my face as I watch him rap Vanilla Ice's lyrics without assistance from the screen. He's good. I think I really have met my match. Musical match, nothing more.

Yeah, keep telling yourself that, woman.

When he starts doing the dance to go with the song, the whole bar cheers, myself included. He's freaking amazing.

When he's done, he takes a bow then points at me and curls his finger, signaling for me to, *Come here.*

"I guess that means you're up, girl. Kick his ass."

Taking a deep breath, I stand up and salute Scarlett. "On it."

The audience is still applauding and shouting for him as I make my way to the stage. As I take his extended hand, he pulls me up on the stage and hands me the mic. Tingles shoot up my arm again, lighting my body on fire.

"Good luck. I look forward to seeing you top that performance."

"I hope you get a good look then," I sass back, trying to play it cool. My heart, on the other hand, has its own agenda and skips a beat. There's something happening between us, and it might be too big for me to contain.

"Oh, I will." He backs away from the stage, eyes firmly on me. The way he said that leads me to believe he's not talking about my performance.

Butterflies flutter in my stomach.

With a deep breath, I give the emcee my pick. He nods, entering it into the machine. The song starts, and I decide that—in order to win—I need to go for it.

That's exactly what I do. I go for it.

Hoping to give Jace the good look I promised.

CHAPTER SEVEN

Jace

I take my seat back in the booth.

The buzz coursing through my veins is not from the alcohol I've consumed but from the gorgeous woman I left on stage. She has me intoxicated.

We've only met this afternoon, and yet I find it hard to keep my eyes and even my hands off of her. When I whispered in her ear earlier, the scent of lime and coconut enveloped me and damn near made my dick hard.

The song starts, and our whole table goes nuts, as do the rest of the people in the bar. I shake my head because I can't believe it—she is going to rap one of my favorites. I have a thing for 90s' rap, especially one-hit wonders. Apparently, so does Rylann.

Eli elbows me in the stomach, taking my attention away from the stage and the girl that has me enchanted. "Oh. My. God. I never thought I'd see it, but here we are."

"What do you mean?" I look over at my brother, who's shaking his head in disbelief as he points a finger at Rylann.

"I mean ... She's got your taste in music. She's competitive, she gives no fucks about getting on stage to rap *Baby Got Back,* and she's fucking gorgeous. She's the total package. If you don't go for it, I will."

"Don't even think about it." I growl, smacking him in the chest.

He gives me that shit-eating grin again, the one he's been giving me a lot lately. The one that makes me want to dick-punch him. Over my dead body will he be going near her.

I return my attention to the sexy woman shaking her ass on stage like she's one of the girls in the music video. All she's missing is a giant peach to dance on. Somehow, she's managed to rap every single lyric from memory and dance like nobody's business.

Groaning, I watch as she bends over and slaps her ass in that incredibly short dress, taking me from semi-hard to full mast in my jeans. Grateful for the lack of light, I adjust myself without getting caught.

"Shit. She's awesome."

"Yeah, she is." An unfamiliar feeling washes over me as I watch the dazzling woman on stage unknowingly dig herself a place inside my chest.

"I think my girl has you beat, Jay," Scarlett states.

"Yeah. She definitely does," I reply, my eyes never leaving Rylann. I feel like she has me in a trance, and I'm absolutely okay with that.

There has to be a way for me to get some time alone with her. The need to talk to her, to see if what I'm feeling is real, is overwhelming. I want time with her. Who am I kidding—I want her.

The rational part of my brain is telling me I'm crazy for feeling like this so soon, but there is this other part of me that's telling me what I feel for her is special.

"So, are you going to go for it?"

"Eli," I warn. I'm not talking to him about ... whatever this is. I don't even know what it is yet.

"What? I'm wondering where your head's at."

Where is my head? It's not thinking about Alina and the dumpster fire our relationship turned into the last couple of months. All my thoughts are on the beautiful brunette rocking it on the stage. I want more time with her. I want to know if her lips taste like the limes she's been sucking on.

"I don't know," I admit.

"I get it. You're both on the rebound. But, when you look at her ..."

"When I look at her, what?"

"The fuck ... I don't know, man. But it's almost the same way Levi looked at Scarlett in Mexico. Besides, I heard you. I don't think I've ever heard you talk like that to a girl before. Definitely not to Alina." He arches a brow at me, waiting for me to disagree.

He's not wrong. I've never spoken to a woman like that before. Only her.

The crowd goes wild, indicating that Rylann's done with her performance. Everyone's eyes are all on her, and I can't blame them. The out-of-character desire to rip out the eyes of every man who looks at her hits me. Hard.

Rylann takes a bow and floats back to the booth, wearing a cocky smirk.

When she reaches the table, I stand and curtsy. "You are definitely the queen tonight."

"And don't you forget it!" She laughs, grabbing her dress at the sides and curtsying.

I tip my head back and laugh and her cheeky comeback. Her sass is oh-so-fucking sexy.

Sliding into the booth, we sit side by side, our bodies brushing against each other. Leaning back with my arm stretched along the back of the banquette, we watch more people perform. Some good, some not. We talk the entire time, joking and laughing.

We both go for another round on stage. I rock Montell Jordan and, of course, she hits me with Tag Team. Yep ... *Whoop, there it is.* She's flipping my world upside down without even trying.

"Alright, everyone, we are heading out," Levi announces, Scarlett giggling in his lap. Those two have no boundaries when it comes to PDA. Totally time for them to go and give me the opportunity to talk to Rylann—alone.

"Lee, why don't you two lovebirds head back, and I will get everyone else to follow."

"That's why you're my best man, Jay." Levi stands up with Scarlett in his arms. "You are mine, Short Stack. Say goodbye."

"Goodbye," Scarlett calls out, blowing us all kisses. She points to me and says, "Take care of my girl, Jay. She's my MOH-fo. I can't live without her."

"Your wish is my command." I'll be doing more than taking care of her if she lets me.

The fuck?

Rylann hugs Scarlett while she's in Levi's arms. They have some sort of hushed conversation that ends with them both gigging. Levi, obviously knowing this could drag out, turns and carries Scarlett out of the bar without looking back.

Scarlett leans back, waving and yelling over his shoulders, "Have fun, kiddos! Please do all the things I would do!"

Giving Scarlett another wave, Rylann watches our friends leave with a smile and a look of longing, like she wants what they have.

I do too.

Taking our seats in the booth, only ten minutes have passed before the itch to head out claws at me. Eli and the twins are laughing and watching the person on the stage butcher an Evanescence song, having a good time. Rylann has become more quiet, and my only hope is that she also wants to get out of here. With me.

"Alright, gang. It's time for us to head back."

I'm hit with jeers from the three musketeers, making Rylann giggle.

"One more round, big bro. Laci and Lexi plan on singing one more song. I'll get the girls home if you and Ry want to head back to the hotel."

"What do you think? Stay or go?" I ask her.

Please say leave.

"I'm good to go. Get back safe. Goodnight."

She turns her back on Eli and mouths, *You owe me.* I give him the finger instead, and he laughs. I do owe him one, but he doesn't need to know that.

I catch up with Rylann as she gets to the door. I open it for her and follow her out into the night. My hand rests on her lower back, the heat of her body seeping through the thin cotton sundress she's wearing setting my blood on fire.

How can this woman that I barely know make me feel like this?

"Do you mind if we walk back to the hotel? It was pretty hot in there, and I could use some fresh air."

"Sure. My shoes might be tall, but they're comfortable enough for walking." Rylann twists her foot back and forth, allowing me to check out her feet.

The shoes aren't the only thing I notice. My eyes devour her deliciously bronze legs. She might be short, but her legs look a mile long in that dress. Legs I wouldn't mind having wrapped around my waist. Spread wide for me as I thrust into her hot, wet body.

I swallow the lump that's formed in my throat and grit out, "Very nice. Shall we?"

As I extend my elbow out, she takes the offer and slides her little palm into the crease of my arm. We walk in comfortable silence for a block before I realize this walk is a lot shorter than I want it to be.

"If we go straight, this leads to the beach. Wanna walk to the hotel from there?"

"I love that idea. We haven't been to the beach yet." Her voice has a hint of sadness to it, like the beach is the one place she longs to be at.

"Let's fix that then."

"Okay," she answers.

"Levi tells me that you're a lawyer too."

"Yep. Family law." I'm not always comfortable talking about what I do anymore.

Alina always had a negative opinion about my specialty. She thought I should be working at a large firm, making more money like her. If not in corporate law, at least I should be handling high-profile divorce cases that could make me a name.

Money. All the shit I couldn't care less about.

"I specialize in a wide variety of custody cases. I enjoy helping children and families with adoptions."

Rylann squeezes my bicep, pulling me to a stop. She looks up at me with such awe and gratitude in her eyes that it makes my chest ache. "That's really amazing, Jace. What you do for those families is wonderful. Thank you. I know those kids appreciate your support and help to make them feel a part of a family."

"Thank you. I don't think anyone besides my clients has thanked me." Confessing this heals a part of me I never knew was jagged and broken.

Her dark chocolate eyes sparkle in the street light as she rewards me with a genuine smile that warms my skin like sunshine. A man could get used to being on the receiving end of smiles like that.

We continue walking towards the beach, her fingers making small circles on my bicep sending prickles of awareness throughout my body. I want to know how it feels to have her hands trail over other parts of my body. Her touch is addicting.

"More people should. Kids need someone on their side."

This woman, whom I barely know, has shown more respect for me and my career than my ex ever did. Every word Rylann utters speaks volumes about what kind of person she is and the kind of heart that beats in her chest.

"It means a lot to me that you understand." It really does. I haven't received this support from anyone besides my family.

"Of course. I love children. I have always pictured myself to be a mom—not that I'm in a rush or anything, but I definitely want kids. A lot of them. I'd love to have a big family. What about you?"

"Same." I've had the best role models. My parents are devoted to each other and to me and my brothers. That's the kind of partnership I hope to have with someone someday. "I want kids. More than one. I have a tradition to carry on. I don't know if you know, but I have two other brothers as well."

Rylann quickly whips her head to the side, sending the intoxicating scent of coconut up my nose. I breathe in her sweet scent, and my dick twitches in my pants. My hands itch to twist the silky strands in my fist and tug.

"*Hello*, I've met them. Mexico, remember?" The "duh" is implicit in her tone.

"Ah, yes. The trip I missed. I guess I like to forget that trip didn't happen."

"Like a tree falling in the forest?"

I bark out a laugh. "Something like that." I wonder how things would have played out if we met then.

"You're close to all your brothers?"

"Yes, it helps that we are all close in age; only two years between each of us. I'm the oldest, then Eli, Mason, and Cameron."

"Four boys so close in age? Your mom's a saint."

"Try more like five boys. You have to count Levi too. We fed him once and could never shake him after that."

Rylann laughs, the tinkling sound settling in my bones.

"True story. Levi can really put away food. His metabolism is insane. In all honesty, though, my parents and I adore him. He makes Scarlett so happy. It feels like he's been a part of our life for longer than six months."

The sound of the waves gets closer, and the beach comes into view. She's lost in her thoughts as silence settles between us. I need to bring her back to the moment, back to me, so I change course.

"You know … Now, don't get mad when I say this …" I take a deep breath. "But when Levi told me he was moving to Oregon, I thought he was nuts. I get it now." I do get it. I would do anything to be with the right person.

Rylann. My heart squeezes at her name.

"I totally understand. It was crazy. You had to be there. It was kind of amazing."

"It took meeting her to truly understand. I've watched him light up when she walks into the room. Hell … you can even tell when he's thinking about her. There's only one way to describe it—soulmates."

Rylann gives me a questioning look, her perfectly shaped eyebrow lifting up. "You believe in soulmates?"

Not until you.

What the hell is wrong with me?

I give her a shrug and smirk. "What's not to believe?"

"Hmm." Rylann tilts her head like she's weighing her thoughts.

Reaching the beach, she takes off her wedge sandals and steps into the sand. I follow her lead and do the same. We walk through the soft sand, our shoes in hand.

I breathe in the salty sea air, and I love how it reminds me of home and my condo back in Santa Monica. I'm not on the beach, but I am close enough to hear the waves crashing at night. Sitting out on my patio at night, unwinding, is my favorite time of the day. Next is sitting on my board at sunrise.

I look out at the ocean, and although it's the same one I see every day, it looks different here. The sound of the waves crashing is louder. The light of the moon reflecting off the water looks like it's covered in sparkling diamonds.

Taking a chance, I reach for Rylann's hand, threading our fingers together. A current passes between us when our palms meet, and she squeezes my hand tightly, her small hand fitting perfectly in mine.

"I never did before." She pauses, picking up where we left off. I can feel her thinking before she continues, "Believe in soulmates. I mean, I did in some ways. My parents are very much in love, but I guess I never thought of them as soulmates. When I saw Levi and Scarlett find each other, I knew then that it was real."

Absorbing her words, I think about all my conversations with Levi. The way he described meeting Scarlett sounded surreal. After everything that's happened today—experiencing the instant spark with Rylann, the way my heart picks up speed when I look at her, the warm feeling in my chest when she smiles, the need to kiss her and hold her—I think I'm starting to understand how real it is too.

The hotel comes into view too soon. I don't want this night to end yet. "Wanna sit on the beach and talk for a while longer?"

"I'd like that." She bites that bottom lip of hers.

I saw her do this earlier, and the same urge to take that lip between my teeth hits me again. I guide her to our hotel's beach access entrance and pull her down into the sand with me, keeping her hand in mine. It feels natural being with her, holding her hand like it's something we've always done.

After a few minutes, she lays her head on my shoulder. The smell of her hair wafts around my nose. Taking a deep breath of it, I commit the delicious scent to memory.

I want her. Something in me says, *Mine.*

The thought hits me like a freight train.

Sitting here with her is easy and comfortable. With my heart still hammering in my chest, I have an indescribable desire to kiss her. I can't describe it, but there is something pulling us together.

"Rylann?"

She hums, tilting her head back to look up with those big brown eyes. Her beauty stuns me.

"Jace?"

My eyes bounce to her pink lips. "I'm dying to kiss you," I confess. "I need to know if your lips are as soft as they look." I inch closer, running the tip of my nose along her jawline.

"Really?"

"Really."

Her eyes search mine. The reality of what's about to happen between us seeps in. If I kiss her, everything will change. I don't think I will be the same man after her lips touch mine. I'm playing with fire, and I don't give a fuck.

She smiles at me, and I have no doubt she can read my mind.

Her breath fans across my mouth as she whispers, "Kiss me."

"If I kiss you, are you prepared for what comes next?"

Her smile grows wider. "What's going to happen next?"

"I don't know, but something tells me it's going to be special. Are you ready for that?"

"As ready as I'll ever be."

I cup her cheek with my free hand, and she melts into my touch. *Fuck me, she's gorgeous.*

"Well, what are you waiting for? Kiss me already, Ace."

"Ace, huh?" I muse. I've never had a nickname before.

"Yup. It fits you."

Our eyes lock. Staring. Searching.

I don't know what kind of magic this is between us, but I don't want it to go away. I want to lean into it and hold on for as long as possible.

Inching my face towards hers, I hover over her parted mouth. Her pink tongue swipes across her lips, grazing mine. My control snaps, and I finally take what I want and cover her mouth with mine in a searing kiss.

The electric current that's been humming and crackling between us explodes like dynamite.

Her lips part, and I don't hesitate to deepen the kiss, sliding my tongue into her mouth. Our tongues caress in a sensuous dance, slow and deep. Her soft moans get lost in the sound of crashing waves.

She curls her fingers through the hair at the back of my neck, scraping my scalp, and fuck if it doesn't feel good. My blood rushes south and as much as I don't want to, I slow down our kiss. Nipping at her bottom lip and planting a few more pecks on her swollen lips, I pull back, pressing my forehead to hers. Eyes pinched tight, I will my thickening cock to calm down.

Opening my eyes I find hers still closed, looking how I feel—overwhelmed, dazed, and yearning for more. I want to kiss her again and never stop. I'll never get enough of her.

"Ry?"

"Yeah?" she whispers as her breath fans across my lips.

"Did you feel it too?"

With her eyes still closed and our foreheads still touching, she nods. "Yes. I felt it," she whispers back. With a soft smile, she opens her eyes, finding mine.

Running my thumb over the two small freckles on her cheek, I know on some basic level that I'm exactly where I'm supposed to be and whom I'm supposed to be with.

"Good, because that was the best damn kiss I've ever had, and we will be doing that again." She leans back on her hands and laughs. "What's so funny, Sunshine?"

Sunshine? Where did that come from?

"You." I frown at her. "Oh, goodness. Not like that. Your honesty is sweet and endearing. You just laid it all out there. I've never met anyone like you before. I like it." She pauses, biting her lip, debating on whether or not to continue. In the end, she does. "Full disclosure, it was the best kiss I've ever had too."

My chest puffs, and I lunge at her. She giggles when my fingers dig into her waist. Unable to help myself, I sink my fingers in her hair and steal another kiss.

With her legs draped over mine, we talk. Between kisses, she tells me about her business, her life back home, and her dreams for her future. I learn that her favorite color is yellow, which she swears has the ability to warm her up when she's feeling down. I find it adorable. Next to Scarlett, her mom is her best friend.

I tell her about my life back home, my family, and my dreams. We talk about everything except our past relationships. It's not like I want to talk about them. But I want to explore us, and I think we need to get it all out there if we want a chance at making this work past this week because a week with Rylann won't be enough.

"Can I ask about your ex?"

"Umm ... sure?" she croaks, and I worry that I've ruined the mood.

"Was it a clean break?"

She looks away at my question. Pinching her chin with my fingers, I bring her eyes up to meet mine.

She likes my honesty, so I'm going for broke here. "I know it sounds crazy and fast ... I would really like to spend more time with you while we're here. Just the two of us. I want to explore this connection with you. There is something here—I can feel it, and I think you can too. But we can't do that if you're holding onto something with him. I'm not holding something for my ex. You're all I've thought about since I saw you. When I'm with you, it's like the past never happened. It's only ever been you and me. Please, tell me you're with me?"

She stares at me for what feels like forever, searching my eyes. For what, I don't know, but she seems to find what she's looking for.

"I want to explore this too. I feel it too. I can't explain it, but it's there." She reaches up, rubbing the scruff on my chin.

Now it's my turn to lean into her touch, relieved that we're on the same page. Her soft hands move from my chin to my hair, her nails gently scratching my scalp.

Fuck, that feels good.

"I have to tell you ... When Scarlett and I got drunk at that airport bar, she made me promise to have fun and to ... *kiss a hottie*," she admits, using finger quotes.

I throw my head back and laugh. "Does that make me a hottie?"

"Oh, hush." She weakly slaps at my chest and turns her big doe eyes on me. "I never expected to kiss you and for it to feel like this. Like there's something more here."

I run my hand up her spine, my need to touch her multiplying every second I'm near her.

"To answer your questions, yes. He made it pretty clear after the second breakup. After months of dating, he gave me the *It's not you, it's me* speech. Pretty cliché." She shrugs, turning her sights on me. "Your turn. Want to tell me about Alina?"

The way she said my ex's name has me flinching, and my stomach flips. "Scarlett told you about the dinner?"

She nods.

Closing my eyes, I pinch the bridge of my nose in shame.

Talk about a shit show. A couple of months ago, Levi brought Scar down to Los Angeles and we met up with them. Alina acted like an uppity bitch the entire time. She made it clear she didn't think much of Scarlett. It got so awkward that Levi threw cash down on the table, grabbed Scarlett, and walked out of the restaurant without a backward glance. It led to Alina and me having a huge blowout fight that night.

"Oh, yeah. Levi was not happy." She shakes her head in disapproval. "I feel like I need to give you full disclosure here—I also heard stuff from your brothers when we were in Mexico."

"Not surprising. Which one was talking shit?" Those fuckers always have something to say, especially Cameron.

Rylann smirks at me before answering, "All of them, Jace. All. Of. Them."

We both burst out laughing. I love that she isn't judging me or saying anything negative in return. Instead, she chose to tease me and take the sting out of the truth. I move my hand to her thigh and give it a little squeeze.

At my touch, she immediately stops laughing and lets out a sexy little groan. Her knees snap together, trapping my fingers between them. It's so fucking hot, the way my touch turns her on. Leaning in, I kiss her again.

She pushes me away, gigging. "Don't distract me with those lips. You wanted this conversation ... Finish."

"I'm regretting this now." I grunt. I want to go back to kissing her. "I met my ex in law school. Back then, she was ambitious but fun. Things were great until we graduated. She went into corporate law and didn't like the area of law I specialized in. The only thing she cares about is becoming a partner at her firm. She's not the same girl I fell for, and our breakup was a long time coming. I skipped the guys' trip as a last-ditch effort to fix our relationship."

We sit in silence, both of us lost in the past. Honestly, ending it with Alina was a relief, like a huge weight being lifted off my shoulders. She didn't want the future I did.

"I'm sorry."

"Thank you. But you know what?"

"What?"

"I'm not sorry. I haven't thought about any of that since I came across this beautiful woman with big chocolate brown eyes and a smile that can light up the world."

I kiss her neck, and she sighs and sinks into my chest a little deeper.

I almost miss her whispering, "Me too," over the sound of the water.

Rylann shifts, moving between my legs and rests her back against my chest. I wrap my arms around her waist.

"Ace?"

"Yeah, Sunshine?"

"Meeting you has changed everything. I don't want to talk about the past. Let's be right here, right now."

Her words are like a fist around my heart that squeezes. The guy that let this amazing woman go was a fucking idiot.

"You got it, babe."

I tilt her chin back and plant a soft kiss on her lips. She accepts my kiss, opening herself to me. A sense of peace washes over me as I taste her sweet mouth.

Here and now sounds good to me.

For now.

CHAPTER EIGHT

Rylann

Warmth surrounds me as the sun rises behind Diamond Head.

The soft orange and pink glow of light breaking into the night sky makes the volcano look inky black, like one of those seashell paintings you find in gift shops.

"I think this is the most beautiful sunrise I've ever witnessed," I tell Jace in awe.

He presses a kiss to the back of my head as I melt further into his body. His strong arms wrap around my waist, pulling me closer to his chest.

The night has passed too quickly. I'm not ready to leave the comfort and safety of Jace's arms, but if the sun's up, we don't have long before we need to meet up with everyone for breakfast.

The hours we have spent alone talking and kissing will be forever ingrained into my heart and soul. Jace is amazing. His honesty and vulnerability took me by surprise. The way he spoke about his life, his family, his feelings—everything—speaks volumes about his character. He personifies all the good we humans search for in life and in another person.

My chest twinges. Twining my fingers with his over my stomach, I squeeze him tight. Something happened between us last night, and there are no words or feelings I can find to describe it. All I know is that without even trying, he has positively stolen a piece of my heart. I think I might be falling for this man. We only met yesterday, and yet somehow, I've known him my whole life.

"We better get back to our rooms. We're supposed to meet everyone for breakfast at 8:30," I say, reminding him and myself.

We might have carved out a moment for ourselves, but we aren't the focus of this trip. Even if it feels like the rest of the world fades away when we're together.

"Shit. You're right." Jace gives my temple a kiss. "Up we go, Sunshine."

He quickly scoops me up in his arms and stands, making me yelp in fear. My arms automatically wrap around his neck, holding on.

"Ohmigod, Jace. A little warning would have been nice."

He throws his head back and laughs. The deep happy sound has me laughing along with him.

I knew he was strong, but he just lifted me like I weighed nothing. Like he could carry me for miles and wouldn't even break a sweat. And I'd let him.

"Where's the fun in that? Then I wouldn't get to hear you scream my name and laugh." He drops my legs, letting them dangle, and pulls us chest to chest. His strong arms clamp around my body, holding me up. "I like hearing you laugh."

I stare into his honey-green eyes, and my heart takes off in a gallop at what I see reflected in them. "Yeah, why is that?"

Gently placing me on my feet in the cool sand, he brushes my hair back, tucking it behind my ear, and cups my face. He rubs his thumb across my cheek, leans down and kisses the tip of my nose, making me giggle like a schoolgirl with a crush.

"You get these two cute little dimples on your cheeks right here, and it makes me want to do this." He drops kisses on the apples of my cheeks. Once. Twice. When he leans back, he has a soft, almost loving look on his face that leaves me breathless.

He captures my lips with his, and I fall right into him. I'm lost in his taste, in desire, in him. He tilts my head, deepening the kiss. Electricity zips from my core to the tips of my toes and fingers. This isn't just a kiss. With the way he holds me close and the sensual way his tongue slides against mine as he pillages my mouth, he's turned this kiss into a promise of so much more.

I really want him to keep kissing me like this and never stop. Unfortunately, we need to get back to our rooms to change before breakfast. Before we get caught together.

I'm not ready to explain what's going on between us. Hell, I don't even understand it. I want to stay in our bubble a little longer. The problem is, I don't know how much longer I will be able to keep this a secret. Being away from him and not touching him while he's standing right next to me is going to be agonizing.

I break the kiss. "As much as I would like to continue this, we need to get changed for breakfast."

"I know." His voice is as somber as I feel. He releases me from his arms but grabs my hand. "But I want the record to show that I am not happy about this. In fact, I am filing a motion that we are to pick this up ... later."

My insides flip upside down at his sweet declaration. He's so freaking swoony.

"I feel the same way." The idea of going to my room alone makes me sad. I don't want to leave his side.

Hand in hand, we walk into the hotel, through the lobby to the bank of elevators, stepping into the awaiting cart.

"What floor are you on?"

"I'm on 10. What about you?"

He pushes the button for the tenth floor, and the elevator doors close. He pushes me to the back of the elevator, crowding me. His deliciously sexy scent floods my senses, making me dizzy.

Electricity flows between us, sending tingles from my chest to my core. I have never felt this kind of instant connection before. Together, we are a flashfire waiting to happen. He ignites this deep need inside that sets my body on fire.

"Interesting. So am I. That might work in our favor ... later." The way he says "later" sends dirty images flickering through my mind.

Biting my lip, I tilt my head back, looking into his eyes.

"Stop that," he growls, sucking my lip from the grasp of my teeth with his mouth.

Fuck, that's hot.

Clearing my throat, I say, "Speaking of later, do you think we can keep this thing between us quiet? I don't want to take away from Scarlett and Levi. This is their week, and I—"

He stops me from continuing, placing his finger over my lips. He tenderly runs his nose up my neck to my ear, breathing me in deep. "Whatever you want, Sunshine."

Goosebumps erupt along my skin, and my eyes flutter closed. My arms instinctively move to his shoulders, holding on. The air around us is thick and electric.

The ding of the elevator doors opening breaks the spell.

My knees wobble, and I swear I feel drunk on Jace Miller. The smug smile on his face tells me he knows exactly what he does to me. The competitive part of me can't let him be too smug.

Straightening up, I pat his chest and push him away. I roll my eyes at him playfully before walking around him and exiting the cart. I make sure to put a little extra sway into my hips for him to enjoy. Glancing over my shoulder, I catch him doing exactly what I want—his hazel orbs are hooded and latched onto my ass.

"I know what you're doing," he grits out between clenched teeth.

"What's that?"

He catches up to me and presses his chest into my back, banding his arms possessively around my waist, pulling me to a stop.

"You're trying to get a reaction out of me, Sunshine. But you don't need to try. You've been affecting me since I laid eyes on you." To prove his point, he pushes his hips forward, pressing his hard cock into my lower back.

My core clenches, and a needy moan slips past my lips.

Nudging my ass back into his thick length, I grind into him, feeling the ridges of his thick cock. His hands circle my waist, gently squeezing and bunching the soft fabric of my dress. The ache between my legs intensifies, my pulse races, and my breath quickens. I thrust my hips again, begging for him to touch me.

He holds me steady and takes a step back. "Let me walk you to your room."

I nod, thankful for his self-control. I can't believe I pretty much dry-humped him in a public space. He places a hand on the small of my back, and we walk the rest of the way to my room.

"Here we are," I say silkily, leaning back against the door. I get in one last look at the handsome man making his mark on me. Disappointment that we won't be able to touch each other for the rest of the day has me pouting on the inside. "Thank you for a wonderful night."

Jace holds my face in his hands as he runs his thumb over my cheek—a gesture I'm quickly becoming addicted to. Instead of kissing me, he drops his hands and steps back. The heat in his eyes burns me to my core. It doesn't feel like he wants to be a gentleman, but he will, and it only makes me want him more.

"I'll see you at breakfast. Be a good girl and save me a seat." His gravelly command hits its mark, and my thighs clench.

I'd much rather be a bad girl.

He starts down the hall. *Fuck it.*

"Ace!" I shout.

He turns around, eyebrows raised. Dropping my shoes and clutch to the floor, I run to him and jump in his arms. I grab his face and press my lips to his in a quick hard kiss.

"What was that for?" he asks.

"To let you know that I can't wait for *later* to arrive."

Surprise washes over his face before it brightens with a megawatt, panty-melting smile.

My breath hitches at the sight.

I drop my legs and turn around, rushing back to my door. I pick up my stuff off the floor, unlock the door, and walk into my room, leaving a dumbstruck Jace in the hall.

I can't fight my grin as I run my fingers over my still-tingling lips. Placing my purse on the table, I chuck my shoes across the room and climb onto the bed, sinking into the soft, fluffy comforter. Even though I haven't gotten a wink of sleep, I'm not tired.

I'm wide awake.

Elated, I stare at the ceiling, replaying the night over in my head. The feel of his arms around me. Our hungry kisses. The deep conversations we shared. The kisses.

Oh god, the kisses. The way he holds me as he ravages my mouth.

Grabbing a pillow, I cover my face and squeal with glee. I don't think I could be any happier than I am right now.

My phone pings. *Scarlett.*

Dragging myself out of bed, I grab my phone from my clutch.

Scarface*: You up? It's almost time for breakfast. Then the beach, you beetch!!!*

Rice Cakes: LOL. Yes. I'll shower now. See you in a bit.

Scarface*: OK. Hurry up. We need to talk about last night.*

Oh, shit. Did she see us? No. No way. Not possible. There was no one around last night or in the lobby this morning. I take a deep breath. I have to play it cool. She doesn't know anything, and I prefer to keep it that way. At least for now.

Rice Cakes: ***thumbs up emoji***

I plug in my phone to charge and hop in the shower. Twenty minutes later, I'm dressed in my white halter bikini, matching sundress, and yellow Ray-Bans.

I forego makeup, only applying some tinted moisturizer and waterproof mascara. Simple and beach-ready.

Grabbing my bag, I slip on my flip-flops and head out. I guess it's time to face the one-woman firing squad. With any luck, I can dodge her questions.

I arrive at the restaurant to find Scarlett and Levi already sitting with Levi's parents. Greeting everyone, I take the seat next to Scarlett, leaving the other empty for Jace.

Leaning over, I kiss the bride-to-be on the cheek. "Hey, babes. How ya feeling this morning?"

"I'm good."

"No hangover?" I ask.

"Nope, totally ready for the beach." She tilts her head to the side, narrowing her eyes at me. "You look different."

"No, I don't." I answered way too quickly. I can feel her gaze burning a hole into the side of my head as I look at the menu. I can't get anything past her. She can read me like a book.

"Mhmm."

"Did you order already?" I try to change the subject.

"No, we were waiting for you, Jace, and Eli. They should be down soon. Lexi and Laci are going to meet us at the beach. They had a little too much to drink and were still sleeping."

"Amateurs." I scoff, taking the distraction and running with it. "Gotta drink that water and take that Ibuprofen before passing out."

"Or stay up getting the D. Right, Short Stack?" Levi interjects, making me snort. How he can carry on a conversation with his parents and whisper dirty things to Scarlett at the same time, I will never know.

"Levi!" Scarlett hisses, clearly embarrassed. "Your parents are right here at the table. Geez."

"You love it, baby," he purrs.

Her face flames, matching the color of her Bloody Mary. Ugh, it's too early for this.

"Seriously, you two," I whisper, pointing between the two of them. "Let me eat before you start with the dirty talk. I need food and a mimosa before I have to deal with you two pawing at each other all day."

Levi's parents chuckle at my not-so-low whisper. Now I've turned Scarlett on me, and she elbows me in the boob.

"Shi— Shoot, Scarface. Your bony elbow hurt my boob." I rub my poor, beaten chest, scowling at her.

"You know you like it rough." She grins back at me, happy with her version of punishment.

Scarlett smirks, and the hairs on the back of my neck stand up, my body sensing him before I see him. Looking up, he hovers over me, nailing me with those sexy hazel eyes, making me melt.

"Morning, everyone," he greets the table, but his eyes never leave mine, and the sound of his gruff voice sends bolts of electricity straight between my legs.

Jace takes the empty seat next to me, sliding it closer, and sits down. His arm brushes mine, and his clean scent invades my space. I think I just had a mini orgasm.

As casually as I can, I glance to the side, taking him in. He looks fresh, showered, and rested. No one would be able to guess he was up all night kissing me. He's wearing flip-flops, black boardshorts, and a sinfully tight white t-shirt that hugs his chest and torso, hinting at all the hard muscle that lies below and abs that I look forward to getting to know better—preferably, without his shirt on.

"Morning, ladies. What's this about liking it rough?" Eli asks, cutting my ogling session short. He sits in the seat across from us.

The server arrives, and thankfully the conversation changes. Everyone orders food and drinks, and when my pineapple mimosa arrives, I take a big sip. The bubbles pop on my tongue, and the sweet tangy liquid tastes delicious.

After a few sips, I feel more calm sitting next to Jace. His presence is driving me crazy. With every brush of his arm or thigh against mine, my skin heats and prickles with need.

He's too tempting. I need space. I attempt to put it between us and slide my seat closer to Scarlett.

Jace considers that a challenge and innocently adjusts the napkin on his lap before slyly reaching over and running his fingers up my thigh and under the hem of my dress.

My breath hitches, and I choke on the bite of my omelet in my mouth. Choking does nothing to stop my body's response to his touch. My skin pimples, and my center throbs.

"Oh my gosh, Ry, are you okay?" Scarlett slaps my back.

"I'm fine," I cough out. Taking a sip of my drink, I side-eye Jace. I don't know whether to smack or kiss the cocky smirk off his lips.

He's going to pay for making me look like an idiot. I'm competitive, and he woke the beast. He may have won this round, but I plan on getting him back.

Game on, Miller.

Trying to tease Jace is going to be hard with Scarlett's hawk eyes. I've never had a secret relationship before. It's both frustrating and hot as hell. But he's made it my mission to make him feel as frustrated as I have this morning.

"Alright, people. It's time to hit the beach. We have Jet Skis reserved for two hours, then lunch, and then chillin' on the beach. Mom, Pop, are you meeting us for lunch?" Levi continues his conversation with his parents, and Scarlett takes the opportunity to whisper in my ear.

"Bathroom. Now." She turns to Levi. "Babe, Ry and I need to use the restroom. We'll meet you in the lobby in five."

Levi nods and she grabs my hand, pulling me from the table with a yank, not giving me a choice.

"Shit, Scar. Slow down."

With a freakishly strong grip, she drags me to the bathroom. "Nope. Nuh uh. You have some 'splaining to do, young lady." Reaching the bathroom, she flings the door open and pushes me inside.

"I'm sorry, Ricky. What do I need to 'splain?"

She smiles at my returned Lucy reference, but it quickly morphs into a scowl. Ugh. Nothing gets past this one.

"Cut the shit. What's up with you and Jace?"

"I'm sorry, what?" I scrunch my eyebrows in confusion and dramatically place my hand on my chest.

"Fine. Play it like that. But I saw him rub *all* up on your leg. You almost jumped out of your skin—it was so obvious. So were all the little brushes and how close he sat next to you. It was like watching me and Levi in Mexico. So dish. Now." She stomps her foot like a petulant child, waiting for me to answer her.

"Damn. You know you could be a detective, right? You see all, and you're relentless with the interrogation."

"Don't you forget it. I'm Detective Sexy, and I know what I saw. So, tell me. Did you two bone last night?" She wiggles her eyebrow at me.

"What in the ... No. I did not bone him." Did we spend the night with our tongues down each other's throats? Yes. My body heats thinking about what a good kisser he is.

Now is not the time for that.

"First, bathroom. 'Cause now I really do need to go."

Walking into the stall, I do my business, thankful for two minutes of reprieve from her interrogation. Scarlett is not going to give up; she's a dog with a bone when she sinks her teeth into something. I need to give her a little something, so she can calm her tits. I take my time washing and drying my hands.

When I look into the mirror, she's staring at me, arms crossed, waiting.

"So?"

"So, nothing happened. After karaoke, the two of us walked back to the hotel together while the twins and Eli stayed later." That was the truth. "We sat on the beach for a bit and chatted." Also true.

"So why all the touching?" She has me there.

"I don't know. He's just being friendly and flirty. I thought you wanted me to 'get my flirt on'?"

"Yeah, I guess. Shit. I'm sorry. I thought ... Nevermind." She looks away, ashamed for jumping to conclusions.

She might have jumped Levi's bones right away, and I don't blame her. I'm not blind—he's hot. Jace and I aren't there yet.

Will we get there? Before last night, I would have said no, but now I'm not so sure.

"Hey." I grab her hand and look her in the eye. "It's okay. I'm not mad. We had a nice time talking. He's a great guy."

I stop at that. She doesn't need to know about all the kissing. Super hot, panty-melting kissing.

Geez, I need to take a chill pill.

Jace and I agreed we wouldn't say anything about what was or wasn't going on between us, at least for now.

"He is great. I think he's into you. I mean, who wouldn't be? You're freaking gorgeous and the best person I know. You deserve to have what Levi and I do. I got excited. Best friends with best friends."

Ah. I get what's going on here. "Levi really did a number on you, sister. You've gone and gotten all soft and mushy."

"Sorry, not sorry about the boning comment."

"It's fine." I chuckle. This is typical Scarlett since Levi. She thinks everyone should be in love and should be going at it all the time like they do.

"I blame Levi for this, you know. He turned you into a lovesick horn dog."

"How dare you?" She gasps. I glare at her, arms crossed. She's so full of it. "Ha! Fine. He did. Can't be helped. He's a sex god, and his cock—"

"Stop! I don't need to hear that." I cover my ears with my hands.

"Oh, please. You know I can't get enough of his sexiness." She gets a dreamy, faraway look in her eye, and I'm officially done with this conversation.

"I know. I heard. I saw. It's why I moved out." I fake a gag, and she sticks her tongue out at me.

"No more fantasizing—save that for later. It's time to go have some fun."

Time to get revenge.

Better watch out, Mr. Miller.

CHAPTER NINE

Jace

Since we left the restaurant, Rylann's been actively ignoring me.

To say breakfast didn't go as planned is an understatement. I think me and my roaming hands have landed me in hot water. I swear, I'd planned on playing it cool, but as soon as I saw her sitting there in that little white dress, all common sense flew out the window.

She looked like an angel, all fresh-faced, innocent, and sexy. No sign of looking tired after the night we'd shared. All I wanted to do was dirty her up. Pull her into my arms and make her messy with my hands and my mouth.

As soon as I took my seat next to her at the table and our arms slightly brushed, those tell-tale sparks between us flared to life. With every brush of our bodies, her breath would hitch and she'd squirm in her seat. I couldn't help getting off on knowing she was as affected by me as I was by her. My presence was making her wet while hers was making me hard. It only made me want to touch her more.

When I stroked her thigh with my fingers, I thought she was going to jump out of her chair and hopefully land in my lap. On some level, I wanted her to break first. Let everyone know what's developing between us.

Instead, she choked on her omelet, catching Scarlett's attention. I pulled back after that and kept my hands to myself. She wants to keep our budding relationship low-key. I'll respect that for now, however, I don't know how long I can keep that promise. I know that's selfish, but that's how badly I want her, want to be with her, hold her, kiss her. All of it.

On the walk over to the Jet Ski rental hut, all I can do is watch Rylann as she laughs and talks with Scarlett. I need her to put me out of my misery. Not having her undivided attention is killing me. Keeping my hands off her is a lot harder than I thought it would be.

When we arrive, the rental guys have each of us sign waivers and review the safety guidelines before fitting us with life vests.

Rylann makes her way to the dock, her swaying hips taunting me. She's so goddamn sexy. Soft and curvy in all the right places. I stifle a groan as she takes off her dress and puts a life vest over her incredibly small bikini.

I turn around and find every guy working at the rental place staring at her. Clenching my fists, I shoot each one of them a scathing look. Fuckers better keep their eyes off. She's mine.

Mine?

Technically, she's not yet. I plan to change that soon.

"Alright, we have three Jet Skis rented, so we'll need to team up," Levi tells us while he and Scarlett saddle up and hit the water.

"Great. Jace, you ride with Ry. I'm ditching you people to go searching for hot girls. See you out there," Eli shouts, shooting me a knowing look. He salutes us and takes off like a bat out of hell, chopping through the waves.

He knows I didn't sleep in my bed last night and assumes I was with Rylann all night. He hasn't pressed for information, and I won't be offering any either.

I turn around and find Rylann checking out my ass. She shrugs, and I flash her a cheeky grin, wiggling my eyebrows at her. She smacks my chest.

"Are you ready to ride, Sunshine?" I grab her wrist before she can get away and pull her close.

She looks around nervously.

I grab her curvy hips and bring our bodies flush together. "No one's around. It's just you and me on this dock."

"I know. I—"

I interrupt her before she can start to overthink things. Without a care as to who is around, I plant a quick peck on her soft lips. She tries to pull away, but I hold her tighter.

"You know, that little stunt you pulled at breakfast didn't go unnoticed. Scar was all over me for information."

"Is that why you were ignoring me?"

She fights a smile and nods. *Fuck, she's cute.*

"Please, don't be mad at me anymore."

"I'm not mad. I'm disappointed." She tries to sound stern, but I recognize bullshit.

"Are you now?"

"Yep." She pops the P, something she does when she's being fresh. It's adorable as fuck.

Bending my knees, I bring my face to hers, our eyes leveled. "I'm sorry. You looked so damn beautiful sitting there. All I could think about was how I got to kiss and hold you last night. I want to do more of that. In fact, I really want to kiss you right now."

"I want you to kiss me too," she admits. I inch closer, but her hand goes up and blocks me. I scowl, and she chuckles. "We promised to keep whatever this is between us for now."

"I know, and I'm starting to think that was a stupid idea."

"Don't pout, Ace." I push my lip out further. She pokes it with her finger with a chuckle. "It wasn't a stupid idea. But ... I am going to make you pay for driving me crazy."

"Please, tell me that's code for 'I was totally turning you on.'"

She pops her hip to the side and says, "Wouldn't you like to know."

"I would like to know," I declare. If she only knew how badly I wanted to shove my hand up her dress at breakfast. I haven't stopped thinking about diving into her hot center and letting my fingers explore her wet pussy.

"Maybe if you're a good boy ... *later*," she sasses, and my dick perks up. "Now, come on. We have to catch up with the others."

"Yes, ma'am."

Jumping onto the Jet Ski first, I hold out my hand and guide her onto the seat behind me.

She wraps her arms around my waist, rests her chin on my shoulder, and whispers into my ear, "Before we take off, Ace, let me clarify things for you. All your touching *did* turn me on. It left me frustrated. Now, it's your turn to be turned on and left hanging with no relief. I'm going to make it so *hard* for you that you'll be begging me to stop. Or maybe you won't. We'll see."

She scrapes her nails across the open skin between the waistband of my board shorts and my life vest. The hair on my arm stands on end, and my cock hardens instantly.

"Fuuuck." I groan, adjusting my board shorts. I am so screwed, and yet I can't wait for her to tease me. This is some of the best foreplay I've ever had.

"Let's go, big guy." She grazes the back of her hand across my tented board shorts before wrapping around my waist.

Such sweet torture.

With a deep breath, I will my cock to go down as much as possible. Starting the Jet Ski, I pull back on the throttle and shout, "Hold on tight. It's time for a long, hard ride, Sunshine."

I grin at my innuendo. It can't be that bad with her at my back.

I was wrong. Absolutely, one-hundred-percent fucking wrong.

I spent the entire time hard as a rock while Rylann tortured me. Most of the time, she wasn't even trying. Her body stayed pressed against mine, rubbing and grinding on me from behind. Her small hands were all over me. My shoulders, abs, hips, thighs.

Every-fucking-where.

Even her sexy laugh had me harder than stone. I'm going to have to beat my dick in the shower in order to be able to walk around without hurting myself.

Blue balls and all, today has been hands-down fantastic. I can't remember the last time I laughed so hard. We had so much fun riding the waves, teasing each other, and talking. Rylann is amazing. She's playful, smart as a whip, and drop-dead fucking gorgeous.

Looking over my shoulder, I find her lying on her towel in the sun. My eyes eat up her curves. Her body glistens in the sun, and the contrast of her tan skin against the tiny white bikini she's wearing has me biting back a groan.

I'm standing in the water with Eli as he scopes out chicks—his words not mine. Levi, Scarlett, and his family are scattered around, doing their own thing. Now is the perfect time.

I ditch Eli and make my way to where Rylann is lying. I plop down on the towel next to her and lay back, closing my eyes behind my shades so I can enjoy the heat. Despite the fact that I haven't slept in two days, I feel invigorated. It's like I've grabbed onto a live wire and it's pumped pure raw energy into my veins. She does this to me.

I move my arm closer to hers and reach out, twining our pinky fingers together. The electricity between us surges to life.

"I know what you were doing," I tell her out the side of my mouth.

"Hmm?" Playing innocent, she turns her head to face me. Her eyes are hidden behind her sunglasses. She licks her bottom lip, and my eyes follow the action.

"On the Jet Ski. Message received loud and clear."

"What message would that be?" she asks sweetly, a smirk on her lips.

"You win, Sunshine."

Rolling onto my side, I prop myself on my elbow, head resting on my fist. Her smirk is now a full-on grin at my admission of defeat. My heart beats double time, stunned by her beauty. I want to kiss her. Just cover her mouth with mine and kiss the hell out of her.

I look around to check for our group, but see everyone is too close. Kissing her right now is impossible. Instead, I use my body to block us from view and run my fingers down her arm. Her soft warm skin pebbles under my touch. Groaning, I imagine all the very ungentlemanly ways in which I want to run my hands over her body. With any luck, I'll be able to get my hands on her soon.

"Jace," she exhales my name, and I wonder if that's how breathless she'll sound when I make her come.

I run circles over her hand with my fingertips. Not wanting to get caught, I pull away too soon.

I clear my throat before asking the question I've wanted to since I found out we only have drinks and dancing plans for the night. Turns out, Levi convinced his bride-to-be to schedule a free night. That leaves me an opening to take Rylann on a date, without Scarlett's observing eyes watching our every move.

"Let's sneak away from the hotel tonight. Before we have to meet everyone, let's get out of here. Just the two of us." Okay. That's not a question, but Rylann smiles and I let out a breath.

"What do you propose we do with that time?" She reaches behind her ear and wiggles her sunglasses up and down. I bark out a laugh at her playful insinuation. "Seriously, though. What did you have in mind?"

"I was thinking we could go for a walk through the market-place. Do some souvenir shopping. Grab some dinner. Grab your sexy body and kiss you senseless. You know, the usual first-date stuff."

"First date, huh?"

"Hell yes. We are doing this the right way, baby." She chuckles softly but still doesn't answer me. "Say yes."

"Yes."

Fuck yeah. I pump my fist internally.

"It's a date." I roll onto my back with a grin.

"Ace?"

My head swivels back to her as she lifts her sunglasses off her face. She sweeps her eyes over my body, stopping at my cock for a full two seconds before moving them back to meet mine. "I plan on grabbing onto you too." Then she drops her shades back in place.

Thoughts of her small hands stroking my cock fill my head and have me swelling in my board shorts. I roll onto my stomach to hide my now fully hard dick from fellow beachgoers.

"Fuck, Sunshine. You're going to pay for that." The words come out more gravelly than stern.

"I look forward to my punishment."

With those parting words, she jumps up from her towel, laugh-ing, and starts towards the water. Over her shoulder, she gives me a teasing finger wave.

I bury my face in my arms, willing my cock to go down.

Two things are for sure.

I'm gone for this woman. And tonight can't come soon enough.

CHAPTER TEN

Rylann

I'm beside myself with happiness.

It's only day freaking two, and I am having the most amazing time in paradise. Sun, laughs, waves, and a hot guy who can't keep his eyes—or his hands—off me. It almost doesn't feel real.

After all the heartbreak I endured back home, my expectations for this week weren't high. Then I met Jace.

The moment our eyes met, everything shifted. Butterflies swirled in my stomach, my heart did this little flip in my chest, and a strange bolt of electricity ran through me when he touched my hand. I don't know how to explain it except to say that we have this instant connection. A chemical bond innately pulling us together.

Although we promised to keep what's going on between us on the down-low, I don't like it. It's making me feel icky. Besides, there's no way in hell we will be able to keep a lid on us. I'm about two seconds away from combusting every time he comes near me.

Jace has already made it clear that he doesn't want us to be a secret, and after our date tonight, I'm going to tell Scarlett because I don't want to keep us a secret either.

When he asked me to go on a first date with him, I almost kissed his sweet, sexy face right there on the beach for everyone to witness. We had a great time on the Jet Ski, flirting and teasing each other. I wasn't expecting him to ask me out when he came over to lay with me. I like that he took the initiative. I'm so excited to go out with him, just the two of us. It will be nice to take advantage of being best-friendless.

While I love my bestie, she's a nosy little thing—always in my business, asking if I notice Jace staring at me. *I do. He looks at me like I'm his next meal.*

Are we into each other? *Yes, we are, and I can't wait to rip his clothes off.*

Jace has this way of saying inappropriately sexy things to me when no one is around, and it's freaking hot. I need to look good for him tonight. After all his innuendos, I want him to be frenzied with the need to touch and kiss me as soon as I open the door.

Scarlett lays her head on my shoulder, bringing me out of my head. "Did you have fun today?"

"I did. What time do you want to meet later?" *Please say after 8:00.*

I look at the back of Jace's head, and his ears perk up imperceptibly. Our group is in the elevator up to our rooms.

"You want to eat dinner together?"

No. I want to meet up with Jace, but I go with, "I was thinking of room service and a bath. Maybe take a nap before we hit up the bar tonight."

"That sounds good."

"Besides, that gives you and Levi plenty of time to get all your,"—I make a gross face and wave my hands over her body—"horniness out. We do not need to be subjected to that all night."

Scarlett rolls her eyes. "Whatever. But fine. I actually like this plan. I'm tired. I'll text when I'm getting ready. Meet up around 9:00-ish?"

"Perfect. I'll be ready to party," I reply coolly. Internally, I'm screaming, *Yes!* while glitter bombs go off.

The elevator dings my floor, and I exit with Jace and Eli. I'm about to reach my door when a warm hand wraps around my wrist and spins me around. My chest slams into Jace's hard torso and into his strong arms.

He looks over his shoulder before placing his hands on my lower back, scantily close to my butt. Those pesky butterflies flutter in my stomach again, and I melt into his touch. I fit perfectly in his arms, and a wave of peace falls over me, reminding me that this is where I want to be. The sparks between us flicker as we stare into each other's eyes.

"I heard you and Scarlett in the elevator. Are we still on for dinner?"

Running my hands up his chest and shoulders, I drape my arms around his neck. "Of course. I was just trying to buy us some more time alone. Scarlett is getting suspicious."

Jace grins and kisses my nose and the freckles on my cheek. "Good. Don't worry about her. Can you be ready in thirty minutes?"

"Ace, I need more time than that."

He reaches up and moves a loose lock of hair behind my ear. "How long do you need?"

"An hour. I'll go fast. That gives us three hours alone."

"I can live with that for now." He leans in and brushes his lips over mine. Before I can return the kiss, he releases me, takes the keycard from my hand, and unlocks my room. "One hour," he says gruffly, holding my key hostage.

"One hour," I agree.

He grins and hands back my key before walking away.

The speed at which I wash, buff, and prime my body is other-worldly. After blow-drying my hair into loose waves, I apply a light layer of makeup and search for the perfect outfit.

After rummaging through the closet—because, yes, I am that person who unpacks on vacation—I decide on my yellow short-shorts, with my favorite black silk tank top with ruffled cap sleeves. I finish off my look with my black wedges. Not only will they give me a couple of inches, but they are comfortable enough to wear all night.

Looking at the clock, I find exactly an hour has passed. Now, what do I do? We forgot to talk about how we'd meet up. Should I call his room?

A flash of anxiety hits me. What if Eli picks up? Before I pick up the phone, there's a knock on the door and relief hits me like a tidal wave.

He's here.

Grabbing my wristlet, I make sure my ID, money, and cell are inside, and head to the door. My stomach flips with nerves. Running my hands down my clothes one last time, I swing open the door.

Standing on the other side, looking sexy as sin in dark jeans and a black button-up shirt with the sleeves rolled up to his elbows, is Jace Miller. Holy mother of god, he looks sex-on-a-stick hot.

My tongue rolls over my bottom lips as I take in the sight before me. Jace does the same. His eyes eat me up from head to toe and back. I love it when he looks at me like I'm everything he's imagined and more. Like he can't wait to touch me.

Surprising me, he pushes me into the room and closes the door before hauling me into his chest by my hips. "You look stunning. So damn sexy and edible. If I wasn't such a gentleman, I would be pushing you up against the wall and burying my face between your legs, having my way with you."

My insides liquefy.

He runs his thumbs over my hips and slides his hands over the globes of my ass. Kissing my neck, he breathes me in and, for some reason, the act seems so erotic. "God, you smell so fucking amazing," he purrs.

My heart is beating so fast it might explode out of my chest. Jace continues to run his nose up and down my neck grazing the sensitive skin with his lips. This man is dangerous, and his words are potent. A lesser woman would crumble under the tender heat of this man's touch. I almost do. Fortunately, I'm stronger than that. Plus, I'm hungry.

Although, putting my mouth all over his body does sound appetizing. *Mmm.*

Reading my mind, Jace smiles. "As much as I would like to eat you for dinner, I think we should get a proper meal first."

On cue, my stomach grumbles, making us both laugh. "The stomach has spoken. Food first, Ace."

"Yes, ma'am. Do you have everything you need?"

"Everything I need is in this little guy." I hold up my small wristlet for him to see.

"I like that you pack lightly. I made a reservation at a restaurant that serves local food. Is that okay with you?"

"Sounds perfect. I love trying local cuisines. It's the best part of traveling."

"God, woman, you know exactly what to say to turn me on." He kisses me and drags me out of the room, and down the hallway.

"Hold up. You're walking too fast. What's the rush?" I yank on his hand trying to slow him down, but he doesn't stop until we get to the elevators.

He pushes the button before answering my question. "I had to get away from your room before I did some very ungentlemanly things to you." He cups the side of my face, rubbing his thumb across my lips, making them tingle. "You look so damn gorgeous tonight. You and your room smell so fucking intoxicating. I was barely hanging on by a thread. Thankfully, your stomach growled before I had you for dinner."

The elevator dings its arrival, and he plants another kiss on my lips before we step inside. Once again, his sweet, dirty words have reduced me to a pile of goo. He has me thinking about how good his hot mouth on my wet center would feel as he made me come and scream his name.

"Stop that." Jace growls, interrupting my smutty thoughts.

"Stop what?"

"Stop thinking about me having you for dinner."

"I wasn't thinking about that." My retort sounds choppy and breathless even to me.

"You're a bad liar. But that's okay. I like knowing you're thinking about what I'm going to do to you … later." He gives me a cocky smirk.

Two can play that game. "I might be a bad liar, but I think it's you that's thinking about all the unlady-like things you want me to do to you … later."

His eyes close as I run both sets of fingers through his thick brown hair, scratching his scalp—something I've learned he likes. My hands make their way down his body, roaming over the back of his neck, his throat, and his strong torso, lingering on the ridges of his stomach until I reach the waistband of his jeans. Curling my fingers over the edge, a few inches above the noticeable bulge in his jeans, I lick my lips and hum.

"Behave, Sunshine," he grits out from behind clenched teeth.

"You behave," I challenge, thrusting my pelvis into his, pressing his hard cock against my mons. My pussy aches with need.

In a flash, he has me pinned against the wall of the elevator. The gold rings around his irises glow as he growls, "You made your point, Sunny."

The elevator opens up into the lobby, sucking the tension between us with it.

"Ugh. I can't eat another thing," I grumble, throwing my napkin on the table in defeat. I'm stuffed.

Jace's restaurant choice was perfect—a cute little spot in the marketplace that offered a tasting menu of all local dishes. Not only was the food good, but the company has been even better.

Jace is easy to talk to; we have no trouble talking about our lives, serious topics, or even funny random subjects. Our conversation has been fun and flirty, and at times, toeing the line of dirty and back in seconds. Our attraction to each other is out of this world. I've never wanted to be with a man physically the way I do with him.

"Are you sure? I think I saw an ice cream shop back that way that could be fun to check out." Jace takes a sip of his beer.

"I do love ice cream," I muse.

He shakes his head and chuckles. "How about we walk around a bit? Maybe buy some souvenirs. Then ice cream?"

"Sounds good to me."

Jace catches the server's attention to bring us the check. I go to reach for the cash I have in my wallet, but his voice stops me. "Don't even think about it. Dinner is on me."

Pursing my lips to the side, I pretend to think about fighting him. He growls, and I laugh. It's fun to bait him. He gets all bossy, which I like.

"No need to growl. Thank you for dinner. It was wonderful."

"My pleasure." I watch him sign the check, and my stomach dips.

We are about to go walking around in public. I should be excited, not nervous. I don't want to feel like this; I want to enjoy my time with him.

I need to talk to Scarlett. I'm shit at keeping secrets.

Jace looks up at me with those piercing hazel eyes and notices the change in my thoughts. He offers me an understanding smile. "Breathe, Sunshine. We aren't doing anything wrong. We're getting to know each other. You can tell Scarlett any time you want. I know she means the world to you. You know where I stand."

His words soothe my nerves, and my heart skips a beat for a completely different reason.

Standing up, he extends his hand, giving me the choice. The choice is obvious. I pick us.

Placing my hand in his, those tell-tale currents of energy shoot up my arm to my heart, confirming I made the right decision.

"Thank you. You don't know how much I needed to hear that. Let's enjoy ourselves, and I'll talk to Scar later. I think I need to, so I can be comfortable. It will be good for us too. Then we don't have to hide that we like each other."

Jace pulls me aside and palms my cheek. "More than like. And I won't complain about getting to be near you without feeling like I have to hold back."

My heart flutters in my chest. *He more than likes me.* I more than like him too. We are on the precipice of something big here. I can feel it.

"This isn't a green light to get handsy," I tease, trying to hide my smile.

He rubs his thumb across my freckles. I love that he is so sweet and gentle, and makes me feel treasured while simultaneously turning me on with his authoritative tone and manliness.

"There they are."

"There's what?"

"Your dimples." It's said with such reverence that it takes my breath away.

He leans in and pecks my lips. He's so open and free with his affection—I love it. I haven't dated many men, and the ones I have never expressed their feelings for me the way he does.

I wish we didn't have to meet up with everyone, so I could express the way I feel about him with more than words.

CHAPTER ELEVEN

Jace

Fuck me, she's beautiful.

That's the only thing I was capable of thinking when Rylann opened the door, ready for our date. I almost swallowed my tongue when I saw her in those sexy yellow shorts, her tan legs on display. Pushing her back in and having my way with her was undeniably my second thought. I had to hustle us from her room as quickly as I could so as not to tempt myself.

She makes me feel alive. Every time we touch, my blood heats, my heart speeds up, and my cock turns to stone. Her smile sucks the breath from my lungs and fills me with a warmth so deep that my chest aches.

No one has ever made me feel this way. Physically or emotionally. We fit together on a molecular level. When I'm with her, my world feels right. I'm going to have a hard time keeping my distance from her tonight.

She squeezes my hand, grounding me. "You okay there?"

"I'm sorry, what?" I look down to find concern etched on her brow.

"You haven't said anything for two blocks. Are you okay?" She pulls me to a stop on the sidewalk.

I escort her to the side. "I was just thinking about how I'm going to have to let you go when we get to the hotel, and I really don't want to."

Her cheeks flush at my confession. Lifting her hand, I place a kiss on the soft skin of her wrist. The scent of coconut washes over me, simultaneously soothing and driving the animal in me wild.

She sighs, a smile lighting up her face. "Me too. You know, since we *are* going dancing, there might be a way for us to stay close." My ears perk, and so does my dick when she places her hand on the waistband of my jeans. "That's if you would like me to save you a spot on my dance card." Her fingers start crawling up my abs to my chest.

"Sunshine, if you think that dance card is going to be filled by anyone else, you are sadly mistaken. All those spots belong to me," I growl.

Her breath hitches, and her gaze turns heated. She likes it when I get growly and possessive. I save that tidbit for later before I get carried away and kiss her out in the open.

An idea pops into my head, and I lead her towards our hotel, through the lobby and toward our destination. I remember seeing a family restroom near the gift shop, and it's the perfect location for what I have in mind. I glance around to make sure the coast is clear before turning the handle down and tugging Rylann inside, locking the door behind us.

"What are we doing in here?" she pants.

I wrap my arms around her back and haul her body into mine. With one hand on her hip and the other in her hair, I tilt her head to the side. "This."

I slant my mouth over hers in a searing kiss. My tongue ravenously curls and lashes around hers. We're all lips, tongues, and teeth. She wraps her arms around my shoulders, twisting her finger through my hair, and tugs, releasing a beastly groan from my chest. Our kiss on the beach was tame compared to this. This kiss is raw, real. I could kiss her all night, and it still wouldn't be enough.

Greedily, I pull her tighter, closer. I need more of her. I place my hands on her ribs, below her full tits. She arches her back, and her nipples scrape my chest. I circle my thumbs over the hard peaks, the fabric doing nothing to conceal her arousal.

She moans, and it's like a siren's call to my cock. My blood rushes south, making me impossibly hard.

Walking her back, mouths still fused, I lift her onto the counter and spread her legs wide. Stepping between them, I grab her thighs, caressing and squeezing, dangerously close to the apex of her thighs. Rylann wraps her legs around my hips, ankles locking me in tight, and grinds her pussy into my cock. She bites my bottom lip, and I almost come in my pants.

This woman has me coming out of my skin. I want to spread her open and bury myself deep inside her.

Loud muffled voices break through the fog, startling her. She pushes at my chest, nudging me away, but I don't stop kissing her—her jaw, her neck, the tops of her breasts.

"Jace." Kiss. "We have to." Kiss. "Stop." Kiss.

"No," I grunt, shoving my tongue into her mouth again.

She gives as good as she gets as I ravage her mouth. She tastes sweet, like the ice cream we shared for dessert.

Someone shouts on the other side of the door, and I break my mouth away from hers. I rest my forehead on her shoulder and shake my head with a groan. She rakes her fingers through my hair, scraping her blunt nails on my scalp. Thoughts of her nails digging into my back as I ram myself inside her hot wet center have my dick growing harder.

I grab her hands from my hair and place them on my chest between us. "Now it's you that has to stop, or we'll never make it out of this bathroom."

Her shoulders shake with quiet laughter. "You're right, even though I don't want to stop."

I lift my head and look her in the eyes, willing her to feel the weight of my next words. "Me neither. I really like your lips on mine. You taste and feel so damn good. I bet you taste this sweet all over." I kiss her neck, and her lids close with a hum. "Hands down, that was the best kiss of my fucking life. I can't wait to kiss you again." I kiss her cheek. "And again." I lick her lips, and she parts them for me. It's the opening I need to kiss her yet again. Deeper.

Fuck. Every time I kiss her, it's the best kiss I've ever had.

This time, Rylann breaks away. "You have to stop saying things like that or we're going to get in trouble."

"Why would we get in trouble?"

I'm purposefully being obtuse, and the knowing look on her face confirms she knows it too. I can't stop myself from giving her a cocky grin.

"Because you got me all hot with that sexy-as-hell kiss and your sweet, dirty words. I'm gonna end up climbing you like a tree right here in this bathroom," she says with a huff.

I bark a laugh. *Fuck, she's so goddamn adorable.*

"That doesn't sound like trouble to me. That sounds like it could be fun. We will have to try it out ... later." I give her my most charming smile.

"You're so bad." She playfully shoves me away.

I drop another quick kiss on her puffy pink lips. I can't help myself when it comes to her. She's irresistible.

"What can I say, babe. You bring out the beast in me. But really, we better get out of this bathroom or I can't be held responsible for what happens next." She lets out a cute-as-fuck giggle and slaps my chest. "Besides, the first time I let you climb me like a tree will not be in a public bathroom."

Her breath hitches, and she bites that sexy bottom lip again. I grab her hand, distracting myself from sucking that plump flesh into my mouth. I kiss her fingertips. She melts under my touch.

I love how her body responds to me.

"What do you say … You ready for some dancing?" I grab her hips and lift her off the counter, placing her on her feet.

She looks flushed and a little sexed-up. Fuck, yeah. I did that to her.

"More than ready. Hope you can keep up with me."

"I can more than keep up with you."

She hums, straightening up and running her hands over her top. She adjusts those sexy yellow shorts of hers, and I wish it was my hands covering her body. Every-fucking-where. Cupping her tits, groping her ass, touching her sweet pussy …

"Jace, did you hear me?"

I tear my gaze from her body. "No. I'm sorry, what?"

Rylann rolls her eyes at me, but I can see the smug little smirk on her lips. "I asked if I should walk out first. Get your head out of the gutter and focus, please."

"Sorry, baby, but my head is not coming out of the gutter any time soon. You are just too damn sexy." I drink her up, lingering on her luscious tits.

She claps in my face, and I give her a devilish look.

"Focus, Mr. Miller."

Fuck. It's hot when she says that.

"Have I told you how smoking hot you are?" She sniggers, shaking her head no. "Well, that's criminal because you are and should be told so constantly."

"Ace," she whimpers.

"I'm focused. Promise. You slip out first. I need another minute." I adjust myself.

"Okay. I'll see you in a few." She reaches up on tiptoes and gives me one last little kiss before heading to the door. "While you force that beast in your pants to go down,"—she points at my crotch—"I'll be running upstairs to change my panties. These are completely ruined thanks to you." She blows me a kiss and hightails it out of the bathroom.

My cock twitches in my jeans. I'm definitely going to be thinking about her wet panties all night long.

This woman is going to be the death of me.

CHAPTER TWELVE

Rylann

I wasn't kidding when I told Jace I needed a new pair of panties. He completely destroyed me with that make out session.

I shake out the lingering tingles left on my skin from his big hands. If that kiss in the bathroom is a prelude to what it will feel like to have sex with him, then *damn*. Just thinking about how I felt his thick cock grind into me in the bathroom has me clenching my thighs on the ride up to my room.

Ah! I need to stop thinking about what went on in that bathroom.

I make it to my room without being seen, and I hate that I'm sneaking around. I need to talk to Scarlett. Things with Jace are progressing fast. I can't explain it, but there is something about him that has me under his spell. When I'm with him, I feel different. In a good way. I feel confident and bold. I like who I am when we're together.

It only takes me five minutes to change my panties and be back in the lobby. Everyone is waiting when I arrive.

"What took you so long?" Scarlett demands, hands on her hips, looking like ball-busting Barbie.

I glance over at Jace. He covers his smirk with a fist, knowing exactly what took me so long.

"Geez, you act like I'm late for your wedding. Chill, woman." I smack her ass and hug her tight.

"You chill. I'm just busting your lady balls 'cause it's fun," she mumbles in my ear.

I love this girl, even when she's giving me hell.

"You're a shithead. You know that, right?" I twist her around, putting her in a headlock. She tries to unhook my arm, but I've got her pinned. "Tap out, or this could get worse for you."

"You wouldn't! Let me go. We don't have time for this, Ry!" Scarlett wails and starts squirming, trying to push me off. It's useless, and she knows it.

"You're being too feisty. Tap out, or I'm going to sit on you."

"I'd pay to see that." I turn to find Eli wagging his eyebrows.

I release my bestie and point at him. "Down, boy."

He laughs, along with everyone else.

Scarlett scowls, smoothing down her hair.

"Don't get them started, E. The last thing I need is to stop one of their wrestling matches in the lobby." Levi rolls his eyes at us.

"Wait. They wrestle? Like, wrestle wrestle?"

Scarlett and I start giggling at Eli's bewilderment.

"Yes, and it's not as exciting as you think it is. It always ends with someone getting sat on."

Do we wrestle? Kind of. Think Monica and Rachel *à la Friends*.

It started in middle school. We were in Scarlett's room one day, and I was having a freakout over a science test. She wrestled me to the ground and sat on me until I calmed down, then gave me a lecture about science not being important because I was going to be an artist. Now, we do it for fun or when one of us wants to get her way.

"Okay, we're all here. You two, knock it off." Levi points to us. "Now, let's get this party started." He hooks an arm over Jace's shoulder and pulls him away, Eli and the twins following behind.

I grab Scarlett's hand, holding her back a few feet before following after the guys. "That was fun."

"No, it wasn't, you wench. I'm going to make you pay."

Ignoring her comment, I continue, "What did you guys do for dinner?"

Scarlett eyes me with suspicion. "Room service. Why?"

"Well, I had a change in plans." I take a deep breath. "Now, I'm kind of freaking out."

"What did you do? Do I need to sit on you?!" she yells.

"Geez, keep your voice down." I look up, making sure no one is paying us attention.

"Okay, okay. Sorry. You're just kind of freaking me out now. What's going on?"

What's going on? Good question because I have no freaking idea. My emotions and hormones are batting it out as we speak. I'm excited, nervous, horny, scared, and happy.

One day into this trip, I met a man that turned out to be amazing, and now I'm crazy about him. I just got out of a relationship—is it really this easy for me to move on? To be with a new guy so soon after breaking up with someone I truly cared about?

Yes, my heart whispers.

"I see you thinking. Where's your head at? You know I got your back, right? No matter what."

"Of course, boo. Ride or die." We bump knuckles, sealing our promise.

"Now, tell me what's got your undies in a twist."

"I didn't spend my free time in my room. I ended up going out on a date. But before I get into that, I have to tell you something else. I know this goes without saying, but I need you to keep this between us."

Scarlett rolls her eyes but follows it up with a verbal confirmation. "Vault."

I look ahead again, making sure we are out of earshot before letting the verbal diarrhea begin. "I lied. By omission! After karaoke, Jace and I walked and talked. All night long. On the beach. It was amazing. He's amazing. He's got me feeling ... all kinds of ways, and I really freaking like him. I feel so torn. My head is in one place, and my hormones are in another ... Ugh. That isn't even the point I am trying to make."

I look at my friend, trying to read her reaction, but all I get is a calm and collected Scarlett. "Take a deep breath. Please clarify what you left out of the story." She waves her hand in a circle encouraging me to continue.

"We kissed. Like a lot. That kiss ... It was earth-shattering. The best first kiss I've ever had. It's never felt that way before with someone. It felt so right. It was hot as fuck. Like panty-melting hot. But now I have a guilty conscience because of Sam. I feel like a horrible person for wanting Jace. I suggested we keep whatever it is between us low-key and continue to get to know each other while we're here. He took me out on a dinner date, and then we kissed again. Boy, did we kiss. It was so freaking hot. Like, burn-you-to-your-soul hot. I want to rub myself all over him, so his scent stays on me. Ugh, listen to me. I sound like a crazy person."

She puts her hand on my arm, and I shut my mouth. "Wow. That's a lot of info to get in thirty seconds."

"Sorry," I whine.

"Don't be sorry. It's fine."

"But—"

She puts her hand over my mouth to stop me. "Breathe. It's my turn to talk. Sam broke up with you. You are a single woman. A hot, desirable single woman. Sam should've thought about that before calling things off. You have nothing to feel guilty about. Whatever's going on with you and Jace is separate from everything else. I mean, you should have told *me* this morning." She swipes at me like a mean old cat with a smile on her face. "Anyway, you are free to have all the fun you want, with whomever you want. As long as you and Jace are on the same page, I find nothing wrong with what you two are doing."

"I know, and you're completely right. That doesn't make me feel any less torn up, though. I mean, we both just got out of relationships. But he does things to me. When he touches me, my skin tingles, my heart races, and my stomach flutters. I want to be around him. I want to kiss him. Shit, I want to *do* him."

We walk in silence for a few minutes, following our group.

"I've never heard you like this before. You know, everything you're saying is how I felt with Levi. So at breakfast, he really was getting handsy with you, huh?" She pumps her brows suggestively and honks the air with her hands, making me laugh.

"So crass. Yes. He said all he could think about was kissing me, so he settled for touching me as much as possible. How can I not swoon at that?"

She lets out a whistle. "So, what happened at the beach? I'm not gonna lie. I saw you two talking, and I could see the sparks. It's been so hard for me not to push for answers. I told Levi something was going on, and he told me to—and I quote—'Calm my tits and leave it alone.' It sometimes amazes me that he's a lawyer." She shakes her head.

Levi does have a way with words, and it cracks me up.

"While we were on the Jet Ski, I gave him a little payback with the touching."

"Payback, huh? I bet you gave it to him good, didn't you?"

"You know it. Let's just say I got a handful myself."

"Ha! You little slut." She cackles.

"Twit. Anywho, I was sunning when he came over to admit defeat and asked me out on a date."

"How was the date?"

"Wonderful. We had so much fun, talking and laughing. We have so much in common. Then right before we met up with you, he dragged me into the family bathroom—"

"Ladies!" Our heads snap up at Levi's shout over the crowded street. He and the gang are waiting for us at the door to the club.

"Give us a second, Levi!" Scarlett yells at him and turns back to me. "Quick. Spit it out."

"He kissed me. No ..." I shake my head. "It was earth-shattering."

"Damn." Scarlett looks at Levi, and I can tell she's thinking about his kisses.

"'Damn' is right." My clit tingles at the memories of Jace's mouth on mine and his hard cock pressed between my thighs. I shiver at the thought.

"Let's talk more later. My advice to you for tonight—don't overthink things. Just have fun. Don't get wasted. Lee wants us to go on that hike in the morning. Deal?"

"Deal."

We both nod and make our way inside.

⁓♡⸬

"Are you feeling better?" Jace asks.

We are sitting at a table in the back, big enough to fit us all. I've been staring at him while he told some story about his and Levi's college days. I got lost in the deep timbre of a voice.

Like him, it's sexy. Deep and warm, like caramel being poured over my body.

"Hmm? Oh, yes. Much better." I stop myself from stammering and take a drink of my margarita.

Scarlett and Levi are slow-dancing in the middle of the dance floor, wrapped up in each other.

"Disgustingly cute, aren't they?"

"They are." I sigh.

Jace covers my hand with his, giving it a quick squeeze under the table before returning it to his drink. I miss his touch immediately.

"You're fucking cute yourself." Jace half-smirks at me and winks.

Swoony fucker.

"Stop that!" I punch his shoulder.

"Ow! You wound me, baby." He feigns hurt, clutching his arm.

"Doubtful." I roll my eyes. "Are you having fun?"

"I'd be having more fun if we were alone. I can't really hold you like I want to."

I glance at the dance floor. "How about a compromise?"

"I'm listening?" He twists his body, his knees knocking mine.

I stand up and hold out my hand to him. "Care to join me for a dance?"

"Hell yes." The skin at the corner of his eyes crinkles with his beaming smile, looking sexy as all get-out.

He takes my hand and leads me to the dance floor. He grabs my hips and pulls me close. My breasts press against his hard chest, and I can feel my nipples harden. I wrap my arms around his broad shoulders, inhaling his masculine scent.

"Jace."

"Rylann."

"I was thinking ..." I lower my eyes to his chest, concentrating on how our bodies feel pressed against each other as we move to the music. Before I chicken out, I ask, "Would you maybe want to come back to my room tonight?"

"Look at me, Sunshine." He tilts my chin up, forcing my eyes to his. "We don't have to rush anything. You know that, right?"

"I know. I thought we could hang out like we did last night. I don't want tonight to end, but I also don't want to get sand all up in my ass again."

He barks a gruff laugh that wraps around me like a warm bath. "I'm always happy to personally help you get the sand out of your ass."

"You're incorrigible."

"Nah, just helpful."

"That's oddly sweet, you dirty man."

He winks at me, and I stifle a laugh. Our bodies continue to sway to the beat.

"I want to spend every minute with you too. We can go as slow or as fast as you want. Whatever you ask for, I will give you."

I melt at the comfort his words give me. He brushes back a strand of my hair, his fingertips grazing the skin behind my ear and neck giving me goosebumps. I really want to pull his head down and kiss the ever-loving hell out of him.

Reading my thoughts, he pulls me closer, his breath fanning over my face. "Me too. You can guarantee that these lips,"—he rubs his thumb over my lips—"will be given my full attention ... later."

My stomach dips, and my knees wobble at his pledge. Our eyes stay locked on each other as we sway to the music. The song switches to one with a faster beat.

We stay pressed against each other, moving to the slow beat only we hear.

CHAPTER THIRTEEN

Jace

When we get back to our floor, I walk Rylann to her door.

I'm high on anticipation. She surprised the hell out of me asking me to stay the night in her room. But I won't lie and say I'm not happy about it; I can't wait to wake up with her in my arms, my body curled around hers.

She opens the door and steps in, waiting for me to follow, but I don't.

"Did you change your mind?" She looks up at me in confusion, her pink lips turned down.

I cup her cheeks in my palms. "No fucking way, Sunshine. I want to spend the night with you. I'm going to go grab some clean clothes and my toothbrush. I'll be back in a few. Go on in and get ready for bed. I'll be right back."

"Okay." Her shoulders drop, and a smile spreads across her face. She hands me her room key. "Use this to come back in, just in case I'm not done in the bathroom yet."

"Good idea. I'd hate to have you answer the door looking indecent, where anyone could see you. You're all mine, baby."

I enter my room, and Eli is sprawled out on the couch. He stops scrolling through his phone and gives me a grin. Ignoring him, I walk over to my bag and grab a clean pair of shorts, a shirt, and boxers.

He clears his throat, waiting for me to talk. I don't give him the satisfaction. Nosy bastard can fuck right off. I grab my toothbrush and deodorant from the bathroom, then wrap them up in my clothes.

"Where ya off to, J?"

"None of your fucking business."

"*Au contraire*, big bro. It's definitely my business."

It's not like he doesn't know where I'm going. He just wants me to say it out loud. *Asshole.*

"No, it's not. But if you must know, I'm going to spend the night with Rylann."

Eli's eyebrows leap to his forehead. By the expression on his face, I don't think he was expecting me to be so honest. I'd rather not waste my time talking to him about things when I can be with my girl.

My girl. I like the sound of that.

"Holy shit! I can't believe you just came out with it. I thought I was going to have to pry it out of you."

"I know you weren't going to let me go without talking. To save myself the pain and agony of hearing your voice for longer than necessary, I'm giving you the truth."

"Well shit, bro. You, like, really *like* her, don't you?"

"Yes. I do. From the first moment our eyes met, I haven't been able to think about anything or anyone else." I huff out a breath. Saying that out loud felt like unloading a weight from my shoulders. "I hope this goes without saying, but I need you to keep this to yourself."

"Of course. Are you ready for this? Not to sound like a dick, but you two just met and you both recently got out of serious relationships. Don't get me wrong—I want you to move on and be happy. Ry is a cool chick, but is it too soon?"

Logically, *yes,* it's too soon. But my gut says no.

"I don't know. What I do know is that things feel different with her. I can't explain it. I'm going with my gut, and it says to go for it." I shrug and grab my stuff and head for the door.

"Wait a sec!" Eli yells, jumps off the couch, and runs to the bathroom. He returns, holding a small box. He slaps me on the back and hits me in the chest with a box of condoms. "Looks like you need these more than I do. Take them. I can get more tomorrow."

I bat his hands and the offending box away from me.

"You're such an asshole." I shove him away and flip him off.

I reach the door and ... Fuck.

I double back and grab the box from him, then stomp out of the room trying to slam the door behind me.

"You're welcome!" he yells. I can hear him howling with laughter as I make my way down the hallway to Rylann's room.

I hope she's still in the bathroom, so I can hide these fucking condoms. I'm not even sure why I grabbed them. It's not like I am expecting to do anything other than sleep with her tonight. The last thing I want her to think is that I'm only here to have sex. I'm in no rush. She decides where she wants this relationship to go physically.

Have I thought about fucking her? Of course I have. I'm a man, and she's the most gorgeous woman I've ever laid eyes on. The mere thought of her big brown eyes, sweet coconut scent, and dazzling smile gets my dick rock-hard.

The kiss we shared in the lobby bathroom was scorching. Our chemistry is off-the-charts hot. Putting my hands and mouth all over her was a wet dream come true. It was physically painful to stop from spreading her open, sinking inside her, and having my way with her.

Thankfully, Rylann is still in the bathroom when I enter the room. I move over to the dresser and pull it open to find her clothes inside. It's cute that she puts her stuff away instead of living out of a suitcase. I smile at the neatly folded piles.

"Ace, is that you?" she calls from the bathroom.

"It's me. I was looking for a place to put my clothes."

The door opens, and I find her leaning against the door jam, looking like a wet dream.

My mouth waters at the sight of her. She looks so goddamn sexy with a loose side braid, a makeup-free face, little black shorts that barely cover her ass, and a see-through white tank top. Her dark nipples peek through the fabric.

How the fuck am I supposed to sleep next to her when she's wearing that?

"I think one of the bottom drawers is empty. Or you can put your stuff on top. I don't mind." She shifts from foot to foot, and I'm pretty sure I'm making her uncomfortable with gawking like a creep. I'm frozen.

She takes a deep breath and makes her way over to me, opens the bottom drawer, grabs my stuff, and drops it in. The box of condoms lands with a thud. She looks down at the drawer and then at me, eyebrows raised in question.

"It's not what you think. Eli was bugging me, and he forced these on me before I left." Squeezing my eyes shut, I pinch the bridge of my nose. "Shit, shit, shit." I'm fucking this up already. She's going to kick me out of her room for being a sex-crazed pervert. I mean, I am sex-crazed for her, but I'm no pervert.

Rylann barks out a laugh, and I can breathe again. "Your brother ... gave you ... condoms. Omigod ... I can't." She's *full-on* laughing at me. Like, "bent over, hands on her knees, and shoulders shaking" laughing at me.

"So glad I can amuse you, Sunny." I chuckle.

"Sorry, not sorry. It's funny that your *little* brother gave you condoms, and your face ..." She starts laughing again. When she gets herself under control, she steps towards me and places her hands on my chest, rubbing small circles. "Let's pretend I didn't see the box. I'm not upset or worried. I trust you. Now, go get ready for bed and when you're done, come join me on the couch."

"Thank you for finding the hilarity in my embarrassment instead of kicking my ass out of your room." I give her a quick, smacking kiss on the lips and make my way to the bathroom.

At superhuman speed, I do my business, brush my teeth, and pull on a pair of athletic shorts for sleeping. I pick up my clean shirt, testing the fabric between my fingers. Fuck it. If she can wear booty shorts and a tank with no bra, I can go *sans* shirt. I throw the shirt on the counter and walk out of the bathroom.

I find Rylann lying across the couch with a Kindle in her hand. She looks relaxed reading in the warm glow of the lamp. Her head is propped up on the arm of the couch, with her legs crossed at the ankle. I could get used to seeing her like this.

"Whatcha reading?"

She glances up from her book, but does a double take. Her eyes zero in on my naked chest.

That's right. Look all you want, Sunshine.

I give my pecs a little flex to mess with her. I'm not going to lie—I like it when she checks me out.

"What did you ask again?" She finally looks up at my face, and her cheeks pinken.

"What are you reading?"

"Oh." She rubs her neck as she swallows. "I'm reading a romance novel. I was trying to keep busy while you were in the bathroom."

I sit next to her on the couch, lift her legs up and drape them over my lap, then rest my warm hands on her cool shins. "What's it about?"

"You really want to know?" I nod. "Well, this one is about a hockey player that falls in love with his best-friend-slash-teammate's little sister."

"Hmm. Is it any good?"

"Yes. It's fantastic. Right now, they are sneaking around so her brother doesn't blow up their love bubble. It's pretty hot."

"Hot, huh?"

"Mhmm." Her eyes flick down and roam over my chest, leaving a trail of heat in their wake. I've never been more grateful to spend my mornings on my surfboard and my evenings running or lifting at the gym.

"What's hot about it?" I ask, drawing her attention back to me.

She takes another hard swallow before answering, "It depends on the story. This one is because she's sneaking into his bedroom while her brother is home, so they can hook up. The fear of getting caught is pretty hot." Her voice lowers, sounding downright sultry.

Talking about her book was a bad idea. We sit there, staring at each other. The energy between us shifts. I'm dying to kiss her soft lips again, and my hands itch to touch every inch of her body.

My hand has a mind of its own and travels up her shin, over her knee to her thigh, and back down. Reaching higher, lingering longer with each pass. She releases a muffled moan. The sultry sound has me cupping the back of her neck and threading my fingers in her silky brown hair.

"I'm going to kiss you now," I whisper against her lips.

Her tongue swipes across her bottom lip. I tilt her head to the side, cover her mouth with mine, and kiss her with everything I have to offer. She tastes minty and sweet. The zap of electricity I get every time we kiss is there, awakening an insatiable hunger deep inside me. I delve deeper, knowing only she can quench my hunger.

Wrapping my arms around her, I shift us down the couch so her luscious body molds perfectly to mine like she was made for me. Our mouths do the talking. I spread her legs and nestle myself between them as she wraps her thick thighs around my waist. Bringing my hands down to her ass, I squeeze the firm globes.

Her hips lift and grind against my cock. I can feel the heat of her pussy through the thin layers of cotton separating us against my cock.

I'm completely lost in her. In the way she smells, the way she tastes, the sexy way she moans in my mouth. I never want to stop kissing her.

She wrenches her lips from mine, throwing her head back into the cushions, baring her slender neck to me. I kiss and lick the exposed skin. She tastes like she smells—sweet and citrusy.

"Yes." Rylann moans, gripping my hair, her nails digging into my scalp and stinging the sensitive skin.

I groan in pleasure as my dick grows harder, pulsing against the apex of her thighs, greedily seeking entry.

Wrapping a hand around her neck, I give it a gentle squeeze, testing her as I feel her pulse race under my thumb. She moans louder, arching into me and thrusting her hips desperately into mine. Letting go of her neck, I grip her gorgeous full tits with both hands.

Fuck, they're big and sexy.

My mouth waters at the sight of hard nipples poking through her shirt, begging for attention. With my thumbs, I rub the hardened peaks before pinching them. She writhes beneath me, and a vision of me hovering over her while I fuck them has my dick weeping with need in my boxers. *Someday.*

I yank her shirt down, exposing her, and take the stiff bud into my mouth, swirling my tongue, tasting her before sucking her deep into my mouth. Even her tits taste sweet like melted chocolate. I release her nipple with a pop and show the other the same attention.

"Oh god ... Don't stop. That feels so good."

I mumble around her nipple, "Not stopping for anything. You taste so fucking good, Sunny."

I take my time alternating between the two. As Rylann's moans grow louder, I wonder if she could come from nipple play alone.

"Mmm." She digs her heels into my ass, grinding herself on my cock. "More ... I need more." She moans.

"I like it when you beg. It's so fucking hot." I smile around her nipple, my tongue teasing.

"Touch me ... *please.*" Her whispered plea sets my blood on fire.

"Where? Here?" I whisper above her skin. I trail my fingertips over the tops of her heavy breasts, making her skin pebble.

"Lower."

My fingertips trail down her stomach, lingering on her hips before traveling over her thighs. I stop at her knees. "Am I closer?" I tease.

"Higher," she grits out in frustration.

Gliding my fingertips up her thigh and over her shorts, I cup her hot center. She grinds her mound into my palm, searching for relief.

"Does your pretty pussy need to come?" I whisper against her lips.

Eyes squeezed tight, she hums and lifts her hips in approval. But I want her words. I want to hear how needy she is for me. I remove my hand from her hot center, waiting for her answer while the heady scent of her arousal invades my nose and sends fire shooting through my veins.

"Please, make me come, Jace. Please." She lifts her hips again, searching for my touch.

"As you wish, Sunshine." I bring her lips to mine in a ravenous kiss while I slide my hand down the front of her shorts, where I am treated to the best surprise. Ever.

No. Fucking. Panties.

A growl rumbles in my chest at the discovery of her bare pussy.

"You're a bad girl, laying here with no panties on. Dripping wet and needy for me." I trace her seam with my fingertips.

"So bad, but only for you." Her breaths are ragged, and the way her body is screaming for me has me fighting for control.

"You're goddamn right, only for me. Now, it's time for you to come all over my fingers." I growl like an animal. A gush of her sweet cream coats my fingertips, and I almost lose it. "You like it when I talk dirty, don't you, my bad girl?" I glide my fingers through her wetness and tease her entrance before pressing soft circles down on her swollen bundle of nerves. I edge her closer to climax without delivering. "Answer me, Sunshine."

"Yes, yes, yes. I like it. So much."

I press my thumb down on her clit and sink two fingers into her silky-tight heat, crooking toward her front walls. I search for her sweet spot. Her pussy flutters when I find it. She hums against my lips as I finger-fuck her.

"You like that?"

"God yes. Don't stop." She keens, her nails digging into the tops of my shoulders.

Fuck. I like when she does that.

She rides my hand with abandon, her pussy clenching as her orgasm builds.

I pump my fingers faster and press down on her clit. "That's it, baby. Ride my hand. You feel so good. So tight. So wet. Come on my hand, Sunny. Now," I growl, biting her nipple.

Like a good girl, she detonates. I watch as she rides the wave of her orgasm, with her head arched back, lips parted, a sheen of sweat covering her skin, and a look of absolute bliss on her face. She is breathtaking.

I tug her to me and devour her mouth until the final flutters of her orgasm fade away. When her muscles relax, I slowly remove my hand from her sopping pussy.

"Look at me," I demand.

Her eyes pop open, completely glazed over. I bring my fingers to my mouth and lick them clean, tasting her sweet arousal on my tongue.

Her eyes round with surprise at my dirty display as she mouths, *Fuck.*

"You taste so damn sweet. I can't wait for you to come on my tongue." I lick her honey on my lips. "Later."

What this woman does to me. Fuck, I'll never get enough of her. She tastes incredible. She tastes like mine.

"So tell me, was that as hot as what's written on those pages?" I nod to her book and smooth the stray hairs around her face behind her ear.

She waits, catching her breath and fixing her shirt before answering, "Wouldn't you like to know."

"You're gonna pay for that sass, baby." I dig my fingers into her side and tickle her.

Her uncontrollable laughter fills the room. I like how easy it is for us to go from being intimate to laughing in a matter of seconds—another new experience for me. I wonder if it will always be like this for us.

"Oh my god! Ace! That tickles. I yield, I yield!" she screams.

I stop and give her a second to catch her breath, resting my head in the crook of her neck, breathing in the sweet smell of her skin. She smells like home.

My chest squeezes. This is exactly where I'm supposed to be. With her.

"Ready to answer the question?" I raise a brow at her, waiting.

She throws her arms up. "Yes. You win. That was hotter."

"Damn straight." I kiss the smooth skin of her throat. "We should get to bed. We've got an early morning with the gang."

With one swift move, I pick her up bridal style and carry her over to the bed. I throw her on the mattress, watching her tits bounce.

She stares at my still-hard cock and bites her bottom lip, not helping my hard-on in the slightest. "Do you need help with that?"

I look down at my tented shorts. Adjusting myself, I trap the tip of my cock under the waistband of my boxer briefs. "Nope. Tonight was all about you. Scooch over." I tap her thigh and she moves over, pulling the comforter down and climbing under the covers.

I turn off the bedside lamp before sliding in beside her and pulling her to my side, resting her head on my chest. We lay there, our breaths evening out and our legs entwined, like two pieces of a puzzle.

Her quiet voice breaks the silence. "Jace?"

"Ry?" I parrot.

"I'm not tired anymore."

"Me neither." I smile into the dark room.

Pulling her closer, I twirl the silky strands of her hair around my fingers. She drags her fingertips across my chest and down my abs, oblivious to sending my dick the wrong message. She quickly sits up, crosses her legs, and faces me. The light of the moon filters through the window, highlighting her face and making her eyes sparkle.

She's so beautiful and real. The little pang in my chest makes an appearance again.

"Let's play a game."

"I was enjoying the game we were playing. It's called, *Come back here and cuddle me, woman.*" I go to grab her, but she slaps at my hands, laughing.

"That's the problem. I liked it *too* much. And you're driving me crazy laying there without a shirt, and that snake in your shorts is not helping."

I throw my head back on the pillow and laugh. I like how she just says what's on her mind. "Oh, like you're making it easy on me with this." I pull at the hem of her shirt.

"What's wrong with my jammies?"

"You call these jammies? Your shirt leaves nothing to the imagination." I roll on my side and rest my head on my hand. With my other hand, I run the back of it across her chest, making her nipples pucker. "And these shorts. We both know they barely cover that sweet little pussy of yours."

She audibly gulps at my crassness. I move my hand to the top of her thigh, where her shorts sit caressing her soft skin, letting my thumb dip under the fabric to the juncture where her inner thigh meets her heated core. Teasing.

Her lust-filled gaze follows my movements. Running my thumb over her wet slit, I watch as her eyes close and her head tilts back. The moonlight bathes her face with an ethereal glow. She looks like an angel brought to earth for me. My angel, come to save me.

Pulling my hand away, her eyes snap open at the loss. She smacks my chest. "Stop that!"

"Stop what?" I give her a smug smile.

"All that teasing and touching." She smacks me again.

"You like it." I cup her cheek in my palm and bring her face to mine.

She melts into my palm. "Do not," she hisses like a kitten against my mouth.

"Liar." I nip her bottom lip with my teeth before soothing it with my tongue.

Her lips part, and I kiss her. She meets me sweep for sweep, our tongues sensually exploring. We lose ourselves in each other. Unable to help myself, I pull her on top to straddle me and grope the delicious globes of her ass, kneading the firm muscles. She swivels her hips and grinds her pussy on my cock.

Shit, I need to slow things down before I lose all sense of control.

Grabbing her hips, I flip her onto her back and situate myself between her legs. She's so small her pussy rests on my lower abs instead of my painfully hard erection. She's making it really hard for me to be a gentleman. With every gyration of her hips, I start to second-guess myself. I'm so close to saying *fuck it* and burying myself deep inside her.

I pull away, pressing my forehead against hers.

She whines. "Why'd you stop?"

"We don't have to rush, Sunny. We have time. When I finally do get to sink my big cock into your tight little pussy, it will be because we both want it. Want more. Not just some vacation fling. You understand me?"

I watch as her gaze softens at my words. Her hands lovingly frame my jaw, making my heart pinch.

"I understand," she whispers.

"Good. Besides, we don't have enough time tonight. Believe me when I say that when we do take this further, I will be keeping you up all night. Once we start, we won't stop. I'll take my time exploring every inch of your body with my hands, my mouth, and my cock."

She shivers beneath me. "I like the sound of that."

I peck her lips and roll to the side. Pulling her back into the position we started in, we lay there, our breaths syncing into a slow rhythm. I could get used to sleeping with her molded around me.

"Jace?" Rylann whispers, and I chuckle. I can't even imagine what she is going to say now. She keeps me on my toes.

"Hmm?"

"You're right about my pajamas."

"Oh, yeah? How's that?"

"They aren't really pajamas, but this was all I had for our sleepover."

I am not sure I want to finish this conversation because I think I know where it's going, and yet I can't stop myself from asking, "Ry, why don't you have pajamas?"

She sighs dramatically, but it's laced with a hint of mischief. "Because I'm not a huge fan of sleeping in clothes. I usually sleep in a pair of panties and bralette or ... naked."

"Fuck." I squeeze my eyes shut and pinch the bridge of my nose. My mind goes into overdrive thinking about her sexy naked body and her golden brown skin against the white sheets.

There goes my dick again.

This woman makes me feel like a horny teenager. I can barely control my own X-rated fantasies. I don't need her to add to them.

Breathe. In. Out.

"You okay there?"

"No. You did that on purpose." Her whole body shakes with laughter. "You're a tease. Now, go to sleep."

"Good night, Ace."

"Good night, Sunshine."

CHAPTER FOURTEEN

Rylann

"Wow. This view is gorgeous."

We are standing at the top of Diamond Head Summit overlooking Waikiki Beach, and the view is incredible. Below, the busy city keeps moving, the beaches littered with visitors. The ocean stretches out from the beach like the world's own perfectly crystal-blue infinity pool.

"I couldn't agree more." I look over at Jace, who is staring at me and not the view below.

My cheeks heat at his sweet words. "Knock it off. No putting the moves on me."

"Wouldn't dream of it." He shoots me a wink and his signature panty-melting smile.

What am I going to do with this man? I never thought someone like him existed. Jace Miller is a freaking unicorn.

He belongs on the cover of a magazine, with his dark brown hair, tan skin, and dreamy hazel eyes that remind me of sunny days in the forest back home in Portland. He's built like a Greek God, with strong rippling muscles and all. It's a good thing he's wearing a shirt covering his delectable abs, or I might have to beat women off him with a stick.

From what I felt bulging in his shorts, he's also packing some serious heat between his legs. The way he made me feel last night was nothing short of spectacular. My hussy of a vagina pulses just thinking about it.

Horny much?

While, yes, Jace is all those things, he's also attentive and sweet. He's thoughtful and caring. He's a wonderful person, and it only drives up his sexy factor. When he flirts with me, my stomach twirls. When we talk, our conversations are effortless. When he touches me, my skin ignites and I'm putty in his hands. When he looks at me like I'm everything he's ever wanted, my heart beats double time. Jace has awakened something inside me, and it's clawing to get out. I find myself easily opening up to him. I can be vulnerable or playful. I can be me.

A part of me wanted him to lose control and ravish me last night. Instead, he confessed to wanting to wait, and it only made me want him more.

He steps behind me and wraps his arms around my waist, pulling me close. I lean into his embrace as he rests his chin on my shoulder. The scruff of his chin scrapes across my neck, sending shivers down my spine.

"Everyone will be catching up soon. They will see us," I warn. Jace hums, acknowledging me, but instead of backing off he holds me tighter.

Scarlett knows we have something going on, but we haven't broadcast it to the rest of the group. On the ride over here, all the guys were debating on who was in better shape. Scarlett suggested that I could kick all their asses because I run daily. Jace, who is super competitive, challenged me to race up the trailhead with him. I saw it for what it was—a chance for us to be alone—so I agreed.

"I don't care who sees us anymore." His lips graze my neck.

"Really?" My heart beats faster.

"Really. I don't want to hide how I feel about you."

I want to ask, "*How do you feel about me?*" Instead, I go with, "How will that work?"

"We can start by sitting next to each other at meals. Holding hands." Jace entwines our fingers together across my stomach and spins me around, trapping me in his strong arms. "A kiss here," he whispers, pressing his lips to mine. "A kiss there." He kisses me again, deeper. His tongue delves past my lips, exploring my mouth and stealing my breath.

When he pulls away, I'm left dazed, watching as he smirks and wipes my mouth with his thumb. Once the fog clears, I look around, checking for a sign of our group, my nerves spiking. This thing between us is moving at light speed. Even though I'm afraid to jump into something with him, there is no way I can stop myself from leaping.

I'm already falling for him.

As if he knows where my thoughts are going, he says, "I know what you're thinking, Sunshine. I feel it too. I know you're nervous, but I feel it—we are gonna go beyond here. You might not see it now, but I do."

"You do?"

"I do." He kisses my nose. "I'll get you to see it too."

I link my arms around his shoulders. "How are you so sweet and sexy?"

"My mom made me that way," he says with a cheeky grin. "You're sweet and sexy too, Sun." My heart flutters when he turns that smoldering grin on me. "I also think your ass is hot as fuck in these skin-tight leggings. Maybe we can explore a little ass play."

My mouth falls open in confusion, curiosity, and a little fear. I glance down at where our hips meet and picture the monster from last night. I shake my head, and Jace throws his head back in a hearty laugh. He pinches my butt cheek, and I jump out of his arms.

"You perv," I scold him. I might like him pinching, grabbing, and maybe spanking my ass, but he's gonna need to work a lot harder before I let him stick his dick inside there.

"I'm kidding, babe. We can save ass play for ... *later.*"

"You're so bad."

"But you like it." He's right. I do. No one has ever talked to me the way he does, and I freaking get off on it.

"Okay, now that we've established that butt stuff is for later, let's be serious. How are you so confident?"

Jace grips me by the hips and pulls me close to his chest. "For many reasons. One, I'm a confident guy. When I want something, I work for it. Two, I sense it here." He places my hand over his heart. "And three, I have good instincts, and my gut tells me that what we are starting to build is something worth chasing."

"I like your guts." I rub his stomach, stealing a feel of the ridges hidden below. I take a deep breath. If he can be honest with me, I can return the favor. I place his hand over my heart. "I feel it here too. My gut is telling me to chase this feeling with you. Which is scary as hell."

"Scary good, right?" I nod in agreement, and he kisses my freckles and flashes me his signature white-toothed grin.

Before he can lean in again, we're interrupted by my kiss-blocking bestie. "Rice Cakes!" We look over to see Scarlett and the gang heading our way.

"Later," he whispers in my ear, and goosebumps break across my skin.

Scarlett approaches us and wraps her arms around my shoulders, stealing me from his arms. "Jace, your time is up, buddy. I'm stealing my MOH-fo bestie. We have selfies to take."

Jace grumbles in protest but lets me go. "Of course. She is all yours." I'm pretty sure I hear him grumble, "For now," before he walks away and joins Levi and Eli at the edge of the lookout to chat.

I grab Scarlett's hand and pull her in the opposite direction, taking in the view below.

"I know I was annoyed that Levi was rushing us to take this hike but ... *Wow*. This view ... It's amazing, isn't it?"

"It's freaking gorgeous. You picked the perfect place to get married. It's beautiful here."

"I bet it." She makes kissy faces at me.

"Shut up!" I push her as we burst out laughing. I won't deny how happy I've been since meeting Jace has made all the difference.

Scarlett takes in my face. "Ooh! You have dirt. Spill."

"Jace slept over last night," I admit.

"For real?" She grabs my upper arms tight and squeals, and we start giggling again. She's Team Jace and wants me to find what she has with Levi.

I want that too. More than anything. The way my heart skips a beat and my stomach flutters when I'm near him, I'm starting to think that maybe, just maybe, I did find it.

"Tell me everything! Did you ...?" The perv shoves her index finger through her fist.

I snort and slap her hands. "Stop that. And no. I'm not that easy."

"Nothing wrong if you were."

"I know. Let me tell you, though—I wanted to. I was this close to jumping him." I hold up my thumb and forefinger with barely any space between them. "We did do *other* stuff."

"That good, huh?"

"God yes." Everything Jace does to me is good. "You almost caught us kissing. You have *impeccable* timing."

"Not my fault you wasted your time talking instead of making out. Besides, I saved you." She waves me off.

"How's that?"

"You would have had a lot of explaining to do to Levi. I thought you two were going to keep quiet."

"I thought so too, but Jace changed his mind. He kind of asked me ... Actually, no—he *told* me he doesn't care who knows we're together."

"Wow."

"I know."

"Is that what you want?"

I nod. "I mean it's so fast, but I'm crazy about him, Scar."

A huge smile spreads across her face. "I am so happy for you, babes. What do you think is gonna happen after Hawaii? Did you two talk about it at all?"

"We did. A little. He's so confident about what's building between us. But honestly, I'm scared. We live hundreds of miles from each other—"

"Answer me this." Scarlett grabs my wrists, getting my complete attention. "If we had to leave today, would you be okay not seeing Jace again?"

"No!" I blurt out. The thought of not seeing him again hurts every part of me. I think my heart would break.

"There's your answer. I know it's scary. You just have to keep trusting your heart. No matter what, I am here for you. Ride or die?"

"Ride or die." I wrap her in a hug. I needed to hear her reiterate my thoughts. "Let's get our picture with the ocean in the background. Then, we can head out. I don't know about you, but I am starting to get hungry."

"Agreed. Poke bowls for lunch?"

"Yes!" I agree.

Scarlett and I spend the next twenty minutes snapping pictures, mimicking the first photo we took all those years ago that still hangs on the wall. In it, we are sitting on the front steps of Grams's house with wide smiles as we hug cheek to cheek. We have loved each other from the start, and there hasn't been a day that has kept us apart since.

"Okay, Scar, now you and Levi. Smile for the camera." I grab her phone and start taking pictures of the two of them. Some posed, some candid. They are so cute together.

I sense rather than see Jace step behind me. My body is already attuned to his.

"Ry! You should take a picture with Jace. Maid of honor and best man at the top of the volcano."

"It's not a volcano," Jace and I declare at the same time. I caught him reading about Diamond Head this morning after I got out of the shower.

"Yeah, I don't like this at all." Scarlett points and circles her finger at us. "Now, come on over here for your photo op. Bride's orders."

"Whatever you say, Bridezilla." I roll my eyes.

Jace leads us over to the railing, the blue ocean stretching behind us. The breeze picks up, causing my hair to whip around my face. He pushes my stray hair behind my ear. "You're so beautiful."

My stomach flips at his gravelly tone. "You're not so bad-looking yourself."

"Alright, you two, look over here for me," Scarlett calls out.

Jace wraps his arm around my shoulders, pulling me close to his side as we turn toward the camera. I place my hand on his chest and smile. Jace lays a smacking kiss on my cheek, surprising the heck out of me. My shock soon morphs into laughter, the two of us lost in our own moment. He makes me so happy that I might be past falling.

"Are you all ready to go?" Levi folds Scarlett up in his arms as she pockets her phone before I can see the pictures.

"We're ready, babe. I'm hungry. Ry and I want poke bowls."

"I think that can be arranged." Levi gives Scarlett a kiss and leads her to the stairway that leads down the mountain.

I'm about to follow when Jace grabs my hand and laces our fingers together. I glance at our clasped hands, then his face. He brings my hand to his lips and kisses my knuckles. "It starts now, Sunshine. Get used to it."

All I can do is bite my lip and nod at his bossy tone. My nipples stand at attention, and my knees wobble. He's really doing a number on my libido and heart.

When we turn back to our friends, we find Levi watching us with his forehead scrunched in confusion. I think Jace and me being together might have surprised him. Scarlett registers his confusion and whispers in his ear. Levi glares at Jace before they exchange a nod one only best friends can understand.

"Do you think he's upset with me?" I ask nervously.

"You? Definitely not. Me? Maybe. I'll talk to him."

"I feel like we're doing something wrong." I try to pull my hand away, but Jace only grips it tighter.

"No. Levi will be fine. I don't know if you know this or not, but he loves you like a sister. You have him and his loyalty. You're his family too. He will be looking out for you and making sure that I don't hurt you."

Tears well in my eyes. Levi thinks of me as a sister. I feel the same way and have for a while.

Jace tugs on my hand, leading us down the trail but, this time, I don't pull away.

"So what you're saying is, Lee's mine now?"

Jace barks out a laugh and wraps his arm around my neck, pulling me to his chest. It's almost comical how he towers over me. I love how his big arms and body envelop me, making me feel safe and cherished.

"Yeah, Sunny. Levi is yours."

"Interesting ..." I tap my lips with my index finger. "While I do appreciate the concession of your bestie, I think I can play nice and share him with you."

"How magnanimous of you, milady." Jace gives me a tip of his imaginary hat.

"Smartass. All I'm saying is that I would never take him from you. Like, if we didn't work out. I would never let him cut you out of his life."

"I know."

"Good, because I never want to come between you." I couldn't be more serious. Best friends like ours don't come along every day.

"I would never let that happen."

I look ahead to see Levi with his arm around Scarlett. I really hope Jace is right and Levi isn't mad at us.

"Besides, I would never let you take him without a fight. You are a small little thing—I think I could take you."

I give Jace a punch in the arm, trying to take him down a peg, but it backfires in a spectacular fashion. All I can think about is how delicious and muscular his strong arms look. With little to no effort, I bet he could lift me up for a long period of time.

Mmm. Like up against a wall. My clit pulses at the idea of wrapping my arms and legs around him while he pounds into me.

"Don't look at me like that."

"Hmm?" My eyes leave his arms and return to his face.

"I know what you're thinking, and if you don't stop it, holding hands will be the least of your worries. I won't be able to stop myself from taking you right here, on top of the world for everyone to see." Jace hears the low moan that rumbles in my throat. "Is that what you want?"

Yes.

"Fuck. I know you're thinking yes. As much as I would like to give you what you want, we need to catch up with everyone else. But this,"—he moves his finger between us—"isn't over by a long shot." He gives me a little kiss and discreetly tries to adjust himself.

I shamelessly check out his hardening cock. "I don't want it to be." I lick my bottom lip.

Jace growls like an animal before dragging me down the trail and cursing under his breath. I think I just poked the horny bear.

CHAPTER FIFTEEN

Jace

Rylann throws her head back in laughter, exposing the supple skin of her neck. My blood rushes south at the sight, and my brain blacks out. Shifting in my seat, I try calming my half-hardening dick.

I watch her continue to tell a story about ... Hell, I don't even know because I can't hear a single word. All I can do is stare at the beautiful woman taking over my every thought. She laughs again, and the sound is like music to my ears. It's warm and larger than life, like the sun spreading its light over the world.

The urge to ravage her sweet mouth on that mountain was fierce, but I kept it together for her. She's lowering her walls but is still cautious. Being honest about my rapidly growing feelings made her feel safe to admit she feels the same. I like that we're on the same page. Now, I just have to deal with Levi.

He's like a brother to me. I can read him like a book, and he wants information. He wants to know whether or not he should kick my ass. I can feel him watching me. I know he's wondering when the hell I started being into Rylann. The answer to that is easy—the moment I laid eyes on her.

I feel a tap on my thigh and cover Rylann's hand with mine, giving her my attention.

She leans in, and I dip down for her to whisper in my ear, "You've been quiet. Everything okay?"

"Everything is fine. I enjoy listening to your stories." I'm so full of shit. I've done nothing but stare at her beautiful face and have highly inappropriate thoughts. Like how I can't wait to drag my lips and teeth across her golden supple skin or suck on her huge tits until she comes screaming my name.

"Sure you do, big guy." She glances down at my crotch and winks. "You have been staring at me like a perv since we got here."

"No, I haven't." *I have. Like a fucking creeper.*

"Sure. But we both know I'm right. I'm going to visit the ladies' room before we leave for the hotel. Don't perv too hard at my ass while I walk away."

"You're a terrible, terrible woman, you know?" I boop her nose, and she snickers.

"Terribly awesome like my butt." She jumps up from her seat with a laugh and shoves her delicious ass in my face before making her way to the bathroom with Scarlett.

I watch her hips sway until they disappear.

Levi knocks on the table. I turn to him, keeping my face as emotionless as possible. I love the guy, but at the end of the day, Rylann and I are two consenting adults.

"I'm waiting," Levi mutters.

Eli laughs, slapping me on the back. He knows exactly what Levi wants and is loving that I'm about to catch shit.

"For?"

"The fuck you mean, *for?* Explain." He throws his hands in the air.

"Rylann and I are together."

"Since when?"

Since I saw her.

"What does it matter?" I know it matters, but he's not the fucking boss of me. Ry and I are consenting adults, and we care about each other.

"It matters. For many reasons. The most important being that she is my family now. I don't want to see her get hurt." The implied "again" reminds me of our past relationships.

The reminder weighs heavy on my shoulders, but I push it away. "Look. I appreciate you looking out for her. She deserves for you to have her back. But I'll tell you the same thing I told Eli—I'm crazy about her. I don't plan on hurting her. Ever." I take a deep breath. "I know this seems out of character for me, but isn't this how you felt about Scarlett?"

"Yes, it is. But Scarlett and I didn't just get out of serious relationships. We weren't rebounding."

"Neither are we," I growl.

His words hit the mark like an ax to my chest. I was expecting him to be more supportive, like his girl was. Yet here I am, having to defend my budding relationship with Rylann.

"Relax, Jace. Look, man. I'm just looking out for you two. You both seem really into each other. It caught me by surprise. But I want you to be sure. If you hurt her, it will cause a lot of problems."

I run my hands through my hair, tugging. I hate that his words hold truth. "I don't want to hurt her. I care about her. A lot. We've been spending time together after our group activities. We have so much in common, and ... Shit, man, she's amazing. I already have feelings for her."

Silence falls over the table.

"Well, fuck. I wasn't expecting that."

"Neither was I."

She came out of nowhere and captured me.

"I was. Ry is a total smoke show." Eli makes a low whistle. I cuff him in the back of the head. "Hey! Whatever. I'm just glad there is no more Alina. She was a fun-sucker."

"No shit," Levi mumbles.

I sigh, taking a drink of water. I wish Rylann would hurry back to the table 'cause these assholes are bringing down my good mood.

"Jace?" Rylann yells from the bathroom.

My body aches as I get up from the couch. It's been a long day. After our hike and lunch, we all went back to the hotel to change for another afternoon at the beach, which then rolled into dinner and cocktails at the nearest beach bar we could find. I'm grateful betrothed couple called it an early night after that. Not only am I beat, but I'm ready to be alone with my girl.

After lunch, we easily slipped into being a couple in front of our friends and family. I even went so far as to kiss her while we waded in the ocean, not caring who was watching. She's unlike any woman I've ever known, and I haven't been able to take my eyes off her. Or my hands.

"What is it, babe?" We decided to rinse off before watching a movie and heading to bed. Striving to be a gentleman, I open the door a crack to see what she needs. "Sunshine?"

"Can you come in here and help me?"

My mouth goes dry and my palms start sweating at her request.

What the hell could she need? The bathroom has an open floor plan, and one of the walls is covered in mirrors. The shower is encased in clear glass and the free-standing bathtub sits in front of the window. She has to know there would be no hiding her body from me. Right?

Opening the door a little more, I avert my eyes away from the clear glass. Away from her. "Forget your towel?"

"No."

"What do you need help with then?"

"Ace, get your ass in this bathroom right now."

I'm not sure what I expected to see, but it sure as hell wasn't a wet, naked Rylann sitting in a bath full of bubbles. The tops of her luscious tits are exposed, and my cock turns to stone at the sight.

"Fu—" I'm frozen. This woman keeps surprising me at every turn.

She rests her arms along the side of the tub, bubbles dripping to the floor. Our eyes lock, and the electricity crackles between us, the air growing thick with tension. I can see the storm brewing in her brown eyes. She licks her bottom lip and bites down on it. She definitely didn't call me into the bathroom for a towel.

"I left the shower on for you to rinse off the sand."

The sound of the shower finally registers in my sex-addled brain. My sole focus has been on her. If this is the game she wants to play, I'm in.

All the fucking way in.

I stroke my stiffening shaft over my shorts before untying them. I leisurely pull them down over my hips and let them fall to the floor. My cock springs free with a slap. Without taking my eyes off of her, I get in the shower. Steam covers the glass, and I can't have that. I want to prolong the sexy game she started. Reaching over, I adjust the temperature of the water, making it cooler to keep the glass from fogging so she has a clear view of my body. Water cascades down my heated skin, not remotely dousing the fire blazing inside me.

That's it. Keep those big brown eyes on me. If she wants a show, I'll give her one she'll never forget.

I grab her shampoo and wash my hair. The smell of coconut and lime assaults my senses. It's pure Rylann. Sweet. Sexy. Stimulating. Seems I found the source of my addiction, and it has my dick turning to granite.

Squirting the matching body wash into my palms, I lather it between my palms. I wash my chest, torso, and abs, making sure to linger over every ridge, putting on a show for her. Gliding my hands down the V-shaped muscles at my hips, I fist my stiff cock.

Pupils blown, her eyes look almost black as she watches me squeeze and stroke my thick length. The surface of the water ripples, spilling over the edge as she slips her hands under the water.

Fuck yes. She's touching herself to the sight of me jacking my cock.

I pick up the pace, moving my hand from root to tip, thrusting my hips. Rylann sinks into the water, resting her head on the edge of the tub. Her lips part as she releases a sexy groan. More water spills over the top of the tub at her movements. The desire to touch her has me turning off the shower and stalking toward her waiting body. While watching her get herself off is hot as hell, I want to be the one who makes her fall apart. I want to feel the tightness of her pussy as her muscles contract and convulse as she explodes. I want to own her pleasure.

"Put your hands on the side of the tub, Sunshine. No touching. When you're with me, I'm the one that will be delivering your pleasure."

Chapter Sixteen

Rylann

My movements halt at Jace's command, his voice sending shivers through my body.

He stalks towards me like a hunter ready to devour his prey, and my eyes eat up every inch of his wet naked body.

God, he's gorgeous.

The butterflies in my stomach soar as he hinges over me, his hard chest and arms caging me in. His eyes glow as they scour my body. I want him to deliver my pleasure as promised.

His erection grazes my hair, and I want to reach out and touch him. Taste him. My mouth waters at the thought, so I boldly tilt my head back and lick the bead of precum leaking from the tip of his thick cock. I moan at his taste—salty and all man.

"Watch it, Sunshine," he growls.

I shake my head. I don't want to watch it anymore. I have an ache only he can relieve.

"What do you want, baby?" Brow arched, he runs his fingers up my arm, over my shoulder, and across my collarbone.

My eyes close as I revel in the fire of his touch. My body vibrates with anticipation.

"Eyes on me," he grunts. My eyelids flutter open, locking on his hazels, the amber around his pupil glowing. "Answer my question, Sunny."

I preen at the endearment. It's like the blazing hot sun on my skin when it slips past his lips.

"You. I want you, Ace. All of you," I confess as I palm his scruff-laden jaw.

His hand possessively caresses my throat, gently squeezing, and my pussy floods with arousal. He tilts my head back, exposing my neck to him. Kneeling down, he removes his hand from my neck, only to replace it with his lips. He kisses me tenderly before cupping my breast with one hand while sliding the other down the center of my body and into the water, pausing below my belly button. I lift my hips, encouraging him to continue.

"Are you sure this is what you want?" he whispers, nibbling my earlobe with his teeth. "Because once I start, I won't be able to stop. Ever."

"Yes. Don't stop. Touch me, Jace. *Please.*"

A cocky smirk spreads across his plump lips. "No need to beg, Sunshine. I'll give you what you want."

I bark out a laugh at his smart-ass comment, but it evolves into a moan as his fingers slide through my slick center. He presses down on my clit with his fingers, rubbing it in tight circles before dipping down to my entrance, pumping his finger in and out of my tight channel, then returning to my clit. He repeats the pattern—the pressure, the tempo, everything. It's exquisite.

My orgasm builds low and warm in my belly before spreading like wildfire. I convulse as he grinds his palm against the swollen bundle of nerves while curling his fingers inside me, pressing against my G-spot.

"I'm so close." I pant, my body coiling tighter. I don't know whether to squeeze my thighs together or spread them wider for him.

"Come for me, Sunny. Let go. I can feel how close you are. Give me what I want."

At his demand, my body snaps like a rubber band pulled too tight. My toes point, heat floods my center, and stars burst behind my eyelids as I fall over the edge. His mouth covers mine, kissing me as he swallows my cries of pleasure. When I finally come down, my body feels like Jello.

"You are so beautiful when you come."

"That was … amazing." Amazing doesn't even do justice to what he does to me.

"You're amazing," he whispers before kissing the freckles on my cheek.

I rub my hand over the scruff of his jaw and imagine it scraping the sensitive skin between my thighs. "I think it's time for you to get in this tub with me."

"Move up." Jace nudges me and climbs in behind me.

I settle in between his long legs. It's tight, but he has his arms wrapped around me like I was made for him to hold. I chuckle when his hard cock nestles between my butt cheeks.

"Care to share what's so funny?"

"I'm just finding it *hard* to get comfortable." I wiggle my butt, grinding against his hardness.

He drops his head onto my shoulders and groans. "I warned you. There is only so much I can take before I snap," he says gruffly.

His teeth nip at my shoulder and I roll my head to the side, giving him more access. He makes another pass over my neck, nipping at my sensitive skin before stopping.

"Hmm." My skin is raw and prickles with a fevered need to be touched. "I thought you said you weren't gonna stop."

He circles my nipples before pinching them, sending a bolt of liquid lust straight between my legs. "I never said I was done. I'm just taking my time. There's no rush."

He releases my nipples and wraps his arms around my waist, pulling me closer to his chest. The water laps around us, dripping to the floor. I adjust my hips, and his cock slips in my ass crack.

Grunting, he squeezes my hips, holding me still. "I'm gonna need you to stop doing that."

"What if I don't want you to stop?" I drop my head on his shoulder and look into his burning green eyes.

"You should have thought of that before you convinced me to get in this tub with you."

"Why? There's plenty of room here."

To prove my point, I swing around to straddle his thick thighs. I glide my hands up his body before burrowing them in his hair. His erection jerks between us. The electricity ricochets between us as we stare into each other's eyes. We both lean forward, and our mouths mold together in a slow, sensuous kiss. It grows deeper and more frenzied with every passing second. He holds my hips tight, and I love the feel of his strong fingers digging into my skin. He controls my movements while I'm lost in his domineering hold on me.

Who knew? I had a "rough and bossy" kink. *No, it's a Jace kink.*

My hips have a mind of their own as I slide forward and back along his massive erection, bumping my swollen clit with his broad tip. Needing more, I break our kiss and push up onto my knees, notching the tip of his cock at my entrance. Jace growls, latching onto my nipple, his teeth scraping the tender flesh.

"More," I beg.

He alternates sucking and biting each hardened peak. My head falls back in pleasure. The need to feel him inside me overcomes me and I slide down, allowing his broad head to breach my entrance.

"Fuck, Sunshine. You have to stop."

I shake my head.

He curses around my nipple but doesn't move his hips. I can feel his restraint teetering on the edge. His cock pulses and my muscles respond, contracting around him.

"No. No stopping." My voice is strangled as I squeeze my eyes closed tight and the last dregs of my control snap. "I can't wait anymore."

Without warning, I drop down onto his thick cock in one fell swoop, sheathing him to the hilt. A pinch of pain has me hissing. He's so big it hurts, but it hurts so good.

"Oh, fuck!" Jace growls, smashing his lips to mine.

He forces my mouth open and fucks me with his tongue while I sit impaled on his hard cock. I start to swivel my hips, but he holds me still and breaks our kiss.

"Hold on tight, baby." Jace stands, hands under my ass, keeping us connected.

I lock my ankles behind his back and my arms around his neck as I hang on for dear life. Water sloshes down our bodies as he climbs out of the bathtub. We don't make it far. He places me on the vanity and pushes my back down onto the cold marble. My breath hitches at the cold contact. Gripping the backs of my legs, he spreads my thighs and stares at where we are connected. My heart speeds up at the animalistic look on his face as he watches himself slide in and out of me.

"Now you've done it. You got me to break, and I'm not gonna stop," he grunts. Without warning, he slams into me to the hilt, his balls slapping my ass. "You feel so fucking good." Thrust. "Is this what you wanted? For me to fuck you?" Thrust.

You have no idea. But the words escape me.

I'm lost in the sensations of him inside me. The way his hands grip my thighs. The way my body begs for more. I feel so full, complete, and yet absolutely ruined at the same time.

Jace stills. "I asked you a question. Answer me, Rylann." Thrust.

"Yes!" I yell, pressing my hands into the mirrored wall behind my head, bracing myself as he pistons into me. Every thrust and grind of his pelvis into my clit has me getting wetter, sending me higher. "Right there. Don't stop. *Please,* don't stop."

"My pleasure," he grits out.

Jace licks his thumb before pressing it to my swollen clit as he sets a punishing pace. My thighs shake and my pussy clamps down around him, squeezing. My vision blurs and I explode, my orgasm rolling over and through me, in delicious waves from head to toe.

Opening my eyes, I find him watching me with a look of awe as I come down from what has got to be the best orgasm I have ever received. The biggest, cockiest grin spreads across his handsome face.

"That was ..."

"A taste. We're not finished yet. We're just getting started." He brings his mouth to mine, kissing me the same way he just fucked me. Deep, hard, and with everything he has to offer.

He scoops me up like I weigh nothing, keeping us connected, and carries me out of the bathroom. He slams me up against the wall and I dig my heels into his ass, using the wall as leverage to bounce up and down his length, meeting him thrust for thrust.

"That's it. Ride me."

His dirty words spur me on, and I slam down harder on his upthrust as I chant, "Yes, yes, yes."

His punishing thrusts hit a deep spot inside me, and when his hand finds my sensitive clit and pushes down, it sends me over the cliff again.

"Fuck me, your pussy is squeezing me so tight." He groans, kissing up and down my neck, pulling inhuman moans from my body.

His ability to wring this many orgasms from me is unheard of. It's like he has a direct line to my body, reading it with perfect clarity so he can deliver me nothing but pure, unadulterated pleasure. My body goes limp as he carries me over the bed.

"You feel so fucking perfect wrapped around me. But ..." He pauses to pull me off his glorious cock and throws me onto the bed, breaking our connection for the first time.

The cool air hits my sensitive core, making me hiss. His eyes feast on my naked body. My legs fall open, showing him how soaking wet I am for him. This position would usually have me feeling vulnerable, but with him, I feel powerful and uninhibited. I want him to know exactly what he does to me. How much I want him.

My eyes rake over his hard muscular body. He's all smooth tan skin and hard lines. His thick erection stands long and proud, painted in my arousal.

"Ace ... Condom. We forgot about a condom."

"Fuck. I'm sorry." Jace rushes over to the dresser to get the box of condoms, ripping it open. He tears one off the strip and throws the rest on the bed next to my head.

"Are you okay?"

"Yes, I'm fine. Don't stop." All my body wants is for him to keep going. To claim me, make me his.

I reach out and wrap my hand around his cock, giving it a few firm strokes up and down.

He groans in pleasure but swats my hand away. "Enough of that, or this will be over sooner than I want it to be."

He brings the foil package to his mouth, rips it open, and rolls the latex over his broad tip and down his thick shaft. I've never thought putting a condom on was sexy, but Jace makes everything sexy.

He grabs me behind my knees and drags me down the bed, placing my ass right at the edge. Dropping down to his knees, he throws my legs over his shoulders.

"Now, where were we?" He kisses my inner thigh. "Here?" He kisses my other thigh. "Or here?"

He spreads me open with his thumbs, flattens his tongue along my center, and licks me from the bottom up, furiously flicking my clit with his tongue. He moans into my pussy like I am the best thing he's ever tasted. His mouth is freaking magical, and he has me cresting towards another orgasm in record time.

Before I can come, he stops and flips me onto my stomach, pulling my ass up into the air. My pussy gushes at the way he dominates my body, dripping down my inner thighs. Over my shoulder, I watch him run his fingers along my spine, down my crack, and through my wet lips. He looks down on my body with a look of such reverence, it blows me away.

"Your pussy is so fucking beautiful. So wet and tight. Perfect." He positions himself between my legs, spreads my ass cheeks, and drives himself inside me until he bottoms out with a groan. "You were made for me."

My muscles quiver at his words.

Jace grunts his approval, his pelvis connecting with my ass with his every thrust. "Fuck yes. I love how your pussy is trying to suck me in deeper."

He leans over me, bringing his chest to my back, and hooks his hands over my shoulders, holding me as close to his body as he possibly can. In this position, his cock is so deep that it reaches places I didn't even know existed, delivering me pleasure like I've never felt before.

"Keep talking, please." I push my ass back against him, wanting more.

"You like my dirty mouth, Sunshine?" He switches his pace from long strokes to short, piercing ones.

"Yes. So much." I bring my hand around his neck, and I pull his head down to mine for a scorching kiss.

The sound of our skin slapping fills the room.

He pistons his hips faster while his fingers find my overstimulated nub. "One more time. I need you to come with me, Sun."

I shake my head. I don't think I can come anymore; my body feels wrung dry.

"Yes. You can. And you will." His fingers work fast, furiously swiping and coaxing my body to do his bidding.

Without warning my body obeys, and I come, hard. "Yes!" I cry out.

"Oh, fuck," he roars, his thrust erratic as he falls over the edge with me.

As the last waves of my orgasm fade away, we collapse onto the bed completely spent. Jace covers my breasts with his large hands, gently kneading them as he pulls out of me. Rolling us to the side, he peppers the back of my shoulder and neck with kisses.

"Ry?" he whispers, pushing my hair behind my ear.

"Yeah?" I mumble, barely able to keep my eyes open. This man just blew my mind, and I'm pretty sure he screwed me into a coma.

"That was fantastic." He places kisses along the back of my neck. "You're amazing."

"You're not so bad yourself, Ace." I roll over to cuddle into his side, resting my head on his chest. I run my fingers through his neatly trimmed chest hair and breathe him in, basking in the comforting warmth of his manly scent.

"I'm going to go take care of this condom and grab a washcloth to clean you up."

"That's okay. I can do it." I start to get up, but he pushes me down.

"No. You stay here. I want to do this. Please, let me take care of you."

I cup his cheek in the palm of my hand and stare into his pleading eyes. "You can take care of me." I kiss his jaw as his lips turn up into a blinding smile. A smile that has me melting into the bed.

"Thank you. After I clean you up, I'm gonna let you get some sleep. And then, I'm going to wake you up because, babe, I plan on being inside you all night long."

My pussy clenches at his dirty promise.

He gives my lips a hard kiss and my ass a little slap before jumping out of bed like he has all the energy in the world. He's so sweet. So dirty.

He's perfect.

True to his word, he wakes me up and makes love to me well into the early hours of the morning. With his body, he shows me exactly how he feels, and I return every touch with the same passion and intention.

CHAPTER SEVENTEEN

Jace

These past few days have been some of the best I've ever experienced, and it's because of her.

Rylann.

I love being around her and her radiant personality. She's everything I ever dreamed of and never expected to find. Everything about us feels right. She's the one person that exists only for me. The other half of my soul.

My sunshine.

For the past two days, we haven't been able to keep our hands off one other. As soon as the door to our suite closes, we tear into each other. I've had her body in every position, on every surface and inch of our room. And it's still not enough. I'll never get enough of her.

I wasn't kidding when I told her that once I started, I wasn't going to stop. She's brought out this domineering caveman side of me I never knew existed. I feel possessed with an insatiable need to be in her at all times. To claim and consume her while delivering unmeasurable pleasure to her with every touch, every kiss, and every orgasm.

Last night, I surprised her with a romantic dinner for two on the balcony, with flowers and candles. She took my breath away as grateful tears flooded her eyes. She jumped into my arms and peppered kisses all over my jaw. It felt so good to receive such gratitude for something so small.

After dinner, I lifted her into my lap for a searing kiss, which escalated into me pulling out my cock and pushing her down on it. With her panties shoved to the side, she rode me as the sun set behind her, casting her in an ethereal glow.

I'd never done that before—needed someone so badly that I'd risk getting caught having sex in public. But fuck ... It was hot. And I'd do it again in a heartbeat.

I smile, sauntering over to the bed, where Rylann is still fast asleep. She lays naked in the middle of the bed with the sheet only covering her peach-shaped ass. Her long brown hair is fanned across her pillow, and she's curled around another. She's breathtakingly beautiful, peacefully sleeping in our bed.

I climb onto the bed behind her back and shoulder. After a few presses of my lips to her skin, her breathing changes and she moans.

"Good morning, Sunshine," I whisper into her ear. Damn, she smells good—a mix of her sweet lotion and me. My greedy dick twitches in my shorts.

"Mmm. Morning," she mumbles, pushing her ass into my half-hard cock.

I grip her hips, forcing her to stay still. "It's time to get up. We promised Scarlett breakfast before you go off to do your thing."

She shakes her head, squeezing her pillow tighter. "I'm too tired. Someone kept me up too late." She grinds her ass into me again, reminding me of all the dirty things we did last night.

"We don't have time for that. We need to start getting ready." I pump my hips, poking her in the ass with my hard-on, giving her a taste of her own medicine. "Later," I whisper, kissing her neck and sliding off the bed.

"Where are you going?" She whines and rolls over, giving me an exquisite view of her tits.

My teeth find my lip, wishing I could feast on them. I grab my clothes from the drawer. "I'm gonna shower. I'll hurry, so you can get one in before breakfast. Be out in a minute," I yell over my shoulder.

Turning on the shower, I let it warm while I strip off my sweaty clothes. I'm in the middle of washing my hair when a rush of cool air hits my skin.

Rylann steps into the shower. My eyes feast on her gloriously naked body. My cock springs to life in an instant. I'm so fucked. *She will be too.*

"Mind if I join you? You know, to save water and all that?" She smirks, batting her long thick lashes at me, the tease. She knows exactly what she's doing.

"Of course. For the sake of the planet."

She flashes me a dimple-popping smile, the mischief in her eyes unmistakable. *She wants to play this morning.*

"Mind passing me the body soap? I think I'm gonna save washing my hair for later, so we can hurry off to breakfast." Her hair is piled on her head, looking messy and sexed-up, just the way I like it.

She squirts gel into her palm and hands me the container. I watch her lather it before spreading it over her shoulders, her tits, and down her soft, flat stomach. The cream-colored tan lines of her bikini stand out against the rest of her rich almond skin. Her chocolate nipples are hard, and all I want is to suck on them, run my tongue all over them, then down her stomach to her warm, hot pussy.

She bends over to wash her legs, and I've had enough. I drop the soap and scoop her up in my arms, her legs automatically wrapping around my hips. Pushing her up against the wall, I slam my mouth to hers, kissing her.

"You done with your little show there?" I nip at her bottom lip.

"Depends ..." Her words are confident, but her pink cheeks betray her vulnerability.

"On?" I ask through clenched teeth, holding back, waiting to strike.

She watches me, the request on the tip of her tongue.

Come on, baby. Tell me what you want. It's fucking hot when she wields that power over me.

Kissing the side of her neck, I feel the vibrations of her moans on my lips.

She wraps her palm around my stiffening shaft, stroking it up and down, taking what she wants. "How much time do we have before breakfast?"

"We will make time. Tell me what you want."

"You ... Fast and hard," she whispers in my ear before biting my earlobe and squeezing her fist around my cock.

"My pleasure." I smash my lips to hers in a bruising kiss and lift her higher.

She notches me at her entrance, and I impale her with my cock, over and over, giving her exactly what she wants, until she's screaming my name and we're exploding together.

With her warm body wrapped around mine, she lays claim to my heart.

CHAPTER EIGHTEEN

Rylann

"If I can get everyone's attention!" Levi stands at the head of the table, holding his glass up, his eyes firmly on Scarlett, who's dressed in a simple white silk sheath dress for tonight's rehearsal dinner.

Our party has grown since more of Levi's extended family has arrived for tomorrow's ceremony.

"I just wanted to thank you all for being here to watch me marry the love of my life, Scarlett. It means a lot to us that you all made the trip across the ocean to share our special day with us."

Jace's fingertips graze my shoulder and twirl my hair. I love that he can't keep his hands off me. I don't think I'll ever get tired of the way his touch lights me up inside.

"Short Stack, I knew the moment I saw you in that bar in Mexico that you were my forever girl. I love you so much, baby. I can't wait to call you my wife. So please, raise your glass to my forever girl, the future Mrs. Walker."

"Cheers!" Everyone clinks their glasses with shouts of, "Kiss!"

Levi leans down and kisses Scarlett.

I wipe away my tears, my heart full. My bestie deserves her happy ending, and so does Levi. They are perfect for each other.

"You okay, Sunshine?"

I nod. "I'm just so happy for them."

Jace wipes away a stray tear before kissing my cheek. "Me too. Are you ready to get out of here?" Jace whispers, sending goosebumps erupting across my skin. He chuckles, grasping my hand in his warm one under the table. "I'm gonna get us out of here in a vain attempt at being the best man."

"Don't you go rushing everyone out for your own personal gain," I chide, taking a sip of my wine.

There is no way I'm going to interrupt Scarlett's evening, even though I've also thought about getting out of here so we could get naked all night long. He looks fucking hot tonight, with his brown mane swooped back and to the side, the sexy-as-sin charcoal gray suit that makes his green eyes pop, and his signature leather and citrus cologne that wafts off his skin, tempting me to bathe in it. In him.

"I will rush anyone and everyone to get more time with you. Besides, if I know Levi, he's just as ready to take Scarlett to their room for the night too. He won't be able to thank me enough for doing my duty as his best man."

The pulsing desire building between my legs builds. Jace runs his hand over my thigh, giving it a squeeze before springing into action.

Scarlett glows as she makes her way over, done for the night, her goodbyes given to Levi's family. She plops down in Jace's empty seat with a sigh. "Tonight was perfect."

"It really was."

"The guys are surfing at sunrise tomorrow, so it's just you and me all day. I have everything packed. We can sleep in a little before heading over to the venue after breakfast. Work for you?"

"Sounds good. I'm all packed up and ready to go too."

"I wouldn't expect anything less."

We sit there another minute, soaking up the silence, watching the guys talk across the room.

"Are you gonna tell him?"

"Tell him what?"

"That you love him."

I turn back to Jace and watch him shake hands with one of Levi's uncles. He feels me staring and looks up. He gives me a wink before returning his attention to the man in front of him.

I want to tell him I've completely fallen for him. But every time I try to, the words stay trapped on the tip of my tongue.

"Don't be scared Ry. Take a chance. You might get everything your heart desires." Scarlett wraps me up in a tight embrace before leaving me for Levi.

They wave back at me before walking out of the restaurant, hand in hand.

Eli heads my way and gives me a lingering hug, hoping to set Jace off. "See you tomorrow, sweetheart. Take care of my big bro, yeah?" He wiggles his eyebrows, and I laugh.

"I will. Good night, Eli."

Jace yanks Eli's collar, pulling him away from me. "Alright, enough of you," he growls.

"Don't be jealous, big bro. I got hugs for everyone. All you have to do is ask." Eli attempts to hug him, but Jace steps around him, dodging his arms.

"Fucker," Jace mutters under his breath and pushes a laughing Eli out of the now empty room before walking over to me. He grips my hips and pulls me flush to his chest.

"Don't be jealous, Ace. He's just messing with you. You know I'm all yours," I purr, running my finger down his chest.

With a flash, he pushes me back until I hit the wall. He presses his hard body against mine, and my body bursts into flames.

Time slows down, and my breaths speed up.

Seizing the collar of his shirt, I pull his head to mine. I watch his pulse hammer against the skin of his neck, the rapid tempo matching my own beat for beat.

Our eyes connect, and the spark between us roars to life, making the hairs on my arms stand up. His hands move from my hips to cradle my face—firmly and tenderly, the perfect balance between possession and worship. Love and devotion.

We are both right there, the words floating in the air between us.

This sweet and sexy man has gotten me to fall in love with him in a matter of days, forever changing me. I wouldn't want anything about this trip to be different. This is where I'm supposed to be. Where *we* are supposed to be. Deep down in my soul, I know being with him feels right. *He* feels right.

Just tell him.

Jace tips my chin up and places a gentle kiss on my lips, stealing the words off the tip of my tongue.

Time catches up.

"It's time to go upstairs. I've been picturing this on the floor, you on the bed naked and waiting for me to ravage your body. All. Night. Long."

His fingers drift down my throat, over my collarbone, hooking his index finger under the soft yellow strap of my silk dress. He slides the delicate material over my shoulder.

My eyes flutter closed as he places feather-light kisses across my exposed skin, the scrape of his scruff sending shivers down my spine, straight to my clit. I moan needily.

"Quiet, Sunshine. We don't want someone to hear you, now, do we?"

I shake my head and bite my lips. I forget where I am when I'm with Jace and his big hands are on my body.

He presses his hips into mine, grinding his hard cock between us, setting my body on fire. "Do you see what you do to me?"

His lips capture mine in an open-mouthed kiss. He sucks my tongue, swallowing my needy cries. The way he owns my mouth renders my panties and my brain useless.

Ripping his mouth away, leaving us both gasping for air, he places my leg on the floor. "Time to go. While I would love to spread you out on that table and eat you, I want you and the sexy sounds you're making all to myself."

Over his shoulder, I spy the table and picture myself laid out for him—ripping and swollen, ready for him to claim me with his mouth.

"Yes, please." Bringing my eyes to his, I reach out and stroke his stiff cock over his pants.

He growls like a feral animal ready to pounce and grabs my wrist, squeezing it with a warning. He twirls me around, pinning me to his chest with his forearm and aligning my ass and his cock. I grind into him, and he swats my ass.

"Time to go, bad girl," he commands. "Don't. Move. Or everyone will see what you do to me. Do you want that?"

My center pulses. The anticipation of him between my legs, showing me how much he wants me, thrums in my veins.

"No," I choke out. And I mean it—he's for my eyes only. Every inch of him.

CHAPTER NINETEEN

Rylann

We burst through the door, desperate for one another.

Our mouths collide in a ravenous kiss as Jace lifts me into his arms. He pushes me up against the door, pinning me in place with his hard body.

"I need you inside me. Now," I mumble against his lips.

I'm going to combust if he doesn't take me right here and now. My body is at a fever pitch, overriding all my thoughts, singularly focused on Jace and the way his hands skim over my heated skin.

His hand slips under my dress and pulls my thong to the side. My sensitive flesh tingles as he traces the seam of my wet slit with the tips of his fingers.

"Fuck, you're soaked for me." He grunts, sinking his fingers inside me.

With a groan, I chase his tongue, sliding it against mine as he finger-fucks my pussy with the same sensuous speed. My body shakes when his thumb circles my clit as his fingers curl, finding that spot deep inside me that only he can touch.

"Yes ... Right there, Ace." I use his shoulders for leverage as I ride his hand.

My pussy spasms, and I explode in a rush of white-hot heat, stars bursting behind my eyelids.

Oh my god, that was crazy intense.

My eyes snap open, pulling me out of my post-orgasmic daze at the sound of Jace's chuckle. "Did I say that out loud?"

He peppers my neck and chest with kisses before removing his fingers and snapping my thong back into place. "Yes."

"That's so embarrassing." I hide my face in his neck, breathing in his citrus leather scent.

"Hey, look at me." I bring my eyes back to his hooded hazels that soothe my beating heart. "Don't be embarrassed. You're a vision when you come."

My pussy gushes, and my body flames to life at his dirty praise. My shame is all but forgotten as I get lost in the way Jace is looking at me with such reverence.

Unlocking my legs from around his waist, I let them fall to the floor and hook my fingers in the waistband of his slacks. I want to show him the same adoration. Jace deserves to be loved, to be cared for, and I plan on being the person who does that.

I glance down at his impressive erection, and my mouth waters with the need to taste him. "Your turn."

I lead him to the foot of the bed. His chest heaves, and his cock strains against his zipper. Jace follows my tongue as I swipe it across my bottom lip. His face transforms into a look of hunger.

"What do you want, Rylann?" His husky voice demands my attention, and my body responds by sending a shot of liquid arousal to my pussy.

He might be bossy, but he'd do anything for me, even if that meant stopping. It's a powerful feeling, knowing I'm in control even though he is physically bigger and stronger than I am.

"Lose the shoes." He toes off his black dress shoes and removes his socks.

"Your turn," he demands, reaching for me.

I step away from his outstretched hands. "Nuh uh. I don't think so."

He drops his clenched fists to his sides and rakes his eyes over my body, lighting my skin on fire.

Stepping closer, I slide my fingers down the front of his body, taking in the ridges of his muscular torso and stopping at the top of his slacks. Removing his belt, I toss it on the floor and release the button of his slacks with a quick flick of my fingers.

"Fuck. You're killing me, Sun."

Good. I want tonight to be burned into our souls forever. I tsk. "Patience, Ace."

I languidly pull the tab of his zipper down and push his slacks over his hips, letting them fall in a pool at his ankles. He kicks his pants to the side, leaving him in only a pair of black boxer briefs. They strain to contain his monster cock.

Okay. I'm exaggerating, but his dick is big. It's perfect.

My mouth waters and I drop to my knees, running my hands and nose up his muscular legs and over his hard shaft, breathing in his manly scent.

"Sunny," Jace exclaims, my name a plea and a warning.

I stare up into his eyes, "I know."

I rip my dress over my head and throw it over my shoulder. I'm left in a strapless bra and a pale yellow thong as I kneel before him. Jace reaches down and unhooks my bra, releasing my heavy breasts. He pinches my pebbled nipples, and my eyelids flicker closed. I couldn't hide the desperate, inhuman moans Jace elicits from me if I wanted to.

"You look so pretty on your knees for me."

My eyes snap open. I want him so badly. But not before I taste him.

I pull down his boxers, releasing his cock. Grasping the base of his length, I lick him from root to tip like a deliciously sinful ice cream cone, before pulling him into my mouth. He tastes clean and salty, and it turns me on. I hollow my cheeks and suck.

"Oh, fuck." He rumbles with a loud exhale. His hands fly into my hair, stilling me. He holds me steady, slowly fucking my mouth.

I look up to find his head thrown back and his mouth open in pure pleasure. The sight sets me off, and all I want is to watch him come with his cock in my mouth. Groping the hard globes of his ass, I take over, diving onto his dick. I take him to the back of my throat, sucking and swallowing around him as fast as I can.

"Sunshine ... You have to stop."

But I don't. I'm hungry for him.

He pulls me off his length with a pop and pulls me into his arms before slamming his mouth to mine in a scorching-hot kiss. He grunts into my mouth with satisfaction as I taste the flavor of his precum on my tongue. With me in his arms, he sits on the bed and spreads my thighs to straddle him.

I break away from his mouth with a pout. "I wasn't done."

He kisses and nips at my neck. "If I didn't stop you, I would have come in your mouth instead of your tight pussy."

His hot mouth latches onto my nipple, lavishing it with his attention, swirling and sucking. My nails dig into his shoulders when he scrapes his teeth along the sensitive bud.

"And this pretty pussy,"—his fingers glide through my wet slit from behind—"wants to come on my cock."

Oh, fuck yes, it does. My body shudders in agreement. I'm so gone for him.

The words come bubbling up to the surface, but I push them down and pull his face to mine, kissing him instead.

Softly. Slowly. I hope he feels the words I'm dying to confess.

He flips me onto my back, positioning me in the center of the bed.

"These have to go. I want you completely bare." Jace pulls my panties down my legs, throwing them behind him. He spreads my legs, hungrily staring at my glistening center. "Now, it's my turn."

He covers my sex with his mouth and eats me like I'm his last meal. His tongue is magical. I feel like my body is floating and on fire at the same time, as my muscles tense and my pussy flutters.

"You're so close. Come for me, Sun." His hot breath fans across my hot, wet center.

He pulls my swollen clit into his mouth, and when he sucks, my hips fly off the bed.

"Jace," I cry in frustration as my body inches higher to climax.

"Now," he growls, spearing me with his fingers.

His command sends me soaring over the edge. With my hands gripping his hair, I ride his face until my orgasm crashes through me and my body falls back to earth.

Jace kisses his way up my body, capturing my mouth with his as he settles between my thighs. My legs fold around his hips, and my heels dig into his firm ass. I notch his cockhead at my entrance, coating it in my slickness.

"So wet for me." He pushes forward, sheathing himself inside me inch by glorious inch, all the way to the hilt. "Look at me, Rylann."

I open my eyes to meet his deep green pools. The golden rings around his irises glow like burning embers in a campfire.

Threading his fingers through mine, he brings them over my head. Eyes on mine, he starts to thrust his hips in unhurried strokes. Long. Deep. He moves in and out of my body, burying more than his hard cock inside me.

This is Jace making love to me.

"Jace ..." I whisper.

"Me too, Rylann. Me too."

The pleasure inside me begins to build again, and my pussy contracts around him. I accept his unspoken words because this man, right here, already stole my heart. And as he picks up his pace, pounding his cock, his unspoken feelings, his everything into me, he's giving me his heart in return.

"Come with me, Sunshine. I need you to be right there with me." His eyes are still on mine. Pleading with me to feel his words.

I hear them loud and clear. "I'm there. I'm with you," I confess. Every last part of me is with him.

My nails dig into his back as the tension in my body finally snaps, and I come apart beneath him in an earth-shattering orgasm. He stills, following me, burying his face in my hair, kissing my neck. Whispering sweet words of praise in my ear.

I am more than in love with Jace Miller.

There are no words to describe the depths of my feelings for this wonderful man.

CHAPTER TWENTY

Rylann

Sunshine,

Sorry for not waking you before surfing with the guys. You looked too peaceful sleeping, the perfect vision to start my morning. Enjoy your time with Scarlett, and I'll see you at the end of the aisle. I'll be the guy waiting for a brown-eyed beauty to appear in a shimmering yellow dress as bright as the sun, like her smile.

— Jace

So fucking swoony.

I clench the small, handwritten note to my chest as the butterflies in my stomach take flight.

Sadness washed over me when I woke up without Jace by my side for the first time since arriving. But this letter—his words—washed those feelings away.

This week has flown by, and at the same time, it feels like a whole lifetime has passed. In the past seven days, I have fallen head over heels for the best man. He'd come out of nowhere and swept me up off my feet.

I am so in love with Jace Miller, and I know he loves me too.

I stretch my hands over my head, feeling my muscles ache in the most delicious way. Jace kept me up all night, delivering me orgasm after orgasm. I lost count after the third round when I woke up with Jace's face between my legs.

My cell dings, drawing my attention to the time.

Scarlett.

I grab it from the bedside table and chuckle at my messages.

Scarface: I'M GETTING MARRIED TODAY!!!
Scarface: **Gif of Monica tripping**

I laugh out loud at Scarlett's texts. Another text dings before I can respond.

Scarface: You better be ready. We need to leave in 30.

Rice Cakes: Just woke up. I'll shower and be ready in time. Meet downstairs?

Scarface: Perfect. Don't be late! Xox

I roll out of bed with a huge smile on my face, completely ready for what today has in store.

The sun is shining, my best friend is getting married, and the man I've fallen for will be waiting for me at the end of the aisle.

I park the jeep in the private driveway and take in the surroundings.

We just arrived at the venue, and it couldn't be a more perfect spot for a wedding. Scarlett and Levi did a good job picking this place. It's so unique and perfectly them.

The venue resembles a squat little hut that looks like one of those cute little hobbit houses in *Lord of the Rings*. I never would have guessed something like this, with its thatch roof and ornate woodwork, existed here on the island. It's surrounded and draped in local ferns, bright hibiscus, sweet-smelling plumeria, and exotic birds of paradise. It seems so out of place amongst the coconut and koa trees, and yet ... I can't picture the cottage anywhere else.

I take in a deep breath absorbing the beauty around me.

"Ry. We forgot the orange juice." Scarlett races to the backseat and grabs her dress bag.

"I got it. You go in, put your robe on, and wait for the makeup artist to arrive. I'll be right back."

"Thanks, Rice Cakes. You're the best." She hands me the keys and strolls off through the gates to the bridal suite.

It takes me twenty minutes to grab a bottle of orange juice from the gas station. My hands are full of bags as I kick open the door. "Bridezilla! I'm *baaack*. I've got the OJ. Now, let's pop the bubbly! What the fu—?"

The bags fall from my hands to the floor. *What the hell is going on here?*

I must have taken a wrong turn because I ended up on the shore. I kid you not, my best friend looks like an amalgamation of those chicks on that crazy reality show, with big hair and overly orange-tan skin.

Her eyes catch mine in the mirror, and I can see the internal meltdown going on in her head. She has a deranged-looking smile on her face as two girls I've never met apply foundation to her face.

Scarlett's eyes are so wide, they are screaming at me.

"So ... Funny story. Not 'haha' funny, but more like 'meh' funny. Anyway, Kelani got into a car accident and couldn't make it. But she sent us back up," Scarlett anxiously explains.

"Ah." I nod, looking at the two strangers working on my friend. It's too bad because Kelani's portfolio was amazing, and I doubt these girls have any experience.

I look back at Scarlett's reflection in the mirror and cringe. The creepy smile frozen on her face is starting to scare me. She resembles one of those freaky screaming goats with big eyes. My lips twitch, thinking about those damn goats, stifling my laugh.

I pull out my phone and snap a picture of her.

"What the fuck, Ry?"

The girl putting foundation on my friend jumps at Scarlett's outburst, stepping back.

"Sorry, babes, but I had to document this moment for the wedding album," I say as calmly as possible.

Her eyes widen in hysteria. *Okay, time for damage control.*

"Hi, ladies. Nice to meet you," I introduce myself to the two technicians. "I need to talk to the bride. Do you mind stepping outside for a bit?"

The girls nod their heads, leaving us alone. I pop the bubbly, passing Scarlett the bottle. I think we are *way* past the pretty-glass phase right now.

She takes a swig, the bubbles dripping down her chin.

"Scarlett. What do you want to do?"

She shakes her head with a shrug and passes me the bottle.

I take a swig and hand it back to her. "Liar. Tell me what you want, and I'll do it."

She sits quietly, taking another sip of champagne.

"Scarlett! We are running out of time. What. Do. You. Want?"

Through clenched teeth, she whisper-yells at me, "Fine! I don't want them to do my makeup. I want them to fucking leave and never come back."

I bark a laugh, and she throws a towel at me.

"That's all you needed to say, babes. Momma's got you." I clap my hands and rub them together.

She rolls her eyes at me. I start to walk away, but she grabs my wrist, yanking me to a stop. "What are you going to do?"

"Well ... First, I'm gonna tip these ladies and very nicely tell them to take a hike. Then, I'm gonna get started on your hair and makeup myself. What do you think?"

Scarlett lets out a high-pitched squeal and jumps off the chair, wrapping me up in a bear hug. "Yes! Thank you, thank you, thank you. I didn't have the heart to say anything to them. They seemed so sweet."

My friend is too kind. She's honestly the nicest person on the planet. But my job as her MOH is to give her what she wants and that means, *Hit the road, ladies.*

"I know." I bring her in for another hug before grabbing my wallet and stepping outside.

I thank the girls for taking the time to come help and explain that we didn't need them after all. I hand each of them a hundred bucks for them to scram, which they do.

"Are they gone?"

I close the door behind me and look out the window. "The coast is clear."

"Good. Now, *please,* get this shit off my face! Levi can*not* see me like this. And you better delete that damn picture," Scarlett wails.

I burst out laughing. "Never gonna happen."

That picture is golden. Perfect bribery material. Her face is orange, she has big fat rollers on her head, and the best part ... She's got those crazy eyes.

"Seriously, Ry! How can you be laughing at me right now? This is a complete disaster. Look at my face—I look like a frickin' Cheeto!" Scarlett yells.

"I think you look more like a pumpkin princess, not a Cheeto."

"You're such an asshole," she bristles, making me giggle. She hits me with a death glare that sobers me up.

I hold my hands up in surrender. "Sorry. I won't laugh any-more. Don't worry. I'll fix this. Promise. Go wash your face, and I'll get everything ready."

Grabbing both our makeup bags, I arrange the makeup and tools on the vanity.

CHAPTER TWENTY-ONE

Rylann

I take one last look at my masterpiece, admiring my work. Scarlett looks every bit the goddess she deserves to be today. Her make-up is the lightly bronzed look she envisioned. Her hair is braided and twisted into a chignon, with yellow plumeria surrounding it and a few wisps of hair framing her face.

I turn her chair around to face the mirror. "*Voilà!*"

Scarlett jumps up, inspecting my work, twisting her head side to side. She's quiet, inspecting her reflection, and I start to worry that I missed the mark.

A broad, blinding smile spreads across her face, and the pit in my stomach disappears.

"Oh my god, Ry, it's perfect. I ..." Her words get caught in her throat as her eyes turn glassy.

"No, you don't! You'll ruin all my hard work." My eyes also water with unshed tears.

"Thank you. This is better than I could have imagined," she says, sweeping her hand over her body.

How could I mess up? This day and every detail about it is all she's talked about for weeks. "You're welcome. Now, take a seat and relax while I finish getting ready."

She plops back in the chair and watches me while I work on my hair and makeup. I keep my makeup simple, as well as my hair, with a waterfall side braid and a trio of yellow plumeria pinned behind my right ear.

"Can you believe it? In just a couple of minutes, I'm going to walk down the aisle and become a married woman."

"That you are." And in a few minutes, I'll get to see Jace. My body hums to life knowing he is just outside, waiting on the beach for me.

"I wish Grams was here." She sighs as a heavy silence falls between us.

"Me too. She would have loved Levi."

"She would have, wouldn't she?" She wipes a stray tear from the corner of her eye.

I bat her hand away and hand her a tissue. "What did I tell you? No crying. You know, if Grams were here, she'd tell you something like ... Stop that fuckin' crying, girl, and drink this."

She chuckles when I hand her the half-empty bottle of champagne. "You're right. Now, what say you about helping me get this dress on?" She points at the gorgeous dress hanging on the door hook.

"It would be my honor."

Pulling her gown off the hanger, I squat down and hold it open for her to step inside. We both let out an audible sigh as I slide the delicate fabric up her body and into place. I go to work crisscrossing the long thin strips of chiffon in the back, twisting them into an intricate knot. The extra fabric falls from the knot like a cape down her back.

My heart swells with love as I step back to look at her in the mirror. She's the picture-perfect bride.

Tears sting my eyes. My bestie is getting married to her soul-mate. All because of a last-minute girls' trip to Mexico. I watch her wistfully looking into the mirror, and I'm taken back to the day we cleaned out Grams's room.

It had taken Scarlett a year before she finally got the nerve. We ordered pizza, uncorked multiple bottles of red wine, and got to cleaning. When we found Grams's wedding album, we cried. Scarlett's Grandpa had passed before her parents, so looking through pictures of her grandparents—young and happy on their wedding day—hit her hard.

We found pictures of them at a little hotel in Mexico for their honeymoon, and that prompted us to go on a last-minute vacation. We booked flights and a week's stay at an all-inclusive resort.

On our first night at the bar, Levi and Scarlett locked eyes from across the room, and that was it. Two months later, he was moving into Scarlett's house. And the rest, as they say, is history.

I know to my bones that Grams had led us there so Scarlett could find Levi.

"Oh, Scar, you look absolutely stunning." I dab at my eyes.

"Thanks, babes." Her voice cracks as she sniffles back tears. "You don't look so bad yourself."

"This old thing?" I wave her off like it's nothing, but really, it's everything. The dress, standing next to her. All of it.

The one-shoulder dress she picked is soft yellow, cinches at the waist, and flows down in a high-low cut. The shimmery fabric overlay sparkles in the sun. I can't wait for Jace to see me in it.

"It's time to get you hitched. I'm gonna go check and see if everything is all set for your grand entrance. Are you ready?" I ask, taking my job seriously. I'm supposed to let everyone know when she's ready to walk.

"More than ready."

With a nod, I leave the bridal suite and head towards the beach, where the ceremony is taking place. I'm excited to get this show on the road for both of us.

I haven't laid eyes on Jace since last night, and I'm anxious to see him. It's only been a couple of hours, but I've missed him today.

As I'm walking toward the ceremony, Eli jumps out at me by the gate to the beach, blocking my view.

"Hey, Eli. I was just coming to see if Levi and the officiant were ready. Scarlett is chomping at the bit to get this show on the road." I'm so focused on my job as maid of honor that I almost miss the anxious look in his eyes. "Is everything okay?"

His brows pinch. He looks ... worried. I try to move around him, but he blocks me. I search his face in question, but he just shakes his head. My heart rate picks up, and a prickle of unease hits me.

"Ry, wait a sec."

"Eli, stop." Now, he's just being too weird. I give him a little shove, creating some space for myself, and move around him, pushing my way through the gate.

Levi is standing at the altar with the officiant, but Jace isn't in his spot next to him. My eyes instantly find him standing off to the side.

Like I've been punched in the solar plexus, the air is expelled from my lungs in a painful rush.

On Jace's arm is a beautiful, tall woman with blonde hair and blue eyes. She's holding onto him in an overly familiar way, and the smile on her face makes me feel queasy.

Oh my god. Please, no.

"Eli, who is that with Jace?" I choke out.

"Fucking shit." Eli grabs me by the elbow, leading me back behind the gate, and I rip my eyes away from the heart-shattering picture before me.

Trying to focus on Eli, and not the horrible feeling growing in my chest, I ask him again. Pleading for him to explain what's going on. "Please," I whisper.

He runs his hands over his scruff, trying to gather his thoughts. "That's Alina. I don't know what she's doing here. She was waiting in the lobby at the hotel when we got back from surfing. I haven't been able to talk to him. I don't know what's going on. He's clammed up and hasn't said a word since he arrived with her."

The uneasy feeling I had before settles deep in the pit of my stomach. Something is wrong. I can feel it. I want to know what the hell is going on.

Why is she here? Why did he bring her? Question after question rolls through my brain.

I shake my head, holding back the tears stinging my eyes. Clearing the emotion from my throat I say, "Okay. Well, tell Levi we're ready. I'm going to go get Scarlett."

Conflicted, Eli pulls at his collar. He clearly wants to say something to ease my mind. There's nothing either of us can do right now—this is on Jace.

"Hey ..." I place my hand on his forearm. I don't want him to feel like this is his problem. All I need is for him to help me get my friend married. "This is Scarlett and Levi's day. I'll deal with this later. Can you please just go tell Levi we are ready?" My voice is eerily calm, refusing to let on that I'm freaking the hell out inside while my heart is breaking.

"Yeah, sure." His sad eyes meet mine. "It's gonna be alright, Ry," he says solemnly.

I nod, but something tells me it's not right. I pat his arm once more, and I run down the path until I'm back in the bridal suite, slamming the door behind me. I throw myself against it, hoping to block out everything on the other side.

Oh, fuckity fuck fuck.

Why is she here? Are they back together? The questions rapid-fire in my brain, setting off my panic attack. My mouth dries, and my throat constricts at the thought. I can't breathe. The weight of an elephant sits on my chest, my head spins, and my stomach flips.

I'm going to throw up.

Scarlett rushes to my side, cupping my cheeks, forcing me to stare into her crystal-blue eyes.

I claw at my neck, gasping.

"What the hell happened out there? Breathe. Shit! You're having a panic attack. Sit down and put your head between your knees." She pushes me down to the floor, taking the place next to me. "You're scaring me. Is something wrong with Levi?"

She rubs my back. With my head between my knees, I vigorously shake it no. I'm incapable of talking.

Alina is here. With Jace. This can't be happening.

There is no stopping the panic from taking hold of me like a vise squeezing the oxygen from my lungs. The pain in my chest expands to a debilitating point, ready to burst.

"You need to calm down. You're officially freaking me out. Please don't make me slap you!" Scarlet pushes me hard down onto the ground, and in one swift move, she pulls her wedding dress up around the top of her thighs and straddles me, pinning my arms to my side. "Get a fucking grip and tell me what's wrong. Is it Levi?"

I shake my head.

"Is it Jace?"

I nod, tears forming in my eyes. "His ex is, h-here," I mutter between choppy breaths. "He's with her."

The image of her on his arm flashes, and my heart bleeds like a knife cutting into the delicate flesh.

"What? Alina? Is here? Like here, here? Like at my wedding, *here?*"

I nod again. My nose tingles, and I'm close to crying.

"Inhale. Exhale," Scarlett repeats, continuing to sit on me like I'm a damn pony.

Oddly enough, it works. The weight of her on me comforts me. My breathing slows, and my tears recede. A few more repetitions, and my heart finally starts to slow, my breath matching hers.

"You know, if Eli walked in on us, we could make some money," Scarlett teases.

I look up at her and down the length of my body. She's right. We look ridiculous. I bark out a laugh, and Scarlett joins, the worry on her forehead melting away.

Scarlett rolls off and lays beside me, threading her fingers through mine. "Ready to tell me what happened?"

I nod and tell her what happened with Eli. "God, Scar, it was awful. She was holding onto him like he was hers. I-I think they're back together."

I woke up so happy this morning, practically floating after the night Jace and I shared, and the sweet note he left behind. We didn't outright say *I love you* to each other, but nevertheless, there was love between us.

But blindsiding me like this? That's what hurts the most. He could have tried to get a hold of me to talk, to figure this out before bringing her here.

"You don't know that for sure. I've seen him with you. You two are head over heels for each other. There has to be more to the story."

I have no doubt there is more. "You're right."

"I know."

"This isn't going to end well." I place my hand on my churning stomach. That sinking feeling hits me again, but I push it down. "Fuck."

"Double fuck," Scarlett whispers.

A loud knock on the door has us jumping out of our skin.

Shoot, how long have we been lying on the floor while I've been freaking out?

"Scarlett? Is everything okay, dear?" Julie, Levi's mom, asks.

We yell at the same time. "Just a minute!" "I'm fine!"

I need to pull on my big girl panties and get my friend down the aisle. I sit up and drag my ass off the floor, and reach my hands out for her to grab onto. Hauling her up, I bend down and smooth out her dress, then my own.

"What do you want to do?" She's worried, but today isn't about me.

"Nothing. I'm going to walk you down that aisle to marry Levi. I'll be your dutiful maid of honor. I will deal with whatever is going on with Jace after your wedding. You are the most important person to me right now."

"Are you sure?"

This woman. I cover her cheeks with my hands and stare at her dead-on.

"Abso-fucking-lutely," I tell her. And it's without a doubt the truth.

She nods, a wistful smile on her face. "I have your back."

"I know. Thank you." I drop my hands and kiss her cheek.

"Anything for you, sis."

"Same." I give her a quick hug and brush back the strands of hair that came loose from her updo. "You look gorgeous, Scar. I love you so much." I grab our bouquets off the table and suck in a deep breath. No more hiding. I can do this.

"I love you too." Scarlett grabs her bouquet and my hand as we walk down the path to the beach. She squeezes my hand tight, offering her unspoken support.

The photographer steps into our path and begins snapping away. I refuse to let my worry take away from my best friend's day. So ...

I smile.

And I smile some more, keeping it in place with everything I have.

All the while my heart slowly breaks inside.

CHAPTER TWENTY-TWO

Rylann

Everything and everyone around me keeps moving forward, living, while I'm suspended in a state of numbness.

It was hard enough to watch Scarlett and Levi vow to love one another forever, but when it was time for the pictures, I almost lost it. I was standing next to Jace, but he might as well have been a million miles away. My heart begged for him to talk to me.

He didn't. Not one word.

Pretending like nothing was wrong, click after click, was downright painful.

I push the food on my plate around. It tastes bland, and what little I've been able to put down sits like a brick in my stomach.

Someone laughs, drawing my attention, and I look up. I've been trying to join conversations, smile, and laugh on cue, but I just can't do it anymore. I can't continue like this. It's too painful. I need answers.

Scarlett pats my hands, drawing my eyes to hers. She's the only one I can manage eye contact with without fear of crying or getting pitying looks. There is definitely an uncomfortable charge in the air that everyone seems to have picked up on.

I wish I could crawl into a hole and cry.

It's really fucking weird sitting here alone tonight, when only yesterday, everyone saw me with Jace. Now, he's sitting with a new woman on his arm as if last night never happened.

It fucking hurts.

To make things worse, he's avoided me completely and treated me as if I'm a stranger, not the woman he's been sharing a bed with since we got here. My heart bleeds with every passing minute.

I know his ex-girlfriend showing up out of the blue makes a mess of things, but he should have had the decency to talk to me before bringing her to our best friends' wedding. He owes me an explanation.

He asked me to trust him, to open my heart to the possibility of a future. The least he could do is talk to me. Tell me the truth. The fact that he can't even acknowledge my existence leads me to believe that whatever he has to say is bad.

In a short amount of time, he's become everything to me. I felt it last night in every touch, every look, every laugh, every kiss. I love him, and he loves me. He's *the one*. The other half of my heart.

I shake my head. I need to prepare for the worst.

Out of the corner of my eye, I see Jace excuse himself from the table and walk toward the exit.

This is it. This might be my only chance to talk to him, and I'm taking it. I can't take this anymore.

Placing my napkin on the table, I go to stand when Scarlett places her hand on my thigh, stopping me. She gives my leg a squeeze and mouths, *Good luck*. I blow her a kiss and, as calmly as I can, I go after Jace.

Fortunately for me, this place is a little quirky, so the bathroom isn't located near where dinner is being served but a short walk away down a path lined with tropical plants.

"Jace!" I yell at his back as I catch up to him on the path.

He stops, shoulders hunched, and turns around, emotionless. His face is a blank mask.

I immediately hate it. He's put walls up between us.

When I reach him, we stand toe to toe, staring. He's so close I can smell his leather and citrus scent. I take a deep, calming breath. Memorizing the way it makes me feel safe and at home.

He's on the verge of tears, and I know he's broken up over whatever has happened. I want to reach for him, comfort him. But I don't.

He breaks eye contact first and stares at his shoes.

"Just say it." My voice is shaky, but I steel myself against the inevitable blow he's about to deliver.

When his eyes find mine, I gasp. The comforting forest green in his hazel eyes is murky like that of a blackened, lifeless pond, and when he lets his mask drop, I can see it all. Confusion and despair. He looks like he's falling apart.

"Alina is pregnant," he whispers, and my knees buckle at his confession.

A stabbing pain pierces through my chest, and my breath hitches in my lungs.

This can't be happening.

I can feel my head shake in disbelief as his words replay in my mind over and over.

She's pregnant.

Oh god. She's having his baby.

I hold myself up and wrap my arms around my middle like armor. I will not fall apart right here.

"Ry ..." His voice cracks. Reaching out for me, he lifts his hands but drops them to his side, thinking better of it.

My body screams for him to hold me. To make all this go away. But it's better if he doesn't touch me right now. If he did, I don't know if I'd be able to let him go.

"I'm sorry. I didn't mean to bring her, to make a mess of this day. I just ..."

I nod, understanding. Because I know Jace, and he doesn't need to explain. He was blindsided too.

"So what happens next?"

Please, pick me! my stupid heart screams. But I push the thought away. I know better, and that can't happen.

"I don't know. I ..."

I look at the man I love as he tugs on his hair in distress. My heart breaks for him. He didn't plan this, and I can see it's tearing him apart. He's hurting.

But I know him. There is no way he can walk away from a child. *His* child.

And I won't let him. I love him too much to make him choose.

"Yes, you do. I know you. I know what's in here." I hover my hand over his heart without touching him, afraid that I won't be able to do this if I do. "You value your family above all else and when you love, you love with your whole heart. So tell me, Ace, what are you going to do for your child?"

This is going to hurt like hell. Even though it's for the best, it's killing me inside. Like my heart is being ripped out of my chest without anesthesia.

But the longer we put it off the inevitable, the worse it's going to be on both our hearts. No matter how much we love each other or want to be together, it won't work. Our homes are a thousand miles away from each other. His life will have a child that needs him more than I do. I need to save us both from the pain.

I have to let him go.

Because that's what you do when you love someone. You put them first. Their needs, their hopes, their dreams—all of it.

He needs to be there for them. It's going to break me to walk away, but I know it's the right thing to do.

"You're going to be a dad, Jace. What are you going to do about it?" I push him, my heart ripping in two.

"I-I feel like I need to do the right thing. For the sake of my child, I need to give them the family they deserve. I have to be there for them."

My beautiful man. His words gut me and make me love him more.

"You are a good man, Jace Miller. Please, don't ever lose that part of you. You're gonna make a wonderful father."

"Ry, I ... I—"

"I know, Ace," I cut him off. I can't have him say any more, let alone those three words, knowing it will be the first and last time. We both deserve to hear those words every day for the rest of our lives. "Me too." If possible, this might hurt more. We love each other, and yet that's all we will ever have—a brief moment in time.

"It was real, wasn't it?" he asks, voice cracking.

"Every single minute," I confirm.

"I don't want us to be over."

My heart skips a beat and dies at the same time. "Me neither. But we'll always have Hawaii." Tears sting my nose as I hold them back.

"Before we say ..." He stops, the unspoken word too hard to say aloud. Goodbye is the last thing I want to say too. The idea of living without him seems impossible. "Can I ask ... Why do you call me Ace?"

Of course, he would ask that. I knew from the moment I met him that he was an ace. One of a kind. Special.

"Aces are the most valuable cards in the deck. Like an ace, you are the most valuable card in the lives you touch. Your family, your clients, your unborn child, me. You, my sweet ace, are everything that is good in the world. You make us all better with your love and support. You're one of a kind."

His eyes shimmer with unshed tears as he absorbs my words of love and praise.

I adore him. Always will. He deserves to be happy, even if that's not with me. He's going to make an amazing father. He has so much love to give. He's given me a lifetime's worth of love in just a few days.

"Thank you."

"Close your eyes." His lids close, and a single tear slips out the corner of his eye. I wipe it away with my thumb, wishing I could wipe away his pain. Our pain. "I wish you nothing but the best life has to offer. You deserve it. You are a wonderful man, and I'll never forget you." Reaching up on my tiptoes, I cup his face, hoping he can feel my love one last time. I give him one last chaste kiss on the lips.

Sparks flicker across my lips, and my heart pinches.

I'm going to miss him so much.

I drop to my feet, taking in his beautifully sad face one more time before turning and walking away. Without looking back, I leave him standing on the path, surrounded by tropical plants and a piece of my heart and soul.

My heart pounds, and I think I might vomit as I walk back to the reception. I can't stay here anymore. I can't sit here and watch Jace with another woman. I may have accepted that we aren't meant to be, but I'll be damned if I torture myself with watching them together.

When I get back to my seat, I notice the plates have been cleared. I couldn't plan my escape any better. With dinner over, it will be easier for me to slip away.

"Are you okay?"

I look over at my beautiful friend and shake my head. I hate that she's more worried about me than celebrating her marriage.

I pat her hand resting on the table and answer honestly. "No. But I will be."

Her smile drops. "What happened?"

I really don't want to say this out loud, but the more I do, the better off I will be. "She's pregnant ... We-We're over." I choke back a sob. The words feel like acid on my tongue. It physically hurts saying we're over.

Scarlett wraps me in a tight hug and I return it eagerly, needing her strength if I'm going to make it through this night. Through this heartbreak.

"I can't stay here. I'm so sorry. Please, don't hate me," I whisper in her ear.

"Never. I understand. Don't be sorry. Go. Take the Jeep. Levi and I can figure out a ride."

"Are you sure?"

She grabs my face in the palms of her hands with so much love and empathy. I know she sees how devastated and heartbroken I am. "One. Hundred. Percent."

"Thank you ..." Tears threaten to fall, but I push them back with a deep breath. I refuse to let anyone see me cry. Least of all *her*. The pain I feel right now is unbearable, and if I let the floodgates open now, I don't know when I'll be able to get them closed again. I need to go home. "Scar?"

Her eyes dim, but she nods in understanding. She knows what I mean. "I know. Text me when you get home."

"I love you. I'll put all our stuff in the back of the car, and I'll use the valet for Levi."

"Okay. I love you. Fly safe."

"Have a great honeymoon." I give her one last kiss on the cheek.

As discreetly as I can, I slide out of my seat and slip out the side entrance leading to the bridal suite, successfully avoiding everyone. In a rush, I gather all the bags from the room in my arms and load the car in one trip. I jump in the jeep and drive away, leaving a part of my heart behind.

Before I know it, I'm pulling up to the hotel's valet station and racing up to my room. As soon as I walk in, I'm assaulted with the scent of us in the air and wonderful memories of our nights together. Shared kisses on the couch, the surprise romantic dinner on the patio, the bed where we made love professing our feelings to each other with our bodies—all of it.

The memory of our love will stay with me forever. A blessing and a curse. A piece of me feels like such a fool for falling for Jace so quickly. So deeply.

But I don't regret us.

I won't.

What we shared was a once-in-a-lifetime love. There are some people that will never experience the kind of love and passion that Jace and I did. I can say that I am one of the lucky ones.

I take off my maid-of-honor dress. My eyes drift over to his pillow, the spot where I found his note, and then on the little scrap of paper sitting on the dresser.

I double over in pain, clenching the comforter in the palms of my hands. There's a hole in my chest that grows with every second I'm away from him.

I can't believe it was only this morning when his sweet words made my heart soar. I was happy. It already feels like a lifetime ago.

I turn back to my suitcase, but a wave of nausea hits me.

Don't do it. Walking away without a trace is the smarter option here. Just leave it behind.

I do the dumb thing, which makes me a masochist because I grab the note and shove it into the pocket lining my luggage. It's all I have left to remember that it was all real.

As much as it hurts, I don't want to forget how Jace made me feel. Jace Miller can keep the piece of my heart he stole because everything we shared was worth the pain of losing him.

I might never recover from the theft, but it was worth it. All of it.

He was worth it.

CHAPTER TWENTY-THREE

Jace

When I finally get the courage to open my eyes, Rylann is gone. Only the sweet scent of her coconut skin lingers in the air.

"Fuck." My steps falter as I follow the plant-lined path to the bathroom.

Leaning over the sink, I stare at myself in the mirror. I look like shit. My eyes are red-rimmed, and my face looks green. I take a few ragged breaths, but they do nothing to quell the pain and regret brewing together in my stomach, making it churn.

I look down, ashamed of the person staring back at me.

What is happening right now? This cannot be my life.

My hands grip the edges of the sink, making it groan from strain. I wish Doc Brown would show the fuck up right now, so I can go back in time and fix this. Change the future.

As soon as I saw Alina in the lobby this morning, a sense of dread slithered down my spine. And now, my sunshine is gone.

Rylann left me, taking the sun with her, leaving me cold. Numb.

I can't believe how epically fucked my life has become in the span of a day. Last night, I spent the night making love to the woman of my dreams and woke up with her in my arms. It was the happiest I'd ever been. I never thought for a second that the note I left for her would be the closest I'd get to telling her how I feel.

Fuck, I love her so much, and I know she loves me too.

She captivated me from the start, with those beautiful brown eyes and a smile brighter than the sun. She was right there with me when the air crackled around us as I buried myself deep inside her and we came together in an explosion.

I felt it out there on the cobblestone path. I wanted to tell her, but she stopped me. I don't know what hurts more—her not letting me speak the words in my heart or voicing them only to never repeat them again.

I'm pregnant.

Alina's bomb replays on a loop in my brain. I didn't believe it at first—we hadn't been together in weeks. But she's thirteen weeks along and, well, thirteen weeks is a long fucking time.

And ... There was that one night.

I remember joining her at a networking event her firm was hosting, and it was the first occasion in a long while where we enjoyed each other's company. She wasn't harsh or disparaging. She was sweet and attentive. I caught glimpses of the old her, the Alina I had fallen in love with in law school.

Then, things went back to the way they were. She was demanding and cold. She shut me out and made work her priority. It was then that I knew I needed to end it with her.

I don't even know how Alina finagled her way onto the shuttle to come with me. It was like my body was allowing this to happen while my head and heart were screaming, *What the fuck, dude?*

I didn't want Rylann to see Alina, but I couldn't stop the shitshow if I wanted to.

Everyone was trying to talk to me, but Alina glued herself to my side. It's like she knew they would try to talk sense into me, and she wasn't about to give anyone the chance. She's acting like we never broke up and, like the stupid fuck I am, I haven't done a single thing that says otherwise.

I'm pregnant.

Those words have completely rendered every intelligent, rational thought I could possibly have right out of my brain like bacon fat.

I can't believe this is happening. More than that, I can't believe I let Alina sink her talons into me again.

The devastated look in Rylann's eyes will haunt me for the rest of my life. I did that to her. I hurt her, and that's the last thing I ever wanted to do. Instead of protecting her, I blindsided her by bringing another woman here. I should have had the balls to talk to her before I let things get out of hand.

This isn't what I had planned tonight. I was supposed to hold her close, tell her I love her and kiss her beautiful lips.

We were supposed to have a future together and, of course, I went and fucking ruined it all by being a coward. I wasn't even man enough to look her in the eyes until after I broke her heart.

I'm pregnant.

It was supposed to be Rylann. She's the woman I'm in love with. The one that makes me feel whole. Only her.

It wasn't supposed to end like this, with me becoming a father to another woman's child.

I think about a future where it's Rylann's belly that's swollen with our child. A baby created out of love. The two of us watching our children grow and experience true unconditional love.

I'm pregnant.

My dreams turn to reality, and my insides wilt. The reality is that the mother of my child will be a woman I no longer love.

I feel sick.

I spin around, throwing open the stall door, and I spill my guts in the small, dank toilet. I take deep breaths, but they keep getting caught in my throat. I throw up until there's nothing left inside me.

"Fuck!" I scream, slapping my hands against the metal door.

Why did I let her walk away from me? I don't want to be with Alina. I want the warmth Rylann brings to my soul. The way she loves me for me and not for who I can be. Rylann doesn't want to change me, just be with me.

What the fuck am I doing?

I can't let her slip through my fingers. It's her.

It will always be her.

I pull myself off the ground and hurry over to the sink to wash my hands and rinse my mouth and face.

I need to find her and tell her this changes nothing.

I need her.

Living without Rylann is the true nightmare. I know that we can make this work. We are meant to be together. I know it deep down in my soul.

I need to go after her.

My eyes search for her along the path and gardens. She's not there, and the sinking feeling in my stomach doubles.

I rush to the reception. I need to find her. To tell her that I choose her. I can love her and my child. She's wrong—we can have it all. She can move to Los Angeles. Alina and I can share custody.

I double over, hands on my knees, my heart racing. "Shit, shit, shit."

This is exactly why Rylann walked away.

She knows me better than I know myself. I can't be a part-time parent. I can't ask her to leave her family and her career to move to Los Angeles. To help me raise a child I share with another woman.

I'm pregnant.

I push the haunting words away and scour the room for her and her shimmering yellow dress. I need to talk to her. There has to be a way for us to have it all.

I won't survive without her.

She's nowhere to be seen, and I can't feel her presence. No hair standing on end, no swirl of electricity. Nothing

I catch Levi's line of sight. He looks pissed as fuck and disappointed. He shakes his head at me, and my already destroyed heart breaks more.

Scarlett catches my eyes, offering me a sad smile before mouthing, *She's gone.*

A pain so fierce stabs me in the chest. With my fist, I rub my breastbone, the ache growing with every shaky breath.

I know down to my soul ... I just made the biggest mistake of my life.

Part Two

Some moments, however finite,
can last a lifetime in one's heart.

CHAPTER TWENTY-FOUR

Jace

SEVEN YEARS LATER

Blaring silence fills my ears as I enter my condo.

With a sigh, I close the garage door and take in the open-concept kitchen and living room laid out before me. The space is painted inky back and, in the dark, looks painstakingly empty tonight. I haven't bothered to decorate it since I moved in after my divorce. Not that it matters. I prefer it that way. At least, that's what I keep telling myself. Maybe one day, I'll start to believe it.

I rub at the hollow ache in my chest. Sadness has a habit of sneaking in when I think about how I ended up in this place. Alone. My home is nothing like how I thought it would be. My life is nothing like I pictured.

I envisioned my home to be full of energy and love. I imagined coming home to someone excited to share life's adventures, all while raising a family together. A home where the walls are covered in happily captured moments. A home filled with the sound of children's laughter.

But that's not how my life has panned out. That dream continues to elude me.

Just as well. I only have myself to blame.

That's why I keep things simple—eat, sleep, work, repeat.

The monotony of my days keeps me from falling down the what-if rabbit hole. Staying busy keeps me from thinking about what could have been. Neglecting family and friends by burying myself in work and keeping myself closed off is how I make it easier to accept my lonely existence.

My stomach sinks, as it so often does when I think about the past and the mistakes I've made along the way that have brought me here. To the lowest point in my life. After years of therapy, I expected to be past this phase of dwelling on some of my more regrettable choices.

Fuck. I need something to bring me out of this funk.

With a sigh, I turn on the lights, toss my keys on the entry table, and drop my suitcase on the floor. I toe off my shoes and place more mail on the already overflowing pile waiting to be opened.

It's been a long day. I've been working myself to the bone on this case. I'm not doing what I love anymore, and it's starting to take a toll. Without my old business partner, it was easier to give up our small practice and go work for a large firm specializing in family law.

I huff at myself. Family law. What a joke. I was brought in under the guise of having the freedom to do pro bono work for kids in need of families, citizenship, or assistance in juvenile court.

Another regrettable choice on my long list of fuck-ups.

My job now consists of filing divorce papers and mediating arguments between bitter couples that use their children as pawns. Case in point, my current client.

He and his soon-to-be ex are at each other's throats over who will maintain legal custody. At this point, I couldn't give less of a shit. The only person I feel an iota of sympathy for is their teenage daughter, currently stuck between her infuriatingly narcissistic parents.

Shaking my head and loosening the tight muscles in my neck, I try to push work out of my head.

I need a change. I can't keep working like this much longer. There is no fulfillment to be had in this line of law for me. It's made me passionless about the career I used to love.

I walk towards my bedroom, flicking on lights as I go. Like my living space, my room is just as empty. The soft gray walls are bare and lifeless. A king-size bed with a tufted headboard sits in the middle of the room, covered in soft navy Pima cotton sheets and a matching duvet while a simple bedside table adorns each side.

Walking into the half-used walk-in closet, I empty my pockets and hang up my sports coat. I finish undressing, grateful to be exchanging my suit for a pair of cut-off sweatpants and a shirt.

A reflection out of the corner of my eye draws my attention to the mirror hanging beside a line of suits. I look at myself, taking in the onset of wrinkles at the corners of my eyes and across my forehead. I'm too young to look so damn old and tired.

I turn away in disgust, grabbing my phone before walking out of the closet, shaking my head at how drastically different my life is compared to how I envisioned it when I was younger.

I make my way back to the kitchen and grab myself a beer from the fridge. Twisting off the cap, I take a swig and make my way out of the back door to my patio. My sanctuary, when I'm unable to make it to the beach for surfing.

I glance over at the blue board, trimmed in pearl white, hanging on the hook. It's been a couple of weeks since I've been out on the water. I blow out a deep breath, my lips rippling, as I stare longingly at the surfboard calling me to use it.

Maybe tomorrow, I'll change that.

Leaning back, chin to the sky, I close my eyes and inhale the salty sea air before plopping down in one of the Adirondack chairs that circles the propane fire pit. Lighting the fire with the remote,

I slump down, getting comfortable, and take another pull of my beer. I drop my head and stare up at the sky. As usual, the light pollution prevents me from seeing the stars blanket the night sky.

My mind drifts back to the night that changed my life.

I was staring up at the stars with the most beautiful woman I'd ever met sitting beside me. My heart pounded a mile a minute as her body pressed against mine, electricity surging through my veins. I can still picture the way her dark eyes glittered in the moonlight as she looked up at me. How her bright smile warmed me like the bright rays of the sun. She was so painfully beautiful that I had to kiss her.

And I did.

The whole world fell away when her heart-shaped lips touched mine.

I close my eyes and let myself remember the sweet scent of her soft skin. Her soft curves. The feel of her body wrapped around me as I explored every inch of her, from head to toe.

My phone pings with a new text notification, pulling me out of another one of my hallucinogenic memories of her.

Digging my phone out of my pocket, I scroll through the numerous missed calls and texts. It's my brothers, going on again about Cam's pre-season game schedule, wondering when I'll join them. I might not make many family dinners these days, but I never miss my little bro's games.

I exit, knowing I'll get back to them later, and look through the rest of my messages. I read a text from my mom, asking me to come over for dinner soon.

I roll my eyes at the text from one of the senior partners I work with, trying to set me up on a date with his niece, whom, coincidentally, I attended law school with. *Pass.* I won't be making that mistake again. Being forced on dates with friends and family of my colleagues never works out.

Because of her.

Grunting at my wayward thoughts, I pull up the last unread test.

It's another simple *Call me back* from another person I've been ignoring. He's been persistent these past two weeks, with both calls and texts. Something pulls at the back of my mind, nagging me to call him back. It must be important if he's reached out every day without fail.

Sitting forward, I stare at the screen.

My heart pounds in my chest as my knee anxiously bounces. I'm equally nervous and excited to hear what he has to say. We haven't spoken in a long time, and I wonder how he's doing.

Thumb hovering over the contact name, I tap it before I chicken out. My curiosity has been piqued by his continued efforts to get in touch. Holding my breath, I bring the phone to my ear and listen as the line rings.

I'm tempted to hang up when his booming voice answers, "Jace!"

"Hey, man. It's been a while."

"It has. Too long if you ask me. How have you been?"

"Good, good. Work's been keeping me busy."

"Hmm."

He pauses, and my palms start to sweat. It's been a while since we've talked, but I know that hum. He knows me all too well and also knows I've been purposefully ignoring his calls and texts. Shame washes over me, but he continues before I can dwell on my cowardice.

"Well, I'm glad you finally got back to me. I didn't want to have to track you down in person." He chuckles.

I wouldn't put it past him to hunt me down or send one of my brothers after me.

"Yeah, sorry about that." I laugh, squeezing my neck. "So, what can I do for you?"

"I was calling to run something past you. I'm hoping you might be interested in helping me out."

That's a new one. I don't think he's run anything past me in years.

"I'm listening." I'm curious as to why he's been determined to get a hold of me.

"First, I need you to keep an open mind. Second, I need you to agree to my request. No questions asked," he says, boosting my interest further.

My leg stops bouncing at his tone.

"Alright. What can I do for you?" I take a swig of my warming beer and lean back in my chair again.

"Nothing. It's what I can do for you," he says like he's about to solve all my problems.

I doubt he can at this point in my life. But I'm willing to hear him out. Not that long ago we used to be close, practically brothers. I trust him. Who am I to disregard him if he thinks he can do something for me? Maybe he's offering the change I need.

"You have my attention." My voice comes out cool and steady, though I feel nothing of the sort. My mind races with questions.

What on earth can he do for me? He doesn't owe me a thing. If anything, I should be trying to make amends with him. He's the one I owe.

"Knew I would." He chuckles.

I can't help the smile that grows across my face as he explains his plans and reason for reaching out.

Without a second thought, I agree to his request. This is the shake-up I've been needing. For the first time in ages, the band around my chest slackens and my future looks promising.

Hopeful.

CHAPTER TWENTY-FIVE

Rylann

Filling the air is the sweet scent of vanilla mint from the surrounding ponderosa trees. Only my home, Pine Hills—a small town outside of Portland, surrounded by ponderosa pines—can smell like this. Taking in a deep breath, I let the earthy aroma soothe my senses.

Today has been hard. I thought I was making strides, but now, sitting out here on the deck of my childhood home, staring at the thick trees extending past my backyard, I'm not so sure.

The black box on the patio table glares at me, screaming for me to open it. I shake my head.

Not today, Satan.

I don't even know why I brought it outside again.

I focus on the trees again until they blur like one of those 3D posters. Maybe an image will reveal itself to me. Or Sam. *Try again, Ry.*

It's been a year since Sam passed, and sometimes I wonder if the hole he left behind will ever be filled.

A whoop of glee pulls my eyelids open, and my eyes find my son, Rhys, playing with his best friends, Lily and Sadie, Scarlett's twin girls.

Scarlett and Levi welcomed them shortly after I had Rhys. They look exactly like her, with golden blonde hair and blue eyes. Experiencing pregnancy with my best friend was an amazing gift.

Hiring Emery was another. Since we were both pregnant and our business was growing, we needed help. She had just graduated from college and was ambitious, creative, and exactly what we needed. She's amazing to work with. Scarlett and I couldn't take a chance at losing her, so we made her an offer she couldn't refuse—a partnership and a stake in the business. Her loyalty and hard work over the last six years have been nothing short of remarkable. Without her in our life, I don't think Scarlett and I would have been able to keep our little boutique business afloat. Especially after Sam got sick.

Emery was really there for me, further proving she deserved a piece of the business. She loves our company as much as Scarlett and I do. I only wish she'd open up more, but that's Emery. Professional to her core.

I watch the kids laughing and having fun, pretending to defend the "clubhouse" Scarlett and Levi have in their backyard.

Our backyard?

It's still confusing. When we moved here six months ago, it took less than a week before Levi tore down the fence between our yards. Without the fence as a barrier, the little troublemakers have nowhere to hide. Rhys loves living next door to his best friends, who always make sure he's doing okay. He's grown especially close to Sadie this past year. Levi will kill me if he hears this, but I look forward to seeing how Rhys and Sadie's relationship grows as they get older. Mark my words, it's gonna be something.

My chest warms watching my little man. He looks so much like me, with his dark wavy brown hair, tan skin, and trademark freckles on his cheek.

Rhys laughs again, and my lips lift at the corners. His smile is infectious. Every day, it reminds me why I keep moving forward. He's my guiding light in the dark. He looks happier than I thought he'd be today. His smile is wide, his dimples are popping, and his eyes are shining.

Moving here was the right call.

When my parents brought up downsizing, I knew it was a ploy. They were worried about me being alone in my and Sam's old home on the other side of town. Rightly so. The old house didn't feel quite the same anymore, even though I didn't want to leave it. Between my parents, Scarlett, and Levi, I gave in.

We usually spend all our time with them anyway. I also think Rhys being closer to our family has really helped him heal. I wish I could say the same for myself. This past year has been really hard. I go through the motions of living, but most days, I feel like there's a dark cloud following me around again like it did all those years ago.

I shake my head and concentrate on the sounds of joy coming from the kids. I can't believe they've all celebrated their sixth birthday earlier this year. I swear they were babies five seconds ago.

Leaning back in my chair, I stare up at the sky. It really is a beautiful day. The sky is blue, there isn't a cloud to be seen, and the breeze doesn't have that usual spring chill to it. I bask in the last of the sun's warm rays, hoping the warmth penetrates deeper than my skin.

The chair scrapes across the wooden deck beside me and Scarlett sits down, grasping my hand in hers. "How are you feeling, Momma Cakes?"

I chuckle at her deviation from the original. "Couldn't have asked for better weather today, could I?" I sigh, hoping she won't hound me over my clear deflection. The fact is, I'm not okay. I haven't been for a long time.

"No, you couldn't. Stop deflecting. You can't ignore me. It doesn't work. Talk to me. Why haven't you opened this yet?"

I don't have to see her to know she's talking about the black photo box on the patio table. The one I've been ignoring for months. I thought I could open it today, but I don't have the heart to do it. It's the last thing I have left of Sam.

She sighs, no doubt worried and exhausted by my silence. "Ry, it's been a year. Sam wouldn't like seeing you like this, and you know it. You've lost your spark. I haven't seen you like this since ..."

I know what she's referring to, and it makes my hackles rise. I don't want to think about that. *Him.*

Anger burns in my chest.

"Yeah, well, I lost my husband. What do you expect, Scarlett?"

She flinches at my words. Shit, I'm such an asshole.

Softening my tone, I say, "I'm sorry. I didn't mean to sound so angry at you. It's just ..."

I can't tell her what I really think. As someone that has her husband, she'll never understand. And I don't want her to. But grief has a way of making me feel irrationally angry, sad, and lonely. It's every negative emotion, all rolled into one and lit on fire in the empty space in my chest.

"I know, babes. I'm sorry too. I get it. You miss him. I miss him too. We all do." She gives my hand three little squeezes like she does with her girls when telling them *I love you* without words.

My nose tingles, and I sniff away the tears. I don't want to feel this way. I don't want to cry anymore. Especially in front of Rhys. He's finally making strides for the better after losing his doting father. Sam was his world.

Who are you kidding? Sam was the entire universe. For both of us.

This past year without him has been hard, and today feels especially so with it being the anniversary of his death. It didn't matter that I knew we were up against terrible odds. Nothing can prepare you to watch the person you love slowly slip away, without a damn thing you can do to stop it. Watching my husband fight a losing battle with his body day after day, watching him accept the inevitable loss of his life ... It's devastating. There were times I wanted to scream at him to fight harder, even though I knew that realistically he was. He did everything he could to be here for us. Unfortunately, it wasn't enough.

Cancer fucking sucks.

Sam warned me all those years ago, when we got back together, that this might happen. It's why he pushed me away in the first place. I didn't care. There was no way I was going to give up on him just because there was a chance his cancer might return, especially not when he gave up on me.

The years we spent together were wonderful. We got married, had Rhys, and bought a home. We had a life, one where we laughed big and loved each other fully. Even if it was a short time, it was a lifetime of wonderful memories. Sam's ability to love me unconditionally, wholly, even when I wasn't whole, will keep me forever in his debt. He brought me back to life and never—not once—did he leave a doubt about how much he loved me or Rhys. We were his reason for living, and he gave us everything with every fiber of his being, until his last breath.

Without him, I just feel ... hollowed out. I've only ever felt this way once before, and Sam—the person that brought me back—is gone forever. I don't know what to do anymore. I need a break or something because I am stuck in this perpetual state of numbness, and I want out. I *need* out for Rhys. He deserves better. I just don't know how to get there.

"But you need your spark. You need to live, Ry. I think you need to start by opening that box. Sam hid it in the closet for a reason. But since you're too chicken-shit to open it, I will. I need you back. Rhys needs you back."

I look over at my friend as she, as nicely as possible, gives me a dressing down. Scarlett releases my hand, and her eyes flash to the table. My eyes follow hers. The box.

Before I can make a move, she jumps across the table and grabs it.

"What the fuck, Scar? Give me that!" I whisper-shout, not wanting the kids to hear me.

"No! You had your chance. Now it's my turn, and I say it's time we open it." She pulls the lid off the box and throws it at me.

Batting the lid away, I leap around the table to snatch the box from her grasp, but she's too fast and escapes to the other side of the table. As she rummages around inside, I hear the sound of rustling paper.

"What's in the box?" I snap at Scar, but she continues to ignore me. "Scarlett! What's in the box?"

"Chill the frick out, Brad Pitt," she deadpans. "You've been too scared to open the box, so I think you can wait another minute to find out."

"Witch," I hiss at her. "You better give me that box right now or I am going to trucking sit on you." I reach out my hand and snap my fingers at her, demanding she hand over the box. She might be my sister-bestie, but I'm about five seconds away from kicking her ass right now.

She wags her finger, fighting a smile like I didn't just threaten her. We stand there, facing off, until she drops the box on the table and doubles over laughing. "There you are. Where have you been, spice?"

"You're such a cornhole," I tell her.

She laughs at my salty language. Well, as salty as it can be when you're a mom and your kid repeats everything he hears. Over the years, we've gotten creative with bad words.

"I know. But you love me. And I love you. You've had me so worried. I know you're still grieving, Ry ... But, come on. This isn't you."

"I know. I'm—" I choke back a sob, and tears spring to my eyes. "I'm sorry, okay? I'm tr-trying, I swear. I just feel s-so lost," I confess, dropping my chin to my chest in shame.

"Ducking-shizz. I'm sorry, please don't cry." Her arms wrap around me in a tight hug.

I can feel the silence before my ears do. Rhys is watching me.

I straighten up and wipe away my tears. He's always watching, gauging my emotions, reading me. Like Sam used to. My little man is entirely too much like his dad, putting my feelings first. Keeping me warm when life seems a little bleak.

"I'm okay, bug!" I shout.

Rhys cocks his head to the side, searching. For what? I don't know, but after a minute, he seems satisfied and goes back to his game with the girls.

That was close. I don't need him fussing and clinging to me again. It should be me doing that for him.

This past year has come with a lot of changes for the two of us. One of those changes is how closely he watches me and has attached himself to my side. *My sentry.* I didn't hide my grief from him. I wanted him to know it was okay to be sad after losing his dad. I want my son to be emotionally strong and capable of expressing his feelings instead of bottling them up.

Of course, my baby is a formidable little guy. His grief counselor, Dr. Frank, thinks Rhys is handling everything just fine and continues to remind me that kids are resilient. He commends my and Sam's choice to be honest with Rhys about his disease from the start. He thinks Rhys is well-equipped to handle his grief with the support system he has and doesn't foresee there being any negative traumatic side effects after Sam's passing.

I have this little niggling in the back of my brain, telling me Sam had something to do with how well Rhys has been handling all this. Those two had a special bond. They also had a lot of "father-son only" talks and outings together.

"How does he do that?"

"Hmm?" I plop back down in my chair with a thud.

"You know, how can Rhys sense when you're upset? It's like he has a radar on your emotions, and he's ready to tackle the problem."

I hum again at her apt observation, considering I was just thinking the exact same thing. "Honestly? I don't know. I suspect Sam had something to do with it. He used to be the same way when it came to me."

"True." She looks off in the distance, remembering how in tune Sam used to be with my mood, knowing exactly what to say and do to make me feel better in any given situation.

When Sam and I got back together, I was not in a good place. I was heartsick. He promised to fight for me. Stand by my side and support me. He did that, and more. He selflessly loved me and put my happiness ahead of his own every day. Even when I kept him at arm's length, he never gave up. He was the best husband, father, and friend. I miss him so much.

I slide the photo box over to my side of the table and sit down in my chair. I found it hidden in the back of Sam's closet, labeled *For Rylann,* when I was packing up our house. I remember sitting in that dark closet, crying with the box clutched to my chest until Scarlett found me. When I finished bawling my eyes out, she put it back on the shelf and told me to open it when I was ready.

I don't think I'll ever be ready. If I know Sam, this is probably a gift of some sort, and opening it seems so final. Like he'll be gone all over again.

Turning back to me she says, "Sam's gone. He's not coming back. I know it hurts. Ignoring this box isn't going to change that. He left this for you. From what I can tell, it's a gift, babes. Levi and I are going to take the kids to get some ice cream. That gives you some time to yourself to go through it. If you need me, text me."

I nod. She's right—it's time. I'm being a total chicken-shit. I need to rip the Band-Aid off and see what Sam left behind.

My bestie gives me a kiss on the cheek before disappearing with the kids.

With a deep breath, I find the strength to take a look in the box.

Inside, I find a neatly wrapped bundle of envelopes addressed to Rhys in Sam's bold handwriting. There's a bundle of photos tied in butcher's string and one letter-sized manilla envelope with a neatly scrawled post-it note attached to it, from Sam to me. It reads, *Open first.*

Here goes nothing.

CHAPTER TWENTY-SIX

Rylann

"Mommy?"

"Yes, sweet boy?"

I tuck Rhys into bed. It has been one hell of a day. I am mentally exhausted, and I still have one more thing I need to do before I can get some sleep.

"Are you sad again?" His little voice is full of curiosity.

"A little bit, bug. It's only because I miss Daddy so much. Especially today."

"I miss him too." He nods in understanding.

"How was your day? Did you have a high or a low?" I ask him the same question every night. Sam started this when Rhys was old enough to remember things on his own.

His little eyebrows crunch in thought as he files through everything he's done today. "High. I ate two scoops,"—he holds out two fingers for me—"of ice cream with Uncle Lee. He said since it was a special day to remember Daddy, I can have one scoop of my favorite flavor and one of Daddy's."

"Well, that explains a lot, my little sugar fiend. I'm gonna have to have a talk with your naughty uncle Levi about that." I boop Rhys's nose with a stern little glare.

I stifle my laugh when his eyes widen in shock like he just remembered he wasn't supposed to spill the beans about eating two scoops of ice cream. He doesn't want his favorite uncle to get in trouble.

"Oh, I'm just kidding, you silly boy," I say with a laugh and tickle his ribs.

He lets out a squeal, his laugh filling the room.

I love that sound. It soothes my soul.

"Aunty Scar said Uncle Lee was going to get in trouble."

"Maybe another time. But today? Nah. No trouble today. Uncle Lee was right—it was a special day today. Daddy would have loved to see this cute, smushy face covered in ice cream." I squish his little baby face between my palms.

He giggles, pushing me away. I let him go, only to ruffle his soft brown hair with my fingers.

"Did you have a high today, Mommy? Or just a low?"

Aye, this kid. Calling me out and seeing everything.

"Let me think." I tap my lips, exaggerating my thinking about it. This is the perfect segway for talking about what I found today. "My high was having a beautiful sunny day to remember Daddy. Aaand ... I also found a surprise in Daddy's box."

"You did? Was there anything in it for me?" Curiosity and excitement fill his eyes.

I nod, and a wide grin spreads across his face. That smile is the best thing I've seen all day, and it pulls a smile to my lips too.

"There sure is. I'm sorry I didn't find it sooner. You were supposed to get it on your birthday."

"Can I have it now, Mommy? *Please?*"

I pull out the letter from my hoodie pocket and hand it to Rhys. "Do you want me to read it to you, or do you want to read it yourself?"

"I can do it."

Rhys stares at the envelope for another second. I can't imagine what he's thinking. Carefully, he runs his finger under the sealed flap and opens the envelope, pulling a single sheet of yellow paper from Sam's legal pad. He reads the letter aloud, with only a little help from me.

> Rhys,
> Happy Birthday, Buddy Boy!
>   I want you to have a wonderful day full of laughs and, of course, music. Make sure you play our song loudly so I can hear it. Make your birthday a fun one, kiddo. If I know Mommy, she made sure the house was decorated with balloons and streamers everywhere. I also know there will be a big chocolate cake waiting for you to bite into. Make sure it's a big bite. Make your wish count when you blow out those candles. Don't waste it on me because I'll always be with you. I miss you every day.
>
>   Remember what I told you. Everything will be okay, son. I made sure you'll have more highs than lows. It just might take a while. I love you three thousand.
>
> Xo, Daddy

I can't help the tears escape the corners of my eyes. Fucking Sam. Forever the perfect father and husband.

While I want to question Rhys regarding Sam's whole *Remember what I told you* bit, I leave it alone. It's important for him to keep some of his moments with Sam sacred.

I know I do.

Rhys looks at me, and I can see the unshed tears pooling in his light brown eyes, irises glowing brighter in the light. I scoop him up in my arms and lay back against the headboard, his head on my chest, my chin resting on his head. I breathe in his orange coconut shampoo.

"It's okay to cry when we miss Daddy, my love."

He nods his head, hiding his face in the soft fabric of the hoodie, silent tears pouring down his chubby cheeks.

I lay there, cuddled up with him until his breaths even out. Thinking I lost him to sleep, I lean over to tuck him in the covers again, but his eyes pop up.

"Daddy promised we would be happy again. Is that gonna happen soon?"

I tilt his chin up, looking him directly in his eyes when I say, "I *am* happy because I have *you*." I kiss his nose for emphasis. "Finding this special birthday letter makes me happy too. Daddy will always look out for us. Each day, we will be a little less sad and a little more happy. I promise."

He nods his little head, his eyelids closing. I drop one more goodnight kiss on his forehead, tuck him in, and head out of his room, turning off the light behind me.

I find myself in the makeshift office I have set up in the guest bedroom, sitting with that damn manilla envelope in my hands. Inside, there were clear instructions from Sam on the post-its stuck on the various letters inside. Each one is numbered in big bold writing. I only made it through the first message, instructing me to give Rhys his birthday letter and then continue to do so with other envelopes for other birthdays and special occasions.

The next envelope, labeled with *Open Second,* made me pause. Inside wasn't a letter, only a small silver USB drive. Etched along the side is *Play This Next.*

My throat tightens, the pit in my stomach bottoms out, and my forehead breaks out in a slight sweat. My head starts spiraling with all the possible things that are on this thing. This is why I haven't wanted to open the damn thing. It's Pandora's fucking box.

"What the fresh hell have you left me, Sam?" I look up at the ceiling, hoping for some kind of sign, a voice—something.

I get nothing. Just silence.

Plugging in the drive, I wait as the download folder opens up. There sits a little icon labeled *For Rylann, when you're ready.* I click on the icon and a video file loads.

Sam's face fills the screen, and I slam my fingers down on the keys trying to hit pause before the video auto-plays.

My heart leaps out of my chest. If he left this behind, what he has to say is too important to write down.

I look at the screen again, and tears fill my eyes at the sight of him. I'm not sure if I'm strong enough to watch this alone. To see him alive, hear his deep voice. It hurts so damn much just thinking about him not being here. Every day, Rhys and I move forward, creating new happy moments. All without Sam, and it fucking kills me. He should be here. He should be with us.

Last week, when Rhys and I were having one of our after-school dance parties, Sam's favorite White Stripes song came on over the Bluetooth speaker and I froze. Rhys did what he always did with Sam. He started bobbing his head and did the air drums. Sam would have been happy to see Rhys smile and dance around.

Looking back, I hate to admit it, but a piece of me knew we would be okay. Or maybe we already were okay and I just didn't notice. I went to sleep crying that night. Day by day, little by little, Sam misses more, and I feel lost moving forward.

Maybe his message can help you move forward without feeling so guilty for living. My shoulders soften at the thought. Sam did always have a knack for saying the right thing and the right time.

I give my neck a little stretch, pull my shoulders back, and with a deep breath, I hit the play button again.

Sam smiles as he begins talking about us sleeping. He's wearing his favorite gray hoodie—the one I gave him for Father's Day—that reads "I'm a Cool Dad" across the front. The one I'm currently wearing.

His hair is buzzed short, and his glasses are a little askew. I can see the dark purple circles under his eyes. Handsome as ever, but I can see the exhaustion lying beneath the surface. He looks worried. Haunted.

I keep watching and, for the first time, what he says is not the right thing nor the right time.

The video stops, and the silence in the office is deafening.

Hot tears pour down my face as I reach out and stroke Sam's face over the screen.

The sparkle of my wedding bands catches my eye, and suddenly, the grief and anger at what he's just told me hit me in the gut. A pain like I've never felt before grips my heart and pulls me under.

How could he do this to us?

My fingers find my rings, and I wrench them off, clenching them in my fist.

Grabbing my cell phone off my desk, I hit call to the only person that can help me. It only takes three rings before my mom's voice comes through, thick with sleep.

"What's wrong, *mija?*"

At the sound of her voice, I breakdown. "Mom, I-I need you." I can barely get the words out between sobs.

"What's wrong? Is it Rhys?" She sounds frantic.

Taking a deep breath, I reassure her Rhys is fine. "Sorry, he's o-okay. He's asleep. I just … I-I need to t-talk to you. There's s-something y-you need t-to see," I stutter.

"I'll get dressed and have Daddy drop me off. I'll be there soon, *mi amor.*"

She ends the call, and I know she'll be here in the next fifteen minutes since it's only a ten-minute drive from their condo.

I'm so lost in my grief, weeping in Sam's brown chair, that I don't hear her arrive with my dad until her arms wrap around me. She holds me until I can control my tears.

Sniffling, I tell her about the video, playing it for her to see for herself. As she watches, all I can think about is how I wish I never found the video. How I wish it wasn't true. How Sam's confession taints the wonderful life we shared.

I am so mad at him. I wish I could scream at him. Shake sense into him.

My heart fucking hurts. His truths have torn me in two—the part that loves Sam for the wonderful husband and father he was, and the part that hates him for betraying my trust. He swore to love and protect me, but this goes against all that. I don't know how to reconcile my feelings of outrage and adoration.

When Mom finally gets me to bed, whispering words of love and support, I'm a shell of myself. She lays with me, caressing my hair until I fall asleep.

The last thing I remember her saying is, "Tonight is for tears, not solutions. So, let it all out. Tomorrow? Tomorrow you will have a whole lot of choices to make, baby girl."

I just hope I make the right ones.

CHAPTER TWENTY-SEVEN

Rylann

With a steaming-hot mug of tea clasped between my cold hands, I take a seat on the soft padded patio chair and tilt my face up to the blue sky. It's chilly out, but the sun's rays still manage to warm my cheeks. Watching the birds squawk and soar above the tree line, I sip my tea, burrowing into my favorite yellow hoodie. I feel like garbage this morning.

My head is pounding like I drank a bottle of tequila last night. My eyes are puffy and swollen. Turns out, crying yourself to sleep can also leave you with a hangover.

I woke up this morning feeling like I went ten rounds with Rocky. My hand is stiff from clenching my wedding rings in the palm of my hand all night. I tried to put them back on, but I just couldn't bring myself to do it. I have a buttload of unresolved feelings rolling around in my head and my heart. I decided to place my rings in the box of letters, along with the USB drive, and put it on the top shelf in my office.

I rub at the ache in my chest, my mind drifting back to the video.

Thank god my mom stayed with me and helped get Rhys out the door for school this morning. She's good at distracting him. He wasn't fooled, but after reassuring him I'd be there to pick him and the twins up for the walk home, like usual, he left for school.

With the elementary school within walking distance, on nice days, Scarlett, Levi, and I take turns taking the kids to and from school—one of the many benefits of moving back home into my childhood home.

Since my dad retired, he has transformed this place into a whole new home waiting for new memories to be made. It's pretty magical, almost like he had me in mind when he remodeled it. My favorite touch is the new, low wooden deck he painted dark gray to match the new shutters. He really put in a lot of effort to make this place an oasis, like the built-in grill and the six-person hot tub.

My dad still comes by weekly to mow the lawn, trim the shrubs, water the flowers, and raise the garden. I couldn't be more grateful for all the help he gives me. Both my parents have been there for me, supporting us every step of the way. Before and after Sam got sick. I don't think I could have gotten through it without them. I still have remorse for displacing them from their home, but this is where Rhys and I are supposed to be.

My phone buzzes on the table, pulling me out of my thoughts. Setting my tea down, I pick up my phone to find a text from Scarlett.

Momma Bear Scar: *Why was Momma Rita dropping Rhys off? R U OK?*

Momma Cakes: I'm Fine. I slept in. She just dropped by to get some Rhysie love. You know how she is.

My stomach sours for lying to my bestie. We haven't talked since she dropped Rhys off last night after ice cream. She wanted to know about the box, but I didn't have answers. I hadn't fully opened my "gift" yet. I'm glad I waited until late last night to watch it.

Momma Bear Scar: *Are we going to talk about the box?*
Momma Bear Scar: ***gif of Brad Pitt screaming***

Momma Cakes: Dramatic much?

Momma Bear Scar: *Tell. Me. Now. Or you'll pay for it, with my ass print on your chest.*

Momma Cakes: Geez, relax Momma Bear. It was a bunch of letters for Rhys. I'll tell you about them later.

Momma Bear Scar: *What about the yellow one?*

Fuckity fuck. My parents know, but I'm not ready to tell Scar about the yellow envelope.

Momma Cakes: I haven't opened it yet. I'm not ready.

Momma Bear Scar: ***angry face emoji** **knife emoji** **finger pointing emoji***

This girl, I swear, is going to be the death of me. I'll tell her when the time is right. Just not now.

Momma Cakes: **middle finger emoji**

Momma Bear Scar: ***gif from Kellie from the office saying how dare you***

Momma Bear Scar: *Family dinner tonight? Pizza?*

Momma Cakes: Sure.

Momma Bear Scar: *Calm your tits down there, Rice Cakes. No need to wet yourself in excitement.*

Momma Cakes: Oh, but I am. I can hardly wait to eat pizza and drink wine with you. I haven't seen you in sooo long. I'm dying without you.

Momma Bear Scar: *That's more like it.*

Between client calls and some last-minute design projects, today flew by. My brain is officially drained, which is what I do to my wine.

We ate pizza outside on the patio, and with the kids finished and playing, it leaves me with Scarlett and Levi. I've been waiting for her to start in on the envelopes again, but she hasn't—yet. She's actually been abnormally chill.

"So, Ry," Levi says, getting my attention. "I have thought long and hard the last couple of weeks, and I've decided we are going on a vacation."

"Okaaay."

Where is Levi going with this? Oh, is he going to ask me to watch the girls while he and Scarlett take some trip? I know their seventh anniversary is next month. The kids will be on summer vacation by then, so it shouldn't be a problem.

I'm about to agree to watch the girls when Scarlett cuts me off. "By 'we', Levi means us,"—she points between herself and Levi—"the girls, and you and Rhys. Like we used to."

Her *before* implied. While I appreciate her not trying to say *before Sam's death*, it still cuts deep.

"Listen to me, Rylann." I turn to face Levi. He pats my hand, and his eyes are full of compassion and understanding. "I know this is hard. Sam was my friend, and I miss him too. But he wouldn't want you to stop living. He would want you to take Rhys on trips. Experience new things. He would want you to be happy. And, sweetheart, you aren't happy. We can all see it, especially Rhys."

"I hate to gang up on you, but it's true. I told you that yesterday. You've lost your spark."

"Yeah, well, I've kind of been through a lot." I try to put some levity in my tone, even though I want to fucking cry.

Scarlett refills our wine glasses as she waits for Levi to continue.

"Next month is our anniversary, and I've decided that Scarlett and I are going to renew our vows. I want to make sure she knows how much I love her."

Scarlett blows Levi a kiss.

I can't fathom going on a family vacation without Sam. The last time I did it was seven years ago.

My eyes widen in understanding. The blood drains from my face.

No! They wouldn't.

"And that means we are doing it all over again ... In Hawaii," Scarlett finishes.

Oh, fuck no.

Words escape me as memory after memory crashes into me, taking me under.

Hawaii. *Him.* Kisses on the beach. The smell of the ocean air mixed with oranges and leather. Love. Passion. Loss. Heartbreak.

Is the universe conspiring against me now? First the video, and now Hawaii.

I grab the glass of wine in front of me and chug. No wonder the sneaky bitch refilled—she knew this was coming.

"I'm taking care of everything. Flights, hotel, food, entertainment. Everything. My gift to you and Rhys. You two need this. This is something I know Sam would want. All you have to do is be there for us like last time and, of course, have fun. Let go a little. Think of this as a fresh start. Besides, this will be great for Rhys. He will have so much fun. He'll have fun just planning the trip."

The panic in my chest loosens its grip at the thought of experiencing Hawaii with Rhys. Watching his eyes take in the beauty, the way I know he's going to ask questions and need the history of ... Well, everything.

But Hawaii? Really?

I don't know if I can face the memories that place holds for me.

"I can see this is a shock. Please, think about it, okay? I have everything on hold. I just need to confirm the details by tomorrow. I'm going to give you ladies a minute alone. I'll see you inside, baby."

Levi gets up and kisses Scarlett square on the mouth, not giving a rat's ass that I'm here to watch him make out with my friend. Even though I'm used to it, it hasn't been easy to watch over the years. Sam and I loved each other dearly, but we didn't have that kind of passion. That need for constant PDA. I've only had that with one person.

I shake that thought away. I refuse to think about him right now.

Levi walks into the house, leaving me with a stupidly grinning Scarlett. She pulls me out of the chair and leads me to the steps off the deck. We silently watch the kids for a few minutes.

I don't know how to process what went down in that conversation. I'm overwhelmed and confused. There is no way I can go through with this.

"You're in, right?"

"I don't know, Scar. This is a lot to take in. I can't just let Levi pay for everything. That's ridiculous. We have work. We can't leave Emery in the trenches."

"No, it's not. You're our family. And too bad!" She shrugs me off. "Emery already knows and will be hiring a temp. Between her, the new assistant, and a temp, they can handle us being gone for two weeks. So you can't use work as an excuse. You're going. You need this. Rhys needs this. Levi and I need this. I hate that Sam's not here. I do." Scarlett wipes away a tear and bumps my shoulder with hers.

I know her and Levi loved Sam and mourned his loss too.

I lean my head on her shoulder. She's been right by my side, through thick and thin. I want to do this for her, I do, but this is a big ask. It feels wrong to go back there.

"Listen. I don't want to hurt you by saying this, babes, but I don't want to let life pass us by in a blur of work and daily routines. I want to experience new things. I want to show Levi that I love him. I want him to know that, no matter what, I choose him. I choose our family. Most importantly, I choose to live and be happy. Be happy with me. Life is too short."

The wine I chugged finally makes its appearance, and my face starts to warm, dulling my anxiety.

"It's getting late. I need to get the girls washed up before bed." Scarlett stands, wipes the dust off her butt, and yells for the girls.

"Do we have to?" Lily and Sadie whine in that weird identical twin synchronous way that weirds me out.

Don't get me wrong, I love their sweet little faces like they are my own, but they can give off a real "redrum" vibe sometimes. If Scar knew I thought that, she'd kick my ass.

"Yes. Now, come on. We have some planning to do. You too, Rhysie." She taps him on the nose.

"What are we planning, Auntie Scar?" He rubs his nose in confusion.

Before I can stop her, she says, "Vacation, silly. We're all going to Hawaii in one month."

The kids scream, jumping up and down in excitement.

What the fuck? I haven't even agreed.

I look down at Rhys, and the grin on his face melts my heart. His smile is brighter than the sun at the mere mention of vacation. My shoulders deflate in defeat.

I can't take this away from him now, can I?

"Good night, you two," Scarlett says, rushing off with the girls, avoiding me. She knows she's in trouble.

I'm going to sit on her, then kick her ass.

Bedtime routine is a breeze today.

I bathed Rhys and let him play quietly in his room while I took a quick shower, trying to get my head on straight. I've decided that we are not going on that trip. I cannot go back to Hawaii. I won't.

I hate having to tell Rhys that his beloved auntie Scarlett is a goddamn liar, but she is.

Walking into his room, I find him sitting at his desk writing something on a piece of paper, the iPad open to a Wikipedia page. Looking over his shoulder, I see that he's already created a list of all the things he wants to do and see ... *in Hawaii.*

"Hey, bug. Watcha doin'?" I run my fingers through his dark brown waves.

He looks up at me, his soft brown eyes sparkling. "I'm planning our trip. Daddy told me one day I would go to Hawaii and have a real adventure. He said Hawaii is a magical place."

"What?" Rubbing my neck, I clear my throat, emotion stuck like a lump. "When did Daddy say that?"

"When he got sick. He told me a story about a surf king that knew how to ride the waves, made friends with sea turtles, and found love in the ocean."

I know what you're doing! I look up at the ceiling, trying to stay strong.

"That sounds like an awesome story, kiddo. But—"

"Here's a list of all the things I think Daddy would like us to do," Rhys cuts me off, his enthusiasm throwing me off center.

I wasn't expecting him to react with such excitement and start planning already. He hands me the list, and in his boyish loopy print, it reads:

<u>Hawaii Things to do for Daddy.</u>

- Learn to surf
- Climb a volcano
- Drink a coconut
- Meet a sea turtle
- Pick a pineapple
- Go snorkeling
- See the biggest waves
- Ride a horse on the beach
- See a sunset
- Find a waterfall
- Do a hula dance
- Go to a luau
- See black sand
- Eat shaved ice
- See a Wonder

"Wow, that's a lot of things to do. How did you figure this all out so fast?"

"I used the iPad." He looks down, his little face guilty for using the pad without permission.

I hate him going onto the internet without me. You never know what the search engine will pull up.

"It's okay, Rhys. Next time, please wait for me to use it with you. Deal?"

"Deal." The smile on his face returns.

Damn, he's so happy about this trip. Maybe Levi's right. Rhys does need a trip somewhere. Maybe just the two of us, though. I can take him somewhere else when they are gone. Somewhere we can make new memories, where the past can't haunt me.

I'll tell him tomorrow about us going on an adventure. I need to come up with an awesome location that he can get excited about. Just not exactly where he was hoping. I'm not ready to dash his dreams tonight.

"It's time for sleep. Go on and get into bed."

Rhys puts his markers away, climbs onto his bed, and gets under his Spiderman comforter. Once he's all snuggled in, I give him a kiss, turn out the lights, and leave him. My little man is a good sleeper, always has been.

I rub my temples, my bed calling me as my head begins to pound. It's been a day—or two—and I need sleep or something that can turn off my brain. I have so much more on my plate to handle and come to terms with.

Picking up my cell phone, I text Scarlett. I need to just rip off the Band-Aid and let her know it's a no-go for us. I'm not ready for a trip like that yet. I'll figure out something smaller and just as fun for Rhys and me to do together.

Momma Cakes: I'm sorry, but we can't go on the trip. Maybe next time.

Boss Bitch by Doja Cat starts blaring from my phone, scaring the crap out of me. Scarlett and her godforsaken need to mess with my phone.

Why am I surprised by the song choice or her need to call me? Of course, she's calling. She's a freaking bulldozer, I swear. She can't take no for an answer.

I hit ignore. I'm not in the mood to get an earful right tonight. Another text pops up.

Momma Bear Scar: ANSWER YOUR PHONE!! I'll just keep calling until you do.

Less than ten seconds later, Doja Cat starts singing again. Might as well get this over with. There's no fighting her, and I'm too tired to try.

"Hello."

"Don't you *hello* me!" she whisper-shouts at me through the line. "You cannot back out. I refuse to let you. It's too late, anyway. I told Levi you agreed, and he booked everything. It's all set. Look in your email."

Frantic, I pull my phone away and go to my inbox. Sure enough, sitting at the top are both airline and hotel accommodation reservation numbers forwarded to me by Levi.

I bring my cell back to my ear. "Scarlett! What the hell? How could you do this?"

"It's for your own good." She covers the phone, and I hear a muffled conversation between her and Levi.

"Ry!" Levi's voice booms through the speakers. "Did you get my emails? I am so happy you agreed to go. It's going to be amazing and exactly what you and Rhys need."

I slap my forehead with my palm. My best friend is a fucking traitor and a huge asshole. "Yeah. I did. Thank you, Lee. I am happy to pay my portion."

"No, you won't. We're family."

I sniffle back tears at Levi's declaration. "Thank you. Again. Rhys is going to be so happy."

"So will you. Here's Scarlett." I hear more muffled sounds.

"Hiya, bestie."

The nerve of the woman to act like she didn't just throw me under the bus.

"You fucking bitch. Don't you use that tone with me. You set me up. I love you, but you are *so* going to pay."

Scarlett laughs, but it's a little too forced. She sounds off, and my hackles rise. "You don't mean that. You love me too much, Sissy. So, yeah, um. I gotta go. Levi is calling me. Um ... I'll see you in the morning. Oh, and ... by the way we, uh... invited Levi's parents and Jace. Okay, love you, byeee." She says that last part so fast, I can barely make out the words before the line goes dead.

When her words finally register, my heart takes flight and my breathing turns shallow.

No, no, no, no.

This cannot be happening.

She invited *him* too?

Oh fuck, oh fuck, oh fuck.

I'm totally fucked.

I need a new best friend.

Because I'm going to kill the one I currently have.

CHAPTER TWENTY-EIGHT

Rylann

ONE MONTH LATER

Looking around the hotel lobby, I can't help but remember the past.

I've been agonizing over this trip for the last month. I haven't let myself think about Hawaii in a long time, but knowing he is going to be here has brought everything to the surface.

Some of the best and worst memories have even infiltrated my dreams. Glimpses of us in the midst of passionate kisses. The way his hazel eyes burned with desire. It also came with visions, of walking away from his dejected face on the darkened path, that kept me tossing and turning in bed instead of sleeping.

Without a doubt, I left the other half of my heart with him that night, knowing I would never get it back. It wasn't easy walking away from him. I had the hardest time letting go and moving on after him. I missed him so much, it physically hurt to think about him. It took months of healing before I could even hear his name without falling to pieces.

I loved him that deeply.

For weeks, I cried myself to sleep playing the what-if game. What if he came after me? What if we tried to make it work? What if we didn't give up on each other?

I eventually stopped playing the game and forced myself to move on.

Despite the years that have passed, I know I'm in trouble. My heart will never be safe where he's concerned, and I'm scared to see him in person.

Might wanna get used to hearing and saying his name.

I internally roll my eyes at myself.

Jace. There. I said it, and nothing bad happened.

"Ry, Hello!" Scarlett calls, snapping her fingers in my face, bringing me back to the present.

"Geez, woman, knock it off." I rear my head back and slap her hand away.

"I've been talking to you and you haven't been listening. You completely zoned out. Are you okay?" she asks with a sigh. She's worried.

"Yeah, yeah. I'm good." I try reassuring her with a smile. It's weak at best, and she sees right through it, eyes narrowing in on me. "What were you saying?"

"I said Lily needs to use the bathroom, so we are going to head up. Check in and then text me when you guys are ready. We can meet back down here for a late lunch and swimming. Levi is at the restaurant, making us a reservation. Work for you?"

"Sounds good." I lean in and give her a hug and kiss on the cheek.

"Rhysie, take care of your mom. I think she's tired."

"I will, Auntie Scar. I always take care of her. Just like Daddy told me to. I'm her man." He points a proud thumb at his puffed up little chest, and mine puffs too.

"That you are, kiddo." Scarlett's eyes glaze over, and she smooths Rhys's hair to the side. She blows me a little kiss and grabs both Lily's and Sadie's hand, then walks towards the bank of elevators.

The receptionist gets us checked in, and I pay extra for the bellhop to take our bags to our room. Since Levi paid for the room, I'm going to splurge on the extras. I take the room keys from the receptionist and tip the older gentleman taking our bags upstairs.

Before I can lead us upstairs to follow him, Rhys stops me. "Can we go to the gift shop right now?"

I look over at the bellhop in question.

"Go ahead, ma'am. I can take care of this for you."

I thank the man and turn back to Rhys. "What do you need from the gift shop? We just got here."

"It's not for me, it's for you. You need caffeine to keep you awake so we can go swimming all day long." He flashes me a wide dimple-popping smile. Like usual, I'm a sucker and cave.

My little charmer.

"That's not a bad idea. Should we get some snacks too?"

"Yes!" He shouts with a fist pump.

I shake my head and laugh. This kid. His ability to make me smile makes my heart swell with love and gratitude. He's my whole world, and I'd do anything to make him happy.

"Alright, then. Let's hit the gift shop."

He grabs my hand and pulls me the entire way, bouncing on his heels.

It takes us twenty minutes to get drinks and snacks, on account of Rhys getting distracted with the magnets, postcards, and trinkets the gift shop has to offer. If he's this excited about the gift shop, he's going to lose his mind like I did when we go to the International Market Place. I want to make Rhys's experience there as memorable as mine.

A memory of Jace and me eating ice cream pops into my head. The two of us walking through the throngs of shopping tourists flashes through my mind. The way he wiped away the sweet cream left on my lips with his thumb and licked it away. How his hungry eyes stared at my mouth when I licked the spoon.

A shiver rolls down my spine.

Jace was so damn sexy.

Stop it, you silly woman!

I've been here less than an hour, and I'm already losing my mind. That's not why I'm here. This trip is all about Rhys.

"Can I push the button?" Rhys asks at the elevators, shopping bag in hand.

"Go for it."

We step into the elevator, and I move towards the back, resting my head on the wall, tired from the flight and countless sleepless nights.

The doors are about to close when someone shouts, "Hold the elevator!"

My stomach drops, the hairs on my arms stand on end, and my pulse races. I'd know that whiskey-smooth voice anywhere.

Before I can stop him, Rhys hits a button and the doors swish open.

Pulling a small sleek black suitcase, Jace steps into the elevator, an older couple following on his heels. He doesn't notice me, only the little brown-haired boy holding open the door.

My heart pounds in my ears- and the butterflies I thought died soar to life.

"Thanks, pal. You're a real lifesaver," he tells Rhys.

"You're welcome, mister." I can't help the smile that pulls at my lips at Rhys's polite response.

"Mister? Wow, you're a polite little dude. Where'd you learn such great manners?" Jace asks, kneeling down on one knee. He looks Rhys in the eyes to chat like he's his equal, and the sight of them together does all kinds of things to me. The way he talks to my son with such warmth and respect in his voice.

My insides melt, and anxiety skyrockets at the same time.

I take a moment to drink in Jace from behind. He's wearing blue jeans, a light gray t-shirt that accentuates his strong wide back, and white sneakers. His hair is longer on top than I remember, but overall, he still looks good. Really good.

Why does he still have to look so damn hot?

Quickly glancing in the mirror, I take a long look at myself.

I look tired. My brown waves are frizzy, I'm not wearing a stitch of makeup, and I have little black circles under my eyes. Rhys wasn't kidding when he said I needed caffeine. I look like I haven't had a decent night's sleep in days. Which is fairly accurate, considering I've been agonizing over this trip for the last month. To make it worse, I'm wearing the least sexy outfit on the planet. I'm rocking a pair of jeggings—because, let's face it, as a mom, what else is cute and comfy besides yoga pants?—and a loose white t-shirt with the words *Just Plane Cute* written across the front.

Great. Everything about me screams hot mess express.

My pits and palms start to sweat. This is not how I envisioned Jace seeing me for the first time in years.

"My mommy," Rhys exclaims proudly. "She says it's important to be polite and helpful. My daddy used to say manners show people your insides are good."

The older woman next to me places her hand over her heart in awe at Rhys's response.

That's right, baby, make me look good.

"Unless you fart. Then it means your insides are baaad," he explains, waving his hand in front of his nose.

Jace throws his head back and barks out a laugh.

I look back over at the lady, whose jaw is now hanging open in shock, and cringe. Yeah, she's definitely not voting for me to win Mom of the Year. At least the gentleman with her has a good sense of humor and chuckles at Rhys's joke.

What can I say? Six-year-olds love potty jokes. That would have killed if Levi and the girls were here.

"You got me there, buddy," Jace agrees, holding out his fist for Rhys to bump, which he happily taps before looking at me with a bright smile.

Jace follows Rhys's line of sight, and it's just like it was all those years ago when our eyes connect. The wings of a thousand butterflies take flight in my stomach, my heart races like a band of horses in an open field, and my breath catches in my lungs. The golden rings around his pupils have me trapped like a fly in a vat of honey while his verdant irises call me home. They still have the ability to pull me under their spell and keep me swimming in their warmth.

Like the coward I am, I break the connection, looking away. My nerves are frayed, and my hand shakes as I extend it out to Rhys.

Jace watches, on his knee, as Rhys clasps his small hand in mine, his eyes widening in surprise followed by understanding.

Yup, he's my son.

"Hello, Sunshine," Jace drawls.

My old nickname sounds like melted caramel on his tongue, and I fight the urge to squeeze my legs together at the sound of his deep voice. He stands, eyes sweeping over me from head to toe, and smiles. My traitorous body bursts into flames beneath his gaze.

"Still stunning, I see."

My heart jumps at his compliment, and I pull Rhys to my side like armor.

"Hello, Ace." His nickname feels both foreign and familiar on my tongue. His lips imperceptibly quirk upward at my reaction. "It's been a while. I see you've met my son. This is Rhys."

"You know him, Mommy?" Rhys asks, tugging at my hand, but my eyes stay glued to the hazel depths before me.

"She does," Jace answers for us.

"Really? Did you know my dad too?" Rhys asks. My chest does that achy thing whenever he talks about Sam.

Jace beats me again, answering Rhys, "No. I'm sorry, buddy. I didn't."

Rhys visibly deflates at Jace's response. It hurts that he's looking for connections to the man that raised him.

"It's okay. I'm looking for a surfer that knows my dad. He said I would find him here and that he would teach me how to surf."

What's that now?

I look down at Rhys, who is staring at his shoes. I wish he would tell me what this is about, but he's just been so tight-lipped about his talks with Sam.

Jace lowers down onto one knee again and tilts Rhys's chin up. "I may not have known your dad, but I do surf. Maybe I can give you a lesson or two while we're here. Would you like that?"

"Yes!" Rhys shrieks, making me flinch.

They bump knuckles again, and Rhys's excitement does nothing to quell my apprehension.

Nope. I can't do this right now.

Like a sign from above, the elevator dings and the doors swing open.

"This is us. Come on, Rhys. Say goodbye to Jace. I'm sure we will see him again."

Pulling Rhys, I jump off the elevator like my ass is on fire, but Rhys stops mid-step, forcing me to stop too.

"Your name is Jace?" Rhys asks, tilting his head to the side, studying the man before him.

"It sure is. And you're Bob, right?"

Rhys laughs. "No, silly. My name is Rhys."

"That's what I said." Jace winks at my son.

My stomach flips.

That wink. I'm so fucked.

"Cool. Bye, Jace." Rhys waves goodbye, his demeanor flipping a complete one-eighty at the last minute.

Hand in hand, Rhys and I walk down the corridor toward our room. Only, we aren't alone. My skin prickles with awareness, but I press forward.

Jace follows right behind, bag in hand.

Stopping at our door, I look over to find him staring at my ass. His eyes meet mine and he shrugs, not caring one bit that he got caught checking me out. I bite my lip in an attempt not to smile at the memory of him staring at my ass like last time.

He pulls out his key, standing at the door next to mine.

You have got to be kidding me.

"Well, look at that. How fortuitous. We're neighbors ... Again." He winks at me, sending a wave of heat straight to my center.

Eyes locked, we stand there, watching the other.

"Cool! Neighbors!" Rhys chirps in excitement.

Like a bucket of cold water, I'm brought back to reality. *Thanks, little man. I owe you big.*

"So cool," Jace says.

Rhys jumps up and down. He really needs to tone down the excitement he has for his new friend.

I look away, shaking my head, and scan my key card over the pad. I need to get the hell away from Jace. The light flashes green, and Rhys turns the handle, opening the door. I watch as he runs in and swan-dives onto one of the queen beds.

"I guess that one's his."

I shiver at the sound of Jace's gravelly voice in my ear. When did he sidle up next to me?

"I'd say." I shrug, trying to ignore the energy fizzing beneath my skin at his nearness. I take a deep breath, and my back grazes his chest. I bite my tongue to stop myself from groaning.

Heat fills the space between us.

Jace places a warm hand on my arm, and I'm hit with that same electrical shock I felt the first time he touched me all those years ago. He turns me to face him, and my heart leaps inside my chest at his handsome face.

I avert my gaze, but he places a finger under my chin and tilts my head up, forcing me to look him in the eyes. He's dropped the smile, his eyes displaying some of that same vulnerability he gave me all those years ago. The chains I've kept around my heart start to unfurl as we stand in the doorway, staring at each other. A million different memories assault me.

There is so much I want to say to him. To tell him. I don't know where to start. My brain and my body are at war. I want to push him away and hold him close at the same time. I need my brain to win. I can't let what happened last time happen again. I need to be smart. I can't just fall into him again. I'm a mom now. My son is my priority. I cannot afford to be reckless with my heart.

While Jace still owns a piece of me—a piece I've been missing for a long time—I'm also incapable of forgetting the unbearable grief I felt when I lost him. I don't want to feel like that again. I've lost so much already. My heart couldn't bear it.

Sam would disagree.

The ball of dread that's taken up residence in my stomach swells, trumping all the other feelings I have.

"Jace ..." I whisper, stepping back.

His hand drops to his side, but the heat of his touch lingers on my skin. "It's really good to see you. I've missed you, Sunshine," he says, with a soft smile.

The force of his words hits me like bullets to the heart.

I nod. I missed him too.

"I look forward to getting to know you and your son. Although, I can positively say, he's a pretty cool kid. Definitely funny. I love that he looks just like you."

The lump in my throat grows. "Thanks. It's good to see you too."

With a final wave, I close the door, leaving him firmly on the other side, where he belongs.

Now, I just need to keep him there.

CHAPTER TWENTY-NINE

Jace

Rylann shuts the door to her room, and I stand there, smiling at the door like an idiot.

This trip was the best idea Levi ever had. I owe him, big time. And not just for the room.

I step to my room next door and unlock it. Walking in, I close the door behind me and place my suitcase by the bed. I look around the small room before heading straight for the bathroom.

I need to cool off.

My body hums with anticipation, and my adrenaline has spiked since standing behind her in the hall. I couldn't *not* be near her. It was instinct to brush my chest to her back, as was the deep inhalation of her sweet coconut scent. I felt the air shift as the link between us awakened and came crackling to life. Her breath hitched—a tell-tale sign that she felt it too. She leaned back for a fraction of a second before putting space between us.

Ripping off my shirt, I let it drop onto the floor, along with my jeans, shoes, and socks, before hopping into the shower. The warm water runs down my body as I stand under the spray, letting it relax my tense muscles.

I can still hear the way she uttered *Hello, Ace* for the first time in years. Every hair on my arm stood up on end, and my dick twitched in my jeans. My first instinct was to pull her into my arms and kiss her like the last seven years hadn't passed us by. But I pushed it down. I don't need her slapping me in the face on the first day.

Problem is, I don't know how I'll be able to hold back.

When her eyes latched onto mine, I felt it. The earth shifted, and everything fell back into place. That same electric current I'd felt before zapped me back to life.

She zapped me back to life.

I picture her and smile. She's as beautiful as ever. It looks like she hasn't aged a day. Her big brown doe eyes still have the ability to take my breath away. As does her body with her bombshell hourglass figure. Just thinking about her full breasts and rounded hips has my dick perking up. Motherhood looks good on her.

I chuckle, thinking about the pun written across her shirt—*Just Plane Cute.* She's definitely cute alright.

Ignoring my growing hard-on, I finish washing up and turn off the water. Grabbing a towel off the rack, I dry myself off before wrapping it around my hips.

I knew I was going to feel some kind of way when I saw her, but I wasn't expecting it to feel like this. Like I still love her and can't live without her. I know it's fucking crazy. She's a widow. She has a son. I can't go in all half-cocked—I have to be sure that chasing her is the right move.

The racing heart in my chest leaps as my rational brain tries to slow me down. I'm done listening to my brain. It's what got me here in the first place. Divorced, lonely, and pining for a woman I let walk away.

Not again.

I don't think I have it in me to stay away and let her leave me behind again. Not without taking a chance. She's still the same gorgeous woman that takes my breath away, and after all these years, the spark between us is still there. The feelings I've kept under key came bursting out of the locked box inside me.

Over the years, I wondered if I'd imagined us, but it's like Rylann said on the dark path—it was all real. Our time together might have been brief, but the love between us was as real as the earth moving around the sun. Every. Single. Minute.

She looked beautiful leaning against the wall, a look of surprise on her face. I doubt she was prepared to see me as soon as she arrived, but I'm glad I caught her in the elevator. There was nowhere for her to hide. It was just us.

And her son.

That's still a tough pill to swallow. Rylann is a mom. She had a child with someone else. She had a whole life without me.

Taking a deep, cleansing breath, I push the negative thoughts away. None of that matters, only here and now.

And Rhys? Well ... He's all the best parts of her. He's adorable and the spitting image of Rylann. From his brown hair to his cute-as-fuck dimples and freckles. Except for his eyes. His chocolate orbs fade to caramel around the pupils, with flecks of gold mixed in.

My fist circles my chest as pressure presses against my ribs. Less than five minutes with him, and I can't wait to hang out with the little guy. He's funny and polite. I have to remember to tell my brothers about his fart joke. They'd get a kick out of that.

I can't thank Levi enough for arranging this. Before that call, sorrow, regret, and longing were my constant companions when my mind would drift to her. I had been living half a life without her.

Now that I've seen her, I know she's the part of my world that's been missing. I can't go back to existing without her.

At least, not without shooting my shot at a second chance.

CHAPTER THIRTY

Jace

Levi: Late lunch, then pool. You in?

Jace: Nah, I'm alright for now. I got to check in at work. But a swim sounds good. Meet you there.

Levi: See you later. I'm glad you're here.

Jace: Me too.

I lied. There's no work for me to do.

I skipped lunch to give Rylann a minute to acclimate to my presence. Seeing me again has to be a lot for her to take in. I know it is for me too. Just not in the same way.

I can't wait to see and talk to her. To find out how she's been. I wasn't lying when I told her I missed her.

But she needs time. So I'm giving her an hour to prepare herself because I am going to make my presence known. And soon enough, my intentions.

I know she's not going to immediately welcome me back into her arms. Hell, I broke her heart. I deserve a kick in the balls.

My balls shrivel at the thought. Okay, I hope she doesn't kick me. I hope she gives me a chance to make things right. It won't be easy, but I'm going to die on that hill, trying to make it up to her. To prove that I won't make the same mistake twice.

I get dressed in a pair of board shorts and a t-shirt before grabbing a towel and my key card to head to the pool.

One look at the ocean, and I head towards the beach instead.

As soon as the water hits my hips, I dive into the waves, letting them push and pull me under. I swim out to the buoy and back, riding the current back to shore. I do that a couple more times before heading back to shore.

The gang wasn't at the pool when I arrived, so I snagged a couple of extra towels from the attendant and laid out some sun chairs under the umbrella for everyone.

My ass barely hits the seat when I hear Levi calling out to me. "Yo, Jace!"

I look up to see Levi and the rest of the clan behind him. My eyes immediately find Rylann. They don't get a chance to linger when Levi grabs my hand and pulls me up from the chair into a bear hug.

"It's so good to see you."

"You too, man." I mean that.

Scarlett leans in and gives me a kiss on the cheek. "Long time, no see. Thanks for coming, Jace."

"Wouldn't miss it."

She hums as my eyes search for Rylann again. She's behind Scarlett and the girls, holding Rhys's hand while she bites her lip nervously. The old urge to bite that lip myself comes roaring back.

Before I can stand, Sadie and Lily attack my legs like the double trouble they are. "Uncle Jace!"

Prying their little hands off my legs, I squat down to their eye level. "How are my sweet tart twins?" I ask. They giggle when I tap their sweet little noses. "Are you ready to go swimming?"

They nod their little blonde heads in unison, making me laugh. I'm surprised they remembered me since I haven't seen them in at least a year. I used to put more effort into visiting them when Levi brought them to visit his family. But it's been a while.

Levi's invited me up to visit them over the years, but I never accepted the offer. It didn't feel right. The thought of seeing Rylann with another man made me physically ill. A piece of me hated him. He had everything I wanted. Everything I could never have. Not only did he get the girl, but he got my friend too.

I ignore that negative inner voice.

My eyes follow Rylann as she takes a seat and starts rubbing sunblock on Rhys's face. I want to laugh at his funny little scowl. The skin between his brows is pinched, and his bottom lip is popped out in a pout.

Damn, he's adorable. Just like her.

Still, on my knee, I watch as she firmly rubs the lotion in and explains to the crabby little guy the importance of taking care of his body. She's so patient with him when I'm sure she must be exasperated by his refusal to cooperate. Yet, she never lets it show. The small smile that graces her lips as she tries not to laugh at his stubbornness proves it even more.

She's the amazing mother I always envisioned her to be. Rylann is a nurturer by nature. She's the embodiment of the sun. Her love is warm. Her passion and fire too.

Breaking the spell, I avert my eyes to find Scarlett watching me watch Rylann. I give her a weak smile and turn my attention to Levi and the girls, who've already gone swimming and splashing around in the pool while I was gawking.

"Cannonball!" I yell, jumping in and landing next to Levi, soaking his face.

I'm not stupid enough to stick around for my buddy's revenge. I swim away from the scene of the crime, but I'm too slow. Four small hands grab my legs, preventing me from kicking. I pause and hold my breath while Levi dives on top of me and holds me down. The hands on my legs release, and I kick myself away. I come up sputtering to the sound of laughter.

"You play dirty, Lee," I pant. Even though I'm in good shape and swim constantly, it didn't prepare me for the adrenaline rush of being held underwater. "Double Trouble, I thought you were on my side?"

"Sorry, Uncle Jace!" they yell in unison, swimming off to play with their friend.

"You alright, man?" Levi smacks my shoulder a little harder than necessary—payback for the tidal wave.

"Yup, all good. Just glad I'm a swimmer. Otherwise, I might've ended up like Doodie, floating in the pool. No one likes a ruined pool," I joke, referencing Caddyshack, which we must have watched a million times.

We laugh and hang back while we watch Scarlett and Rylann swim races across the pool with the kids. I'm a little disappointed I missed seeing her get into the pool. I was hoping to watch her peel the sundress she was wearing off.

I shake my head. It's only been a couple of hours, and I'm already perving over her. Picturing her perfect body, her soft curves.

I reach over the edge for my shades and slide them on. You know, to block out the sun, not casually check out a wet Rylann.

Levi and I continue catching up on work and other things. My eyes never leave Rylann as she plays with Rhys. I track her every move. She swims over the ladder and pulls herself out of the water.

Holy shit!

I think I died and went to heaven.

Water drips down her body as the sun's rays bounce off her skin, making her glisten. My eyes take her in from head to toe and all but stay glued to her round ass as she bends over and grabs a towel. She dries her legs, then stands and turns around, giving me a view of her front. My mouth waters, watching her large, round breasts jiggle and overflow from the top of her bathing suit. That piece of material might have been chosen with support in mind, but it's barely doing the job. I couldn't be more grateful.

She looks like a goddamn walking wet dream in that yellow bikini.

A wave of water hits me in the face, and I choke. I wipe my face, sputtering at the taste of chlorine on my tongue.

"You alright there, bud?" Levi asks, snickering at my blatant ogling.

"Yup." I clear my throat. "Great." I cough. " Thanks for that," I say, grateful for the reality check.

The last thing I want is for her to catch me gawking at her like a fool.

"I got your back, dude. Gotta keep it PG in front of the kids. You can perv on her later in private."

My head jerks in his direction, and he laughs.

The fuck?

He's not mad at me for gawking at his friend. I thought he'd for sure be more protective. Warn me off or something.

Instead, he's smirking at me and winks, like he knows the way my head and my heart have been going since I saw her again.

CHAPTER THIRTY-ONE

Rylann

The hot sun feels amazing on my skin, despite the cold unease unfurling inside me.

Jace's presence brings back so many memories, most of them wonderful. We had such an amazing time here together. Every day was the best day of my life—until that final day, when everything came crashing down and our romantic bubble epically popped.

Seeing him in that elevator shouldn't have been so surprising, but it was. I thought I had more time before I had to see him.

I tried to swim and play with Rhys but gave up. He and the girls are too much sometimes. With everything going on in my head, I decided to sit down for a while. I couldn't stop glancing at Jace every damn second to concentrate on my own kid.

I was relieved when he didn't join us for lunch, but I knew better than to get used to his absence.

Sure enough, he's at the pool with towels and lounge chairs reserved for all of us.

Why does he have to be so damn sweet? And sexy? Why couldn't he have a belly or something to keep me from staring at him? The bastard still resembles a GQ cover model, with his gloriously hot body and panty-melting smile. That damn smile had my thighs clenching in the elevator.

Scarlett plops down on the lounge chair next to me, pulling me from my thoughts. I don't know how long I've been laying here, lost in my head.

"You want to talk about it?" Scarlett asks.

I turn my head, sunglasses firmly in place, hiding my eyes. Hiding the anxiety that lurks inside. I can already sense the freaking dumpster fire that is going to be my life on the horizon.

"I'm good."

"Liar."

"What do you want me to say, Scar?"

"I don't know, something. You've been quiet. You haven't been yourself for a while. And I'm talking more distant and tense than usual this past month. Talk to me."

I want to talk to her so badly. But I can't. At least, not yet.

I pinch my lips together and shake my head.

"It's him, isn't it?"

She nods towards the pool, where Jace is standing in the middle with Sadie in his arms. He throws her up in the air, and she lands with a splash. I take in his worried face as he wonders if he threw her too hard. But when Sadie pops up out of the water with a huge smile on her face, he visibly relaxes. He's still the same man, worried about the people in his life. A true caretaker.

The smile on his handsome face grows larger when Rhys and Lily cling to his arms, begging for him to throw them too. My stomach fizzles with anxiety. I wish it was only about Jace and the way his smile makes me melt.

Sam's final words flash in my head, and I stare at Rhys. He looks so happy, swimming and playing. He has been since Scarlett and Levi forced this vacation on me. I've missed seeing him look so carefree, like a six-year-old should. He's been through so much this past year, and he deserves to keep living like this.

Sam was right—I see that now.

I haven't been living. I need to. For me. For Rhys. He needs me to be stronger and make more of an effort at being happy. No more going through the motions or trying to do everything on my own to prove I'm fine. 'Cause I'm not.

"Honestly? Yes." I confess. Well, as much as I can, anyway. The emotions I've kept buried have been digging themselves free since I saw Jace this afternoon.

"I get that, babes. It must be hard seeing him after all these years. I know it was a little mean of us to force this on you. But Levi convinced me it would be good for all of us. It will be less intimidating when Bob and Julie get here. They can help be a buffer."

Buffer, my ass. Rhys is already obsessed with Jace. How can I buffer that?

"Doubtful. Look at my son."

Returning our attention to the pool, the scene before us makes my insides melt and wilt a little at the same time. I watch Rhys laughing and hanging onto the back of the man that still sends my heart racing. Rhys looks so damn happy.

"Like mother, like son. Defenseless against Jace's irresistible charm," she teases, slapping my thigh.

"I hate you sometimes," I mutter under my breath.

She hears me, though, and grins with satisfaction. "If by hate you mean love more than life itself? Yup."

I roll my eyes at her behind my glasses. She's ridiculous. Even if she is right. I'm still annoyed with her for making this happen.

"It's going to be okay, Ry."

"Scarlett ..."

I want to admit why I have reservations. Why I've been so off, but she cuts me off.

"No, listen to me for a minute, will you? I know things didn't work out with Jace last time."

Understatement of the fucking century.

Pulling my shades down, I stare at her. If looks could kill, she would be dead.

Scarlett holds up her hands in surrender. "I'm not telling you to go down that road, but please keep your heart open. Or at the very least, an open mind. You both have been through a lot. This trip is supposed to be healing. Please, just let yourself be happy. Let go of everything that's happened and live in the moment. For Rhys's sake. He needs this."

"When did you become so wise?" My voice cracks. She knows exactly how to get through to me. Damn besties for knowing your weaknesses.

"Not gonna lie. I totally stole that from Levi, and he's right. If you tell him, you're dead to me." She holds her pinky out to me and I take it, sealing the promise. "I want you to know that I *really* wasn't sold on this whole idea at first. Levi had to talk me into it. I knew how hard seeing Jace would be for you. I wanted to protect you and Rhys. However, the more I thought it over, the more I thought this could be exactly what you need. Please don't be mad, but ... babes, I don't think even Sam made you as happy as Jace did for those few days you shared together."

Tears well in my eyes. As I sniff them back, she grabs ahold of my hand and squeezes.

Jace did make me the happiest I'd ever been. What we shared was so intense and passionate. I felt alive with him by my side.

"That was a long time ago."

"It was. Will you look at this for me?" She takes out her cell and pulls something up on the screen before handing it to me.

"How?" I gasp, cupping my hand over my mouth.

"I saved them. Something always held me back from deleting them. Please, tell me you see it too," she says.

There are no words. All I can do is nod.

There we are, frozen in time. Jace and I.

I remember when she took these pictures. We were at the top of the summit at Diamond Head National Park. He just finished telling me that he refused to hold back. If he wanted to kiss me or hold me, he was going to. No matter who was around to see it. Nothing would stop him because we were so much more. He made me feel desired and treasured at the same time. Knowing that he wanted me that badly had both my heart and my panties melting.

Somehow, Scarlett captured all those sentiments in one picture. With the ocean behind us, Jace and I are staring at each other with wide beaming smiles. Jace is tucking a strand of my hair behind my ear, my cheeks are flushed, and I swear it looks like we have hearts in our eyes. *We look so ... in love.*

My stomach lurches, and I sit up. A surge of guilt floods my chest, and I hand her the phone. "I need to—"

"Mommy, look at me!" Lily yells.

We watch as Levi throws her in the air, and she lands with a splash, the water sucking her under, along with my need to confess.

Rhys and Jace seem to be having some sort of conversation. The smile on my baby's face soothes some of the aches I feel in my stomach.

"Let's pick this up later. Looks like the kids are ready for some mom love now." I push the photo and all the feelings it brought up to the back of my mind.

I need to focus all my attention on Rhys. It's the only way I might be able to make it out of this trip with my sanity—and maybe even my heart—intact.

CHAPTER THIRTY-TWO

Jace

Levi and I have been throwing the kids across the pool for the last hour, and they don't seem to be letting up anytime soon. I knew kids had a lot of energy, but I never realized exactly how much. No wonder Levi is exhausted all the time—raising twins can't be easy, but he has Scarlett by his side.

I wonder how Rylann is doing, taking on the responsibility of two parents—being not only Rhys's mother but in many ways his father too. Being a single parent and grieving can't be easy for her. Her parents, as well as Levi and Scarlett, probably lend a helping hand with Rhys when they can, but who takes care of her?

If I know Rylann, she's bearing all the weight on her own shoulders. She won't let herself be a burden to anyone. She takes care of everyone she loves before she takes care of herself.

As if by magic, my eyes find her.

She hasn't moved since she got out of the pool, sunning in one of the chairs. Scarlett has joined her, and the two are talking. Rylann looks a little sad and worried. I would think it's because of me that she's feeling like that, but when I saw her earlier, I noticed her brightness has dimmed. She's still gorgeous, but something tells me she's lost some of her luster.

"You're definitely a better thrower than Uncle Lee." Rhys swims up to me.

Levi and I have been competing for the title of Strongest Man—their words not ours—as we took turns throwing the kids in the pool.

Surprisingly, I've thrown Rhys too. He seems completely un-phased by the fact that I'm a virtual stranger. In fact, I think he likes me.

The feeling is mutual. I could hang with him all day.

"I heard that, kid." Levi points at Rhys.

"You were supposed to!" Rhys sticks his tongue out at Levi, making me laugh.

This kid. He's a funny little dude. He reminds me so much of Rylann and her teasing. Their mannerisms are so similar. It's a trip to watch.

"I'll remember that next time you want something from me."

"Don't be like that, Uncle Lee. You know you're my favorite uncle."

"I'm your only uncle," Levi grumbles, making me chuckle. He's fighting with a kid.

"True. You could be a sucky uncle. But you're cool. So, you're my favorite." The little stinker smirks.

Rhys 1: Levi 1.

"Little shiii ..."

"Oooooo, Daddy said a bad word," Lilly and Sadie sing-song, and Rhys laughs.

Levi picks him up and throws him across the pool, Rhys's laughter dies as he hits the water.

"Who's next?" Levi asks the girls, who eagerly fight for his attention.

Rhys swims back over to us and sits next to me on the bench. He's a damn good swimmer for a six-year-old. He quietly watches

Levi and the girls this time around, and the look on his face pulls at my heart as I watch the light dim from his eyes. And if that didn't kill me inside, the way his bow-shaped lips turn down into a frown surely does.

Oh, fuck.

He's probably thinking about his dad right now.

"Hey, bud. You're a pretty good swimmer. You take swimming lessons or something?" I hope to distract him from whatever sadness is creeping in.

He nods his little head, sending water dribbling down his face. His shoulders deflate as Levi kisses Sadie on the cheek and blows a raspberry on it.

"Hey, Rhys. Look at me." I put my forefinger under his chin and tilt his face up so our eyes meet. "I know you miss your dad. It's okay to be sad. I'd bet anything that your dad misses you too."

His little eyes fill up with tears, but he sniffles and forces them back. Strong little guy. I hate seeing him hold back his feelings.

"Did your dad bring you here before?" *Please say no.*

I know it's completely fucked up for me to hope that this place belongs only to me and Rylann, especially when this sweet little kid is hurting.

"Nuh uh." The tension in my gut releases at his answer. "He said Hawaii was a magical place for adventures. He was too sick to bring me and Mommy."

"I heard. I'm sorry he's not here."

"S'okay." He shrugs.

I can't imagine how this poor kid must feel losing his dad at such a young age. I'm in my thirties, and I don't think I'd be half as brave as him if I lost my dad.

"He's right. This place is magical."

"Really?" he asks, eyes wide with wonder.

The way he's looking at me makes me feel like I have the key to unlocking the magic here on the island for him.

"Really. It's been a long time, but the last time I was here, I had so much fun. And I fell in love with the most beautiful woman in the world."

Why the hell did I say that?

"Gross. Did you go on adventures?"

I laugh at his response. Leave it to a little boy to think loving girls is gross. He'd probably hate me if he knew I was referring to his mom.

Rylann is definitely not gross. She is the epitome of every-thing that's beautiful in this world.

"I did. I went snorkeling with the fish. I rode a jet ski. I climbed that summit over there." I turn and point out over the beach to the top of Diamond Head sitting in the background. The lush hillside towers over the island, reminding me of how I kissed his mother at the top, overlooking the cerulean blue sea.

"Cool! I made a list of things I want to do here."

"Awesome. Did your mom help you with that?"

"No. Google did," he says. Like, *duh,* I should know this stuff.

"Oh, right. Google. Good call. It has all the answers," I agree, tapping my temple.

"Yeah. I got in trouble for using the iPad without asking first. But my mom forgave me."

"Well, that was nice of her."

"She promised to take me to do all the things on my list. She's the best."

That she is, kid.

"Is that right?"

"Yup. We're gonna eat shaved ice, pick a pineapple, swim with sea turtles, see the biggest waves, watch surfers, find a waterfall, climb a volcano, watch a sunset, and drink from a coconut. Did you know they use a big knife called a machete to cut the top off so you can drink it? I saw it on YouTube. I want to chop a coconut." He slices the air like he's chopping a coconut in half, making me chuckle.

Rhys's enthusiasm is infectious. I find myself wanting to do all these things with him. Watch his eyes light up with every new experience.

"I don't think it's safe for you to chop a coconut, but we can definitely watch a guy at the Aloha Flea Market do it. We have to make sure you keep all these fingers." I grab his middle and give his stomach a tickle.

He throws his head back with a laugh, and the same dimples that adorn his mom's cheeks pop on his too.

I imagine this smile on Rylann's face. I have a feeling it's been a while since she's smiled like this. It's a shame because I haven't felt the warmth of her smile in far too long.

That pull I felt in my chest when I met this little guy in the elevator tightens around my heart. Making his vacation dreams come true has become my number one priority, only second to winning back Rylann's heart. If I play my cards right, giving Rhys what he wants might give me what I want. I have a feeling the only way I'll be able to get through to her will be to forcibly insert myself into her vacation.

"You know what, kiddo?"

"What?"

"I'm gonna help you check off that list of yours. Only, we're gonna make it even better. What do you think?"

"Really? How?"

I tap the side of my head again. "I'm making a plan already. But ... I'm gonna need help convincing your mom. You think you can have my back on this?"

"Totally!" he exclaims, his face beaming with excitement.

There is no way I'm gonna let this kid down. He deserves to have the best time ever. So does Rylann.

Based on our little run-in, I can tell that she's tired. She's lost her light and likely needs more help than she lets on. More support. I want to *be* that support.

I plan on breaking down every stone she's built around herself. If using Rhys to bulldoze my way into her life is the only option, then that's what I'll do. I'll do anything to spend more time with her. With them.

There is just something about him. I feel like we already have a connection. There's this voice inside me, telling me to protect him, make him happy, give him everything and more.

The simple act of making him smile today, when he looked down, was rewarding enough.

"First up. You gotta tell your mom I'm coming with you on all your adventures. Then, I'll take care of the rest." I hold out my fist for him to bump.

He does, sealing our deal. "Do you think my mom will let you come with us?"

"Yes. Your uncle Levi and aunt Scarlett will be with us too."

"Will you teach me to surf?" He tilts his head to the side.

"Of course, I will. I'd like that very much."

"Awesome," he says, face lighting up. There goes that twinge. *Fuck, this kid.*

"What are you two over here chatting about?" Rylann's sultry voice interrupts, sounding like the sweetest music to my ears. She takes a seat on the edge of the pool, legs dangling in the water.

"Mom, Jace is going to come on our adventures," Rhys boasts. She shoots me a look, brow arched.

Did she really think we wouldn't spend any time together? *Better get used to it, Sunshine. 'Cause I'm here to stay.*

I return her unsaid question with a smug smile while Rhys continues, "He said we can find a coconut cutter at the Aloha flea bag market. Do you think there are real fleas there? I don't like getting bit. Being itchy is the worst."

Her concern falls away as she throws her head back and laughs. Rhys's cute misunderstanding has me barking out a laugh too.

"You mean the Aloha Flea Market, silly boy. A flea market is like a big garage sale. Lots of people have tables where they sell food and other stuff. Not fleas. I promise."

The worry in his eyes disappears at her reassurance of a parasite-free shopping experience. "Cool. We should go. You like shopping, and I want to see a man chop coconuts."

"We'll see, baby boy."

"Mom!" he whines. "I'm not a baby."

"You'll always be my baby," Rylann croons, pushing his hair off his forehead.

He groans at the gesture.

Watching them together does something to me. It's like peering into the past and watching my mom with me and my brothers as kids.

Rylann and I turn to face each other. Even wearing sunglasses, the electricity swirls around as we engage in a silent stare-off. I can't bring myself to look away. There is so much I want to say. The magnetic force pulling me towards her is so strong. I have to fight hard against the need to touch her. To press my lips to her soft pink ones.

I flash her a smile. The one that used to make her weak in the knees. Her breath hitches, and I wish I could see her eyes. I know she feels the spark between us.

I'm right here with you.

She looks away first, breaking our connection, focusing back on Rhys and ignoring my presence. Like that will make everything disappear. It won't. I know it, and she knows it.

Even if she won't admit it. Yet ...

Better hold tight, 'cause I'm coming for you, Sunny.

"Mom, can Jace come with us? He's my friend. I would like to have a friend that's not a girl."

"Hey! What am I, chopped liver?" Levi splashes Rhys with water.

He and Scarlett have quietly made their way over to join in on our exchange. Not surprising. Scarlett never left Rylann's side before, so it's no different now. It's good to see some things don't change.

"What's chopped liver?" Rhys's face twists in confusion.

"It's an old expression that means you're being ignored," Rylann explains.

"You people are old." Rhys shakes his head.

The adults, on the other hand, crack up.

"Back to your question," Rylann says, her eyes briefly finding mine before returning to Rhys. "Jace is welcome to join us for the group outings. Tomorrow, we are going to the pineapple plantation. Remember?"

I don't miss the way she emphasizes the word "group", and I smirk at her. She can think that for now.

"Yes! Pineapple ice cream. My favorite!" Rhys pumps his little arms in victory. "Sadie! Did you hear? We're getting pineapple ice cream tomorrow."

He swims off in search of his friend, and I vaguely remember Levi telling me they were going to take the kids on a few outings. All these little excursions have been planned by the little guy that just swam away.

I glance over at Levi, who's watching me put the pieces together. He nods his head in confirmation.

This really might work in my favor and make it easier for me to worm my way into her heart. I'll start with group outings and work my way to some one-on-one time. Maybe even plan something extra special for just her and Rhys.

She can try keeping me at arm's length. She can try keeping her walls up and her feelings locked up tight, but I'm out to bring them down or, at the very least, die trying.

I'm determined to show her that I can be there for her. I won't let her down this time. I'll be there every step of the way.

And in the process, bring back her light.

CHAPTER THIRTY-THREE

Rylann

Standing at the valet stand waiting for the guys to return with rental cars has me on edge.

Today is the first group outing, and while I knew I was going to be spending time with Jace, thinking about it and living it are two completely different things.

It was naïve of me to think I could keep my distance from him physically.

First, I have Rhys, who cannot stop talking about Jace and how cool he is. He even personally invited Jace to join us on every adventure we have planned.

What did you expect? For him to stay in his hotel room doing nothing all day?

I growl at my inner voice.

Then, there's me. From the moment I ran into him in the elevator, he's consumed my every thought. *Déjà*-freaking-*vu*.

I wasn't able to ignore the pull he had on me then, and I doubt I can do it now.

I spent the night tossing and turning, thinking about the past, the present, the future.

Jace.

Did I think about Jace? Yes. All. Night. Long.

How could I not?

I had to witness him playing with the kids in the pool, looking all sexy. Like, Greek-god-carved-out-of-marble sexy. He has aged to perfection and looks even better than I remember. All corded muscle and abs for days that are downright frickin' lickable. His wicked smile still gives me butterflies in my stomach and incinerates my panties.

I wasn't the only one staring either. His piercing hazel eyes followed me the entire time. I could feel his gaze raking over every inch of my body.

I know I shouldn't like it, but I do.

His attention makes the hairs on the back of my neck stand up, my skin prickle, my blood boil, and my clit tingle. His current presence in my life is like a light switch to my libido.

And then there's Scarlett, who is of no help whatsoever. Her showing me that picture messed with my head. I'm glad she kept them from me, but the other, bigger part of me hates it. If I had seen it all those years ago, I might not have been strong enough to stay away from him like I did. I would have broken all my promises to get to him.

It would have changed everything.

Guilt settles heavily in my heart.

If I had done that, then Sam wouldn't have had the life he did. He would have been alone during all of the pain he endured. He needed my support. He was there for me when I was at my lowest, and I will not regret returning the favor.

The years Sam and I shared together were wonderful. He wasn't perfect by any stretch of the word, but he treated me and Rhys like precious treasure. We were his greatest joy, and he showed us that every day.

"Daddy!" Lily screams, jumping up and down.

I look up to see Levi stepping out of a minivan, followed by Jace.

Looking over at Rhys and Sadie, I see them still playing rock-paper-scissors. Scarlett and I joke that those two will get married someday. Levi does not like it one bit. Any mention of the words "daughter" and "dating" in the same sentence, and he becomes an overprotective papa bear. He's gonna be in for a real treat. Call it mother's intuition, but Rhys and Sadie are going to cause us a lot of trouble when they hit puberty. I can't help smiling to myself at that thought.

"Hey there, Sunny. What's got you smiling this morning?" Jace's question interrupts my daydream.

My smile slips at his surprise appearance at my side.

A dejected look flashes across his face. I'm a horrible person. I don't want to hurt him, but I also don't know what else to do to protect myself.

"Jace!" Rhys hollers.

He recovers quickly, turning his attention and smiles on Rhys.

"Hey, bud! Wanna ride with me today?" He picks Rhys up and throws him in the air.

Rhys giggles and shouts, "Heck yes!"

Wait? Ride with Jace. What the—

Realization dawns on me. Levi's parents, Bob and Julie, arrived last night, which means there is no room for me and Rhys to ride in the van. That explains the minivan and sedan the guys just pulled up in.

I swallow a groan. I could kick myself for not putting two and two together sooner. I had breakfast with them. I know I've been lost in my head all morning, but dang. This is a lot to process.

I leave Rhys talking to Jace and walk over to my bestie. "You are on my list, woman."

"What did I do?"

"How about not preparing me for today's driving arrangements?"

"Are you sure about that?" She looks at me in question.

"S'cuse me?" She searches my face with a sad smile, and it clicks. "You told me at breakfast didn't you?"

She nods. "Are you going to be okay?"

"I have to be, don't I?" I pout.

"Sorry, babes." She bites her lip, hiding a smile, and nods.

I have the sudden urge to punch her and run away. Then hide in my room all day. I wonder if I can still make a run for it.

"Don't even think about it. I'll take you down right here," she warns, pointing at the ground.

"You don't know what I'm thinking," I grumble. Even I can hear how petulant I sound.

"Wrong. You want to punch me or run. Am I right?"

Sometimes, it sucks having a friend that knows you so well.

"No one likes a smartass." I stick my tongue out at her.

"Wrong again. You love my smart ass," she sings.

"I really hate you." I cross my arms and give her my best *I hate you* sneer.

"And I really, really, love you." She puckers her lips and air-kisses me.

"Now, I hate *myself* for loving you."

Scarlett laughs at me and my sourpuss attitude.

This is going to be the longest day. I need to keep my head out of the clouds and concentrate on what's going on around me.

Over my shoulder, I watch Rhys hang onto Jace's every word. My son is already infatuated with him.

I feel you, baby. He's a hard one not to fall for.

Unfortunately, falling for him also means hitting the ground without a parachute. I'd hate for my son to feel the pain of losing someone again. He doesn't need that kind of heartbreak.

"You got this. Just put on some jams, and let Rhys steal the show."

I give her a curt nod.

She's right. Rhys will steal the show, and I can continue to ignore Jace and the way my body reacts to him.

I make my way back over to my guys.

Guy! Singular. Just one—Rhys.

Mm hmm. Keep telling yourself that, lady.

This is exactly what I'm worried about.

Cruising down the highway towards the pineapple plantation has been a real treat. I stare out the window while Jace gives Rhys his undivided attention, leaving me to myself just like I wanted.

If it's what you wanted, then why is it bugging you so much?

I can't explain it, but his lack of attention is annoying me. I know that makes me a hypocrite, but why does he have to be so damn perfect and respectful, giving me the silence and space I want?

I shake my head and concentrate on Rhys talking about his vacation to-do list. Jace responds with his opinion on all the best things to see on the island.

At my limit with the silent treatment, I reach into my purse and pull out my phone cord. Without a word, Jace watches me plug it into the car's stereo system and hit play on Rhys's favorite songs playlist. The two chatterboxes quiet down as the bass notes to my kiddo's favorite song fill the car. When the drums come in a few counts later, Rhys is ready to play them in the air.

Twisting my body around, I watch him turn into a rockstar in the backseat.

Jace watches Rhys in the rearview mirror as he sings along and plays the drums with the Red Hot Chili Peppers like he's an unofficial member of the band. When he looks at me, he has the hugest grin on his face, clearly enjoying Rhys's show.

"It looks like he got your love of music," he finally says to me.

And dammit if his acknowledgment isn't like a balm to my earlier irritation. I hate that.

Liar.

"He did."

Jace smiles and turns his eyes back to the road.

I take a minute to check him out. His sunglasses are hooked on the collar of his sage green t-shirt that makes the gold in his hazel eyes pop, and he's wearing gray shorts. His jaw is covered in a day's worth of scruff, and it looks sexy as fuck. I bet it would feel good scraping the tender flesh of my inner thighs as he buried his face between my legs while his tongue lashed at my needy bundle of nerves until I screamed his name.

Crossing my legs, I look away, embarrassed and turned on by my thoughts. The temperature in the car goes up ten degrees, and I adjust the air vent and turn up the AC.

"He also inherited horrible taste in music." I say the last part a little louder for Rhys to hear me.

I love teasing my kid. He has great taste in music, very eclectic. He appreciates all different genres without bias.

Except for my 90's playlist. For some reason, he really hates it. In his defense, I might play it more often than should be allowed.

"I heard that!" he yells during his drum solo, making me laugh.

"Why does your mom think you have bad taste in music?"

"Because I told her music from the '90s is for old people."

Jace barks out a laugh. The rich vibrations brush over my skin, making me shiver and my stomach flip.

"I don't know why you're laughing. You like 90's music as much as I do. And you've got years on me, old man," I tease, ignoring how normal it feels to banter with him.

"Hey, now. Them be fightin' words, Sunshine. Sounds like you're begging for a rematch. This time, I won't be a gentleman and let you win," he says, making me scoff.

"Please, I wiped the floor with you last time. I'd do it again in a heartbeat. No contest, Miller."

Jace glances over at me, and we both burst out laughing thinking about our karaoke rap battle. I won fair and square, and he knows it. He's jealous I can shake my ass better than him.

"Jace, why do you call mommy Sunshine?" Rhys asks, his innocent and yet deeply personal question sobering me right up.

I don't know why Jace calls me that either.

"Well," Jace starts, looking over at me adoringly, and I swear my heart is beating so fast it might jump out of my rib cage. "The first time I met your mom, she gave me the biggest, prettiest smile I'd ever seen. She had these cute dimples on her cheek, just like you do, and well, her smile made me feel all warm inside. It reminded me of warm sunny days."

I'm a puddle of ice cream on the sidewalk. Melted. That has got to be the swooniest thing I have ever heard.

"Plus, she was wearing the brightest yellow pants I had ever seen. I was blinded. It was like staring at the sun," he says, winking at me before looking back at the road.

Brushing off the effect his wink has on my lady bits, I roll my eyes at his ribbing. He's right, though—I was wearing my neon yellow leggings because they made my ass look good and were comfy as hell. I can't believe he remembers that.

"She always wears yellow. It's weird," Rhys says, and I mock-gasp at the criticism.

"So I've noticed," Jace agrees, his eyes roaming over my body. They inadvertently light my insides on fire.

Rhys starts laughing, and it's like a bucket of cold water.

I look down at my outfit. I'm wearing black and yellow sneakers, paired with some white shorts and a pale yellow halter top.

Touché, boys.

Fine. I do rock a lot of yellow.

"It's okay, Sunshine. Yellow looks good on you."

Jace reaches over and gives my thigh a tight squeeze. His warm hand sends an electric charge directly to my clit, making it pulse. I glance down at his hand, then back to him. He just smiles and slowly drags his fingertips over my heated skin before placing his hand back on the steering wheel.

The air in the car shifts, and the ever-present energy between us sparks to life. My skin pebbles and burns at the same time.

Trying to ignore how affected I am by his touch, I throw my walls up and act like nothing happened. I make idle chit-chat and sing along to the radio with Rhys for the rest of the drive.

When we arrive at our destination, I jump out of the car, leaving Jace to help Rhys get out of his booster seat.

I need air. I need space. I need ... Something.

My heart is pumping a hundred miles an hour. Between the sweet explanation of my nickname and that touch—as simple and as innocent as it was—I'm freaking out. A tsunami of emotions is storming inside me.

Attraction.

Loneliness. Guilt.

Longing.

Panic. Fear.

Love.

I rub at the ache in the center of my chest, where the panicky feeling is growing.

What I feel scares the absolute shit out of me. Without a doubt, a part of me still loves Jace and probably always will, but I'm not prepared for him now. I should be, but I'm not.

All those years ago, I knew he made his mark deep. The days we spent together were unbelievably special and will always be some of the best in my life. Jace made me feel loved and cherished. The passion between us was so raw and intense. He is ingrained into every fiber of my being.

But that was then.

Everything that happened after is why I find myself holding back. I wanted Jace to come for me then. To fight for me. But he didn't. He let me walk away.

You didn't fight for him either.

My stomach drops. It's true—I didn't fight for him. But the timing wasn't right for us. He had other obligations. I accepted that a long time ago and went on to build a wonderful life with someone else.

What about now?

I take in a deep breath and exhale, mulling that over.

I don't know. There's so much left to be said between us. I have Rhys. He is my life and my number one priority. I can't let myself get caught up in Jace again. I'm not young and carefree anymore. I'm a mom.

"Don't think too hard, Sunshine. You might hurt yourself," Jace drawls in my ear.

"Huh?" I look up to find him walking alongside me, his sunglasses on his head, his hazels more green than before.

"Nothing. I was just teasing you. You've gone quiet on me again." He blatantly checks out my legs and gives me a small smirk.

I fight the shiver.

"I did, didn't I? Just jet-lagged, I guess." The lie slips easily off my tongue, and I hate myself for it.

He runs a hand through his hair. "I'm sorry I upset you by talking to Rhys and for touching you in the car." He glances down at my thigh, and I swear I can still feel the warmth of his palm lingering. "I overstepped, and I hope you'll forgive me."

Why does he have to be so damn sweet? "It's fine."

His lips turn down, and I know I'm getting side-eye under those glasses. He knows I'm lying.

"Please, don't shut me out. I want this to be a fun vacation, and I would really like to get to know you again. Do you think we can do that?"

We've stopped walking, both of us staring at each other. He lifts his sunglasses off his head and swipes his tongue across his bottom lip. For a second, I wish it was my tongue instead.

Fuck, he's dangerous to my heart and my lady parts.

"Okay," I choke out. The happy smile that breaks across his face weakens my knees. Clearing my throat, I continue, "Thank you for indulging Rhys. And you didn't make me uncomfortable. You just caught me off guard, is all. It was nothing. Forget about it."

"Not gonna happen. Everything that happens between us means something. Always did. Always will.". His voice is steady as he not-so-subtly lays his cards on the table. He turns and starts walking backward. "Now, come on, slowpoke, we have some pineappling to do."

I move my mouth to say something—anything—but nothing comes out.

Before I can stop him, he puts his sunglasses on, spins around with a cocky grin and saunters down the path towards the rest of our group, taking his place next to Levi like he didn't just drop an emotional bomb on me.

Everything? What does that mean?

My mind plays with endless possibilities.

But I know Jace. He's a genuine "tell it like it is" kind of man. He doesn't play games. He says what he means and means what he says. Every word he speaks is done with purpose, and right now, it seems his purpose is to make me remember things that should stay buried.

And yet ...

My heart wants him to keep digging.

To fight.

CHAPTER THIRTY-FOUR

Jace

Walking away from Rylann is a hard feat when all I want to do is pull her close and kiss her.

Even though it's the right thing to do. She needs more time to process. I meant what I said. Everything that happened and will happen between us means something. What we share is too significant for it to be meaningless.

Squeezing her leg was only meant to be a playful gesture, but as soon as my hand made contact with her silky skin, I felt the electricity roar to life. She's kidding herself if she thinks there was nothing there. The way her breath hitched and her thighs trembled tells me otherwise. She felt the energy shift between us.

We'll never be *nothing*.

The connection we shared all those years ago runs too deep; it's impossible to be forgotten or erased. She's just in denial. Fighting the truth of how good we were together. The passion we shared.

She's purposefully forgetting all the wonderful parts about us. Her fear has her focusing on the wrong things, but I'm going to enjoy making her remember. However, I need to tread carefully with her. She needs a little time to let my words sink in because I plan on getting to know her and spending time with her again.

This must all feel like an emotional overload to her. She's been through a lot this past year. But I'm here for her now. She doesn't have to do this alone. I'm going to prove it, little by little.

Rhys's question about her nickname cracked open the door for me to tell her how she made me feel then and still does now. I want Rhys to know that I care about his mom and that we have a past connection. He is Rylann's entire world. I know she isn't the only one I have to win over this time around.

Since being here, I've learned two things.

One, I still fucking love Rylann. I never stopped, and I want her back. I don't want to miss another minute of life without her. Two, the same goes for Rhys. I can't get enough of that kid. He's easy to love, and I want to be the one that loves him.

I snag a spot next to Levi and his father, Bob, waiting in line to buy tickets for the train tour around the farm. A glance over my shoulder reveals Rylann joining Scarlett and the kids as they wait off to the side.

"How was the drive?"

"It was good. Rhys kept me entertained. That kid is something else."

"He is. He's my little dude." Levi sighs. "I was so worried about him after Sam passed. It's why I helped Ry's parents convince her to move in next door. We all thought he would need more support. We were wrong, of course. That kid is special. He's been the one supporting us. Especially his mom. He—"

Levi cuts himself off, making me curious, and Bob excuses himself so we can talk more privately.

"Has she been having a more difficult time since losing her husband? Is she ..." I don't even know how to finish the sentence out loud. She's a different woman, not as easy with her smiles, guarded.

Levi tilts his head to the side in thought, weighing his words as we watch the women we love chatting from afar. "Yes and no. Yes, because how could she not? She watched him waste away right before her eyes. Fuck, Jay. It was awful. He was so sick. She never left his side. And no, because Rylann is strong as hell. She's just ... not herself anymore. We sometimes catch glimpses, but then it's gone in a flash. She holds it all in, carrying all the weight on her shoulders."

I guess I'm not the only one who sees that she needs more support than she lets on.

"Listen, the only time she's happy is when she's with Rhys. He's the only thing that makes her truly smile anymore."

I take in Rylann sitting next to Scarlett. Her sunglasses sit on top of her head, her silky brown hair is braided to the side, and her yellow top dips low, giving me a glimpse of the tops of her breasts. My eyes skim up her toned legs, and my mouth waters. She looks fucking gorgeous.

Scarlett says something to her and she laughs, and that's when I see it. Her laugh isn't like I remember or like the one we shared reminiscing in the car. Here, her dimples don't pop and her eyes don't twinkle. It's a half-laugh at best. Wooden.

"I see." I turn back to Levi, finding him watching me, an odd look on his face. "What?"

"Nothing."

"Okay. You're getting weird at your old age."

"You would know, old man." He chuckles and slaps me on the back.

"That's the second time I've been called old today." Gotta say, I'm not a fan of getting older.

"Interesting." His eyebrow arches, waiting for me to divulge.

"Rhys was carrying on about 90's music being—and I quote—*for old people.*"

Levi throws his head back and laughs. He's definitely heard this argument before. "He loves to get a rise out of Ry with that one. It's one of the few times we see her real smile."

Little turd. But then I recall how her face lit up at his teasing. It was the first time I'd seen a smile reach her eyes.

Rhys is Rylann's rock. Her everything.

Make him happy, make her happy.

"I know that look, Jace. What are you thinking?"

I don't want to let Levi know how I feel. I'm sure he has suspicions. I'll talk to him about my feelings and intentions eventually, just not yet. I need more time to perfect my plan, and Rylann needs more time to come to terms with her feelings.

Although, if I'm going to have any luck, I'm going to need Levi's help so I have to give him something.

"I want to help Ry find herself again. I think the only way we can get her out of this funk is for me to help her remember what it's like to live."

To love.

I keep that part to myself. I'm not sure I can get her there in such a short amount of time, but I'm sure as hell going to try. This time, I'm going to fight like hell.

"If you can get her to come back to us, you have my support. Scarlett's too. Just don't hurt her, man. Or Rhys. If you do, I will have to hurt you this time. I really don't want to have to kick your ass." Levi shakes his head and winces pointing at Scarlett. "Actually, my wife will kick your ass. She will hunt you down and rip your balls off. So let this be a warning. If you go down the road I think you're thinking of going, don't fuck it up and go all in. There is no other way. Got it?"

"You have my word."

I wholeheartedly mean that. The last thing I want is for either of them to be hurt.

But who will be there if I'm the one that gets hurt?

"Come on, Jace, we have to beat everyone to the end!"

Rhys and I are currently teamed up, walking through the farm's garden maze. His excitement is palpable.

We've been at this hunt in the sprawling two-plus mile maze for the last thirty minutes. He's helped us find four of the stations and isn't even winded.

Levi and I made a game out of the walk. Our goal: Find all the secret stations and get out of the maze as fast as possible. The first team out wins, and the last team out has to buy the winners' ice cream.

It's me and Rhys against Levi and the twins.

I haven't had this much fun in ages. The last thing on my mind has been work or the achingly lonely life I live.

Rhys has garnered all of my attention. He sat next to me on the train tour, which I was more than happy about because it meant Rylann had to sit next to me too. The three of us shared a seat, and damn if it didn't feel good to be sitting next to them.

Since starting the maze, Rhys has opened up about school, sports, and things he likes to do. And his mom.

He really loves his mom, but our earlier conversation has me concerned. We had just found the first secret station when a sad look crossed his face.

"Are you having fun?" I asked Rhys.

"Yes."

"Then why do you look so sad all of a sudden?"

"I was thinking about my mom."

"She's okay. She's with your aunt Scarlett."

"I know, but she's probably sad without me."

"Why do you think that?"

"She's sad a lot when she's alone. I want her to be happy again." His admission was like a punch to the gut, expelling my breath from my lungs and knocking me down. I'd known Rylann was sad, but if Rhys saw it, things must be worse than I'd thought.

"Is your mom sad?"

He nodded. *"She tries to hide it. She doesn't like me to see her sad. But I hear her cry at night sometimes."* His confession tore at my heart—it fucking ached for him. For Rylann.

I cleared my throat, my mission clear. *"What do you think about me making her happy while we're here? We could team up?"*

"Really?" Rhys grinned at me.

"Really."

That was the end of it. We found the second secret spot, and he's been focused on winning this game since. The pep in his step is unmistakable. I've given him a new purpose.

I only hope I don't let him down. I want him to see me as a friend. Someone he can talk to. Trust.

He's ridiculously smart and sees a lot. I loved listening to him ask questions and thoughtfully listen to the answers the tour guides gave during the train ride. He knew a lot of answers to the trivia. I have a feeling he'd gone onto Google before he came here. The look of pride on Rylann's face proved she didn't mind his googling.

At his age, I was a curious kid too. I had to know everything. Drove my parents crazy. Only then, we didn't have Google. We still used encyclopedias because the internet was too new for some older teachers who wanted us to use real resources for research.

Damn. Rhys is right—I am fucking old.

We exit the maze first, and Rhys does a happy hype dance. Fist pumping, he kicks his little leg while he hops. Levi and the girls come out next, followed by Rylann, Scarlett, and the grandparents.

I watch as Rhys jumps into his mom's arms, celebrating his victory.

"Nice start," Levi states, jerking his head towards the happy scene.

My chest puffs with pride. I helped Rhys put that smile on her face. She is glowing with a bonafide "Rylann sunny smile".

Fuck me. I want to rush over there and kiss those tiny divots on her cheeks.

"Uncle Lee!" Rhys comes barreling into Levi, jumping into his arms, the two of them laughing as Levi tickles his sides.

Jealousy hits me. I want Rhys to jump into my arms, not Levi's.

"For my reward, I want two scoops of ice cream." Rhys tells Levi, holding up two fingers.

"You got it, Rhyses pieces. Just don't tell your mom, or she won't let us have dessert after dinner."

"Deal."

"You good there, Jace?"

Levi puts Rhys down, and I stare at him as he runs off towards our group. That uncomfortable feeling is still coursing through me.

"Yeah, yeah. All good." I try to shake it off.

"Alright, let's get these people some lunch. Then ice cream."

I stand a ways away and watch my friend beeline straight for his wife, wrap his arms around her, and kiss her. Another pang of jealousy quickly washes over me.

I want that. A loving wife, a family, happiness.

"They're still as gross as ever, aren't they?" Rylann's sultry voice cuts through the fog.

"Definitely."

"Thanks for helping Rhys win the race. He's extremely happy. I bet Levi's already promised him two scoops of ice cream for his victory. Am I right?" She looks up at me, waiting for me to answer.

I pretend to zip my lips and throw away the key, making her laugh. It's not a full-blown Rylann laugh, but it's getting there. It's breathy and rough, but it still makes my heart and my dick jump.

I glance over, to see Rhys watching us. He shoots me a thumbs up, which has me chuckling, and I give him one back.

"You feeling hungry?" I place my hand on her lower back.

"Starved," she whispers.

"Then let's get you fed. Can't have you getting 'hangry', now can we?"

"I'd be more worried about Rhys getting 'hangry'. He can be a real pain when he's tired and hungry."

"Can't imagine where he gets that from," I joke.

Rylann digs her elbow into my ribs. In mock pain, I clutch my side, making her laugh again.

"Shut up. Everyone gets cranky when they're hungry." She shakes her finger at me, pulling a smile to my face. I don't know how she does it, but damn, she really knows how to make me feel like I'm floating.

"Touché, Sunshine. Shall we?" I lead her toward the group.

For the rest of the day, I watch Rylann and push her boundaries. I count and measure her smiles. I sit a little too close at lunch, which doesn't go unnoticed by Levi, who chuckles. I watch her drift off during conversations, chewing on her cheek instead of listening. I stand by her side, making contact with her body with a brush of my arm. I watch as her breathing speeds up when I'm near. I watch every fucking thing about her.

When I'm not staring at her, I'm talking to Rhys about all the activities he wants to do. I dub his itinerary Rhys's Kickin' Hawaiian Adventure List, which gets a real laugh out of Rylann.

I also get burned by Scarlett's scrutinizing glare. Levi was right—if I mess this up, Scarlett will never forgive me.

On the way back, I stop on the side of the highway where a sign for fresh coconuts is displayed. We lucked out, and the guy working the stand has a huge-ass machete. Rhys watches in awe as he slices away the hard green shell, sliver by sliver, to reveal the nut inside. He is even more excited to drink the water straight from the coconut.

When we arrive back at the hotel, our group's energy has finally faded. The kids are all asleep. Levi and his dad carry the girls while I carry Rhys, only after Rylann gives me a hard time about it.

I will not let her carry the burden alone while I'm here. If I can help, I will.

She needs to know that I'm here for it all. I know Rhys is part of the package. And I got to be honest, it's a pretty fucking awesome package.

With promises to meet for dinner later, we say our goodbyes to everyone at the elevator.

As we step off the elevator, I lean over and whisper in Rylann's ear, "Since we aren't taking the hike with everyone until mid-morning, would you be open to letting me take you two out surfing tomorrow morning?"

"YES!" Rhys yells, startling us.

I guess the little stinker wasn't asleep after all. His arms circle my neck, clinging to me while he pleads with his mom.

I give her an apologetic smile, hoping she forgives me for putting her on the spot. Not that it makes a difference—I'm not letting her get out of this.

She bites her lip, and Rhys gives her puppy dog eyes and a pouty lip. It's his signature move to get what he wants. He better not turn it on me because I'll give him whatever he wants. Same as I will Rylann.

"Ugh, fine, you win." She reaches over and musses his brown locks, his face glowing, his fist pumping the air. "What time should I have him ready?"

Nice try, Sunshine. But you're going.

"You *both* should be ready by 7:00 tomorrow morning. Gives us plenty of time to get a little breakfast before we hit the waves."

There's no way she's going to let me take Rhys alone. She's just being stubborn. We arrive at their door, and I place Rhys on his feet. "I have some things to do before we all have dinner. Save me a seat?"

"Okay. You can sit next to me and Sadie," he says.

I squat down on my knee, and we bump knuckles before Rylann opens the door. He races inside like he's just had a vat of coffee. I shake my head in wonder at his energy.

When I stand to my full height, Rylann looks up at me with her deep brown eyes. I feel like she wants to say something, but I stop her. I don't want her to overthink right now. I know there is a lot for us to talk about. Just not yet. We'll get there.

Without thinking, I push the little strands of her hair behind her ear, grazing the sensitive skin with my fingertips. A little touch to hold me over.

"See you *later*, Sunny," I say.

Her lips fight a smile at my intentional use of her nickname.

I hurry to my room, fighting the urge to kiss the crap out of her. She's not ready, and when I do finally kiss her again for the first time, she needs to be because I won't stop kissing her. Ever.

I can be patient.

Besides, I have surfboards to rent and some shopping to do.

CHAPTER THIRTY-FIVE

Rylann

A loud knock on the door sounds, and I look at the clock.

Jace wasn't kidding when he said he'd pick us up at 7:00 on the dot.

"Jace's here!" Rhys screams, jumping off the bed.

Don't act like your coochie isn't jumping for joy too.

Fine—a teeny tiny part of me is excited too. But it's nothing in comparison to Rhys's excitement. He's so eager to learn to surf and hang out with Jace that he was up at six this morning, driving me crazy with his non-stop chatter.

This little outing Jace has planned for Rhys is extra thoughtful and generous. It's sweet how he's going out of his way to bring my son joy. That's Jace, though—if he can find a way to make people happy, he'll do it.

I was only half serious when I tried to skip. I wouldn't miss Rhys's first surfing lesson, and even if I was serious, Jace would never let me miss it either.

Rhys opens the door, and there he is, all 6'3" of him looking handsome as ever in a tight black rash guard that hugs his broad chest and boardshorts.

"Good morning, Sunshine," he croons, walking in and shutting the door behind him. He hugs Rhys and makes his way to me, leaning down and pecking my cheek, right over my freckles like he used to.

His manly scent envelopes me, and my knees quiver. My heart pounds so loudly in my chest, I wouldn't be surprised if he could hear it.

He steps back, taking his heat with him, a cocky smirk on his lips. He knows exactly how he affects me.

"What's this?" I point to the two brown shopping bags in his hand.

He holds them out to me and Rhys, waiting for us to take them. "Just a little gift." I push the bag away, but he stops me. "It's nothing big. I promise you're gonna thank me. You'll need it for today."

I look over at Rhys. He's staring at me, pleading with those big brown and gold eyes to let him take the present. Like I can say no to that sweet face.

I look over at Jace, and he winks at me. Sexy fucker.

"Go ahead."

"Yes!" Rhys celebrates, grabbing the bag and digging inside. He pulls out a long-sleeved, marbled royal blue and white rash guard, matching board shorts, and water socks. "Sweet! Surf clothes! I'm gonna go put them on now."

"Manners!" I shout at his back.

"Thanks, Jace!" Rhys calls out, rushing to the bathroom.

I look back at Jace, and he lifts the bag higher, giving it a shake. He's holding back a grin and failing. He's so irresistible, I don't know whether I want to smack him or kiss him.

Kiss him.

"Your turn, Sunshine. I hope you like it." He wiggles his eyebrows at me.

As indignantly as I can, I snatch the gift from his hands and dig inside. I pull out a black and neon yellow long-sleeved rash guard and a matching pair of water socks. I laugh at the color. It's almost the same shade of neon as the leggings he told Rhys about.

It's very sweet and thoughtful of him to think about our comfort and take care of us.

"My favorite color. How'd you know?" I tease, batting my lashes at him.

"Lucky guess," he says.

I look at the material, and reality settles in. I'm going to have to do this. Running is more my speed. But surfing? I've never been interested in surfing, and frankly, the idea of it scares me a little. My gut churns. I'm a fairly adept swimmer, but I'm not the greatest. It's why Sam and I made sure Rhys took swim lessons as a baby. He was a natural and took to the water like a fish.

"Thanks for this. It's perfect."

"My pleasure."

Rhys exits the bathroom and poses in a surfer stance. He looks the part, with his long shaggy hair and new clothes. He's so happy. I wish I could be as excited.

"Your turn, Mom. Let's go," Rhys urges me to hurry.

I try to move, but my feet are stuck to the fluffy carpet.

Jace notices my hesitation and rubs his hand up my arm, soothing my nerves. "Hey, Ry. Look at me." Jace bends at his knees, bringing us to eye level. His eyes are dark green today, but it's not the color that gets me. It's the way he's looking at me. All humor gone, he says, "Today is all about having fun. To help you get out of your head. I promise that the instructors I've hired are the best in town. I'm taking you both to the safest place on the island for your first time out. I will be by your and Rhys's side the entire time. I will not let anything happen to either of you. Do you trust me?" His eyes search mine, imploring me to trust him. Begging me to give him a chance.

Without question, I trust Jace with my life and, by extension, Rhys's. I know he would never let anything happen to us. *Plus, Levi would kick his ass if either Rhys or I got hurt.*

I take a deep breath and nod. "Yes, I trust you."

$$\sim \heartsuit \cdot \cdot$$

We pull into the parking lot across the street from the beach, and it's breathtaking. The turquoise waters glitter in the morning sun, and white fluffy clouds paint the exotically blue sky.

Grabbing my beach bag, my nerves make another appearance. I can't decipher if I'm nervous about surfing or spending time away with Jace. I watch him help Rhys out of his booster and place him on his shoulders. The picture they paint together looks so natural, an everyday occurrence for them.

I listen as Jace explains how the Waikiki Beach walls break the tide, allowing the waves to roll more smoothly instead of swell and crash to the shore. Rhys is eating up every word.

"Mommy, I'm hungry," Rhys complains.

"Again? Didn't you just eat a bowl of cereal and a waffle at the hotel before we left?" Hands on my hips, I eye him curiously. I swear this guy eats non-stop.

"That was *first* breakfast. I need *second* breakfast now." Rhys rolls his eyes like I should know this stuff.

I bite back my smile at his cheekiness. Jace huffs out a laugh, and I give him the mom glare.

He holds a hand up in surrender, the other wrapped around Rhys's calf. "Sorry, but I'm with the kid. I need some sustenance before we surf." He throws his thumb over his shoulder at the café behind him. "We have time. Our lesson doesn't start for another thirty minutes."

"Fine. But I'm not liking this." I point to the two of them. "No ganging up on me."

"Deal!" Rhys shouts while Jace makes no promise to do the same.

He just flashes me a mischievous smile. One I'm well acquaint-ed with. The same smile that got me in trouble before.

We share cranberry macadamia nut muffins and bananas before we walk across the street to a yellow school bus outfitted with surf and paddle boards.

Jace got us the VIP of all surf lessons. I'm impressed with his choice and his continued ability to calm my jitters. Giving me what I need without having to ask for it.

Check-in is quick as we are shuffled into the bus to watch instructional videos. The staff is amazing, and I feel comfortable with the idea of Rhys doing this. Me? Not so much, but I'm determined to make the best of the day for Rhys and Jace.

Rhys is in his element the entire time. We've been doing part two of the surf lesson on the beach, and he's been entertaining his instructor with jokes and, well ... being Rhys. He's so charismatic and sweet. Undoubtedly destined for greatness, with his big per-sonality.

Jace, with his waterproof-cased phone, captures every minute, promising to text me all the pictures and videos. Again, he's thought ahead and is giving me what I need. His attentiveness and generosity are breaking through the walls I've erected around my heart.

He turns his camera on me while I practice bringing my knees to my hands before standing into a squatting position. I'm not as quick a learner as my son, who is a natural.

"Looking good, Sunshine." Jace gives me a flirty wink.

Why does that wink have to do it for me? I stick my tongue out at him, making him laugh. He knows what he's doing, and he's using it to his advantage. Ignoring him, I go back down on my stomach to repeat the process as explained by the instructor, Shawn, who is a mocha-skin hottie with toned abs. It's a shame I'm into hunky lawyers that look at my son like he's the fucking sky.

I watch Jace watching Rhys, and my heart flutters.

I let my eyes roam over Jace's body, lingering on his firm butt. Absolute, biteable perfection. I imagine pressing my teeth into his supple skin. Running my hands over his shoulders and down his hard torso, stopping at his boardshorts and ...

I bite my lips and inwardly groan, forcing my lusty thoughts away. I need to stop thinking about Jace like that.

"Alright, alright," Shawn shouts. "It's time to put these skills to use, yea? Grab ya board. Let's paddle out. Remember, ya gonna paddle out to Leo waiting at the line-up." He points to a shirtless blond man straddling a board in the ocean, waving back to us.

Rhys and Jace lead the way, walking down to the water and climbing onto their boards. My nose tingles with unshed tears as I watch them paddling out like two peas in a pod.

Pushing my thoughts away, I follow them. I concentrate on my movement as I slice through the waves with my arms, paddling away from the beach. The combination of the cool water licking my skin and the warm sun on my back feels good. Relaxing, even.

I can see why Jace likes this sport. With the sound of the ocean and birds in the background, everything slips away at the feel of the waves beneath me. And for the first time in a long time, my mind feels quiet.

Maybe Jace was right. I do need to get out of my head.

When I reach the line-up, the instructor is walking us through the steps again. Since Rhys is the youngest, he gets all the attention and is instructed to lead off. On his first try, he makes it to his knees. On his second, he makes it to his feet but falls over into the water. My insides lurch forward, and I start to swim toward him when his little head bobs up out of the water. He grabs his surfboard and before I move, Jace is right there, helping him get back on and encouraging him to try again. He's there like he promised he would be.

I watch Rhys try again and again until he finally stands up, nailing it. He rides the wave for a good twenty feet, the crowd around us cheering and applauding his effort and success.

"Way to go, Rhysie!" I shout like the proud mom I am.

Jace looks over at me, our eyes locking, and something more powerful than I'm ready for passes between us. All I can manage is a mouthed, *Thank you*.

I truly am thankful. As much as I wanted to fight him and his involvement on this adventure, it was what both Rhys and I needed. We needed a moment to just live.

Jace's smile grows wider the longer we watch each other bobbing in the waves. He humbly inclines his head and mouths back, *Your turn*.

I shake my head at him.

He paddles over to me. "You can do this, Sunshine. All you have to do is try."

"I'm scared," I confess, unsure what I'm really scared of, but I don't think it's surfing.

Jace brushes a wet strand of hair behind my ear and whispers, "Me too. But if you don't try, you'll regret it. You can do this, and I'll be right here for you." The way he looks at me when he speaks those words lets me know he means every word and they're not limited to surfing.

"Okay."

"There's my brave girl. Now, show Rhys where he gets his skills from." Under his penetrating gaze and unwavering support, my frayed nerves stitch themselves together.

I forgot how confident Jace makes me feel. Stronger. Braver.

It takes me longer to stand, but when I do, pride fills my chest. I whoop in victory, arms high in the air. Damn, it's good to accomplish something different. Get out of my head.

"Way to go, Momma!" Rhys screams behind me, making me smile.

I try looking for him but lose my balance. Jace's proud voice is the last thing I hear before falling into the water.

I did it. My tired body buzzes with adrenaline and life. My shoulders are lighter, and for the first time in a while, I'm ... happy.

It's all thanks to Jace. He did this for me. For Rhys.

Oh, crap.

He's doing it again.

He's making me fall.

CHAPTER THIRTY-SIX

Rylann

Standing at the top of Diamond Head again feels surreal. The island below looks exactly how I remembered it and yet completely different ... Or is that I'm different?

A long arm wraps around my shoulders, pulling me close. Scarlett's strawberry scent penetrates my nose, and I breathe her in. My sister-bestie.

I wrap an arm around her waist, resting my head on her shoulder, my eyes never leaving the view spread out below. "Where are the kids?"

"With Levi and Jace. I came over to check on you."

"Thanks. I was just looking at the view. It looks the same but ... different."

"It does. Did you have fun this morning?" she asks, looking forward.

I soak in the silence for another minute before answering. "Yes. It was fantastic. Rhys had an amazing time. Thank you."

"Why are you thanking me? I didn't take you surfing."

I roll my eyes at her. "Not that, you dummy. For this." I wave my hand at our surroundings, but really, I mean for everything.

I'm incredibly grateful for her friendship and support over the years, and for forcing this trip on me too. She and Levi might have been right—this was the push I needed. Things have to change, not only for Rhys but for myself too. It's what Sam wanted.

His words flash across my brain. *Live. Life is too short. Find happiness.*

I'm not sure what true happiness is for me now, but I'm starting to be at peace with the past, and the future doesn't seem as bleak as it did before.

Truth be told, Jace is the reason I feel lighter today. He showed up for me and helped me and Rhys find extra joy in trying something new. I couldn't be more grateful for his support. I don't know how he knows what I need, but he does. He's always understood me on a deeper level. It amazes me that he still gets me. Sees me.

As I mentioned to him earlier, I'm scared. What happens if I keep letting him in? I don't think I can go through losing him again. My heart isn't the only one at stake.

"I'm always here for you, ya know? Now, turn." Scarlett turns us around and pulls out her phone. She flips the camera to selfie mode and snaps photos of the two of us. She switches over to her camera roll and pulls up the picture. "Hmm."

"Did I close my left eye again? You better delete it. I don't need you holding another gross picture of me over my head." Her payback since the pumpkin princess debacle.

I grab the phone from her hands to double-check. She's messing with me. We look good. We're both smiling wide. But something looks different about us. I can't put my finger on it.

"It looks good. Deletion not required," I approve, handing the phone back.

"You don't see it, do you?"

"See what?"

"It's coming back."

"What's coming back?"

"Your spark. It's coming back."

I reach for her phone again to see what she's talking about, but she slides it into her leggings pocket.

"Aunty Ry! Rhysie needs you!" the twins cry out, skidding to a stop in front of me. They point over to Rhys, who is standing on the roof of a crumbling cement platform looking freaked out.

My stomach drops as I race to my baby, praying he doesn't slip and fall. I rush over, but Jace gets to him before me. A strange sense of relief washes over me. He wouldn't let anything happen to Rhys.

"Hey, buddy. It looks like you got yourself into a jam."

Rhys nods his head, his eyes wide with fear.

I join Jace at his back, fisting his shirt in the palms of my hands. He reaches behind, squeezing my hand in reassurance. He's got this. As much as I want to intervene, my gut tells me to let Jace handle this.

He reaches out to Rhys, who looks down over the summit's edge. His little body shakes, and tears well in his eyes.

"Eyes on me, Rhys. Don't look anywhere else. I got you. I won't let anything happen to you."

Rhys looks back at Jace and nods like it's just the two of them.

"That's it. Now, I want you to get on your hands and knees, and crawl over to me."

Slowly, Rhys gets down on all fours as instructed.

"You're doing great. That's it, keep coming. Now, stop. Sit on your butt and scooch yourself over to the edge, and let your feet dangle over."

Rhys sits and inches his butt forward.

Jace attempts to walk forward, but I pull him back, my hands clutching his shirt tight. Reaching back, he pats my hip, reassuring me. He's got this. I let go.

He stands below Rhys, less than a foot between them, and reaches up. "You're doing great. Now, you're going to drop right into my arms. Think you can do that?"

Rhys shakes his head no.

"I think you can. It's scary being brave. But you're not alone. I'm right here. I promise. I won't let you fall. Now, on the count of three. One. Two. Three."

Jace's words wrap around my heart and squeeze as I watch Rhys push himself off the edge, and—as promised—drop into Jace's waiting arms. With a sigh of relief, I rush over to Rhys and pull him from Jace's arms into mine for a tight hug. He wraps his arms and legs around me, nuzzling his face in my neck.

"What were you thinking, climbing up there? You could have gotten hurt, my love," I softly scold, checking over every inch of him.

"I'm sorry, Mommy. I wanted to stand on top of the world. But then I looked down, and I got scared."

"Oh, you sweet, silly boy." I kiss his face all up, making him giggle, the scary ordeal already behind us.

Holding Rhys, I lean into Jace's warm touch. He's been silently supporting me, his hand at the small of my back the entire time I comfort Rhys.

"Thank you."

"Always," he whispers in my ear. He rubs my back, sending shivers up my spine.

Rhys lifts his head off my shoulder and reaches out to Jace, who ruffles his wavy hair and takes him back in his arms.

"Thank you for helping me get down, Jace."

"You're welcome, bud. I'm proud of you for being brave when you were scared. Next time, I'm gonna need you to read the sign and follow directions, okay?" Jace points to the side of the pillars, where *Keep Off* is spray-painted.

Rhys's eyes pop open. He missed that sign. I bite my lips, trying to hold back my smile.

"I'm sorry," he mumbles, his little voice shaky.

"It's all good, kiddo. Now, how about we get out of here? I'm hungry. Care to join me for a burger?" Jace tickles him until he agrees, then places him on his feet.

"Yes!" Rhys grabs both my and Jace's hands, and pulls us down the mountain.

Together.

CHAPTER THIRTY-SEVEN

Jace

My fingers tap the counter while I check the clock again.

I'm going to be late for breakfast if these people don't get off Hawaiian time. I don't want to miss my date with Rylann and Rhys. Okay, so it's not an official date. But any time I get with Rylann feels like it.

Another couple of minutes pass without a peep, and I start to worry. I placed the reservation online late last night because they had what I wanted. After yesterday, I wanted to make today extra memorable for Rylann and Rhys. The smiles I put on their faces with those surf lessons felt fucking fantastic. The hike also helped propel my relationship with Rylann forward. Rhys getting stuck was an opportunity for me to prove that I'm there for her. Stepping in to help him felt like second nature. I would do anything to keep him safe. Rylann recognizing that and handing over her trust to me was a huge step for her. She's the one that always fixes the problems, and while that makes her a wonderful mother, she can't be everything all the time. I fully appreciate the faith she had in me to take care of her son.

When I found out the plan for today was to drive the North Shore, I talked Levi into upping our agenda with a few more stops. I really want to make this trip unforgettable for Rylann and check off all those boxes on Rhys's bucket list. Levi was happy to go along with the updated plan and even suggested I exchange the rental car for something more fun.

"Sorry about that. Thank you for being patient. My nephew did not put the key in the right place. Teenagers." The lady behind the counter—who I assume is the owner—huffs and playfully rolls her eyes. "The car is in the side parking lot. You can't miss it. When you return the car, you just park in the same spot and drop the key here with my nephew."

"*Mahalo*," I say, thanking her.

Key in hand, she wishes me a good day and I rush out the door.

The car is exactly where she said it'd be, looking like a dream. Rhys is going to flip. Starting the car, I pull out of the lot and head back to the hotel.

I need today to go well, so Rylann can continue to relax and embrace these moments. I finally saw it yesterday. Her real smile. It came out when we were surfing. Ear to ear, dimples popping, and eyes shining, her smile took my breath away.

Fuck. Thinking about the way her face lit makes my chest puff. She looked so brave and strong riding that wave, a look of pride on her face. She was a vision.

I wasn't the only one to notice either. The possessive caveman in me wanted to knock some damn heads. I made no attempt to hide annoyance either, glaring at each one of those asshole instructors staring at my girl. I had to stop myself from wrapping her up in my arms and kissing her. Laying claim to what's mine. Because she is mine. Mine to watch, to protect, and to take care of. She's mine to love.

She needs more time and proof that I'm here for her. Ease her into us. We're getting there. We've already come a long way in the last two days.

I chuckle, thinking about how she tried to ignore me on the drive to the pineapple plantation. She was kidding herself thinking she could keep me away. But I'm like the fucking Kool-Aid man, fully prepared to break through her walls at all costs.

When I arrive at the hotel, I park next to Levi's minivan in the guest lot and rush to the restaurant, where everyone is eating breakfast.

"Jace! You're here!" Rhys jumps into my arms, taking me by surprise by wrapping his little arms around my neck in a tight hug.

I squeeze his little body back. He smells like waffles and maple syrup—sweet.

"Of course I am. I can't miss breakfast. It's the most important meal of the day." I take his seat, place him on my knee, and bring his plate closer.

He tucks back into his breakfast without missing a beat.

"Everything all set?" Levi asks.

"Yup, good to go."

Levi slides an untouched omelet toward me.

It's my favorite—veggies, ham, and cheese with a side of toast. "Thanks, man. How'd you know?" I ask, placing a bite in my mouth.

"Uncle Levi didn't order you food. Mommy did," Rhys says matter-of-factly.

My eyes jump across the table to her. She watches me, and I arch my brow at her in question. Her cheeks pinken and she nods, a small smile on her lips.

Fuck yeah.

"Thanks, Sunshine."

She shrugs me off like ordering my breakfast was nothing. *Little liar.* It might seem insignificant, but this is huge for her. For us. She remembered.

A grin pulls at my lips, and I give her a wink. She was thinking about me. I eat my omelet quietly, not wanting to draw too much attention to Rylann's gesture, but I'm peacocking hard on the inside.

Once breakfast is done, Levi and I excuse ourselves to bring the cars around.

"How many stops do you have planned for today? Scarlett wanted to know. The girls were asking us a million questions, and I didn't have answers. You might not be used to driving with kids, but you should know they are relentless. It's easier to tell them what's next to avoid getting a headache."

I'm frozen. I'm still not used to having Levi on my side. I was expecting pushback and have received the opposite. He's been nothing but supportive.

"Jay? What are the plans?"

"Sorry, I spaced for a second there. I have it down on my phone."

I pull up my notes and send him the details, including the couple of reservations I made for the entire group. He looks through the itinerary, then hops into the minivan without another word.

I get in my car and turn the key, the engine roaring to life sending a thrill through my veins. I plug my phone into the aux and start up my 90's playlist before hitting the button to bring the top down.

Pulling out of my parking space, I follow Levi to the front of the hotel. Everyone comes into view when we turn into the roundabout, and damn, I wish I set up my camera to video Rhys's reaction.

He's standing on the curb with his mouth hanging open and his eyes popping out of his head in awe. His mom, on the other hand, is a tougher nut to crack. I can't tell what she's thinking. She's standing next to Rhys with her eyes hidden behind a pair of black and yellow sunglasses, her teeth sunk into her bottom lip, and her arms crossed under her chest, lifting her ample rack up. She looks fucking exquisite.

And maybe a little pissed.

I can't help but run my eyes over her again. Her long brown hair is twisted into a braid. She's wearing a white wrap dress with lemons on it that hugs her body to perfection, accentuating her soft curves in all the right ways. She's the perfect combination of sexy and sweet in that dress. I can practically smell her sweet citrusy scent from here.

My dick twitches at the thought of eating her up.

"Are we really driving in that?" Rhys yells, forcing me to tear my eyes away from the vision that is his mother.

"Only if you want to. Do you want to?"

"Hell yeah!"

"Rhys!" Rylann scolds as I slap the steering wheel with a laugh.

His reaction was better than I could have imagined.

Rylann turns her angry mom glare my way. I put my hands up in surrender, fully chastised for my parent-unapproved reaction.

"Sorry," Rhys bemoans.

"I forgive you, but please watch what you say, kiddo. You are not a grown-up."

"I won't say it again. Promise." He crosses an X over his heart.

"You." Rylann points at me. I point at myself in question. "Yes, you. What's the meaning of all this?" She steps closer and waves her hand at the car.

Alright, so it's a little much. That's not the point of this, though. The point is for her to relax and have fun. And this car is the epitome of fun.

"What do you mean? It's a car," I say innocently.

She rolls her eyes at me. Over her shoulder, I see Scarlett cover a smile with her fist.

"I know that. Why are you driving a white convertible Mustang? What happened to the other car?" Rylann starts tapping her foot, waiting for me to answer.

"Had to exchange it."

"Why?" She's not going to let this go.

"Why not?" I shrug. I can play this all day. I'm not gonna change the car and cave. She's going to get in this car and enjoy herself, even if I have to sit her down and strap her in myself.

"Because this is ridiculous. We don't need all this."

"Speak for yourself, Mom. I'm riding in this with Jace. It's awesome!" Rhys opens the passenger door and climbs into the backseat, where I set up a booster seat for him.

I exit the car and walk over to where Rylann stands, glancing over at Scarlett, who gives me a thumbs-up.

Scarlett leans forward and whispers in Rylann's ear, loud enough for me to hear, "Live a little, Rice Cakes. He went out of his way to do something nice for you and Rhys."

She deflates before my eyes, and Scarlett smacks her butt before grabbing her girls and walking away.

Getting out of the car, I walk toward her. I need to see her eyes. I don't want her to admit defeat; I want her to accept this for what it is—a little adventure. Fun.

Taking a chance, I lift her shades onto her head and tuck a sliver of her silky hair behind her ear. I don't miss the shivers as I graze her sensitive skin. I rake my eyes over her beautiful face, cute little freckles decorating her cheek calling to me to kiss them. So I do.

The electricity crackles between us.

"What do you say, Sunshine? Wanna go for a ride with me?"

My eyes flick to her mouth as her pink tongue gently swipes her bottom lip, where her teeth left an indentation. I'd give anything to press my mouth to hers, taste her.

Questions, desire, and indecision all lurk behind her eyes.

"Why are you doing this?" she whispers, so low that I almost miss it.

Ah, Sunny. You're not ready to hear why yet.

Instead, I settle for, "Because I want to."

She places her hand on my scruff-covered cheek, and I lean into her warmth.

Dropping her hand, she clutches it to her chest. She's still scared, but she has nothing to worry about. I won't leave her again.

"Okay." She clears her throat.

A shit-eating grin takes over my face at her acquiescence. Picking up her travel bag, I place my palm on the small of her back, leading her to the car and opening the door for her. She climbs in, and I put her bag behind her seat before sliding into the driver's seat.

Twisting my body, I double-check Rhys has his belt fastened properly. "You ready, buddy?"

"Oh, yeah."

"Good surprise?"

"The bestest ever. This car is sooo cool."

"I knew you'd like it. Now, we are ... What did you and Scarlett call it?" I ask Rylann. I snap my fingers pretending not to remember.

Her lips fight a smile at the memory. Before she can answer, I press my finger to her plump pink lips. Her smile widens. I can't wait to feel those soft lips against mine. I pull my hand away, like the gentleman I need to be.

"Island style," I say, my voice gravelly.

She nods, biting her lip.

"Are you having a good time?"

Between driving in a convertible with the top down and her being glued to Scarlett's side, we haven't spoken much today.

Rylann and I stroll side by side around the grounds of the Japanese Temple, one of the stops I added to our island tour. It's a nice spot for the kids to get out some energy with a walk around the gardens and Koi pond. We watch kids up ahead. The three of them get along so well. Rylann and Scarlett have done a wonderful job raising them.

"I am. It's beautiful here," she answers. She looks less tense today.

"I'm glad."

"You know, you didn't have to do all this for Rhys's benefit."

Yes, I did. And I'd do it again.

"Meh, where's the fun in that?" I give her a wink, and she shakes her head at me.

"Thank you, Ace. You've made Rhys's day. That means more to me than you will ever know."

Fuck me, she called me Ace again. I missed hearing that name on her lips. "What about your day?"

"What do you mean?" She tilts her head to the side, confused. She can't possibly think I didn't do all this for her as well.

"Is this making your day? I didn't do all of this just for him. I did it for you too."

Rylann stops on the path. She looks surprised at my confession, her mouth flopping open and closed, speechless.

"Don't look so surprised, Sunny."

"I ... don't know what to say." She averts her gaze and stares at the pond.

"Just answer the question."

Taking a chance, I cup her cheek in the palm of my hand and turn her face towards mine. The urge to kiss her intensifies.

As if she can read my mind, her breath hitches. My eyes dip down to her mouth and back.

"Yes," she whispers. She looks at me expectantly, but she's way off. I'm not kissing her now.

"Good." I drop my hand and start walking again. I look back at her. "Let's get out of here and get some lunch. Can't have you getting 'hangry' now, can we?" I tease.

She crosses her arms under her chest, lifting up her big tits. She has to stop doing that. I can't help the way my eyes eat up the view.

I look away.

Fuck. She's so beautiful in that sexy little lemon dress and sneakers.

When I peer back up at her, she's hiding a smile. I wiggle my brows at her and give her a toothy grin.

Yeah, Sun. I was looking at you. What are you going to do about it?

"You're incorrigible." She slaps my chest and walks away, leaving me to stare at her ass.

Don't think I don't see the extra sway, Sunshine. I see everything you do.

♡

I take a seat next to Rhys on the soft white sand. He's been sitting in the same spot, eyes glued to the surfers riding wave after wave. He looks so much like Ry at this moment.

We sit and watch as a young girl attempts to ride some pretty big waves. I'm quite impressed, but she rides a little too slowly off her bottom turn, letting the white water at the top overtake her.

"See the surfer over there?" I point in the direction of the girl on her teal and white board, with ocean bleached highlights.

"Uh huh."

"She's new to taking on these bigger waves. Watch how she loses height when she turns at the bottom, trying to get back to the top of the wave. She keeps her arms too low. If she threw her arms up over her head, she could get more height and speed."

"Wouldn't that make her fall off?"

"You would think, but when you're on the water, all you have is your body to help you move. If you move your body in the right direction, the surfboard follows you."

"Really?"

"Yup."

"How old were you when you started surfing?"

"I was way older than you." I scruff his hair, making him laugh. "For real. I was fourteen the first time I got on a board. Now that I live closer to the beach, I go out on the water every day. Well, I used to."

"You live on the beach?" he asks, curious.

"Not quite. My house is a couple of blocks away. But, late at night when everyone is asleep, I can hear the ocean from my backyard."

"That's cool. I live near the forest. All I hear are bugs. But I get to see lots of stars."

"That's awesome. I don't get to see many stars in Los Angeles." I point to the ocean where a bunch of guys are bobbing in the water on boards. "Do you think any of these guys knew your dad?"

"No. It was just a story my dad told me to make me feel better. Because he was dying."

His words hit me hard and my throat constricts, making it hard for me to breathe. The desire to wrap him up in my arms and protect him takes over. I want to comfort him. Tell him everything's going to be okay. That his dad will always be here with him in some way. That I'm here for him now and always will be.

I can't make those promises, though. I need Rylann to let me in before I can.

"It's okay. I'm not sad anymore. My dad made me a promise, and I think it's gonna come true."

"What promise?"

"I can't tell you. It's a secret. I'm not supposed to tell anyone," he says, staring back at the ocean.

Interesting. While I'm intrigued, I don't press further.

"I understand. If you ever want to talk, I'm here for you. And I know your mom is too. She loves you so much."

"I know. My dad told me she loves me more than him."

I chuckle at that. It sounds like something my dad would say about my mom.

The more Rhys talks about his dad, the more curious I get about the guy. He's kind of a mystery to me. I made it a point never to ask Levi about him. I felt irrationally jealous of the man that got to marry Rylann. He must have been a good guy to deserve her and help raise a strong, sweet kid like Rhys.

I take a deep, cleansing breath of the salty air and wrap my arm around Rhys, bringing him closer to my side.

CHAPTER THIRTY-EIGHT

Jace

After yesterday's car debacle, Rylann's let loose and has been enjoying herself more. She's opened up to me, talking about her work, family, moving into her childhood home with Rhys, living next door to our friends, and all things Rhys.

Her whole face lights up when she talks about him. I can feel her love for her son with every word, glowing with pride at the mere mention of his name.

My eyes are trained on Rylann as she waits in line to get shaved ice with Scarlett and the kids. We are at the best sweet shop on the island, and while they get dessert, I've been tasked to save a table.

Rylann throws her head back and laughs at something Scarlett says while Rhys puts his hands on his hips and shakes his head. I wonder what they said to annoy him.

Troublemakers.

My mind drifts back to the first time I saw them together. Scarlett was draped over Levi, drunk as hell, and talking shit to Rylann, calling her a she-devil. Seems like they're still at it.

I like that some things don't change.

While Levi and I haven't been as close as we used to be, I appreciate the effort he put into getting us here again. I'm being gifted with another opportunity to make so many wrongs right. With him, with Rylann.

"Hey, man." Levi takes a seat next to me at the metal bistro table I've been saving.

"Where'd your parents take off to?" I glaze around the small little strip of shops and restaurants.

"You know Ma. She's dragged Dad off to the souvenir shops."

"Are the girls having a good time?"

Levi smiles in the direction of all his girls. "They are. I was a little worried it would be too much, but they're having a blast. Good looking out." He reaches his fist across the table for me to bump.

We watch our little group move closer to the front a bit longer before Levi breaks the silence. "You know, what you're doing for Rylann and Rhys is great. I haven't seen them smile this much in way too long." He rubs his hand across the scruff of his jaw in thought, still watching his waiting family, contemplating his next words.

I brace myself, unsure where this conversation is going.

"Listen, Jay. There's a lot you don't know when it comes to Rylann and Sam. I know you never wanted to talk about it, but I need to say this. They were best friends more than anything. She never looked at him the way she looked at you, and he never once complained. He, on the other hand, looked at her like she hung the fucking moon. He gave her and Rhys everything and more. He was a good man. He became a good friend to me too. Over the years, he would ask about you. He wanted to know what kind of man you were—"

"Hold up ..." I interrupt Levi, but he holds his hand up, stopping me.

Why the fuck would *he* want to know about me?

"Let me talk. I promise there's a point to this, and I want to make it before the girls come back. I told him the truth. That you are an honorable man, a great brother and friend. You always do the right thing, even when you shouldn't. And when you love, you love hard."

I cross my arms, waiting.

Levi sighs and looks me in the eye. "I'm thankful you're here. I'm not gonna warn you about hurting them because I know you wouldn't do that. But I gotta prepare you. Rylann isn't the same girl you fell in love with all those years ago. If you want her, you're gonna have to chase her. Hard. You're going to have to push to make it happen. She's closed-off. She hasn't been herself since we left this island seven years ago. The last year, with Sam's passing, has only made it worse."

"Fuck." A pain throbs in my chest.

I knew I hurt her, but this? This information is hard to swallow.

"Yeah, 'fuck' is right. Just know that Short Stack and I are rooting for you to get the girl. And keep her this time." He taps the table with the palm of his hands and gets up to help Scarlett and Rylann carry the containers of shaved ice back to the table, ending our conversation.

I'm reeling. That was a lot to take in. Now, I have more questions than answers, and the time to get them is quickly running out.

She hasn't been herself since we left this island seven years ago.
I'm not sure if this is good or bad.

The part of me that longs for Rylann believes it's a good thing because, in a lot of ways, I feel the same. I lost a part of myself all those years ago, and I haven't been whole without her.

Rhys is passed out in the back seat, snoring, as we drive back to the hotel. He's beat after all the stops we made checking off items on his list. He wasn't happy when we told him we had to put the top up for the ride back to the hotel. It was the first time I witnessed him get smart.

I itched to get involved but resisted. Watching Rylann handle his attitude with such grace was such a fucking turn-on. She was patient and calm. When he got in his seat, he brooded but was asleep in less than five minutes. I'm surprised there weren't other incidents during the day.

Besides our serious talk on the beach, he was great. He talked non-stop about his likes and dislikes. He listened when I gave him extra details about the island. Spending the day with him was nothing short of awesome. He's smart, funny, and a whole lot cheeky. He's the coolest kid I've ever met. Watching him experience new things was truly something else.

So was watching Rylann get some of her light back. She said I didn't need to do more, but the soft, happy look on her face was worth the extra effort. She was less lost in her head, and she laughed a lot.

She deserves to have fun on this trip too. Hell, she deserves to have someone in her corner, making sure she's taken care of. I want to be that someone. I'm going to prove that I'm that person.

The remaining clouds in the sky glow orange in the setting sun's light. The view is almost as beautiful as the woman next to me. She's looking out the window, her pink lips mouthing the words to the song playing softly in the background. Her scent fills the car in the same coconutty citrus scent I remember, bringing me both peace and hell. I want to bury my face in her neck, breathe her in, and devour her.

As casually as I can, I adjust myself in my shorts. Being so close and yet so far from her is sweet torture.

The hotel comes into view, and I hate that tonight is coming to an end. I'm not ready for us to go our separate ways.

"Jace?" Her raspy voice breaks the silence.

"Yeah, Sunshine?"

"Thanks again for today. You made the drive better than I could have. I appreciate what you're doing for Rhys. For me."

Her gratitude makes my chest bloom with warmth. *I'd do anything for you.*

"You're welcome. I've had fun planning and going on all these little trips with you two."

She glances over her shoulder at Rhys and smiles. I can feel her love for him in that look, and it makes me love her more. Her being a wonderful loving mom is fucking hot. I finally understand the MILF hype.

"It was pretty amazing. I have to say, I wasn't sure how today was going to go—you can never tell with kids. But I think he managed pretty well there until the end. Sorry you had to see that."

"Are you kidding? That was nothing. I've seen Double Trouble losing their shit during a visit to Bob and Julie's. Made me thank the stars that twins don't run in my family."

Rylann throws her head back and laughs, the delightful sound filling the interior of the car stealing my breath away. I'm mesmerized by her beauty.

"Same. Those two ... "

I chuckle as she shivers in mock horror.

"I'm guessing there are some stories there?"

She nods her head and laughs again as I park the car. "You could say that. Remind me to regale you with some twin-tude stories. Teenage Sadie and Lily are going to be the death of Levi."

She laughs again, and I find myself staring at the length of her neck, the way her chest rises and falls. She's the most beautiful woman I've ever seen. I need to get out of this car before I kiss her.

"Come on, Sunny. Let's get this monster to bed."

I exit the car, walking around to the passenger side, and open the door for her. She takes my extended hand, and I help her out of the car. Moving the seat forward, I grab her day bag, handing it to her.

"Why don't you carry this, and I'll carry Rhys upstairs?"

She hesitates for a second before agreeing.

Scarlett walks over to us as I unbuckle Rhys and lift him into my arms. When I have him situated on my hip, I see the twins with Levi, wide awake and arguing with each other. I bite my lips, trying to stifle my laugh.

Scarlett points her finger at my face in warning. "Don't start."

"Yes, ma'am."

Rylann laughs, and Scarlett punches her in the shoulder. "I fucking hate you guys. Stop making fun of my girls."

"Hey, now, we didn't say a thing," I say in our defense, even though we were talking shit about the twins.

"Lying sacks of crap. They aren't trouble," she huffs, and we crack up. Rylann doubles over in laughter while I do my best not to wake Rhys. "Dicks. I came over to ask if you wanted to leave Rhys with Julie and Bob so we could get a drink. But since he's asleep, I'm guessing you're out?"

"Yes. How about tomorrow night? Oh, shoot. We have the luau dinner tomorrow night. Let's plan for the night after. It would be nice to have some grown-up time."

"I'm holding you to that. You too, Jace." She wraps Rylann up in a hug before hollering over her shoulder. "I'll see you two in the morning!"

We watch her catch up with her family as we slowly follow behind.

Rylann is quiet on the ride to our floor. Rhys is still snoozing, with his head resting on my shoulder. My chest warms, and I hug him tighter. I like the three of us together like this.

As asked, I lay Rhys in his bed. I go to leave but stop at the door.

I watch Rylann tuck the little guy in and kiss his forehead goodnight. He's in pajamas already, and I didn't understand why she made him change after dinner. I do now.

Rylann gazes down at him adoringly.

I can't tear my eyes away from the achingly tender moment, so I watch her watch him. As much as I can see her love for him, in this moment, I can feel it. It's fucking remarkable. *She's* remarkable.

When she finally looks my way, her lips lift in a sweet smile. My body aches to hold her warm, curvy body. Breathe in her sweet scent. Kiss her soft lips. Worship every inch of her. She's the siren calling me home, only she doesn't know how her magic has captured me, body and soul.

Unhurriedly she walks my way, her steps muffled by the thick white carpet. She stops in front of me and presses her palms to my torso. Shock waves wrack my body at her touch. My cock hardens, and my scalp tingles.

"You waited?" she whispers.

"Always," I confess, fists clenched at my sides.

We stand there, staring, and what I wouldn't give to know what she's thinking.

Unable to stop myself, I place my hands on her small ones, pressing them harder into my chest. Her touch ignites the fire inside me and soothes it at the same time. My eyes dip to her mouth.

Fuck, I want to kiss her so badly. Her tongue swipes her bottom lip, and I lean down.

"Mommy," Rhys mumbles, breaking the spell.

Slipping her hands from my grip, she steps back, hugging herself. She's not ready.

"Goodnight, Sunny. I'll see you in the morning." I press a soft kiss to the corner of her mouth and promptly slip out of her room and enter mine.

Emptying my pockets, I place my stuff on the bedside table before stripping. I need a shower. I wanted to kiss her so fucking badly, but I'm not sure it would have been the right move. I'm glad Rhys interrupted us.

When I finally kiss her again, I want it to be because she wants me to. I have more work to do on that. I need to prove that I will be there to take care of her. Prove that she can depend on me. Prove that I have her back. My support is unconditional and permanent.

An idea takes root as I recall Scarlett mentioning having some grown-up time. Rylann needs to take baby steps before I can get her to leap with me.

To get there, I'm going to need everyone's help.

CHAPTER THIRTY-NINE

Rylann

Burnt orange and red paint the horizon as the sun sets. The sound of waves crashing has me drifting back to the first night I spent with Jace on the beach. The night I fell for him.

He was handsome and charismatic. Making me laugh at dinner and flirting with me at karaoke. But on that beach, alone together, he was so much more. He showed me a vulnerable side of himself that was sweet and endearing. My gut told me he was sincere, and I let myself be open. Our meeting was fate bringing him into my life. Being with him felt right. He felt like home.

We've been here for five days, and I'm starting to feel it again. Jace is worming his way into my heart again. He has done everything in his power to make this trip a dream come true for Rhys. And as much as I don't want to admit it, for me too.

His thoughtfulness cannot be rivaled. He's gone above and beyond planning extra things for us to do and enjoy. This is what Jace does—he goes out of his way to make the people around him happy. He is a man of action, and his actions speak loud and clear.

He wants me, and he's willing to prove it. That almost-kiss last night shook me. I might have kissed him if Rhys hadn't woken up.

I'm not sure I'm ready, but I'm getting closer. Every time he goes out of his way to show us he cares breaks down my walls a little more.

Like this morning.

After breakfast, he surprised me and Scarlett with massages at the spa. He promised that he and Levi would take the kids so we could enjoy some grown-up time of our own.

I almost cried at his gift. It reminded me of the mom dates Scarlett and I used to take before Sam got sick. I didn't realize how much I missed spending time with my friend away from the kids. I didn't realize how much I needed alone time and to be pampered for a change.

I don't understand how he knows what I need, but he does.

After our massages, Scarlett and I made our way to the beach. I found Rhys building sandcastles with Jace, laughing and having a good time

Joy and guilt hit me in the gut. Their budding relationship concerns me. It's going to be hard to protect Rhys from getting his heart broken at the end of this trip, when Jace leaves. Because he *will* leave.

"Go on a date with me?"

I scream at the sudden voice in my ear, my arms swinging. I turn around and smack the owner of the voice in the chest.

Warm arms wrap around me before the scent of citrus and leather hits me.

"Gah, Jace. I hate being scared!" I shout, slapping him a few more times for good measure. I was so lost in memories, I didn't hear him approach. He could have been a damn serial killer, and I wouldn't have noticed until it was too late. "Why would you do that? You can't just go sneaking up on unsuspecting women."

"I'm sorry, Sunshine." He lets me go and steps back, laughing.

"Are you seriously laughing at me right now? You're the one that came out of nowhere and scared the crap out of me," I say, hands on my hips.

He tries pulling himself together, stifling his laughter. "Sorry, you're right. But you went from scared to angry and slapped the shit out of me in one second flat."

"I did not." I *so* did.

"Sure you didn't," he says smugly.

"Why are you sneaking up on me out here anyway?" I know why he's here—I heard him.

"I saw you slip out, and I followed. I just wanted to make sure you were okay, but then I saw you standing there, looking so beautiful staring at the sunset, I didn't want to disturb you. So, I watched over you for a minute." He slides his hand through his hair nervously.

"That's creepy," I lie, fighting a smile.

He smirks and continues, "I'll admit that it's creeper-ish, but then I was back to the first night on the beach. Just the two of us. Do you remember that night?"

It's baffling that we were thinking the same thing.

"How could I forget? It was a great night," I muse.

"It was. I got to spend it with the most beautiful woman on earth."

My cheeks heat. He has a way of making me feel seen and sexy.

We share a look, both of us reflecting on the past. The amazing days we shared.

I clear my throat, but when I go to speak, he does the same and we end up speaking at the same time.

"Jace, I ..."

"Go on a date with me, please?"

He approaches me like a scared animal, ready to run. I'd laugh if it wasn't true.

I shake my head at him. It's not an answer to his question, but a response to my conflicting feelings. "I—"

He cuts me off before I can finish, "Hear me out. I know you're scared. Understandably so."

He closes the distance between us, centimeters separating us, and smooths loose strands of hair behind my ear. His fingers graze my sensitive skin, sending shivers down my spine.

Eyes closed, I breathe his clean manly scent. This time, it soothes my nerves.

"I'm scared too. I'm so fucking sorry for what happened then. I know my apology is seven years too late, but I mean it. I didn't follow my heart, and I have regretted that decision every day since. But what I'll regret more is not following it now. I know it's asking a lot, but I would love to take you out on a date. Just the two of us. Rhys will already be with Bob and Julie, and I know Scarlett and Levi would love a date night alone, so it's the perfect opportunity."

I'm stunned silent, the words trapped on my tongue.

"Are you hesitant because of Rhys?"

I nod yes. *You have no idea.*

"Let me talk to him. See if he'd be okay with it."

I sigh. He's putting Rhys's feelings first, and it's got to be the hottest thing he or any man could do—understand that I'm a mom first. "J—"

He presses his large index finger against my lips, shushing me. I fight the upward curve of my lips.

"If he's uncomfortable with us going out, I won't be offended. I know he's the number one man in your life. I wouldn't expect anything less from you. You're a wonderful mother, and you put him first. Like a good mom should. You're doing a fantastic job raising him."

"Thank you." My voice cracks at his compliment. I don't think he knows how badly I needed to hear that, especially when I feel like a failure most days.

"I only speak the truth. His approval means something to me too. Rhys is special to me. He's the most beautiful parts of you put into a cute little package."

Okay, no, *that* was the hottest thing he's ever said to me, and he's said some really hot and dirty things to me before. My damaged and confused heart doesn't stand a chance against him.

When did it ever?

Never. Besides, I owe it to both of us to try. We deserve a chance to at least talk openly.

"What do you say? If Rhys says yes, we can go out. Get to know each other again. Talk. Anything you want. I just want to spend more time with you."

A squeaky, "Okay," leaves my mouth. "But only if Rhys is okay with it," I joke. I'm going, no matter what. Rhys won't understand. He'll probably ask if he could go with us.

Jace gives me a sexy smile, and my knees wobble at the potently beautiful sight. "He will be," he says with a cocky tone.

"Ace." I want him to know I said yes because I wanted to. Not because he thinks he needs Rhys's approval. Although, him looking for it only makes me want to go out with him even more.

Jace reaches up and places his hand on the back of my head, curling his possessive fingers in my hair at my nape. It's strangely comforting. My heart thumps wildly and my stomach somersaults in his hold.

"You called me, Ace. Say it again." His words are firm, voice gruff.

"Ace?" I whisper, confused, planting my palms on his hard, warm chest.

The honey in his eyes sparkles in the tiki torch light. I breathe him in, and this time, I do want him to kiss me. To press his plump lips to mine.

Instead, he lifts my palm up and kisses my wrist. "Not, yet." He shakes his head. "We'll get there, love. All in good time. I promise it will happen. Later."

Love? Later? What the heck is he doing to me?

"How about we head back to our table? The hula dancers are about to start, and I'm pretty sure Sadie is going to force Rhys to go with her," he continues like he didn't call me his love or hint at *later* like he used to. All sexy and seductively.

"She probably will. But don't let him fool you. He'll do anything she tells him to," I say with a laugh.

"Oh, I see ... My man." He chuckles.

I elbow him in the ribs in warning. "Don't let Levi hear you say that. He's living in denial. My gut says those two are ... something. It's gonna be a sight to see."

Jace crowds me with his big warm body, crouching down to my eye level. His breath fans across my lips, making them tingle with anticipation. "I hope they realize it before life takes them down different paths. It's a shame when you let the one get away," he admits.

His eyes capture mine, and I know he's referring to us, not the kids.

Time slows.

He inches forward.

His breath fans across my lips when he says, "Have I told you how beautiful you look tonight?"

"You might have mentioned something along those lines," I reply, breathlessly.

Zaps of electricity pass between us. He brings his hands to my face, cupping my jaw. Slowly, his hands trail down my neck, shoulders, and arms. My body automatically responds to his touch. Skin pebbling, clit throbbing, and nipples hardening. He twines our fingers together and starts walking backward, pulling me with him. Breaking the seductive spell he put on me.

"Come on. You know you don't want to miss Rhys doing the hula." He smirks.

His smile and tone are playful, but he can't hide the way his eyes blaze honey-gold with desire. He rolls his tongue over his bottom lip, biting down. Heat floods my face, skin, and core. He knows exactly what he's doing.

I roll my eyes at him, letting him lead me back to the table, pretending he didn't just get me all worked up. I'm so turned on, I think my nipples could cut glass as hard as they are.

When we arrive at our table, he pulls out my chair before taking the seat beside me, pulling me closer. He drapes his arm across the back of my chair in a sweetly possessive move.

Searching for Rhys, I find him at the front of the stage standing next to Sadie, his little brows pinched in concentration. He's watching the instructor's arm and hip movements, trying desperately to mimic the moves. He's so stinkin' adorable.

I look over at Jace who is watching Rhys. Jace shifts closer to me, but his eyes stay glued to my son. He runs his hand over his scruff-covered jaw, and I can't stop myself from wondering how it would feel to have his coarse stubble scrape the sensitive spot between my legs.

Jace's lips curl up in amusement. I can't tell if it's from my staring or the kids dancing. I wiggle in my seat, trying to adjust the shot of liquid lust that vision hit me with.

It doesn't help. I'm worked up and annoyed with myself for it.

I look over at Scarlett, and she looks at me, holding my gaze as we converse silently.

What's going on with you and Jace?

Nothing. I shrug.

Do you want something to go on? She arches her brow.

I don't know. I shrug again.

She bites her lip, thinking a bit before her next question pops up. *Are you unsure because of Sam?*

Yes. I nod.

It's going to be okay.

I know. I nod.

Her eyes soften. She mouths, *I love you,* and I return the sentiment.

I jump at the hot breath that hits my ear.

"You talking about me, Sunshine?" Jace asks.

"What? I haven't said a thing," I try playing it off.

"I saw you and Scarlett doing that thing you two do."

"What thing?" I ask, playing dumb.

"You're having one of your silent *tête-à-tête*. I know you were talking about me. You tell her how hot you are for me?" he grunts, low and rumbly, making my stomach dip.

I keep my head forward, focusing on the kids, desperately trying to keep cool. "Cocky much?"

"Nah. Just hopeful, Sunny." He runs his nose over the lobe of my ear before leaning back in his chair, giving me space.

For the next twenty minutes, we watch the kids put on a hula show.

When it's over, Rhys comes running back with a triumphant look on his face. "Momma, did you see me?"

"I did, bug. You were amazing." I pull him into my lap and wrap him up in a hug, smacking a huge kiss on his cheek, making him giggle. "Did you have fun?"

"Yup," he says proudly.

"Good job, buddy." Jace reaches over, and they bump fists.

"Thanks! It was so cool. Did you know hula dancing tells a story with the song?"

"That is pretty cool. What story did you tell with your moves?" Jace asks.

"It was a love story." Rhys groans, sticking his finger in his mouth fake-vomiting.

The entire table erupts into laughter.

Dinner flies by in a blur of laughs and amazing food. We all tried a variety of traditional dishes and desserts—even Rhys. He hated the poi but loved the dessert. Watching him try and experience new things has been such a blessing. I'm thankful my friends forced me to come on this trip. I miss feeling happy like this, burden-free. I can't remember the last time I laughed so freely, let alone smiled.

A memory of the last time I felt this happy flicks through my mind.

Our family ski trip.

The picture hanging on my wall comes into focus. Our cold, red faces beaming. Happy. It was the last trip we took before Sam got sick. Before he left me all alone. Without a safe place to fall back on when everything turns to dust.

A wave of sadness rolls over me as Sam's loss hits me hard. Grief, guilt, regret, sadness, anger, love, fear, anxiety, hurt, loneliness, longing ... fucking everything and more pull me down.

My breath hitches, strangling the flow of oxygen in my lungs. Tears flood my eyes, and I squeeze them tight, holding them back.

Please don't cry, please don't cry.

My heart starts punching through my ribs in panic.

Just breathe.

I repeat the mantra, but the panic sets in anyway.

"Hey, now. Don't slip away, Sunshine. Stay here. Stay with me," Jace whispers in my ear. He slides his warm hand over my shoulders, cupping the back of my neck, pulling my face to his chest. Comforting me from the stinging pain trying to claim me. "I got you. Come back to me, baby."

Come back to me. His words bounce around my foggy brain.

He rubs my back as I keep my face hidden, too embarrassed by the sudden change in my mood. Leaning into him, I greedily inhale his soothing aroma, finding solace in the familiar scent.

Jace pulls me closer, dropping his cheek to the top of my head. Being enveloped in his warmth and compassion feels incredible. I soak it up like a sponge until my shoulders release the tension and the tears recede.

"It's okay, Ry. It's okay to be happy. He wouldn't want you to be sad. He would want you to make new happy memories with Rhys and your family," Jace croons.

He's right. Sam would want all those things for me.

I don't know how long I stay in Jace's arms, but when I gain the courage to look up, our table is empty. My eyes automatically search for Rhys.

"He's with Scarlett and Levi. They went to the beach," Jace assures me, knowing what I need to hear to stay calm. His fingers continue to rub soothing circles on my back. "Don't worry, Ry. We got you. We told him you just needed a minute. I promised to take care of you for him."

Jace promised to take care of me?

Tears sting my nose. I hate shutting down like in front of Jace, let alone Rhys. I don't want to be this emotional mess.

"Thank you."

"No thanks required." He tilts my chin up, forcing my gaze to his. His green and gold orbs search mine. I can't take the sympathy I see in his eyes and look away.

I hear Jace's exasperated sigh, and it hurts my heart to pull away.

"Is it time to leave?"

"It can be if that's what you want."

"Please?"

"Of course. Let's get Rhys, and I'll take you both back. Maybe a hot shower and a good night's rest will make you feel better."

Jace stands, stalling for a second, but whatever he was going to do, he decides against it. He makes it a few steps away from me before I leap out of my chair and grab his wrist. He can't walk away without knowing how much I appreciate his support.

He glances at my hand wrapped around him, and I tighten my hold.

"Ace. Thank you. I ..." I shake my head, unsure how to start.

"You don't have to explain anything to me, Sunny. You lost someone important to you. I understand grief more than you know. I'm here for you. I may not have been before, but I am now. And I'm not going anywhere," he says, definitively.

I've learned the hard way that sometimes life is too big for words to hold their promise. But tonight, I want to believe his promise.

Stepping into him, I bring us chest to chest. I lift onto my tiptoes, curl my free hand around his neck, and pull him closer, shortening the distance between us. The air crackles like it does every time we are together. I don't let myself overthink. I do what my heart wants and kiss Jace.

My lips tingle as I chastely press them to his. The tingle spreads across my body, and this kiss isn't enough.

Jace stands still, letting me lead, soaking up what I'm willing to give him, as I press kisses to his upper and bottom lips, lingering on each for longer than I should. Willing him to feel my gratitude.

I'm not ready to say the words aloud quite yet, but I want him to know he means everything to me. Now and always.

I release his lips, landing on my heels. "Come on, Ace. Let's get out of here. We have a big day tomorrow."

Not ready to let him go yet, I slide my hand into his, twinning our fingers together. Hand in hand, we walk toward the beach to find my son and our friends.

A warm breeze caresses my face, lifting my hair, and a flicker of hope grows inside me, warming me from the inside out.

I hope you're right, Sam.

CHAPTER FORTY

Jace

I'm about to go to jail for indecent exposure or murder.

Rylann is a fucking vision. An angel brought down to the heavens to torture me. She somehow gets more stunning every time I see her, and I'm not the only one who notices. If I see another man dare to stare indecently at her again, I think I might blow a gasket. Not that I could blame them—she's that beautiful. Inside and out. She is the epitome of grace and beauty. I don't know how I'm going to manage keeping my eyes off her myself.

Fuck the exotic fish—she's the only thing my eyes want to see.

Today, she's wearing a white and baby blue striped one-piece with lemons and a million straps that crisscross her smooth back. She could be on the cover of the swimsuit edition. Thank fuck she's not. I'd go broke trying to make sure I owned every single copy made, so no other motherfucker could see how gorgeous she is.

I know I sound like a perv, and you'd think she was wearing some skimpy bathing suit. It's not that—it's all her. She's starting to shine. Her confidence is growing. She's finding more of herself.

Rylann rubs sunscreen across Rhys's scowling face, and like the creeper I am. I can't tear my eyes away from her body. Her heavy breasts jiggle with each movement. If I wasn't a boob man before, I would be now watching those masterpieces bounce.

She bends over to grab something out of her bag. My cock stiffens. Fuck me, I think I'm going to blow.

I can't wait to see what she decides to wear tonight for our date. Yeah, that date is happening. Even if I have to bribe Rhys, I'm taking her out tonight. That's a fucking promise.

"Take a picture. It'll last longer," Levi says, smacking me upside the head. I'd be pissed if he wasn't saving me from looking like an ass.

"Sorry ... not sorry." I toss my hands up.

"Yeah, yeah. I get it. I see Scarlett the same way. The only difference is, I'm allowed to stare. You're not."

"Yet," I mumble.

Levi grins. "How's that going for you?"

Levi is like my brother, so it's always been easy to talk to him. He has my back on this, so if anyone understands, it's him.

"Honestly? I don't know." I rub the back of my neck.

Rylann confuses the hell out of me. Don't get me wrong—I understand. Her life is different now. She's a single mom. She's still grieving. But I also want her to open her eyes and see what's right in front of her.

Me.

We are meant to be together, but right now, she's still fighting it. So I have to do all the fighting for us.

"Just keep doing what you're doing, man. Scarlett and I see it. She's starting to come around," Levi claims, making my spirit lift.

"You're right," I think aloud. She's definitely getting there. But will she get there fast enough? "She kissed me last night. After I held her and you all left for the beach."

Levi's eyebrows fly up, waiting for more information.

"It wasn't a full-on kiss. It was tentative. Sweet. But the sparks? They were still there. We still have ..." I pause, not wanting to sound like a cheeseball.

"Magic," Levi finishes for me.

We share a look, and I repeat, "Magic."

That kiss, as chaste as it was, still burned. Scorched my lips and singed my soul. I can still feel the softness of her mouth on mine. I felt her gratitude in the tenderness of her lips. I felt her desire as she lingered. I felt it *all* in that kiss.

Standing side by side, Levi and I watch our crew put on fins and goggles.

Scarlett spots us and yells, "Come on, you two. Stop staring at the goods and help out."

"Coming, dear," Levi retorts with a salute.

"Guess we're busted. We better not keep your wife waiting. I'd hate for her to embarrass me in front of the girl I like."

Levi throws his head back and laughs. "She so fucking would, Jay. My girl is cold. Hot, but *cold.*"

We laugh our way back to the group.

The teal waters of the cove glitter beyond the railing and seemingly go on forever. The view is beautiful, but not as beautiful as her. Rylann is all I see.

She looks happier today, carefree. I was worried after last night, but if Rylann is anything, it's resilient. It turns out, last night's emotional release was good for her. Cathartic.

She's been in a good mood all day, and it shows. Our relationship is slowly progressing, as is my relationship with Rhys. Everything is coming along.

The three of us enjoyed time away from the group to explore. Rylann and Rhys held onto my shoulders while I navigated us through the waters searching for sea turtles. Having them at my back was a dream come true. We easily fit together, like pieces of a puzzle. We might not have had any luck spotting said turtles—much to Rhys's chagrin—but I did get him a natural wonder to experience.

The thirty-foot geyser shoots up as I watch Rhys look on in wonder, snapping pictures with the waterproof camera I bought him. Rylann wasn't happy about that gift, but I don't care. She better get used to it. If I can make him smile, I'll do it. Same for her. I'll give her anything and everything to ensure she's happy and the smile never leaves her face.

My eyes instinctively find Rylann. She's leaning over the rails on her elbows, taking in the view. The breeze picks up, and her hair swirls in the air. She's wearing a loose white shirt and jean shorts, and even dressed simply, she stands out. She's the most beautiful woman in the world.

Rhys plops down on the bench, surprising me.

"Hey, bud. Are you having fun?" Inquiring, I look over to find him clutching his new camera tight.

"Yup. I got some cool pictures. Wanna see?" He shows me his pictures, and his eyes light up as he describes each shot.

"These are really good. You'll have to print me some copies so I can put them in my living room." He has a good eye, no doubt getting his artistic abilities from his mom.

"Really?"

"Definitely."

His dimples pop as he says, "Awesome," to the camera.

That full feeling in my chest makes an appearance as we sit quietly together.

"Are you excited to have a sleepover with Sadie and Lily tonight, with Grandma Julie and Grandpa Bob?" I like that he calls Bob and Julie Grandma and Grandpa. I think of them as bonus parents myself.

"Not really. We have sleepovers all the time," he grumbles with a shrug.

I snicker.

This kid. He has so much personality. I love it.

"Since you're busy and all, is it alright with you if I take your mom on a date?"

"Can I go?"

"Not this time."

He bites the corner of his lip, his little teeth digging in, obviously thinking really hard. "Will you take me on a date?"

Laughing at his question, I answer without hesitation, "Yes. I'd like that. We can do anything you want."

I'd love to take him out, just us two guys. The three of us. Anything, as long as we're together.

"Cool." He jumps off the bench and takes off, our conversation over.

That was easier than I thought it would be. For sure, I thought he'd hit me with a million questions. He's inquisitive like that. This means he has no idea what going on a date with Rylann implies.

Glancing up, I discover her staring at me from the metal railing she's perched on. She winks at me with a teasing smile. She knew he wouldn't understand or care. She had already decided to go out with me no matter what.

Fuck yeah.

I hope she's prepared because I'm about to woo the fuck out of her.

Picking up my phone, I text Eli, who's been helping me with my side plans. I was nervous about bringing him into the fold. He

lives to give me shit, and I didn't really want to deal with his nosy
ass. To my astonishment, he was more than happy to help.

Jace: Did you finish?

*Eli: Chill the fuck out, dude. I said I'd do it, and I did. Check
your email, dick.*
*Eli: I'm still at work, you fucker. Not all of us are on vacation
with a hot-as-hell MILF.*

Jace: **middle finger emoji**

Damn, it's late back home. I'm not surprised—Eli is married to
his career.
A text from Mason pops up, and I realize my mistake.
My message went to the group.
I roll my eyes at the shit I'm sure to hear from Cameron. He
always has something to say, whether we want to hear it or not.

Mason: Why are you still at work?

*Eli: My job requires me to be at the office. Not all of us can
work from home in our jammies.*

I bark a laugh at Eli's comment. He loves to goad Mase. Working in tech affords Mason flexibility. He travels a lot, and he's way
too high-strung to wear pajamas while working. Which is why Eli
loves to poke the grumpy bear. Okay, we all do.

*Mason: **middle finger emoji***

*Cameron: **tears laughing emoji** **tears laughing emoji***

Mason: What's your plan for tonight?

My mouth morphs into the biggest grin, thinking about my date with Rylann.

Jace: Dinner. Just the two of us. I'm thinking karaoke after. Like last time.

Eli: *Noice. Make her remember she once had the hots for you. Too bad you blew it.*

Jace: Who's the dick now?

Cameron: *Let's go back to this whole MILF thing. She has a kid now?*

Jace: Yes. A son.

Mason: *You ready to be in this kid's life too? You do this, and he's a package deal.*

Eli: *Good point.*

Why would they think this would change my mind?

I love every part of her, and that includes her son. Having a kid isn't a deal-breaker for me. Never has been. I've always pictured myself being a father one day. It doesn't matter that Rhys doesn't belong to me—I'd love and care for him like I would my own flesh and blood.

Jace: I know. I'd be in if she had 5 kids.

Eli: *Props.*

Cameron: *She still hot as fuck?*

Jace: Don't talk about her like that.

Cameron: Touchy.

Jace: Not that it's any of your business, but yes. She's still hot AF. And mine.

Cameron: Don't worry, bro, MILFs aren't my cup of tea. No, thanks. Hard pass on kids.

Mason: Grow up Cam. There's more to life than banging jersey chasers.

*Cameron: **middle finger emoji***
Cameron: Why fuck regular girls when jersey hoes know the score? In and out. Literally.
Cameron: I don't need complications.

Mason: Charming as ever.

Eli: He's not wrong.

Cameron: See?!

Eli: Kid, just make sure you wrap it up or your dick's gonna fall off. I've seen some of those chicks.
*Eli: **GIF of Jerry Seinfeld shivering***

Mason: Agreed.

I laugh out loud. I want to feel bad for the kid, but he really does need to keep it wrapped up. I've been to a few of his games in L.A., and some of the girls hanging outside the locker room are questionable.

Cameron: Fuck off! I make sure the chicks are quality.

Eli: Sure you do, kid.

Mason: More like quantity.

Shaking my head at their insanity, I check the time. Five minutes until I pick up my girl for our date. I need to put an end to this before it goes on all night. I have better things to do than listen to my brothers rip on each other.

Jace: I didn't text you assholes for this shit. Why I text in the group is beyond me.

Cameron: It's cuz you miss us, bro. Can't go a day without us.

Jace: No, I don't.

Eli: Liar. Now, stop bugging me. I have shit to do.
Eli: Oh ... And don't fuck it up this time.

Cameron: Yeah, woo the fuck out of her.

Mason: For once, I'm with them. Good luck, bro.

Eli: Seriously. Don't fuck it up. We can't deal with you being a sad sack anymore.

Jace: I'm not a sad sack, and thanks for the vote of confidence.
Jace: And I'm not going to fuck it up.

Cameron: *We'll see. 50 bucks says he shits the bed.*

Jace: You're a dick, kid.

Eli: *I'm in. I'm always happy to take your baseball money. Big bro isn't going to fuck it up this time.*

Mason: *I'm with E. I look forward to getting that 50. You got this, J.*

Jace: Thanks.

I switch over to my email, and just like Eli said it would be, the confirmation emails are sitting in my inbox.

My other surprise for Rylann is also ready to go with the concierge. Excitement courses through me. With any luck, Rylann will be willing to take a chance and go on an extra adventure.

Pocketing my phone, room key, and wallet, I'm out the door.

CHAPTER FORTY-ONE

Jace

Rylann swings the door swings open, taking my breath away with it.

Fuck me dead.

My jaw hits the floor, struck dumb by how unbelievably stunning she looks. My cock springs to life in my pants and wants to forget all about dinner.

"Do I look okay?"

Words evade me as I openly ogle her in the middle of the hallway, checking her out from head to toe.

Her long brown hair is curled and pinned on one side, leaving her neck bare, except for the thin gold chain. Her bronze skin glows in contrast against the white flowy jumpsuit she's wearing. The V-shaped neckline dips low, providing me with an eyeful of cleavage. If I could bury my face in those glorious tits, I'd die a happy man. The tie at her waist accentuates her curves. Wide pant legs with thigh-high slits show off her toned legs. Legs I picture wrapped around my hips as I pound into her all night long.

She's sheer per-fucking-fection.

"Jace?"

My eyes slowly drift up her body until they reach those rich brown depths that sparkle at me. I'm drunk on her already.

Ry smiles, her cheeks lightly flushed. Reaching out, she shuts my mouth. Twisting her body side to side, I watch the fabric swish teasing me with those silky thighs.

"I take it you like my outfit then?"

"You look fuckin' stunning." My voice sounds gravelly. Down-right lust-filled.

She bites down on her glossy bottom lip, and I swear my dick is going to explode in my pants.

My control slips and I grab her hips, pulling her flush to my body. I run my nose over her neck, breathing in her coconutty scent before placing a kiss on her jaw.

"Ravishing," I praise.

She responds with a sigh that has my dick growing harder. I need to get us out of here.

Grabbing her hand and lacing our fingers together, I pull her out of the room and march us to the elevator as quickly as I can.

"Ace!" She yelps, laughing, struggling to keep up with my long strides.

There is no way I can slow down. At the elevator, I push the call button roughly. Three times. I need this stupid-ass elevator to hurry. I have a plan, and I refuse to let anything get in the way. Even myself.

"You know, this reminds me of something," Rylann her lip with her finger.

Of course, I do.

Arching my brow, the caveman in me growls, "Really? You want to bring that up?"

Her eyes widen, our past conversation playing loudly in the silence. The same need that had me wanting to do some very *ungentlemanly* things to her then overwhelms me now.

"Yeah, that's what I thought," I grunt.

The elevator arrives, and I place my hand on the small of her back, guiding her on and leading her to the back corner, away from others.

She clears her throat. "So, where are we going for dinner?"

"I reserved a table at the same restaurant as last time."

"Really?" She lights up with excitement.

"Yes. Would I lie?"

"Never," she whispers, wringing her hands nervously.

"Hey, are you good?" I tilt her chin up to look into her eyes. She's trepidatious. A lot has changed rapidly between us on this trip, let alone over the past seven years. "Breathe, Sunny. I'm right here with you. I promise."

I've never meant it more.

I pull out Rylann's chair for her to sit, then take my seat across from her. It's surreal, being back in the same restaurant with her. The decor is the same though moved into a different configuration. The ambiance is the same as I remember, serene and tropical.

Rylann brings her menu down to her chest and leans forward to whisper at me like we're in on some crazy conspiracy. "It feels the same but looks different. Doesn't it?"

"I was thinking the same thing." We share a smile.

She's much calmer after the elevator ride and the walk here. Our conversation was light. We spoke about Rhys and how much fun he had today. I got another earful about the camera, but she laughed, so I don't think I'm really in trouble over it.

The waiter arrives, taking our food and cocktail orders. We opt to share a bottle of wine and a deconstructed poke bowl appetizer. For the main course, Rylann asks the waiter for his suggestions. The older gentleman happily explains the menu, and they chat about food for a bit before he walks away. I didn't hear a word—I was too busy watching her.

"What did you decide on?" I ask.

Rylann beams. "I went with the sea scallops. Olly said the saffron risotto with spicy shrimp oil is to die for."

"Sounds delicious, Sunshine." I love that she's on a first-name basis with the waiter like they've been friends forever.

Olly returns with our wine and places the appetizer in the middle of the table.

Rylann then proceeds to torture me. First, she licks away a droplet of wine from her bottom lip and hums. Then, she leans over, takes a bite of food, and moans in what can only be described as ecstasy. My cock hardens at the sound. She moans again, and it reminds me of the ones she made mid-orgasm. When she licks her bottom lip, catching the juices with her tongue, I'm done. She has me close to blowing a load at the table. She wipes her mouth with the cloth napkin and places it back in her lap, oblivious to the fact that she's turning me on.

"You have to try some of this." Holding out her fork, she offers me a bite.

I grasp her wrist, lean forward, and bring the bite to my lips. Focused on my mouth, her eyes widen as she watches me wrap my lips around the tines of her fork.

I hum at the explosion of flavor in my mouth, the same way she did.

"You're right. That's good." I watch her run her fingertips over her neck.

She bites that sexy lip again, looking turned on as fuck.

I'm right there with you, Sunshine.

When we've finished our entrée, I take a deep breath and steady myself. What I'm about to suggest is a big ask. But it's now or never, and never isn't an option.

"Ry, first off, thank you for coming to dinner with me. Thank you for spending time with me and allowing me to get to know you and Rhys. Second, and I know this is seven years too late, but I am so sorry. Not a day goes by that I don't regret how things played out—"

"Jace ..." she interrupts, but I shut her down. I need to get this out.

"Shh, Sunny. Please let me finish. I hate the way we ended. I treated you and our relationship horribly. I was an idiot. Please forgive me. I ..." My voice cracks.

Rylann places her delicate palm on the back of my hand, calming the ache in my chest. "No. There is nothing to forgive."

I shake my head—there is.

I let the best thing that ever happened to me walk away without giving us a real chance. I've had to live with that guilt and regret every day since.

"I didn't handle things well either. We both gave up. But we can't change the past. We have to keep moving forward. That's one of the hardest things I've learned this past year."

"You're right. We can't change the past." I take a deep breath. "You know, being back here has put a lot of things in perspective for me." I pull at my collar, my heart hammering away.

She probably thinks I'm going to profess my undying love. Which I would, but even I know she's not ready to hear that. We will get there.

"Spending time with you and Rhys these last couple of days has been amazing," I confess.

"I agree," she says with a sweet smile. "Everything you have done has made this trip amazing. It means so much to me. The way you supported me yesterday, I ..." She gets choked up. "It just means a lot to me. *You've* always meant a lot to me. Jace, I need you to know—"

I cut her off. I don't want her to thank me for comforting her. I would do anything to make her feel better. To make her happy. "I really hope I don't scare you here, but I would like to take you and Rhys to the big island for a few days. Just the three of us. We still have something here, and I want to figure that out together. Whatever we are includes Rhys. I know that. I want him too. Let me do this for you two. Let me show you how good things can be. What do you say? Are you willing to take a chance and go on a little adventure with me?"

Chapter Forty-Two

Rylann

My mouth falls open. I'm in complete and utter shock. My brain synapses have come to a complete halt.

Did he just ask me—us—to go on a trip with him? Just the three of us.

Yes, he did.

He's insane.

I don't know what to say. My heart soars and dips at the idea of the three of us doing our own thing. No distractions. It could be the perfect opportunity.

"Umm ... Mmm." It suddenly feels like I'm dining inside a fiery volcano. Throat dry, I reach for my water, and—hand shaking—I take a long sip.

I need to slow this crazy train down a touch. I can't bring myself to say yes. Yet.

You know you're going to agree.

It's true. I can't say no to him. It's always been that way when it comes to Jace.

"You okay there, Sunshine?" He laughs, his knee bouncing under the table assuring me I'm not the only one nervous in this situation.

"Why couldn't you ask at the end of the date, like a normal person?" I toss out, and Jace scoffs a laugh.

"I'm sorry. I don't need your answer now. You have time to think it over and give me your answer ... later?" He winks at me, and my knees snap together.

Why does he have to say "later" all silky and rough like that?

"I think that would be best. Let's see how this date goes first." Putting down my water, I pick up my wine and take a swig.

"I'm about to wine and dine you so hard, you won't be able to say no."

Now, it's my turn to scoff at his cockiness.

He's exactly the way I remember him. Unapologetic about going for what he wants. His honesty, vulnerability, and charm are all qualities that won me over then and keep chipping away at my resolve now.

"This could end up being the worst date ever. You never know." I shrug and take another sip of wine.

"Fat chance, love. It's going to be the best night of your life. You can count on it," he says like it's a foregone conclusion.

I grin at him like a goofy idiot. I wish I understood the power he has over me.

I pick up my glass, lifting it up for a toast. "To the best date of our life ... maybe."

"Definitely."

I roll my eyes at the smug grin on his face as he lifts his glass to mine.

Dinner was fantastic.

Even though I'm getting to know Jace all over again, he is still very much the same. Through dinner we chatted easily, getting reacquainted with each other. With no further mention of his offer, our conversation focused mostly on my life back home and all things Rhys.

I forgot how easy it is to talk and banter with him. It feels as though no time has passed between us, and yet everything has changed. While we briefly hit on the past, there is still more we have to discuss. I know I need to put on my big-girl panties and have a real conversation with him about some things, but I just don't want to.

I'm being selfish. I want to enjoy this moment before real life hits us upside the head. When I'm with him, everything else melts away and it's easy to pretend I'm not addled with anxiety or crippled with anguish and anger on a daily basis. Make-believe doesn't hurt like reality.

My reality is having Rhys to worry about and a business to run. There is no way either of us can just pick up and move. It wouldn't be unfair to ask him to give up his life for me. He has his own business and family to worry about.

That leaves us with Hawaii. Same as last time.

My stomach sinks, thinking about walking away from Jace. Or him walking away from me, which is more likely.

His fingers squeeze mine, bringing me back to the present.

Excitement fizzles in my stomach when I glimpse down at our joined hands. He's held it ever since he picked me up at my door, his mouth hanging open. The butterflies in my stomach make an appearance, remembering the way his eyes heated as he checked me out.

We reach a white building with a neon sign reading *Blue Hawaiian Blues* above the double door, and I know exactly what he's doing. He's reinventing our first moments together.

"Fair warning," he says, opening the door for me, "this place is new, but it should still bring back a few memories."

He lets go of my hand only to replace it on the small of my back. My body heats and whizzes with excitement at his touch.

I walk into an all-white vestibule, and I'm hit with the smell of greasy food and alcohol. The hostess stands at a small desk and smiles, the blue and green neon sign glowing behind her flickering.

Thumping bass notes begin to vibrate, and then I hear it. The wailings of an unprofessional singer ring in my ears. I knew it.

Unable to help it, I throw my head back in a boisterous laugh. "How did I know you were going to bring me here?"

He wraps his arms around my waist, chin resting on my head, bringing me back to his chest. My body automatically melts to his hold. "It worked last time. Why mess with a good thing?" He kisses the back of my head and greets the hostess.

She leads us down a long hallway to an open room with a wall-to-wall bar decorated with a tiki flare. Banquets and tables surround the stage. The hostess seats us at a small cocktail table, letting us know a cocktail waitress will be by shortly, leaving us to ourselves.

"Well, now that you got me here, what are you going to do with me?" I tease. I haven't stepped foot in a karaoke bar since the last time I was in Hawaii. Too many memories.

"As I see it, I think I'm owed a rematch."

"You are, are you?"

He nods sharply. "You cheated last time."

I gasp at his accusation, hand clutching my invisible pearls in exaggeration. "I would *never*!"

"Oh, but you did, Sunny. You got up on stage, shook your sexy ass all over it, and made all the men,"—I raise a disapproving eyebrow at his comment—"*and* women in the room cheer and fawn all over you. It's supposed to be about the singing, not the dancing. Thus, you cheated."

"You loved it when I shook my ass." Batting my lashes, I lean forward and rest my chin on my fist.

He copies me, and whispers, "I loved it more when you let me grab it and bite it."

"Jace! You perv." His unexpected dirty words make my sex clench. I teasingly punch his bicep. His very hard, bulging bicep.

"I saw you checking me out." He lifts his dress shirt, flashing me his washboard abs.

I was watching him at the beach. Him in those board shorts that hug his firm ass and thick, strong thighs. His naked chest glistening with droplets of water I wanted to lick up.

I pinch his stomach and he yelps, pulling his shirt down.

"Maybe. But you're the one that was being a horn dog watching me put on sunblock. Your tongue was practically buried in the sand, you were perving out so hard."

He barks a laugh and shrugs, not bothered in the slightest by being called out for being a creep. Not that I cared one bit. I felt his eyes linger on me, trail over my body, scorching my skin. I don't have to see him to know he's watching me or that he's near. I feel him.

"I wasn't trying to be stealthy, Sunshine. Wherever you are, whatever you're doing, I'm watching. You have all of my attention, always." Jace places his hand on my knee, sending a jolt of electricity through me, making my clit pulse.

"You sound like a stalker. Should I be worried you're going to become obsessed with me and follow me around from now on?"

He runs his hand up my thigh. "You're not ready for me to answer that question."

Well, fuck me sideways.

The waitress shows up, diffusing the tension. Jace orders us a round of margaritas, bringing back more memories.

I get it. This whole night is about getting me to remember the past. How we fell.

"Relax. We're here to have some fun." He leans in and kisses my cheek.

I nod, looking toward the stage. My nerves spike. I don't want to get up there and sing in front of everyone. Past me would have been up there in a heartbeat. I miss that girl. But that girl is long-gone these days.

I continue to sip my drink, and people get up and sing their hearts out.

Jace leans in, his leathery cologne invading my senses and his warm breath tickling my ear. "Time to get out of that head and let go."

Turning my head, our noses bump lightly, barely an inch separating our lips. Sparks flare in the space between. His pupils dilate, and his nostrils flare.

I shiver as he tucks a lock of my hair behind my ear.

"Sunshine?"

"Hmm?" My eyes bounce from his eyes to his lips.

"It's my turn. You sit here and keep looking at me like that."

The edges of my mouth quirk up at his smug comment. He glides his thumb over my bottom lip. The urge to bite the pad of his finger and suck it into my mouth overwhelms me. I shut it down.

"Now, be a good girl and cheer on your man. I'll be back." Dropping his hand, he walks away. All swagger.

Sucking in a ragged breath, I watch him take the stage. Microphone in hand, he waits for the song to start. He's wearing a light gray dress shirt, with the top two buttons undone, dark gray jeans, and black sneakers. He looks especially sexy.

He catches my eye and flashes me a sexy wink. My heart flutters, and my pussy pulses with desire like it did the last time we were together.

The song starts, and the opening beat to *No Diggity* begins.

I grin at him. This is one of my favorites, and an innuendo if I ever heard one. I watch him rap and dance around a bit, but it's nothing like it was all those years ago.

"Not bad, Ace," I shout over the cheers as he sits back at our table.

"I know," he declares. "It's your turn next."

I shake my head. "Oh, no. I can't."

"Yes, you can."

After another margarita and a whole lot of Jace's trash-talking, I find myself on the stage. I guess I'm still not one to back away from a challenge.

If he wants to rap about sex, I can return the favor. The intro for Salt & Peppa's *Shoop* starts, and the words fly out of my mouth. Muscle memory has me dancing to the beat, and I finally let go.

When the song ends, Jace is up from his seat, clapping and rushing me as I approach the table. He wraps his arms around my waist, lifts me in the air, and spins me around.

He plants a kiss on my forehead and places me back on my feet. "You're amazing. Let's get out of here."

CHAPTER FORTY-THREE

Rylann

My body is still humming from the excitement of being up on stage as we walk back to our hotel.

I haven't tapped into that part of myself in so long that I forgot how amazing the adrenaline rush feels when I take on a new challenge and just roll with it. The excitement. The freedom. The fun.

I hate how sad and boring my life has become. Not that I don't love my life. I do. Rhys is my everything. I cannot imagine it without him. Being his mom is the greatest joy in my life. Motherhood comes with a whole new set of priorities. It transforms you into a different version of yourself. Mom life makes it easy to forget the person you were before.

With Sam passing, all the parental duties are mine to carry. I'm both of Rhys's parents, and it's doubly exhausting. I miss having someone to hold me when things get hard. I miss having someone care for me too. Someone to wake up with. Someone to share life with.

I sigh at my wayward thinking.

"Penny for your thoughts?" Jace's question snaps me out of my head.

"I was just thinking how great it felt up there, then my mind started to ..." I circle the air with my index finger. "Spiral."

Jace pulls me back flush against the building, pressing his chest to mine. My body heats at the contact. He tilts my chin up, and our eyes lock.

"Life gets heavy sometimes. That old adage, *Time heals all wounds* is garbage. We just learn to live with the pain. To keep going. Every day, it hurts a little less. But you don't have to do this alone anymore. I'm here now. I've got you."

"Ace," I whisper, tears stinging my eyes. His words are similar to the ones my mom repeats to me daily. At this moment, there is so much I want to tell him. Instead, all that comes out is, "Thank you."

He nods, backing up, taking the heat of his body with him. He holds my hand again, guiding us back toward our hotel. We walk in comfortable silence for a few blocks. Disappointment pools in my stomach. I don't want the night to be over yet.

"Would you be interested in sitting on the beach for a bit?" I ask Jace, flipping the scene.

Jace's mouth turns up in a smile. "I'd love to. I'm not ready for the night to end."

"Me neither," I confess.

Instead of sitting on the sand, Jace finds us an oversized lounge chair close to the hotel. We sit side by side, leaning back, our fingers still clasped together. I don't know if it's the sound of the lapping ocean, the cool breeze kicking off the sea, or the small scattering of stars in the distance, but a feeling of peace falls over me.

It's none of those things.

It's him. Jace is the reason I feel lighter.

"Ry?"

"Yeah."

"Did you have a good life?"

"I did." I really did.

"I'm glad. I missed you."

"Me too." I squeeze his hand tighter. Because I did miss him. So much. Curiosity gnaws at me. "Were you?"

"Happy?"

I nod.

"No," he answers sadly.

"Do you want to tell me about it?"

"Are you ready to hear about it?"

I turn onto my side to face him, and he does the same. I'm greeted with sadness and regret swimming behind his hazel gaze, and it breaks my heart.

"I want to know everything about you, Jace Miller. I always have."

A soft smile graces his lips. "I was never truly happy after ..." He pauses. He doesn't have to say it for me to know. "I tried to be. I really did. But I just couldn't ever get back there with Alina. The only time I was remotely happy was when I thought about being a father." His eyes close in pain at the memories. Cupping his face, I run my thumb over his cheekbone, wishing I could take away his hurt with a touch. "There wasn't anything either of us could do. This sort of thing just happens, no rhyme or reason. One month, there was a heartbeat, and the next, there wasn't. I took it harder than she did. I was so angry with her for that. I wanted to blame her for ... everything." Agony morphs his features.

Instinctively, I move closer, draping my arm over his waist, and hug him tightly to my chest. It's obvious, despite the years, that his memories still torment him.

"What happened with her?" A part of me doesn't want to know, but I do. I've always been curious. My first impression was that she was beautiful, with her long legs, blonde hair, and blue eyes. She was regal-looking, sophisticated. But she also looked too put together and cold.

My exact opposite in every way.

He brushes my hair behind my ear before pulling me to his chest, resting his cheek on my head. "Long story short. After we lost the baby, I was broken up. Went to therapy. Alina was ... Alina. She buried herself in work while I grieved. I was angry with her, with myself, with life. I was in a dark place. We fought constantly. I tried to make our marriage work. She'd all but given up. That went on for a few years until I finally convinced her to do marriage counseling. That lasted one session. She confessed to not wanting a baby and being relieved she didn't have to become a mother."

My jaw drops at his rushed confession. How could she say that to him?

Jace goes quiet, and I squeeze him tighter. I hate that he went through all this alone because I know Jace. There is no way he told his family about this.

"You don't have to answer this if it's too much, but why? Why would she say that to you?" How callous is this woman that she would say that to him? Being a parent is a gift.

He kisses the top of my head, pulling me closer to his side, and takes a deep breath before continuing. "That same session, she also confessed to having an affair with a partner at her firm. He was older and married. She told me that they had been together before we broke up and that she loved him. He ended their relationship before she found out she was pregnant. Since there was overlap, she wasn't sure if the baby was mine but couldn't bring herself to have an abortion. She married me to save face with her family. I should have known something was up. Things were off for months before we called it quits. She railroaded me into getting married. She knew that I would do right by her. The lies are the thing that kills me the most. She knew I would do anything for my family, and she used it against me. Like a fool, I let her."

I gasp as red-hot anger burns in my stomach. I understand not wanting to give up your child, but she's a coward.

The nerve of that woman hurting this wonderful man. A man that gave her his heart. His everything. All so she wouldn't look bad. "That's fucking awful. I'm so sorry she did that to you."

His confession is like a punch to the gut. My held-back tears finally spill free. This poor man has endured so much; while I was off having a wonderful life, he was hurting.

He wipes my tears away with his thumb. "Shh, please don't cry, Sunshine. Don't feel bad for me. I made my choices, however wrong they were. I still chose them." He's right, but it still hurts me.

"Where is she now?" I ask.

"After our divorce, she moved back to New York for work, and about a month after the papers were signed, she was engaged to another lawyer."

"Wow, what a fucking bitch." I slap a hand over my mouth. I didn't mean to say that out loud. I hate talking negatively about anyone, even if all signs point to them being a bitch.

Jace throws his head back and howls with laughter. The rich and rumbly sound is infectious, and I laugh with him.

"Shit, I needed that. Thank you. And you're right. She is a bitch," he says, which sends us into another laughing fit.

Jace readjusts us, resting my head on his shoulder while he lays on his back. My body fits perfectly in the nook of his arm. Like this spot was made for me. I burrow in deeper, hating the fact that our night is ending.

"It's getting late," he says.

"I know," I agree.

Neither of us moves for a few more minutes

"Come on, up you go." Swinging his legs over the chair, he stands, towering over me.

Without a word, he scoops me up, my legs dangling in the air, and I giggle. Another reminder of our all-night talk on the beach.

He places me on my feet, takes my hand in his, and steers us inside the hotel. The air is thick with a newfound tension between us. It skirts the lines of longing and desire, mixed with excitement and a dash of fear, at least on my end.

When we arrive at my door, he places his hands on my hips, turning me to face him. My gaze bounces between his mouth and his eyes.

"I really want to kiss you," he whispers. His hazel eyes reflect the same burning desire I feel inside.

This is a bad idea.

"I really want you to kiss me," I reply, licking my bottom lip.

Slowly, Jace bows his head, brow arched, giving me one last out before he continues. I nod, reaching onto my tiptoes and pressing my lips to his.

Our mouths meet in a kiss that's been years in the making.

He takes his time exploring my mouth, his tongue massaging mine in a sensual dance, slow and deep.

My knees give out as the earth falls beneath my feet.

His arms circle my body, holding me up, as we cling to each other. He tastes like my favorite drink, sweet and sour with a hint of tequila, and all him.

Gliding my palms over his shoulders, I thread my fingers in his hair, tugging the soft strands, pulling him closer. My body is in total control. There is no more thinking, only doing, and right now, it wants to do Jace.

Badly.

The deep vibrations of his groans roll through my body like little bolts of electricity making me hot and needy. Our kiss goes from sweet to full-on turn-the-burner-up, flaming-hot in seconds.

He grinds his very stiff cock into my lower stomach, triggering a deep ache in my belly that makes my whole pussy pulse with need. Throbbing, I lift my leg, wrapping it around his hip, grinding my hot center into him. He grips my upper thigh, and my back hits the hard surface of the door, deepening our kiss. His lips on mine are a reminder of the passion we shared. No one has ever brought my body to life like Jace.

A sudden ding from the elevator has us ripping our mouths away and me dropping my leg to the ground. Our quick breaths mingle in the small space between our lips. Jace covers my body, hiding me from view, as a group of people walk down the corridor.

Thank god for the interruption because I'm not so sure we would have had the willpower to stop. That kiss was without a doubt next-level explosive.

Jace steps back, watching me, waiting for me to retreat. But after that kiss, I don't feel like running or fighting anymore.

"I need you to open your door and go inside, Sunshine." The firmness in his tone has me pulling out my key.

I do as I'm told.

When I open the door, the room is lit with a hundred electric votive candles, and yellow flowers cover every surface.

What in the world ...

Jace comes to stand behind me, wrapping his arms around me and resting his chin on my head.

"What did you do?" I whisper.

Instead of answering me, he leads me to the bathroom, where more candles and another bouquet of yellow flowers await me. "I know leaving with me on a mini trip is a big ask. It doesn't only mean new experiences for you and Rhys; it also means you're open to the possibility of us. I know what I want, Sunshine. You. Rhys. All of it. Now, when I leave, I want you to take a bath, relax, and really think about what you want. If you don't want to go, that's fine. I'll cancel everything. I will be here waiting, no matter how long it takes."

I turn and bury my head in his chest, hugging him tightly. Tears sting my nose at his thoughtful gesture. Yes, he's being pushy as all get-out, but he's also giving me the opportunity to choose. He's giving me space to figure out what I want. It's terrifying because what I really want is him.

I want him to be there for all the small things. The big things. All of it. I want him to be the one that takes care of me. Be my biggest supporter. My everything. And I want to be the same for him.

It's just ...

Leaning back, I stare into his eyes. "Thank you, Ace. This is the sweetest thing anyone has ever done for me."

"You deserve to have someone take care of you. I want to be that person. But I also want you to know there is no time limit on us. This is our new beginning. Now, give me your cell."

"Why?" I pull my phone from my clutch.

He grabs it, holds it up to my face, then types something on the screen. A second later, a muffled buzz sounds from his pocket.

"Now you have my number. When you decide, you call me. I'll be waiting." He hands me my phone.

I look at the contact information and smile. He listed himself as *Ace of my Heart*. The crazy man in front of me is exactly that.

"Nice," I say, pointing at my phone.

He responds with a cocky smile that I happily return.

"I had a wonderful night."

"Me too." He cups my face and runs his thumb over my cheek as if I'm his most precious possession, and kisses it. "Good night, love. I'll be waiting for your call."

I nod, and he walks out the door, leaving me still standing in the bathroom, surrounded by candles and the sweet scent of flowers.

Filling up the tub with hot water, I strip and get in.

For the next thirty minutes, I pretend to think about the pros and cons. I should say no to him. Slow us down and move out of the fast lane.

It's the smart thing to do.

But I'm not smart. Not where Jace is concerned. He makes me love-stupid.

CHAPTER FORTY-FOUR

Jace

The hot water burns my skin, loosening the tension in my neck as I shower.

Walking away from Rylann after that hot-as-fuck kiss was not easy though necessary. I am finally making headway, getting her to drop her walls and let me in.

Reaching for the shampoo, I wash my hair before grabbing the soap and squirting some gel on my palms, working them into a lather. My cock hardens, thinking about our kiss in the hallway.

I didn't expect our first kiss to be anything more than sweet. I only wanted a little taste to hold me over. I should know better when it comes to Rylann and our intense connection. As soon as my lips molded around her soft ones, it was like seven years' worth of combustible chemistry coming to a head.

I fist my hard cock, stroking it from root to tip, using my soap-covered hand as lubrication. She was so responsive, her body melting into mine, begging for more. When she wrapped her leg around my hip and ground her hot pussy into my thigh, I almost lost my mind. We went at each other in the hallway, grappling, kissing, and moaning into each other's mouths. Hands down the hottest first kiss I've ever had.

Stroking my dick harder, I recall Rylann's hard nipples brushing against my chest. The sweet and tangy taste of her lips on mine. I can't wait to taste her sweetness again.

My balls tingle, signaling my orgasm, and I can't stop taking my fantasy further.

I picture her soft curves under my hands as I run them up her thighs and spread her legs wide. I run the head of my cock through her wet folds before thrusting forward and filling her completely. Her head bangs against the tiled wall as I piston in and out of her tight, wet heat under the shower's spray.

With her name on my lips, I explode, emptying myself onto the shower floor.

Fuck. I don't think I've ever made myself come that hard or that fast before.

After a couple of calming breaths, I feel more relaxed.

Quickly rinsing off, I turn off the shower, dry up, and throw on a pair of boxers for bed. Laying down, I pick up my phone. No message yet.

I hope I made the right choice by giving her time to think.

Our talk on the beach was intense. Talking about Alina is a challenge for me. We didn't touch on the subject of Rylann's marriage, other than her saying she was happy. I have a lot of mixed emotions about him. Them. Their life.

As much as her good life pains me, I'd never want her to be anything less than happy. I love her too much.

After hearing about the disaster that was my marriage, Rylann was so quick to comfort me. It both broke and healed me. Even though I hurt her, her compassion knows no bounds.

My phone beeps, and my heart leaps in my chest.

My Sunshine: Are you still awake?

I tap her contact info and call, needing to hear her voice. It rings once before she answers.

"Hi," she murmurs softly. The sound of water lapping in the background catches my attention. Fuck me, she's still in the bathtub.

My dick thickens as visions of her naked and wet fill my brain.

"Hey," I grit out between my teeth.

"Are you okay?"

"No," I grunt.

"What's wrong?"

"Sunshine, you're calling me from the bathroom, where I know you are lying naked and wet in a tub full of water. What do you think is wrong with me?" I all but growl, and she giggles.

She fucking giggles, and I'm a goner. As is my dick that is now standing at full attention.

When her giggles subside, she says, "Ask me again."

My pulse races, my heart working double time. *Please say yes, baby.*

"I'm leaving for the big island tomorrow. Are you going to take a chance and go on a little adventure with me?"

The line goes silent, except for the sound of the water lapping.

"Yes, Ace. I'll go with you," she squeaks. "We'll go with you."

Fuck yes! I sit up in bed, bringing my back to the headboard. I'm wide awake now. My mind and body are reeling with the possibilities. "So, I was right then—best date ever?"

"It was pretty good." I can hear the smile in her voice as she answers blandly.

"Not going to make it easy for me, are you?"

"Where would the fun be in that?" she muses, making me grin like an idiot at my phone.

"Fair enough. I'll just have to do better … later." Her breath hitches, and I can't stop myself from picturing her hands under the water, between her legs. Touching herself to thoughts of me. "Goodnight, Sunshine."

"Goodnight, Ace."

She cuts off our call as I sit there, phone in hand, unmoving, and undoubtedly the happiest man alive.

She agreed to take a chance on us.

My alarm goes off, pulling me out of sleep. Stretching out the kinks and yawning, I hear my text notification go off. The fuck? It's too early for this. Checking my cell, I have four notifications.

I answer Levi first.

Levi: Breakfast at 8:00. See you there. Did she say yes?

Jace: I'll be there. She said yes.

I smile to myself. I told Levi my plan yesterday, hoping that if she said no, he and Scarlett would be willing to help persuade her. Luckily, I won't be needing their help.

Swiping out, I switch to the group chat, named Bro-tally Awesome by Cameron. Seems like everyone wants to know what happened.

Eli: What's the verdict?

Cameron: Did she say yes or what? You're killing us over here.

Mason: I'm with them. Tell us already.

Jace: She said yes.

Cameron: Fuck yeah! Now, you just have to seal the deal.

Mason: *Take it easy, kid. Not everyone thinks with their dicks.*

Eli: *Only the smart ones do.*

I roll my eyes. Eli jokes and talks a big game, but deep down, he's not that guy. Sure, he flirts and used to sleep around, but I know he wants more than just sex. He hasn't been with anyone in a long time.

Not since ... I shake my head. I can't even remember.

Cameron: *LOL. True story, bro **Eggplant emoji** **Water emoji***

Jace: Enough. I'm going down to breakfast. Then, I'm off to the big island. I might be incommunicado for a few days.

Mason: *Sounds good, J. Good luck and have fun.*

Eli: *Please don't fuck it up. Or I'll have to fly there myself and steal her away from you.*

Jace: **Middle Finger emoji**
Jace: You can't have her. Ever.

Cameron: ***GIF of Dwight from the Office saying We'll See***

Eli: ***Finger pointing up emoji***
Eli: *What he said.*
Eli: *Don't forget the condoms!*

Cameron: *Oh, yeah. Def wrap it up, brother.*

Bunch of fucking assholes. I'm not thinking with my dick. This trip is about so much more.

Locking my phone, I put it on the side table and get up. After pulling on some clothes and brushing my teeth, I pack my bag, leaving behind a few things since we will only be gone for a few nights.

Pocketing my phone, room key, and wallet, I leave my bag, knowing I'll need to come back upstairs to help Rylann carry her and Rhys's bags.

Walking into the restaurant, my eyes automatically search for her. She's at a table with everyone, menus in hand, and an empty seat awaits me beside her.

"Jace! Over here!" Rhys yells from across the room.

My heart grows three sizes, like Grinch's, every time he sees me and his face lights up.

"What's up, little man?" I mess up his mop of hair, and he giggles. He's adorable. I can't wait to take him on this trip. He's gonna have a blast.

"Morning, everyone." I pull out the chair and sit down. I lean over and whisper in Rylann's ear, "You saving this seat for me, Sunshine?"

Goosebumps break out along her arm at my breath tickling her ear.

See what I mean? Responsive.

I can't help but smugly grin at her.

She glares at me, fighting a smile. "Don't make me regret it," she sasses, making me laugh.

I love when she gets saucy and playful. A fierce urge to kiss her hits me. I tuck that feeling away and peck her cheek. I gotta do this all the right way.

"So, what's on the agenda for today?" Scarlett asks, playing ignorant. Such a little shit-stirrer, that one.

"You're such a brat," Rylann mumbles to her friend.

I twist my body to face Rylann. "If it's okay with you, I was wondering if you wouldn't mind if I talked to Rhys myself after breakfast. You know, man to man."

I swear I see hearts in her eyes when I suggest talking to him myself. My internal fists pump in the air.

This is exactly what I need to keep doing. Showing her how important Rhys is to me too. Prove to her that I am all in with her, and that includes her son.

"That would be wonderful, thank you. He doesn't know yet. I wanted to wait for you."

My heart leaps in my chest at her admission. "Thank you," I whisper.

Unable to resist touching her, I place my hand on her exposed knee under the table. She stills under my hand before relaxing into my touch. She places her hand on mine, keeping it there for the rest of our meal.

Breakfast flies by in a flurry of stories and laughs. It feels damn good being at this table full of wonderful people. Levi and Scarlett are still sickeningly happy and in love. I envy them. I want that kind of relationship with Rylann. I want us to look at each other with the same love and devotion.

Looking around, I take in everyone at the table. The kids are laughing, Scarlett and Levi are kissing, and Bob and Julie are chatting to themselves. Everyone is together, enjoying themselves and having fun.

I haven't been on a family trip like this in so long. I only ever see these people briefly, and usually during the holidays. It's been ages since I've done this with my own family.

A small wave of sadness washes over me. I've spent too much time away from my family and friends. I'm close with my parents and brothers, but my relationships with them aren't as close as they used to be. We text and talk all the time. But it's not the same. In the past, we used to do everything together: dinner, vacations, hangouts. Everything.

Then I became so self-involved trying to fix my failing marriage or focusing on my career that I overlooked all my relationships.

I let too many calls go unanswered and family dinners go unattended.

Sitting at this table has given me the push I need to fix that when I get home. I know they all understand how things have been for me, but I need to show them how thankful I am for their support. Especially my brothers. They have really been there for me when things got bad. I might not have told them everything that happened with Alina, but they were always there to drink a beer with me or sit on a board out in the ocean. Even now, they've all been so supportive of my plan to win Rylann back. They want me to be happy. They want their brother back.

"Hey." Levi is staring at me. He lifts his eyebrows, waiting for me to say something.

Shit, how long have I been checked-out overthinking?

"Take a walk with me," Levi says.

"Sure."

Placing my napkin on the table, I turn to Rylann. "I'll be right back for Rhys, okay?"

She looks at me, worried. I can almost hear the questions dancing around in her head. I don't want her to think this has anything to do with us.

"We're still going. I haven't changed my mind. This isn't about us. I'll explain later. I promise."

Rylann nods, and I push her soft brown locks behind her ear. I love when they fall loose around her face. Brushing them back is my favorite thing to do.

I follow Levi to the hostess desk. He covers the bill, even though I offer to pay. He refuses. He still won't let me cover anything.

"Talk to me. I saw you slip away," Levi says, concern etched on his forehead.

I grab the back of my neck, squeezing. "Yeah, I just started thinking about how much I've missed. Not just with you guys, but with my own family too. I feel like I've been a shit brother and son."

"Jay, we all love you. You've had a rough couple of years, is all. We don't blame you. That's over now. Right?"

"It's in the rearview," I confirm.

Because it is. I am not going back, only forward, and forward is with Rylann at my side. Going on family vacations, dinner, all of it.

"I have to know that you're not doubting things with Rylann. I can't let you or her go through all that again. I just got you back, and you're bringing her back too. Scarlett and I were talking last night. We can see it happening, and it's because of you. But if you're not sure or all in, I need you to walk away now."

"Fuck no! It's nothing like that. She's it. I know it deep down, right here." I bang my fist to my chest. "Not a single one of my thoughts back there was about her. She's the only thing keeping me here and looking forward to the future. I just got all up in my head, but that has more to do with me than her. You know?"

"Okay. Well, then. You better go talk to Rhys. I know he's gonna be excited. My parents said all he did last night was sing your praises. I think you have a fan on your hands."

I grin. Hope blooms brighter, knowing Rhys likes me.

"Well, I'm a big fan of his too," I say, making Levi smile. "You gotta know I'm all in with them. This time, I'm leaving here with her. With him. Them. They're mine."

Levi pulls me in and we hug it out, back slaps and all. "Good. Like I said, I'm rooting for you. It's good to have you back, buddy. I've missed you."

"Me too." Levi having my back means a lot to me.

We break up the love fest and return to the table.

I lock eyes with Rylann to make sure she's still fine with me talking to Rhys. Giving her one last out of the trip.

She gives me a reassuring wink. Fuck, she's so damn beautiful. I want to pinch myself to make sure I'm awake every time I look at her, afraid my second chance is all a dream.

"Hey, buddy, will you take a walk with me?" I ask Rhys.

"Sure," he says, climbing off his chair. He wraps his tiny hand in mine and looks up at me with his big honey-brown eyes. He looks so much like his mom, down to the matching freckles on his cheek. "Where are we going?"

"Just over here for a minute. I wanted to ask you something."

I lead us over to the benches and take a seat. Lifting him up, I plop him on my knee. He tilts his head to the side, staring at my face, trying to read me.

Fuck, he's adorable. I hope he doesn't ask for anything because I might buy it for him, and I'm pretty sure Rylann would kill me.

"So, you know how some of the things on your list we haven't been able to do, like see a sea turtle? What if I told you I could take you to see not just one but many sea turtles?"

"For real?" His eyes bug out of his head.

"Yes, but we have to fly on a plane to get there. Would you want to go?"

"Can Sadie go?"

Well, look at that. Rylann is right about him and Sadie.

"No, she has to stay here with her parents. It will be just me, you, and your mom. What do you think? Up for a little adventure?"

"What else are we gonna see?" He crosses his arms over his chest.

I hold back my chuckle. "Let's see ..." I tap my lips, pretending to think. "Sea turtles."

"You said that already."

"Oh, I did, didn't I? Hmm ..." I fight the smile pulling at my lips. I start to tick off the things I have planned. "A real volcano. Manta rays. A waterfall." His eyes grow wider with every word. "There's also a black sand beach we can see. We can go horseback riding, and we can't forget driving around in a super cool car. What do you think? Should we go?"

"Heck yeah!" He leaps off my lap and starts jumping around, dancing and thanking me.

Not gonna lie ... When he said I was awesome, I almost did a dance too.

This right here. This is exactly what I had hoped for. A chance to make this guy happy.

For us to create some new and unforgettable memories together.

CHAPTER FORTY-FIVE

Jace

Two and a half hours later, the three of us are sitting in a small plane on the runway, waiting to take off for Kona.

"How long does it take to fly to the big island?" Rhys asks.

"Fifty-five minutes."

"That's forever. Can I have a snack?" he gripes.

Rylann pops her eyebrow at him, her "mom" face saying it all.

I look away, ducking my head to avoid her gaze. I don't want her to catch me laughing and turn that evil eye on me.

"Please!" Rhys amends. Clearly, he knows what that face means.

"Of course, bug." She opens her purse and hands him a baggie filled with a variety of snacks for him to choose from. I make a note to remember that kids need snacks.

Rylann leans back in her seat and rolls her head to the side, facing me.

I copy her, sitting back and turning my face to her, our eyes locked over Rhys's head. The sparks between us flicker, making me hot. I want to touch her. My eyes drop to her mouth, and her tongue swipes across her bottom lip, teasing me.

Looking her in the eyes, I mouth *later* to her while pumping my eyebrows suggestively.

She covers her mouth with her hand, hiding her smile, and shakes her head.

Completely unaware that his mom and I are locked in an eye-fucking contest, Rhys continues to talk and eat his snack.

Teasing her, I rub my thumb over my bottom lip and nod. She blushes, and my cock twitches. She shakes her head no, but it's weak and I know she doesn't mean it. She wants me to kiss her, and I will—she can fucking count it. I'd kiss her sweet lips all day, every day, if she'd let me.

She crosses her legs, and my eyes instinctively dart down to stare at the smooth expanse of her skin. She looks beautiful today, wearing that sexy little lemon dress again. I wish I could untie the little bow at her side, letting it fall open so I could lick the valley between her full breasts. She's wearing a thin gold necklace with a small R charm around her slender neck. My lips itch to kiss the smooth stretch of her skin. My gaze slides to her soft pink lips again.

Flashes of last night's kiss flit through my mind. Rolling my tongue over my bottom lip, I fight the desperate feeling I have to lose myself in her. After devouring her body with my eyes, I bring them back to her face. She looks flustered. Her eyelids are hooded, and her chest rises and falls too quickly for sitting down. I'd bet my entire life savings she's thinking about that kiss and that her panties are as wet as my dick is hard. It physically hurts keeping my distance from her when I want nothing more than to pull her onto my lap and kiss her. Taste her sweet, pouty lips over and over.

Discreetly, I adjust myself in my seat. I don't need to be getting hard in front of Rhys.

"Can't you control yourself?" she whispers, fanning her face.

"When it comes to you, Sunshine? Never." I flash her a dazzling smile.

"Insufferable," she taunts, making me snicker.

I love this Rylann. She's a relaxed, playful version of her old self.

"You mispronounced 'charming'," I tell her.

She rolls her eyes at me, but the cute smile on her lips gives her away. This is exactly what I need to keep doing—charm the shit out of my woman.

My woman.

Fuck yeah, she is. It feels right saying that. Even if it's just in my head. She is my woman. I won't let her slip through my fingers this time.

Pulling out my cell phone, I open up the camera and flip it to selfie mode. "Alright, you two, squeeze in."

Wrapping my arm around Rylann's shoulders, I pull her closer, squishing Rhys between us, and snap a few pictures of the three of us smiling. I also snap a few more photos of Rhys attempting to make cross eyes at the camera. Without thinking, I send the first picture of the three of us smiling to my brothers, then turn off my phone.

Proof of life. A life that will soon include Rylann and Rhys.

We take off, and I spend the rest of the flight telling Rhys all about the big island. He eats up every word.

Once we land, I gather our bags, and we make our way to the car rental counter. This time around, everything runs smoothly. Less than ten minutes later, I have the key in my hand as we stand in front of the white jeep with extra large tires for off-roading.

"What do you think? Cool enough for you, kiddo?" I ask Rhys, whose eyes are bugging out of his head.

"Ooooh yaaaa," he says, making me laugh. "Those tires are huge. Like monster-truck *huge*. So cool!"

My chest puffs with pride. I'm batting a thousand right now. I only hope I can keep up the momentum. The happier these two are and the more fun they have, the better my odds are at making them mine.

Rylann shakes her head in disapproval.

"Sorry, not sorry, Sun." This car is kickass and perfect for what I have planned. She'll see.

She sighs and climbs into the jeep behind Rhys.

"This is us." I open the door to the suite I reserved.

Rhys runs in and jumps on the couch. His excitement is apparent in the way he's smiling brightly.

Checking out the main room, I see it looks comfortable enough with a couch, two matching armchairs, and bright tropical pillows that match the art on the walls. There's a small kitchenette with a mini fridge and sink. I'll have to ask Rylann if we need to go to the store and grab a few essentials for Rhys.

The view from the balcony will be perfect for watching the sunset. I can picture us out there, a glass of wine in hand, Rylann tucked into my side. I can see myself tilting her chin up and kissing her senseless. Stealing her breath like she's stolen my heart.

I shake my head, bringing my focus back to my plans for the day. I double-check my watch to make sure we have plenty of time to change and get something to eat before our horseback riding reservation on the beach.

"Ry, we need to be in jeans for horseback riding. I should have mentioned that sooner. Do you need to go out and get anything?" I run my hands through my hair. How did I not think to prepare her?

She puts her hand on my wrist, her touch calming. "I packed for all possibilities. We're good."

I sigh in relief. I thought I messed up for a minute. "You're amazing. You know that, right?"

"I'm just a mom. Thinking ahead kind of comes with the territory," she replies, shrugging me off.

I reach out, palming the nape of her neck, and I shake my head at her flippant comment. "You're amazing. Don't underestimate yourself." The temptation is too strong—I lean in and place a feather-light kiss on her lips. "Why don't you get ready? Then, we can get some lunch before our drive. Sound good?"

Rylann sways on her feet before turning to leave the living room. I give her sexy ass a little tap, unable to resist pushing her physical boundaries.

She looks over her shoulder, a look of surprise on her face. "You're getting a little handsy there, Mr. Miller."

"Mr. Miller, huh? Careful there, Sunny. I like a good scolding every now and then. You gonna spank me and call me a bad boy too?"

Her eyes blaze before she rolls them with a smirk.

If I didn't know she liked it, I wouldn't push her as hard as I am. But the signals her body is giving me tell me she does. Fake eye roll and all. I saw the way her pupils dilated and the pulse at the base of her neck sped up. She likes it when I flirt, tease, and talk dirty to her. It turns her on.

I follow her down the hall to the two bedrooms. One has a king bed and the other has two double beds. Both have small ensuite bathrooms.

Rylann takes in the two rooms. She's quiet, and I'm starting to worry she doesn't like it.

"Is this okay with you? I am more than happy to share the room with Rhys or take the sofa. I want you two to be comfortable. You're my priority." I grab the back of my neck.

She places her palm on my chest, reassuring me. "It's perfect, Ace. I'll be good here with Rhys."

Placing my hands on her hips, I pull her flush to my body, searching her eyes for distress. I want her to be honest. I meant it when I said I want her to be comfortable. She's my number one priority on this trip. If she wants the master bedroom, she can have it.

"I'm sure. Now, let me get changed. I'm hungry." Her stomach growls, punctuating the seriousness of the situation, making me laugh.

"You got it. Leave in ten?"

She agrees, calling Rhys back to the room to change.

Over lunch, Rylann and I slip into conversation easily, planning out our days together. It feels like this is the norm for us. It doesn't surprise me that we already work together so well. We've always seen things eye to eye.

That's us—we fit together.

Always have, always will.

CHAPTER FORTY-SIX

Rylann

"Did you have a fun day, bug?"

"Best. Day. Ever," Rhys says with a yawn.

We are snuggled up on the bed, talking. He should be asleep, but he's that crazy mix of tired and amped-up only kids can embody.

"It was a pretty great day, wasn't it?"

Great doesn't even begin to cover our eventful day. Jace went all out, and it's only day one. Horseback riding, swimming with manta rays, and even driving around in a monster jeep have already turned this into a once-in-a-lifetime vacation.

Jace has gone out of his way to show Rhys a great time and me how much he cares. In these few short days, he's seen what others don't—the spa date, the flowers and candles set up, the surf lessons ... all of it—has been him taking care of me.

"It was." Rhys nods.

Thinking back, today felt so ... normal. We felt like a family.

Trying to ignore the heaviness the word "family" brings to mind, I keep Rhys talking. "Wanna fill me in on your high and low for the day?"

"My high was seeing manta rays at night. That was so awesome. There were *sooo* many of them swimming around us."

"A whole group," I concur.

Jace signed us up for a family night dive. Dressed in wetsuits and the appropriate gear, we were securely strapped in rafts that shined light into the water, attracting the rays for viewing. I was worried that something would happen to Rhys, but Jace—sensing my apprehension—was by my side, assuring me that everything was going to be fine. He promised he would never let anything happen to Rhys. I already knew that, but looking in his hazel eyes, I knew he meant it down to his core. I could feel the certainty in his voice and the steely determination in his eyes to protect me and Rhys with everything he has to give. Jace held Rhys the entire time, keeping him safe and protected. The sight made my insides warm. I love the way Jace cares for my son so selflessly.

"It's called a squadron, remember, Mom?"

"How could I forget? You keep reminding me." I tickle his sides, sending him into a fit of giggles. I love the tinkling sound of his laughter. "What about a low? Did you have one of those today?"

Rhys purses his lips, thinking. "The horses, for sure!"

I fight a shiver as flashes of Jace's large hands on my hips cross my mind. How he lifted me on and off my horse, purposefully scraping my chest down the path of his large body each time. The charge between us snapping like static electricity, making the hair on my arms stand on end.

"Really? I thought they were beautiful, and I had fun riding on the beach."

"My horse pooped, and it smelled awful!" Rhys retches, his tongue sticking out.

I throw my head back and laugh. "You're right—that was pretty gross." Climbing out of the bed, I kiss his head one more time before tucking him in tight and switching off the bedside lamp. "Okay, bug, it's time to get some sleep. We've had a big day, and we have another one tomorrow." I pull up the blanket to Rhys's chin and kiss his cheeks one more time before walking away.

"Mom?" His soft voice stops me.

"Rhysie?" I respond back, fighting a smile.

"I think Daddy would have liked Hawaii. And Jace." He looks up at me with his big brown eyes. The moonlight catches the gold in his irises, making it glimmer. My heart stops at the sight of his penetrating stare.

"Yes." My voice cracks, and I clear the emotion from my throat. "He would have liked Hawaii ... and Jace."

"He's funny. I like him. Do you?"

My pulse pounds in my ears. I know it's an innocent question, but it also feels weighted with curiosity. "Yes, I like Jace. He's a good man. He likes you too. That's why he brought you on this special trip."

He nods. Thinking.

I wait, wondering if he has something else on his mind. Instead, he rolls over and says goodnight.

"Good night. I love you, sweet boy." With one more glance over my shoulder at my strong guy, I sigh. I'm playing a dangerous game with not only my heart but Jace's and Rhys's too.

After a hot shower, where I decided to shave my entire body for no other reason than to be ready for tomorrow, I finally find the courage to make an appearance in the living room. The room is dark except for a small lamp by the couch illuminating the space. My eyes dart to the glass door of the patio.

Back to me, Jace is sitting out on the balcony, a glass of wine in hand, his form silhouetted by the light of the moon. He's staring out at the ocean, waiting.

I'm at a turning point with him. Accepting this invitation was me giving us a chance at reconnecting. A way for us to figure out how we feel about each other. Well, more how I feel. I know how Jace feels.

Since our date, he has increased his flirting and touching. He teases me with that sexy wink and panty-melting Miller smile of his. It feels like the old us. The us that couldn't get enough of each other.

Before I let myself get lost in him, we still need to dive deep into the past, so we can get through to the future. I'm worried I will get distracted by the sexiness that is Jace and forget what I'm supposed to say. I'm scared of what will happen when he learns about Sam.

I need to power through it and talk. No kissing or touching of him of any kind. I need to keep my wits about me. But it's hard. He still has a tight grasp on my big, weak heart.

I watch him as he sits, the sound of the waves crashing in the distance. He looks sexy as hell with his legs spread, looking calm and collected. He's so handsome it makes my chest ache.

A memory of a younger me straddling his lap on the balcony as he fucked me slow and deep invades my mind. I bite my lip, hoping to stifle the groan and the throbbing between my legs. He's the only one that's ever made me feel insatiable and needy for a man to rule my body for both our pleasures.

"I've been told that if you take a picture, it lasts longer," Jace teases, his voice cutting through my dirty thoughts.

"How did you know I was standing here?"

"Same way you know when I'm watching you. I feel you, Sunshine," he replies, sipping his wine.

Fair—my body does sense him. My skin prickles with awareness, and my heart beats double time. I didn't know he experienced the same sensations I do.

Stepping out onto the balcony, I settle into the chair next to him. He pours wine into an empty glass and slides it my way. I take a sip and let the cool, crisp liquid coat my parched mouth.

"Thank you so much for everything you've done for me and Rhys today," I say, breaking the silence.

Jace shifts, angling his body towards me, and turns that hazel gaze on me. "You're welcome. Thank you for trusting me enough to join me."

His eyes drop, roaming over my body. He quirks a brow at my yellow sleep shorts and matching tank, and I can't help smiling to myself.

Yes, Ace, I have real pajamas this time.

He's wearing a white t-shirt paired with gray sweatpants cut off at the knees. Did I mention the gray sweatpants?

I tug at the hem of my shorts and shift in my seat as my center pulses with need.

When his eyes meet mine, they are filled with lust. The green of his irises glows brighter as his nearly blown pupils overtake the gold. My breath quickens as he swipes his tongue across his bottom lip. I imagine it swiping across something else.

I break the intense connection and reach for my wine, taking another sip. As much as I want him to put his mouth all over me, I need to calm my tits and talk to this man. With words. Not my lips, hands, or vagina.

The slutty bitch squeezes at the thought.

It doesn't go unnoticed.

Jace's fist tightens around his glass, knuckles whitening. Ever the gentleman, he graciously guides our conversation to safer topics. "Did Rhys have fun today?" His voice is gruff, laced with desire. Eerily similar to the way it sounded when he used to whisper dirty words in my ear while exploring my body in the most delicious ways.

I push those thoughts away and concentrate. "Are you kidding? He's having a blast. You're spoiling him. There's no way I will ever be able to live up to the standards you're setting."

Jace laughs, placing his hand on my thigh, squeezing, scorching my skin. An uncontrollable shiver runs down my spine.

He smirks, knowingly, at my reaction. "Thanks for the ego boost. But you're an amazing mom, and he loves you. Every vacation will be fun. There isn't anything you can do that would let him down."

His praise makes my heart twinge. I don't know how he manages to say the sweetest and most thoughtful things when I need to hear them, but I never want him to stop.

"Thanks. But seriously … I can't believe you pulled all this off for us on such short notice. Where did you have the time?"

"My brother helped me," he confesses, massaging the back of his neck.

"Which one?" I'm curious. Do they all know about me? About Rhys?

"Eli. I begged him to help me. It's going to cost me, but you and Rhys are worth it. Watching the two of you smile today is worth whatever favor Eli is gonna cash in on."

He strokes his thumb up my thigh, and my brain shorts and my blood sizzles beneath the surface.

"Ace …" I say his name—a plea on my tongue.

I wish he would run his hand higher, to the apex of my thighs. Desire runs through my veins. I'm slipping under his spell, and there's no way to stop it. I'm not even sure I want to anymore. My body most certainly wants me to let Jace take control of it.

I try to concentrate on what we were talking about before his hand. Something about his brother …

"Do you think Eli will give you a hard time?" I ask thickly, closing my eyes.

"Probably. It's Eli." He shrugs.

I can feel him watching me.

"So, he's as cheeky as ever?"

Jace barks out a laugh. I'm not surprised to hear Eli is still a rascal.

"That's one way to put it," he says, and I laugh with him.

We sit in comfortable silence for a beat, listening to the sounds of the island. His hand still rests on my thigh.

"So ... You know everything that happened between me and Alina. Would it be too much to ask for your story?"

I turn to face him. So many questions swirl behind his hazel orbs. My palms sweat. "What would you like to know?"

"Everything. You said you were happy. Tell me about that."

I break eye contact.

This is it ...

I stare out at the ocean, the light of the stars glittering atop the surface. I hate what I have to say about Sam and my life. I feel guilty for having a good life. Unlike him, I had an incredible marriage. Sam was my best friend, and our relationship was great. Nothing like what it would have been with Jace, but wonderful nonetheless.

"Sam and I had a good marriage. He was my best friend. Well, second to Scarlett. Please don't tell her I said that—she'd kill me," I jest. It's hard to talk about this to Jace. "Sam was there for me when I needed someone to lean on. To hold me up when I couldn't do it myself. He loved me."

Jace's hand freezes on my leg, and I wince. I know that's not easy to hear. Seeing the person you love with someone else is painful. Thinking of him with Alina is like getting punched in the stomach.

I push through with my story. "When I arrived back home, Sam was sitting on my doorstep, waiting for me. I broke down and told him everything, from start to finish. I didn't leave anything out, especially not you." Taking a cleansing breath, I can feel the weight on my chest begin to lift. "Sam held me while I cried. He apologized for hurting me. For everything that happened to me. Even though I was torn up, in lo—" I stop myself and shake my head. I need to stick to the bullet points because—at least for me—even after all these years, the heartbreak still stings. "Sam didn't care. He fought for us. He asked me to give him a chance, and eventually ... I did. It wasn't easy for me, you know. I was—"

Jace's jaw clenches, and I cut myself off. I don't want to hurt him, but he needs to know the truth. I didn't snap my fingers and turn off my feelings for him. I couldn't. But, as best as I could, I did try to move on like he did.

Even now, I can recall with absolute clarity the ache in my chest when I saw Alina holding onto Jace. The realization that we were over. The thought of them together makes my stomach bottom out. I mourned what could have been between us for weeks. During that time, Sam did anything and everything to show me that he would never leave me. That he loved me and supported me. He was as close to perfect as you can get.

"After we found out about Rhys, we got married at the courthouse."

Why did I say that? He doesn't need to know that I chose Sam because Jace married another woman. It's not fair to him or Sam for me to confess that out loud.

"Sam was a good man and father. He did everything he could to make me and Rhys happy. Even when he got sick, he still put our needs first."

I close my eyes, remembering the way Sam would hide the side effects of the radiation so he could make it to Rhys's kindergarten class for parent read-aloud days. How he would push through soccer games and hid his worry with blinding optimism when he knew the treatments weren't working. He took any and every opportunity he could to spend time with us and fit a lifetime of memories into months. His leaving behind all those handwritten letters was his way to remind us how much he loved us. Even when he knew he wouldn't be there.

And the video.

He left that, knowing I would need it to find my way out of the darkness—his way of helping me move on and be happy. Still taking care of his family when he's gone. His intentions were good, but the damage had been done. Everything I thought I knew about my life and my husband is now muddled. He cast a shadow on the wonderful life we shared together. I can't even be mad at him because he's not here to defend himself.

My nose prickles, and I can't stop the tears that flood my eyes, my emotions getting the better of me—again. I hate putting Jace in this awkward position of comforting me once more.

He lifts me out of my seat and places me on his lap, holding me tight as silent sobs wrack my body. His arms wrap around me tighter, feeding me his strength. "Shh. It's okay, Sunshine. I'm here now."

He kisses the crown of my head, running his fingers through my hair as I bury my face in his firm warm chest. Finding solace in his arms. I've been so alone in my grief, it feels good to have someone hold me while I break apart. Mourn. I haven't permitted myself to let it all out. Instead, I've been carrying it all on my shoulders, letting it eat at me. Keeping on a brave face for Rhys when all I wanted to do was fall apart.

"He didn't deserve to die, Jace. He deserved to live a long life. What sucks the most is that he knew he never would. When he got sick, he tried so hard to be optimistic for me. Watching him slip away a little more each day was excruciating. I felt so helpless." Now that the vault is open, I can't stop. "This past year, I've been so damn lonely ... and angry. I'm so tired, Ace. I have all these problems that I don't know how to fix and thoughts that are eating me alive. I-I don't even know where to start there. Now I'm here, and this place is bringing up all these memories and feelings. You're just as wonderful as you were then. And I'm not even sure I deserve your kindness. I'm not sure I deserve to be happy at all anymore. Sam, he—"

Jace growls, tightens his grip around me, and lifts me up. On instinct, I wrap my arms around his neck, clutching on tightly. He carries me inside, bridal style, and places me on the sofa like I'm precious cargo.

"Stay," he commands.

I do as I'm told, pulling my knees to my chest and resting my head on them, bewildered at the change in his tone. He sounds irritated with me.

I watch Jace walk to the patio, collect the wine and glasses, and return to the living room. He places everything on the coffee table in front of us and sits down. After filling up our glasses, he pulls me back onto his lap like it's where I belong. I look up at him, and my stomach flips at his angry face.

"I don't ever want to hear you say that you don't deserve to be happy. That is the farthest thing from the truth. I know your ..." He hesitates, refusing to say "husband". "Sam would want you to be happy. If he's anything like me, those words are ripping a hole in his chest from beyond. You are strong, compassionate, kind ... Hell, I could go on forever because, babe, you're fucking beautiful inside and out."

"But—"

"No." He grabs my jaw, gently but firmly, and continues, my eyes secured on his.

"You can be sad, angry, confused—all the feelings. That's living. But I never want to hear you say that you don't deserve happiness. That's a crock of shit, and you know it. If anyone deserves it, it's you. You and Rhys. You both have been through so much. Losing your family and having to rebuild is hard. I know this. But no matter what, you absolutely deserve to have a life filled with happiness, laughter, and love."

I'm at a loss for words. The passion behind his anger for me is astounding.

With a softer voice, he says, "You are not alone anymore. I'm here, and I'm not going anywhere."

I shut my eyes at his words as hot tears pour down my face. Jace cups my cheeks in his big hands, his thumbs wiping them away. His words soothe the lonely ache that's settled deep in my bones.

I don't want to be alone anymore. I dreamed of him coming back to me, and now that he's here, I never want to let him go again.

He's really here. In the flesh. Saying and doing all the right things. Giving me hope. Reminding me of how much I loved him and still do.

When I open my eyes, he's watching me with a mix of pain and anger, and it has my heart skittering to a stop. Those feelings aren't aimed at me; they are *for* me.

My eyes flick to his mouth. Rolling my tongue over my bottom lip, I tip my chin up in invitation. We close the distance between us together.

Our lips meld in a sweet kiss. We take our time exploring. Saltiness flavors our lips as Jace works to expel my heartache and replace it with comfort with every kiss and caress of his tongue.

Breaking our kiss, I open my eyes to find him watching me again. This time, his green eyes sparkle lovingly and it takes my breath away.

There's no mistaking it—Jace loves me.

Grabbing Jace's shirt, I pull him close and crush my mouth to his in a searing kiss, full of love and fierce passion rolled in desire. I curl my fingers through his hair, unleashing my feelings into his mouth. I need him to know that I do give myself over to him. Body and soul. He has it all.

I want him to feel my love and know that this is real for me too. I never stopped loving him.

My body is on fire under his large hands. Adjusting my legs, I turn and straddle his lap, aligning my pussy on his hard cock. We moan at the contact. His hands roam up my legs, under my shorts, to the crease where my hips meet my thighs. He rubs his thumbs back and forth, staying away from where I want them. Need them.

My clit pulses with each stroke of his fingers. I moan into his mouth, gliding my body along his hard cock. He slows the kiss, but I tug him closer. I don't want to stop.

He pulls away, tearing his mouth from mine with a smack.

Did I read this all wrong?

Like a bucket of cold water, I look away, afraid of what I'll see, and try to escape his lap.

His hands grip my thighs, squeezing, locking me in place. "Don't you dare move another inch."

CHAPTER FORTY-SEVEN

Jace

My fingers dig into her thighs, pinning her to my lap.

She looks away, and I hate myself for making her walls go back up. If she thinks for one second that I'm stopping because I don't want her, she's out of her damn mind. Never in my entire life have I wanted someone more than I want her. My body craves hers. I want to worship every inch of her and never stop.

Be that as it may, she just finished pouring her heart out to me, confessing that she feels undeserving of happiness. Fucking gutting me. I knew she was hurting, but this is too much. My sunshine has surrounded herself in dark clouds, and I will not accept a life in which she is broken and unhappy. I refuse to let her stay in the dark. I want her to shine brightly.

I want to give her more than a physical release; I want to give her everything. When we do cross that line, I don't want her to regret a single minute. While I want to make her body feel good, I need her to know I'm here to support her heart too.

Running my hands up her thighs, over her hips, her stomach, the sides of her breasts, and her neck, I cup her cheeks between my palms. "Look at me, Sunshine."

She takes her time bringing her gaze back to mine. Her little mouth is turned down, and her chin wobbles. My heart lurches in my chest at the dejected look on her face. She can't possibly think I'm rejecting her. If my hard-as-steel dick isn't proof that I want her, we have bigger problems.

If I thought she was ready, I'd already be buried between her legs, demonstrating all the ways and positions in which I want her. But she's not. At least, not completely.

I pepper kisses on her forehead, eyes, nose, and mouth. Her body softens with every press of my lips.

That's right, my love. I've got you.

"Now, you listen to me. Do not second-guess us. Make no mistake—I want to be buried deep inside your tight body while you scream my name. Badly. Always have. Always will. Are you following me?"

She doesn't answer, her eyes wide in shock at my dirty mouth.

I pump my hips up, pressing my rigid cock against her thinly covered pussy, grunting in satisfaction at the feel of her heat seeping through our clothes. She holds onto my shoulders for support as her eyes flutter closed at the friction.

"Open."

Her eyes pop open at my order, making me growl in approval. Her compliance has my cock growing harder. But I ignore that greedy fucker. Tonight is about her and what she needs.

"Thank you for talking to me. I'm honored that you're willing to open up and let me in. There is no need for us to rush. We have all the time in the world. Believe me when I say I'm all in."

She opens her mouth to protest, but I cut her off, cuffing the nape of her neck, bringing us nose to nose.

I stare into her eyes and repeat, "I'm. All. In."

I mean it. She's mine. Rhys is mine. They are it for me.

She nods and whispers, "Kiss me again, Ace. Please?"

Indicative of the whipped man I've become, I oblige, covering her mouth with mine.

Fuck, she tastes so good. Like crisp green apples from the wine and her own dulcet flavor. The greedy bastard in me deepens the kiss. Sliding my tongue against hers and tangling it around hers, I explore every inch of her delicious mouth.

Rylann swivels her hips, rubbing her hot seam along my hardness.

I can't stay in this position if I want to keep myself and my angry, hard dick in check. I twist us around on the couch, bringing us chest to chest, her legs draped over mine.

Like that first night, we lay there making out like teenagers, lost in each other. Rylann throws her leg over mine and straddles me. Her hips swivel, and a desperate mewl escapes her throat. My carefully constructed control is slipping with the heat of her pussy against my cock.

I try pulling away, but she refuses to let me go. "Don't stop. Please. I need this. I need you."

Her words are my undoing.

If this is what she wants, I'll give it to her. I'd give her anything.

Weaving my fingers through her hair, I tug, bringing her mouth back to mine. Hands pressed into my chest for balance, she begins to swivel her hips and glide her pussy along my hardened length, using me and the ridges of my cock to bump and rub her clit. I lay there, kissing her, a slave to her every need.

"That's it, love. Use me. Make yourself feel good," I growl.

My cock grows thicker with every grind of her pelvis, with every whimper that escapes her lips. I kiss and bite at the tender flesh of her neck. Her honeyed scent invades my nose, and the beast inside me claws at my chest. She smells and tastes exactly how I remember, like coconut and limes. Like *mine.*

I suck her nipple through the thin material of her shirt and bite down on the hardened tip. She moans loudly, and it's like a shot to my dick. I should muffle her sounds, but I don't. I want to hear every sexy noise she makes and drown in the sound of her pleasure. The pleasure only I can give her.

I missed her so fucking much. The feel of her skin under mine. The way she moans and cries my name as she comes.

Her legs begin to tighten and shake with every stroke, drawing her closer to the orgasm building inside her. I grab her hips and drag her faster along my erection, and it does the trick.

I watch with rapt attention as she reaches her peak. Neck arched, eyes squeezed tight, and mouth parted, Rylann shatters above me. Jackknifing up, I cover her mouth with mine and swallow her screams of my name. As her arms give out and she falls to my chest, I vow to be the one to catch her. She tucks her head under my chin and I caress her back with my fingertips, until her breathing evens out.

"You look like an angel when you come," I whisper against her lips. My cock twitches in discomfort, so I roll us onto our sides, resting our heads on the cushioned armchair.

"I don't think I've done that since I was in high school," she says with a laugh, her eyes still closed. The light sheen of sweat covering the tops of her breasts glistens in the soft light.

I lick a line from her collar bone to her ear before whispering, "Happy to be of service."

She shivers and her eyes slowly open, locking on mine. A lazy smile takes over her face and sucks the air from my lungs.

She's an angel fallen from heaven. Her beauty is so otherworldly it physically hurts to look at, and yet I can't look away. Couldn't even if I wanted to.

I lean forward and kiss her nose, and she giggles. The sweet sound hits me in the chest, burying itself inside me. Warming me from the inside out.

"You can use me anytime you want, Sunshine. I quite enjoy watching you get yourself off on top of me." I smirk, pushing her hair behind her ear.

"Ace," she admonishes, slapping my chest and making me chuckle.

Discreetly, I try to adjust myself, but she notices and stares at my cock.

"My eyes are up here, Sun."

She blushes, glancing up at me. "Do you ..." She shrugs, pointing at my hard dick.

There is no way in hell she's reciprocating. Not tonight. Not ever. I love pleasing my woman. Besides, I need her to accept that I'm here to stay before I do all the dirty things I've been dreaming about doing to her.

"That big guy? Don't worry about that big guy." I wink, making her laugh again. It's a sound I crave to hear.

Needing to touch her, I drape my arm over her waist and let my fingers drift under her shirt, playing circles over her warm skin. Breathing out a deep contented sigh, I realize I haven't felt this complete since the last time I was with her. I've thought about her over the years, but I never believed it was possible for us to have a second chance.

"Did you think about me?" I blurt.

Rylann hisses.

I slam my eyes shut.

Why the fuck would I ask her that right now? *Way to ruin the afterglow, dumbass.*

"No," she whispers, and I swear my heart falls out of my ass. She flattens her hand against my chest like she's trying to take away the pain her words brought to my heart. "Jace, please look at me."

I open my eyes to find hers filled with remorse and unshed tears.

"I said no because I had to force myself not to think about you. Losing you was one of the hardest things I've ever had to go through. It hurt so badly to let you go. To hear that you were getting married to someone else. To know you were moving on. It broke my heart."

A tear breaks free from the corner of her eye. My heart splinters at her confession. She was right there with me all along. I hurt too.

Watching the wrong woman walk down the aisle toward me was agony. It all felt wrong. Right from the start. But I felt trapped, and I couldn't see a way out. I tried to escape the night before, but when Levi told me Rylann was moving on, I figured she was happy, so I went through with the wedding. I thought I was doing the right thing.

All I did was hurt us more.

If only I had the courage to run out on that wedding and go after the woman I really loved, so much could have been avoided.

"I understand more than you know." I kiss her freckles. If only we hadn't wasted so much time apart.

No. I can't think like that. Her life gave her something—no ... *someone* ... wonderful. Rhys.

He is a precious gift, given to the best woman I know. She deserved to be happy and live out her dream of becoming a mother. I would never change that, and I refuse to let the past haunt us in the present. Our time is now.

"I missed you. I'm glad you're here with me now."

"Me too, Ace," she says with a yawn, her eyes droopy.

"It's time for bed. We have a long day ahead of us."

I roll off the couch and hold my hand out for her to take. She places her small hand in mine, and I pull her to her feet. Unable to help myself, I kiss her pink swollen lips.

Grabbing the bottle of wine, I place it in the fridge and turn off the lamp.

Waiting for me in the hallway is Rylann, looking unsure. My heart leaps at the idea of her sleeping with me instead of the small bed inside the room with Rhys.

"Whatcha' waiting for, Sunny?" I ask.

A confused look crosses her face before she bites her lip and shrugs. "I don't know, actually."

I can't help grinning at her answer. I understand. She doesn't want to leave my side. While I don't want her to either, she needs to sleep in the bed next to Rhys. For now. We'll get there.

Us being together is as natural as the tides of the ocean. It's hard to fight, I know. I gave in on day one. Twice.

She's so close to coming back to me. I can feel it. I'm a patient man, and she's worth the wait. Now that she's within my grasp, I'll wait for her for as long as it takes because she's worth it. *We're* worth it.

"Go to sleep. I'll be right here in the morning, waiting for you. I'm not going anywhere." I push back the loose strands of her hair, grazing her sensitive skin with my fingers.

She grabs my ears and yanks my head down, kissing me hard on the mouth. She surprises the hell out of me, and before I can kiss her back, she's down on the balls of her feet, retreating to her shared room.

"Goodnight," she whispers over her shoulder before closing the door.

"Goodnight, my love," I murmur to the empty hallway.

I head to bed alone but relieved. It won't be long before the woman that owns me, heart and soul, will be in my arms again. Every night for the rest of our lives if I have my say in the matter.

CHAPTER FORTY-EIGHT

Jace

"Slow down, buddy. You're gonna choke on all that pancake," I say with a chuckle.

This kid is hilarious. With his sweet, silly personality, he continues to steal my heart one beat at a time.

"Nu uh, I haff a big mowf n I ungry," Rhys mumbles around a mouthful of his macadamia nut pancakes.

"Rhys!" Rylann chides, shaking her head at his antics, a vain attempt to mask her smile. She wipes the dripping syrup off his chin between bites.

It's only mid-morning, and we've already had a busy day. Settled in at a diner, the three of us are stuffing our faces with breakfast in a cute little pancake house on the northeast shore.

Rhys was so excited, he was up at six this morning, begging us to get a move on. His enthusiasm was contagious. I immediately jumped in the shower, had clothes on, and was ready to head out the door twenty minutes later.

Even Rylann was ready. I remember that she liked to sleep in, but I guess kids break you of that habit.

We ate breakfast in the car as I drove us to the waterfall trails. The entire hour's drive was filled with music and laughter. I adored watching mother and son sing along to the music. When we parked at the waterfall trailhead, Rhys was bouncing off the walls. He settled down about a quarter of the way in. Taking me by surprise, he held both our hands the entire way up the trail. I loved listening to him chatter about his love of school, soccer, and Sadie.

Honestly, I could listen to his little voice all day. He has this spirit about him that just draws you in. He's funny, sweet, and a little snarky—like his mom.

The moment he saw the double waterfall and looked at me in awe, something inside me shifted. The way his little fingers were wrapped around my hand, they also wrapped around my heart, and this ball of warmth swelled up inside me. My future flashed before my eyes.

The three of us on vacation, at home watching movies, dinners full of laughter, nights in, snuggled up on the couch. I could picture it all. Me, a permanent fixture in their lives.

"You okay there, Jace?" Rylann asks, her head tilted to the side, watching me stare at Rhys.

I lift my eyes to her and give her a reassuring smile. "Yup. All good. I'm right where I'm supposed to be."

Reaching under the table, I squeeze her thigh. She blushes, and I would give anything to kiss her right now. It's been difficult keeping my hands to myself.

She bites her lips and shakes her head at me. She knows what I'm thinking.

I mouth *later* to her, and her face lights up.

"What are we doing next?" Rhys asks, interrupting like a good little cockblocker.

I sit back and sip my orange juice.

He looks at me, waiting for the answer, eyes glowing in anticipation.

"Next up, swimming at the beach. After that, lunch. Then, we'll drive to Volcanoes National Park—closer to sunset, so we can see the red glow of the volcano better. What do you think?"

Rhys nods his head in excitement, his bottom bouncing in the booth. "Wow, a real active volcano. So cool."

"Active volcano, huh? Do you know a lot about volcanoes?"

"Yep, I read a book at school and I watched a video about them online."

"You're a regular volcanologist then, aren't you?" I tease.

"A vull-can what? I'm not an alien," Rhys grumbles, crossing his arms over his chest.

Rylann and I bust up laughing at his mix-up.

"No, kiddo, volcanologists aren't aliens. It means you study volcanoes," Rylann explains.

"Oh," he says, happily returning back to his pancakes. "You think the volcano will spit lava for us to see?"

"That does sound pretty cool, but I hope not. I'd prefer *not* to have my buns melted by lava." My joke hits, driving Rhys into a fit of giggles.

"You're funny," Rhys says, slapping the table.

Obviously, butt jokes are funny to six-year-olds. I shoot him a wink that he tries to copy, but both his eyes twitch closed instead, making it look like he is squinting at me.

I glance over at Rylann to see her watching us. Her face is etched with something I can't quite put my finger on.

But before I can think on it further, Rhys pushes his plate away announcing, "I'm full. Can we leave now?"

"In a minute. Let's go wash up and use the bathroom before we leave." Rylann pulls a disgruntled Rhys out of the booth, leading him to the back of the restaurant.

Unable to help myself as she passes, I reach for her hand and kiss the inside of her wrist. She sighs and our hands linger, sliding apart as she walks away.

Fuck, it feels incredible to touch her.

While I love having Rhys around, I can't wait to get her alone again tonight. Hold her in my arms. Kiss her freely.

I call the server over and pay the bill. Figuring I have a few minutes while they're in the bathroom, I follow suit to take care of business.

Rylann steps into the hallway alone as I approach, and my pulse races.

"Is something wrong?" I look behind her, searching for Rhys.

Grabbing my wrist, she shakes her head, calming me down.

"No. Everything is fine. Rhys wanted to have,"—she uses air quotes—"privacy to go pee. I swear, he just makes this stuff up to see how far he can push my buttons."

Stepping closer to her, I whisper in her ear, "I like pushing your buttons too."

She shivers, and I step back. I open the door to the other lavatory and look in. It's clean, with a huge counter and sink. It reminds me of that hot make out session we had at the hotel. When I turn back to her, she has that luscious lip of hers trapped between her teeth, looking past me to the counter.

"Bathrooms, am I right?"

Her lids are heavy when they meet mine, burning with desire. Mouth parted, her breath short, she stands still. Watching me. I do my best to be casual, but there is no stopping the smug grin spreading across my face.

The door opens and Rhys walks out, distracting her, so I slip into the bathroom, closing the door. Leaving her to stew on hot-as-fuck memories of us.

Walking out of the restaurant, I find Rylann and Rhys waiting at the jeep. Rhys is standing in the back seat, jumping around and playing pretend while he holds onto the bars. She throws her head back and laughs at something he says.

Warmth floods my veins at the sight of them waiting on me. Rhys looks like his mom, with his dimpled smile and long brown hair. I feel ten feet tall watching him play around, having a good time. I don't mean to be cocky, but ... I did that. I made him smile. I want to rush over, pick him up, and squeeze his little body tight.

I love him. I might have fallen for him the moment I met him.

Then, there's Rylann.

The siren that's captured me, body and soul, from the moment her big brown eyes locked on mine. Her thick brown hair, sultry curves, and the heart of gold she carries around make her the most beautiful person in the world.

These two have dug themselves into every fabric of my being by their mere existence. They make me feel complete. Part of a whole.

"Jace! Over here!" Rhys yells, waving at me.

I chuckle and make my way over. "I see you're enjoying the monster jeep, but it's time to buckle up. Are you ready for some beach time?"

"So ready!" Rhys plops down and buckles himself into the booster seat.

I open the passenger door for Rylann and gesture for her to climb in. "Time to go, Sunny." I flash her a cocky grin.

She rolls her eyes at me, pretending my bossy tone doesn't turn her on, but I see the way her knees slam shut and her thighs clench. Grabbing her hips, I lift her into the seat, letting my fingers linger on her waist before sliding them down her thighs. Her breath hitches, and my cock flexes in my shorts.

Fuck, she's sexy.

She's wearing another pair of those short-shorts that leave her legs looking long and grabbable. I can't wait to spread her thighs wide and bury my face between them.

"Buckle up, baby." I slam her door shut.

It's going to be a long day if I keep having thoughts like this.

I adjust myself and walk around the car, taking my time to calm down. I climb into the driver's seat and she looks over at me, eyebrow arched. I give her a bright smile, shake my head at her, and mouth *later*.

She purses her lips, hiding her smile, and mumbles so low that I almost don't hear her response. "What in the world am I going to do with you?"

I chuckle to myself and start the car.

Everything.

She is going to do everything with me.

Always.

CHAPTER FORTY-NINE

Rylann

Music plays in the background of the car as I stare into the darkness. I'm exhausted and in desperate need of a shower. It's been another active and emotionally taxing day.

I look over at Jace, who's concentrating on the road as he drives us back to the hotel. He has once again planned another wonderful day, full of activities, somehow piecing together a day full of everything Rhys and I love to do.

As if he knows I'm thinking about him, he turns his face and smiles at me. My heart skips a beat. He's so damn handsome. Inside and out.

"Hey." His gravelly voice caresses my insides, lighting them on fire.

"Hey," I whisper back.

He places his hand on my thing and continues driving.

He's made it impossible not to fall for him all over again. With his help, I've found myself again. He's made me smile, laugh, and live in the moment. He's done everything to help me forget my pain and hold me tight when the pain is too much to bear.

And it's not just me. He has been there for Rhys. He treats him with such respect, patience, and—dare I say—love. Watching them together is something else and every time I see them together, I don't know whether to smile or cry. It's so beautiful. If I'm not smiling or holding back tears when I watch them, I'm swooning. I swear, when Jace makes Rhys laugh, my ovaries get an erection. An ovar-ection? Is that a thing? If it's not, it should be because that's what Jace gives me. Every time that hot-as-hell man tells a super dorky joke and my kid laughs ... *Pop!*

Jace is quite possibly the most amazing man alive. He's thoughtful and kind. He's a giver by nature. He enjoys taking care of people, and it's not specific to his family but to everyone, and he expects nothing in return.

Well, not nothing. This time around, he does expect something in return from me. Another go at us.

Tearing my eyes off him, I stare back out the window.

Deep down, I want nothing more than to give us a chance. I'm trying to give him what he wants, even though we still have obstacles ahead of us. He makes us being together seem easy when, in reality, it's not.

My chest aches, and a pit forms in my stomach.

"What are you thinking about over there, Sunshine?" Jace's thick voice draws my attention back to him.

"Nothing," I mumble, trying to muster up a smile for him.

"You and I both know that's a lie." He sees right through me, even with his eyes focused on the road ahead. He knows me so well.

"I was just thinking about today. It's been amazing. Thank you for ... Well, everything," I speak the partial truth.

"Thank you for coming with me. For giving me a chance. I've loved spending these past few days with the two of you."

"Well, Rhys certainly had a great time." I throw a thumb behind me at the sleeping kiddo, making him laugh.

"Finally," he says with a huff.

I understand. Kids are a lot, especially if you're not around them 24/7.

He glances at me before looking back at the road. "Not that I'm complaining because he's great, but does he have an off switch?"

A loud, uncontrollable laugh bursts out of me. Slapping a hand over my mouth, I look back at Rhys—who is still sleeping in the back seat—and shake my head at Jace. Rhys is a sweetheart and highly energetic, but he rarely stops. He's like the energizer bunny.

"He does not." Resting my head back, I stare at the big man beside me.

His brown hair is disheveled from the wind, and his square jaw is covered in scruff. The t-shirt he's wearing is working overtime, the sleeves stretched tight around his bulging biceps and over his strong chest.

A vision of me bearing down on his pecs as I ride him flits across my mind.

I can still feel the heat of his hands on my hips as I ground my clit along his hard cock, using him to make myself come. Hot shivers race down my spine as I remember how good it felt to shatter above him, his dirty words making me wet and his praise burrowing deep into my heart.

My needy pussy spasms, and my cheeks flush. I've been consumed by these memories the entire day. He consumes me.

Glancing my way, he winks, making the butterflies in my stomach flutter. Like usual, I want to grab his smug scruffy face and kiss him. Then, I want to run. Run my hands over his hard chest and scratch my nails down his back while he—

Oh god, what is wrong with me?

"What was that?"

Did I say that out loud?

"What? Nothing. Just thinking again." I gasp, nervously, my heart speeding.

Jace runs his thumb back and forth across the sensitive skin of my thigh, driving me insane and setting my body on fire at the same time. Everything Jace does sets me on fire. He's the gasoline, and together we're combustible.

He looks over, with one of those smoldering, all-knowing smirks of his. My panties flood with arousal, and my damn thighs contract at the impact.

Damn, that cocksure Miller smirk of his.

Biting my lip, I turn away, my face hot. He has been such a flirt today. Every little touch and graze of his hands on my body has been deliberate. The smoldering looks that linger and hint at so much more, feel salacious and provocative. Each one awakens a hungry desire deep in my belly that can only be satiated by him.

"Oh, I'm *sure* you were, Sunshine," he says smugly.

I roll my eyes at him, pretending like I wasn't envisioning him driving into me while fighting the hot chills my thoughts give me. I need to find something to talk about that will keep my head out of the gutter.

Swiveling my head towards him, I ask curiously, "Can I ask you a question?"

"You can ask me anything." He peers at me for a second, unsure where I'm going with this.

I pause, trying to figure out how I want to ask this. It's been niggling at me since he asked about my relationship with Sam. "Did you doubt your choice?" I think I know the answer, but I want to hear it from him.

"Every day." He squeezes my leg.

The tightness in my chest lessens. I know it's horribly selfish, but that knowledge eases an ache in my heart.

"Me too," I whisper.

I still doubt my choices. I'm torn between guilt for moving on with someone new, regret over the time I lost with Jace, and fear that he'll reject me again. It's a lot to handle.

The two of us stay silent for a beat, thinking about all the what-ifs.

"Did you ever try to call me?" I ask, curious again.

I mean, seriously, what is wrong with me? Why do I want to keep torturing myself with what-could-have-beens?

"Once, but that is a story for another night," he laments. I can hear the despondency in his admission, making me wonder.

Maybe there is hope. Maybe we can make peace with the past and move forward. Maybe he'll understand. If he can understand how I felt after we went our separate ways, we might be able to navigate the future.

"Okay."

"Did you?" His knuckles whiten like he's bracing himself for my answer.

"Every day, for weeks. I even looked up your work email once. But I … I chickened out. I couldn't bring myself to write you an email. Seemed so impersonal after all we shared. Besides, I wanted you to be happy. I stopped, though … When Scarlett told me you were getting married, I never let myself look you up again." I exhale, a small weight lifting from my chest.

I didn't want to let him go, but I had to for the sake of my own broken heart. I had already been so depressed. For weeks, I dreamed he would show up at my door and sweep me off my feet. He never did.

"I'm sorry. For so much. I—"

"No. Don't," I interrupt, not wanting him to feel an ounce of guilt or regret. Life happens. All that matters is how we move forward now. "You don't have anything to be sorry for."

"Yes, I do. I hurt you, and that kills me. I will regret doing that to you, to us, for the rest of my life. I never wanted to hurt you," he states gruffly, bringing my hand to his lips and kissing the tips of my fingers.

"I know. I have my regrets and apologies to give too," I profess. *Now is the perfect time.*

"What do you have to feel sorry about? It's me that let you walk away," he blurts, cutting me off.

I sigh, trying to form my thoughts.

He doesn't get it. We are both culpable for what happened after Alina showed up, but when he takes all the blame, it makes me scared he won't be able to move on from past hurts. Jace can be stubborn and blind when he focuses on something he wants.

"Jace, when I returned home, I was a complete mess. Completely heartbroken. I shouldn't have walked away. I should have fought. I should have reached out. There are so many things I wish I could have done differently. But it's too late, and I need to tell you—"

"Mommy." Rhys's sleep-filled voice jolts me from divulging more.

Twisting around, I give Rhys my attention. "What's wrong, bug?"

His hair is all mussed, sticking up in the back, and his eyes are barely open. I'm pretty sure he's still half asleep.

"I need to pee. It feels like my penis is going to explode," he whines.

"What the f—?" Jace barks a laugh, trying to look back at Rhys but can't.

"Can you hold it?"

"Mom, didn't you hear what I said? My penis is going to explode. I need to go now," he says, making me groan.

I wish he would have stayed asleep until we got to the hotel.

"Hold on, kiddo. I'll find you a spot," Jace assures him.

Less than a minute later, Jace has us pulled over on the side of the road. He refuses to let me out of the car, insisting for me to stay put.

I watch as he and Rhys laugh, watering the plants together.

CHAPTER FIFTY

Rylann

Leaning against the wall, I watch Rhys sleep for a minute.

He's finally tuckered out and curled up into a ball, snoring. After his emergency restroom break, he caught a second wind and was wide awake when we got to the hotel. At Jace's suggestion, we took him for a night swim to help tire him out again. Of course, it worked. Jace has this special power over me and Rhys. He is so attuned to our needs that we've become putty in his hands. Hands that have begun to remold us into our old selves.

This is exactly what Sam wanted for us.

Smiling to myself, I push off the wall and head into the bathroom. Turning on the shower, I let the water warm while stripping out of my bathing suit. I hang it over the shower rod before stepping under the hot spray to wash my hair and body. I close my eyes and let past memories of me and Jace flood my brain.

The first time our eyes locked, knocking the sense out of me. The electrical current that zapped between us when his hand took mine. The first time his lips touched mine, setting me on fire. Getting lost in darkened corners of the marketplace, filling them with secret kisses. Staying up all night, watching the moonlight glitter across the ocean like a sparkling blanket. Cool sheets tangled around us as we talked about anything and everything. The way he set my body on fire with just one look. One kiss. One touch. The weight of his body on mine as we became one. The look of love in his eyes that sent my heart soaring and tethering itself to him for all time.

It's him. It's always been him.

My pulse speeds up, and my hands feel clammy. Now's the time. I can do this. I can tell him. We can get through this together.

Hopping out of the shower, I dry up as fast as I can. Newfound determination runs through me as I tie my wet hair into a messy bun before putting on my sleep shorts and tank.

When I walk into the living room, Jace stands up from the couch, and my determination goes up in flames at the sight of him in nothing but those sexy-as-sin gray cut-off sweatpants.

Holy fuck, he's so hot.

His hair is damp from his shower, and I can smell his sexy orange leather scent from here. My mouth waters as I take in his muscular torso and well-defined abs. My nipples harden, and my fingers itch to touch him.

When our eyes meet, goosebumps skitter across my skin. Heat burns in his eyes as he looks me up and down, igniting flames deep in my belly. Gulping, I watch his irises glow like molten honey rather than the warm green they are in the light of day.

He reaches out his hand, beckoning me. "Come here, love."

I dutifully follow his instruction and inch my way toward him, one step at a time, and take his hand. When his tongue swipes along his bottom lip, my clit pulses, and my pussy floods with arousal.

Jace leads me to take a seat on the couch. He takes the spot beside me and reaches for the remote before asking, "What do you want to watch?"

Wait, what? I don't want to watch a damn thing.

"I don't care. You choose," I mumble. clearing my throat. My mouth feels dry like sandpaper. and my heart is beating a mile a minute. All I want is for him to touch me.

Clicking through the channels, he puts on some random movie starring one of the Chrises. I recognize it, but I don't care which movie it is. The only thing occupying my brain right now is the sexy man sitting next to me. Tucking into his side, I try concentrating and rest my head on his chest to no avail. The heat of his body and the charged particles of energy bouncing between us are too distracting.

Jace runs his fingers over my shoulder in lazy circles, and my sensitive skin tingles. My body feels like it's on fire and the lone cure is for his hands to douse the burn.

"Jace." My voice sounds scratchy and thick.

"Rylann," he grunts.

Okay. So maybe I'm not alone in this fiery, lust-filled haze. Even if he's on the same page, I hesitate with a sigh. I hate that I'm not the same woman I used to be. The one that just went for it. Took what she wanted. I've lost that part of me.

Jace turns his attention away from the TV and watches me. Waiting. This dense, heady sense of hunger stirs inside me, begging to take over. I want him so badly, I ache.

"I can hear you thinking. What do you want?" His thumb brushes over the apple of my cheek. My eyes close to his touch, and my breathing increases. "Open your eyes."

My eyes fly open at his command.

Jace is watching me, the hungry look in his eyes matching my own. While it appears like he wants to devour me like his last meal, he holds back.

My confidence falters, and the words stick on my tongue. I know he wants me to be sure about us before caving into what our bodies want. I'm purely certain about one thing—him.

Jace is the man I want. I want all of him. The same way he wants all of me. Consequences be damned.

With my eyes, I give him the only answer there ever could be when it comes to him. *Take me. Claim me. Make me yours. Body and soul.*

He twists his body, and his hands land on my hips. Shifting closer to him, I place my hands on his shoulders.

"Are you sure?" He whispers the words, his breath fanning over my lips.

"Yes," I croak.

Lifting me onto his lap sideways, my ass firmly planted on his straining erection, he tangles one hand in the hair at the back of my neck. He grasps my waist with the other and pulls me millimeters from his mouth.

"I've waited so long for you to be back here with me. This is where you belong, isn't it, Sunshine?" he rumbles over my mouth.

My heart soars.

He's right—this is exactly where I'm supposed to be. Where I want to be. Everything feels right when it's just us. The rest of the world melts away.

"Yes," I whimper with need.

"Please tell me you feel it too." Eyes on his, I nod my head.

I can feel it. Our connection. It's as real and tangible as the big fat cock I'm sitting on.

Bringing his hand up, he sweeps his thumb over my bottom lip, pulling down. A zip of courage hits me, and I dart my tongue over the tip of his digit, licking it with a moan.

"Fuck," he grunts, shifting me on his lap, and his hard cock pulses beneath me.

Lust pools in my belly, urging me to embrace the moment and drop my guard. Leaning into my desires, I grab his wrist and lift his hand. Slowly, I wrap my lips around his thumb and suck. My eyes never leave his as I twirl my tongue around the tip and bite down.

A noise that sounds more like a feral growl than a groan resonates in his chest, and his cock twitches under me. My thighs clench in response. He pulls his finger from my mouth with a pop and crashes his lips to mine.

The fire inside me burns. My hands take purchase on his broad shoulders before sinking them into his hair. I draw him closer, deepening the kiss. Our tongues stroke and swirl in a fight neither of us wants to end.

His hands slide down my chest, kneading my breasts, testing their weight in his hands. His thumbs stroke over my hardened nipples, and I arch into his touch. Jace pinches my nipples between his fingertips. The mix of pleasure and pain is delicious, and it sends bolts of liquid lust straight to my center. He swallows my moans, bringing my body closer to the edge.

Achingly slowly he slides one palm over my stomach, down between my spread legs, teasing me. Grazing my wet pussy with the back of his hand, he pauses, testing the heat seeping through the thin fabric of my sleep shorts. Tormenting me in the most tantalizing of ways.

Urging him to move the offending material and alleviate the ache building between my legs, I lift my hips. He ignores my request and continues his journey down my body, driving me crazy with need, making sure to touch every inch of my skin. When his hand starts traveling up my body, ignoring the place I want his hand to be, I can't take it anymore.

Breaking our kiss, breaths mingling, I declare, "It's time to take me to bed, Jace."

"Thank fuck," he groans, kissing me again.

I get lost in his lips before pushing him back, shaking my head. His heart thumps wildly under my palm. "Now. No more waiting. Make me yours."

"My pleasure, Sunshine," he echoes the same words he used all those years ago.

CHAPTER FIFTY-ONE

Jace

In one fluid motion, I stand from the couch with Rylann's soft body nestled in my arms.

Clasping her hands around my neck, she looks up and my steps falter what I see in her eyes. There is no mistaking the lust-filled yearning staring back at me from the face of my gorgeous girl.

For some reason, my heart squeezes with uncertainty. I know she wants me to take her to bed, but I need to be sure this is the right step for us. We have time this go around, and I have no problem waiting if it means I get to keep her forever.

"Are you sure you're ready to do this? Because once I start, I won't be able to stop."

A sly smile curves her lips at the same warning I gave her the first time we decided to make our relationship physical. A reminder of the past that brought us together then and brings us together now.

She peppers kisses on my jaw and runs her fingernails over my scalp, making it prickle and my cock jump.

"I'm sure, Ace. Please," she whispers, tugging my hair, and encouraging me to move.

I don't need to be told a third time. If she wants me, then that's what she will get. All. Of. Me.

Without further delay, I carry her to our room.

A vision of me carrying her in a white dress over the threshold of our home flashes before me. My chest floods with warmth, and a wave of happiness washes over me. Not a single doubt creeps in as I think about our future.

This is exactly where she should be—in my arms, in my bed, woven deep down into every thread of my being. I want to cherish her and make her mine until the end of time. Make sure she never leaves my side again. She's it for me. By the end of the night, I hope she has no doubt about it.

Taking a deep breath, I focus on the present. On her. I place Rylann on her feet in the middle of the room. Backtracking to the door, I close it and flip the lock. When I turn around, I'm stunned silent at the sight before me.

Rylann is silhouetted in the pale moonlight as it casts a halo of light around her head, illuminating her beauty beyond belief. She's breathtaking when even looking vulnerable, unsure of what to do next with her lip trapped between her teeth, fidgeting with the hem of her shirt.

"Relax, Sunshine. You're in charge. I'll help you along the way, but I will only do what you want me to do. Do you understand?" My need to take care of her outweighs any need I have to ravish her. Even if my angry, hard cock disagrees.

"Yes, I understand," she says with a nod. She worries her tongue over her bottom lip, drawing my attention to it.

My need to taste her has me stepping forward, bringing us chest to chest. Pushing her hair behind her ear, I wait for those telltale goosebumps to erupt across her skin, and I smirk when her flesh pebbles. Her eyes dart away, and I almost growl. Tilting her chin up, she closes her eyes and takes a shaky breath.

"Look at me, Rylann," I demand, waiting until her lids slide open and her eyes are on me. "Tonight is all about you. I was teasing earlier. If at any time you want to stop, all you have to do is tell me and I'll stop immediately. Got it?"

I mean it. I will never put my needs before hers. She comes first, in every sense of the word. Always will.

Releasing her lip, she nods, dropping her hands to her side and pulls her shoulders back with confidence.

"Use your words, Sunny."

With little to no light in the room, her eyes look like endless black pools, but nothing hides the flickering desire in them. My heart hammers in my chest. The buzz of anticipation makes my blood boil beneath the surface.

"Yes. I'm in charge. If I say stop, you stop," she retorts.

I smirk at the sass in her tone. It turns me the fuck on.

That's right, love. Let's let that little vixen in you out for some playtime.

"Good girl. I like it when you listen," I grunt.

My words are like gas to the fire. Her eyes burn with pure fucking lust. She's so aroused I can smell it coming off of her droves, fogging up the air between us. My cock grows harder, and my mouth waters.

She wants me, but she's not completely confident in asking for what she wants me to do to her. It's my job to get her there. To encourage her. To give her the confidence to speak her inner desires aloud. Take what she wants. I'm hoping that if I go slow enough and make her a needy wet mess, she'll forget about everything else and give into her baser instincts.

I take my time trailing my fingertips up her arm, over her collarbone and her neck. Walking around her body, staying as close to her as possible, I repeat the same trail down her other side. A wispy moan breaks loose from her throat as I stand in front of her again. Leaning down, she shudders as I run my nose up from the base of her neck to her hair and inhale her intoxicating scent.

Grazing my lips along her throat, I stop and whisper in her ear, "Do you want me to kiss you now?"

"Y—"

I crush my lips to hers before she finishes responding, swallowing her answer with a searing kiss.

Her small hands grip my forearms for balance as I grip her hips, pulling her flush to my chest. Her pelvis thrusts forward, and I slide my hands over her backside, squeezing her deliciously thick ass while I fuck her mouth with my tongue. When I break our kiss, I watch her chest heave as she tries to catch her breath. I want her so badly, I'm tempted to rip her clothes off. But I want to drag this out. Take my time with her.

"It's time for less clothes. What do you think?"

She nods, and I lift my brow at her. She knows what I want.

"Yes," she says breathlessly.

Stepping away from her, I grab the bottom of her top and drag it up over her body, my fingers creeping up in a deliberate sensual caress. From hip to neck, I enjoy the feel of her skin under mine. Dropping the shirt to the floor, I take in the sexy woman before me.

"Fuck, you're beautiful," I say, my voice thick. My cock grows painfully hard as my eyes feast on her curves.

She hums as her eyes close and that won't do. I want her to watch me as I worship her body.

"Eyes on me, Sunshine."

Her eyes snap open at my command, and my cock jumps in my shorts. I love when she follows my direction. I've only ever been this way with her. Tamping that part down a bit, I bring my eyes back to her body, exploring every inch of her skin with my eyes.

"Jace?" Her sultry voice pulls my attention back to her face.

"Yeah?"

"Please touch me," she whispers.

Fuck yes, there it is. I knew if I went slow enough, teased her enough, she'd eventually ask for what she wants.

My eyes land on her large tits and those chocolate-colored nipples. Bending my knees, I crouch down, bringing my face to her chest. Damn, her tits are perfect. She arches her back, presenting her breasts to my mouth, begging for my touch.

I look up into her dark brown eyes. "Do you want me to use my hands or my mouth?"

"Both." She sighs.

My chest puffs at her request. "Greedy girl," I murmur, leaning closer. "I like it."

Her nipple puckers under my hot breath. My chest vibrates with a moan as I swipe my tongue around the hardened peak before bringing it into my mouth, sucking. She whimpers as I simultaneously pinch the other between my fingertips. Pulling off her tit with a pop, I proceed to lavish the other with the same generous attention. Alternating between the two, I take my time licking, pinching, and sucking. She tastes amazing.

Her mewls get louder as I nip the underside of her breast with my teeth, marking her. I want her to see them and remember that it was my mouth worshiping them. That she belongs to me.

"You like it when I put my mark on you. Don't you, Sunshine?" I ask around her nipple.

"Mhmm." She arches her back further, inviting me to keep going. Her thighs tense, and her knees tremble.

Lowering to my knees in front of her, I kiss my way down her soft stomach, licking the soft white scars below her belly button. She inhales sharply and grasps my shoulders for balance.

Eyes locked on mine, just the way I want, I tug at the band of her sleep shorts. "Can I take these off?" My mouth waters thinking about tasting her sweet pussy.

She audibly swallows. "Please."

I shouldn't be surprised, but I am when I pull the shorts over her hips and down her toned legs.

"Fuck, no panties," I hiss. Leaning in, I inhale her scent at the apex of her thighs, making her moan. "Just the way I like it."

"Fuck," she keens.

I run my nose up and down her slit. Her gaspy mewls fill the air.

"Quiet now. We don't want to wake anyone up, now, do we?"

"No, I-I'll be quiet," she sputters, dragging in short, shallow breaths.

"Good girl. Now, where were we?"

Placing my hands on her ankles at a crawling pace, I glide my palms up her calves, over her knees, coming to a stop at the tops of her thighs. Her skin pebbles at my touch. I love how responsive her body is to mine. Her eyes close again like she's trying to catch her bearing. I don't want her to think. I only want her to feel.

Removing my hands, I repeat, "Eyes on me. Do not close them. Be here with me."

She nods, eyes wide. "Okay."

"Do you still want me to touch you?"

"Yes." She nods, her bottom lip trapped between her teeth.

She's out of breath, looking needy for my touch. It's hot as fuck and if my dick gets any harder, I'm going to burst out of these shorts.

"Where?" I ask.

She just her hips forward, shoving her pussy in my face.

I know what she wants. With my palms on her hips, I push her back a few steps, until her knees hit the bed and she falls back. Leaning back on her elbows, she watches me as I crawl to her, spreading her knees open.

She's soaking wet. I stare at her glistening pussy in the soft light. Kissing her inner thigh, I tell her, like the pushy bastard I am, "Use your words, Sun."

She does more than that. She grabs my hair and leads my mouth to her wet center. "Put your mouth on me, Jace. Please. I need you to make me come with your tongue."

That's my girl.

Eyes still on her, I lurch forward, burying my face in her pussy. Her mouth falls open, watching me lick up her wet seam. Lifting her legs over my shoulders, I use my thumbs to spread her open before I eat her like she is my last meal. She tastes sweet, tangy and utterly Intoxicating. I'll never get enough of her and, like a starving man, I devour her. I rub my face in her essence, hoping her scent seeps into my pores so I can always smell her as I swirl my tongue over her clit in quick punishing flicks.

She pants my name. I spear my tongue into her hot center, lapping at her juices before moving back to her clit and lashing at the swollen bundle of nerves, until her thighs shake and her pussy quivers. The taste of her cream on my tongue has me ready to blow .

"I need this pretty pussy to come all over my face right the fuck now."

She pulls at my hair and grinds her pussy into my face, riding it.

"That's it. Ride my face. Take what you want," I mumble before flattening my tongue. I swipe it from the bottom up before flicking her clit.

When her pussy begins to pulse again, I bury two fingers deep into her tight channel, curling them up, massaging her G-spot until her body explodes, spasming around my fingers.

"Yes!" She screams as her arousal floods my mouth.

I lap at her center, collecting every bit of her honey with my tongue. I watch as she rides out the waves of her orgasm. She looks ravishing with her chin tucked to her chest, her mouth open, and her chest heaving. When she opens her eyes, a shy satisfied smile graces her lips.

I want to pound on my chest in triumph. I did that.

Dropping her legs to the floor, I rise onto my knees. Curling my fingers around the nape of her neck, I pull her face to mine and my lips to hers. Shoving my tongue into her mouth, I kiss her, hard and deep.

She kisses me back, moaning as she tastes herself on my lips. She wraps her arms and legs around me, and without breaking our kiss, I stand up with her clinging to my body. I hold her up, kissing her with everything I have. She tries to grind her pussy against my cock, but I pull away, pressing my forehead to hers.

"Let's get you into bed, Sunshine." I kiss her head.

"No." She leans back to stare me in the eyes.

"What do you want then?"

She unwraps her legs from around me, sliding her wet pussy down my body and over my cock until she's on her feet. Tugging on my shorts, I grab her wrists, stopping her. She looks up at me, shock followed by shame flashing across her features before her eyes dart away.

Oh, fuck no. That's not happening.

"Hey, look at me."

She shakes her head.

"I need you to look at me."

She brings her eyes back to mine.

"Hear my words, love. Feel them. I want you. But I'm not going anywhere. There is no rush. I will always give you whatever you want, but you have to be absolutely sure. There is no going back once I make you mine."

I search her eyes, making sure she understands. I want nothing more than to be inside her, but I want her to be sure. We can't go back. *I* can't go back after having her in my arms again.

"I'm already yours."

My heart bashes against my ribcage, but I don't move. I let her words sink in.

I'm already yours.

I let go of her wrists and let her continue.

She pulls my shorts down, my cock springing free, and stares at it while licking her lips. My cock has a mind of its own as it bobs, jumping at her attention. I would love to see her puffy pink lips wrapped around my dick, but not tonight. She just admitted that she was mine, soothing the ache in my soul.

Before she can fall to her knees, I lift her up in my arms. "Wrap your legs around my waist."

She obeys immediately.

Turning us around, I sit down on the bed and move up until my back's against the headboard. Her legs straddle me, my hard cock nestled against her wet center. The sight takes me back to the first time we had sex. I smile, thinking about the tub. She was so fucking sexy and brave, laying in that tub, making the first move.

"What's got you smiling?"

"Just thinking about our first time. How you were such a tease sitting in—"

"The tub," she finishes my sentence. "Oh, I remember. You were just as sweet then as you are now."

"Is that right?" I smile. I don't quite remember being so sweet with her. I remember taking her in the tub, on the counter, against the wall, in the bed ... and none of it was sweet. It was fucking, and it was hands down the best I've ever had. "I was definitely no gentleman, babe," I say, nipping at her neck.

"Yep." She pecks my lips. "You were. And you were so ... dominating." She shivers, kissing me. "Giving." Kiss. "Sexy." This time, when she kisses me, her hips glide forward, soaking my length in her wetness.

A growl rumbles in my chest, the heat of her pussy driving me crazy. I claim her mouth, sliding my tongue around hers as we hold onto each other tightly, tugging and pulling. Seeking to get closer. My desire to push inside her and never leave grows. My cock pulses at the vision of slipping inside her hot wet heat.

Rylann begins to swivel and grind her hips. When her movements have the head of my cock notched at her entrance, she stills. Pulling her lips from mine, she sits up on her knees, keeping my tip gripped between her slit. She reaches between us, stroking my stiff cock. Her arousal drips down my shaft. Without thinking, my hips lift, my cock spearing her and spreading her open, breaching her tight hole.

"Do you remember what you said after I rode you in the tub?" Her eyes are heavy with desire, bouncing between my face and my nearly swallowed cock.

I remember every word. Every kiss. Every touch. Every orgasm. Every. Fucking. Thing.

"Yes," I grit out between clenched teeth.

"Tell me again." Her tone is sweet and sticky. She smirks, giving the head of my cock a squeeze.

This is exactly what I want for her—to rediscover the confident, sexy woman I know she is. It's one of the many parts of her that had me falling in the first place.

She loves having me by the dick. And I love her *on* it. She owns me, and I'm okay with that. She can do whatever she wants to me.

But it's a two-way street, and I can only hold back so much. Rylann turns me into a feral, out-of-control beast.

Gripping her hair at the nape of her neck, I tug, reminding her that I let her be in charge. For now. She moans, and I grit my teeth. I might let her lead, but her body tells me a different story. Her body craves for me to own her. To own her pleasure.

"I said ... Hold on tight," I grunt through my teeth.

"Hold tight, Ace," she says before slamming down, impaling herself on my stiff length, taking every inch of me like she was made just for me.

"Oh, fuck." I groan at the feel of her tight channel around my cock.

She gasps, head thrown back, her lips a perfect O. I stay still, letting her get used to my thickness. To being full of my cock. When her muscles relax, her eyes open to mine. I'm struggling, barely hanging on by a thread; she feels so good wrapped around me. I wait.

She leans forward, and her hard nipples brush against my chest as she whispers in my ear, "Fuck me."

My hands grab her hips tight, lifting her up before repeatedly ramming her back down on my length. Her nails dig into my pecs as she proceeds to ride me like the queen she is. My eyes attempt to roll to the back of my head, but I refuse to take them off of her.

The way her tits jiggle as she bounces on my cock. The way her neck looks when I pull her hair, tilting her head back. The way her eyes glaze over in ecstasy, her mouth open and panting for breath.

She's fucking perfect.

"Do you like being in control, Sunshine? Do you like riding my cock?"

"Oh, god yes. You feel so good." She slows her pace, grinding her clit on my pelvis harder every time she bottoms out.

I let her find her rhythm, watching in awe as her greedy pussy inhales my cock. I love seeing it coated and glistening with her arousal.

"You're stunning, but right now, baby, you look fucking fantastic stuffed to the brim with my cock."

My dirty words spur her on. She increases her pace, bouncing faster. Harder.

Reaching between her legs, I rub her clit in tight circles. "I need you to be there with me, Sun. Come all over my dick." I grunt, my other hand squeezing her ass. I'm so fucking close, I can feel my balls tingling, my cum ready to explode inside her.

"I … I'm there. Yes. Oh, Jacccce," she cries, her pussy clamping down around me.

Her muscles spasm hard, and the grip she has on my dick sends me soaring with her. Thick ropes of my cum empty inside her, coating her womb and marking her as mine forever. She falls forward onto my chest, both of us panting, bodies spent and covered in sweat.

Okay, maybe that was the best sex of my life. Always is with her. It's our connection. The physical and emotional ties that bind us are so twisted up that it comes out in uncontrollable passion.

"That was amazing. You're amazing, Sunshine."

"That was pretty amazing, wasn't it?" She leans back, panting, bringing us nose to nose.

"Fucking hot, baby." I grip her face in my hands and kiss her.

We shift, and my dick slips from its home. Glancing down, I watch as my cum drips out of her, pooling between us. I tamp down the urge to push it back inside her as my cock perks up, ready for round two. Twisting us around so we lay side by side, we stare at each other. Her eyes sparkle as a shy smile graces her lips.

The words dance on my tongue. I refuse to be scared this time around.

I kiss her nose and brush her stray hairs back from her face, in the way I know she likes, then go all in. "I love you."

Her body stiffens, and I think I've fucked up until she whispers, "I love you too."

Tears well in her eyes, and her face lights up with a smile so bright my heart stops. If you tried to tell me it's impossible for someone to visibly melt, I'd call you a damn liar because that's exactly what happens to her in my arms—she melts at my words.

"I love you, Sunshine. I always have and always will," I confess. Then I kiss her. I kiss her until she's a breathless, panting mess. And then, I make love to her all over again.

CHAPTER FIFTY-TWO

Jace

I watch Rylann sleep for a little longer.

She looks like a beautiful sleeping angel, peaceful. A soft smile plays on her lips. I love seeing her like this, wrapped in the sheets of our bed.

I admire her strength in tackling the past year, which I know hasn't been easy on her. Now that we've found our way back to one another, she won't have to do life on her own anymore. We were robbed of having a future before, but that's all behind us now. I plan on being there for her and Rhys from now on. Whatever they need, I'll get it for them.

Which is part of the reason I'm about to wake up sleeping beauty. I want to watch the sunrise together. Like we did that first night. Today is the mark of a new stage for us. The beginning of a new life. One we forge together.

"Ry, I need you to wake up, baby." I run my fingers through her hair and kiss her cheek. "Hey, sleepy head. I want to share something with you."

"Hmm. Do I have to?" She whines, snuggling back into her pillow.

She's so cute. If I didn't have a plan, I'd watch her sleep for the rest of the day.

"Yes. Now, come on." I climb out of bed and slide on my shorts and a hoodie. I place her pajamas—if you can call them that—and the hotel robe next to her. "Put this on."

"Ugh, fine," she grouses, throwing the sheet off her body and dragging herself out of bed.

My eyes linger on her nakedness, and my dick perks up. Fuck, she's gorgeous.

"Nope. None of that." She points at my hardening cock.

I look down and shrug. "Can't be helped, love. You're fuck hot and he,"—I point down—"loves being inside you."

She blushes at my dirty mouth and, under her breath, mumbles, "Oh, I bet he does."

Chuckling to myself, I watch her put her pajamas back on under the hotel robe I have laid out for her. When she finishes putting her hair in a messy bun, I grab her hand and lead her outside to the patio.

"Jace, it's still dark out. Why are we up?"

"We're up to watch the sunrise."

She gives me a sleepy smile, appreciating my sentimentality. Dragging the largest lounger to the middle of the space, I lay down, bringing her with me. She curls into my side as I cradle her tight. Kissing the top of her head, I breathe in her soothing scent. A sense of calm takes over my senses.

"Did you know that the minutes leading up to the sunrise are called the blue hour?" I ask into her hair.

She shakes her head.

"During the blue hour, the sky and earth are coated in a blue so deep and vivid, it's become its own time of day. Not quite dawn or twilight. That's what we've been living in—the blue hour, the time before the sun rises shining its light on a new day. I don't want to live in the blue hour anymore. I want to live in the daylight. With you. When the sun rises in a few minutes, it will be a new day for us. We will be starting anew. This is our time, Sunshine."

"I like the sound of that. But how will we work in the real world?"

Her question is loaded with concern. Rightfully so. Anything worth having is worth fighting for. She's worth the fight. I know that now.

"We'll go slow. We will talk on the phone. Text. Video call. We'll visit. As soon as we get home, we'll sit down with our calendars and create a plan. There's a lot of summer left. That gives us time. I'll visit you, and you and Rhys will visit me."

"What happens when school starts and work gets away from you?"

She's worried. I get it. Long-distance relationships are hard to navigate, especially when there's a child involved. But I'm already planning my next moves—the things I need to do to ensure I can leave L.A. behind and start my life with them. I don't want to freak her out, so I'll keep that to myself.

"Don't worry about that. Concentrate on us. I won't let anything come between us again. I promise." After everything that happened in the past, I know it's hard for her to accept my words as the truth.

"Do you really believe that?" She looks up at me with worry in her big brown eyes.

"Of course I do." I cup her cheek. "You and me, we are meant to be," I profess before pecking her lips.

"Please don't make promises you can't keep." Her eyes gloss over with unshed tears.

"I plan to keep every single one. You'll see. I know you're scared, but there isn't anything holding us back this time. I love you. I love Rhys. I know you're a package deal. I wouldn't say any of this if I didn't one hundred percent mean it."

"But. I-I—"

I cut her off from whatever she was going to say. I don't want her doubting us. "Shh. It's okay to be scared. But I got you this time. I won't let go. I promise."

Rylann leans in and kisses me. I pull her tighter, deepening our kiss. Forcing her to feel the depth of my love for her. Our tongues lazily tangle together in a slow and passionate kiss.

I want this to last forever. This feeling of being home. I can feel it soul-deep that we are going to make it. We're a family. I'll never choose another again. She and Rhys will always come first. It might take some time, but it's happening. I will be a part of their lives from here on out. She's mine, and I am hers.

The glass door swooshes open, and she pushes me away, scared of being caught. I snigger and wink at her. She rolls her eyes at me. She can pretend to be annoyed all she wants. We're completely blocked; the little person that opened the door couldn't have seen us kissing.

"Mommy, why are you outside?" Rhys's voice is thick with sleep.

"Come here, bud," I call out before she can answer.

He pads across the patio to us. When he nears, I pull him to my side, opposite Rylann.

"We came outside to watch the sunrise," I explain, kissing the top of his head, smiling to myself when I catch his sweet scent.

Rhys yawns and curls up in the nook of my arm and shoulder, mirroring his mother. My heart never felt as full as with the two of them in my arms.

"Can I see it too?"

"Of course, bug. Are you cold?" Rylann reaches over and rubs his arm.

"Nuh uh." Rhys shakes his head, burrowing further into my side.

Warmth floods my chest and spreads throughout my body knowing he feels warm and safe in my arms. My throat tightens with emotion. Hugging Rhys's tiny body tightly to my chest, I kiss his head again, fighting the tears that gather in my eyes. There is no way I can live life without the two of them in it. This sweet, adorable little boy has wormed his way into my heart. I know without a doubt I love him with every part of me. I would do anything to protect him, to ensure his welfare and safety at all costs. He's mine. Same as Rylann. *Mine.*

I know it's fast, but I will do anything within my power to have them in my life everyday. With them, I feel complete. Happy. We feel right together. Our love feels right.

"So, kiddo, did I make good on checking off that vacation list?"

Rhys yawns again, forcing his eyes to stay open. "Best vacation ever."

I chuckle at his response. "We have one more thing to do before we leave here."

"Really?" He looks up at me with his honey-brown eyes.

My heart swells with love at his sweet face. "We sure do. I promised sea turtles, and that's what I plan on delivering."

"Awesome," he whispers. Lowering his head back onto my chest, he snuggles close, wrapping his arm around my stomach. In a matter of seconds, his breathing slows and he's floated off back to sleep.

Taking a deep breath, I cherish the moment. We watch the blue sky turn red and gold with the rising sun. I have my two favorite people in my arms, and I feel like life can't get better than this.

I don't think I have ever seen a sunrise so beautiful. So full of hope.

The last couple of hours have been a whirlwind. I was able to drive Rhys down to the lowest point in America to see the green sand beaches and to go off-roading to see a flotilla of sea turtles sunbathing on the black sand beaches of Punaluʻu. Since we couldn't go near them, we took a bunch of funny pictures with them in the background. He really got a kick out of that. I managed to make it look like he had a sea turtle in the palm of his hand, sitting on his head, and his favorite was a turtle pinched between his fingers while he pretended to kiss it.

Now, I'm standing on the beach with Levi, watching the kids toss a frisbee back and forth. Well, I should say attempt to toss a frisbee as much as a bunch of six-year-olds can.

"So, how was the trip?" Levi asks.

"It was good. Rhys had the time of his life."

I pull out my phone and show him the pictures of Rhys but scroll to the far left. Before I can stop it from happening, he gets a glimpse of the picture I took of Rylann sleeping.

I couldn't help snapping a few pictures of her. She looked so beautiful asleep, with her rich brown hair spread across the pillow and the sheet draped around her but still covering her nakedness beneath.

"So ..."

Levi and I share a look. I know what he's asking, but I'm not about to give him details.

"I think we made a lot of progress."

"I'll say."

"Fuck off, Lee. It's not like that. I love her."

"I know you do. I never doubted that. Is she there with you?"

We stand there, shoulder to shoulder, watching the kids.

Is she there with me?

Isn't that the million-dollar question? She told me she loves me. I know without a doubt that's true, and yet this morning, I'm questioning it. She's still holding something back.

"She says she loves me too. But ..."

"She's still holding back," he says, repeating my thoughts.

When we left for the airport, she started to retreat. I asked if she regretted anything, and she vehemently shook her head. But

I can't get that fake smile she gave me out of my head, the kind of smile someone uses when to mask their real feelings.

I nod. "Yes, exactly. I don't know what to do. How do I get her to see what I do? We are meant to be together."

"Just give her time, man. She's been through a lot. Just keep meaning what you say and proving it with actions. She'll come around. She really loves you. Always has."

"You think?"

"Scarlett says yes, and she's never wrong. Well, that's not true—she's wrong about a lot of stuff. But not when it comes to Ry."

"Hmm."

"If you tell Scar I said she was wrong a lot, no one will find your body, *capiche?*"

"Mum's the word." I mime zipping my lips and throwing away the key.

"Why don't you go and see if the ladies are ready? It's about time to start, and I want to get the ball rolling. I can't wait to leave the kids with my parents for a few days and spend some time alone with my wife."

"Sounds good. And … thanks. For listening. I appreciate your support."

"Always. It will work out. I have faith." He slaps me on the shoulder.

"Thanks."

I leave him on the beach and head for the bridal suite. I feel like I'm walking on air. This trip has brought me so much happiness. I feel like myself again. I feel whole. And it's all because of her and her sweet boy.

I can't stop the grin that spreads across my face or the swagger in my step as I approach the door to the bridal suite.

This time, I won't miss seeing how beautiful she looks in her yellow dress. I won't miss telling her I love her under the stars. I won't let her go.

CHAPTER FIFTY-THREE

Rylann

I walk out of the bathroom and find my bestie twirling in the mirror. Her skin is glowing, and her blue eyes shine with what can only be described as pure happiness.

My stomach twinges in jealousy then roils in disgust at myself for having such a reaction. It's déjà vu. Only this time, everything is going to fall apart because of the untold truths I've been sitting on.

We are in the same bridal suite, getting ready for the simple ceremony Scarlett has planned, on the same white sand beach where she married Levi seven years ago, and I'm about to lose it. I've been trying to keep it together, but looking at her now, standing in front of the mirror so happy, in love, and looking so beautiful, I can't. The significance of today comes crashing down on me. Seeing her in her dress feels like a bad omen. Not for her—for me.

My beautiful friend is about to renew her vows to the love of her life. A man so wonderful, he's become a brother to me. Here I am, same as last time. A mess. In the eye of a storm that I know is about to hit.

I'll watch Scarlett get her happy ending all over again while mine disappears into a pile of volcanic ash.

Since the sun rose this morning, I've had this horrible feeling in the pit of my stomach. I knew that once we got on the plane my chance was over. I've officially become a horribly selfish person. Everything has come full circle, only this time, it's me that's about to not only decimate my own heart but the heart of the man I love too.

"Scarlett, you look stunning, sis …" I pause, trying to hold in the sob that wants to escape. Losing the battle, tears stream down my face in waves.

My best friend rushes to my side, pulling me into her arms, hugging me. "Why are you crying, Rice Cakes? You're scaring me a little here."

"I … I'm sorry. There is so much I haven't told you. I am so screwed, Scarlett. I've been the worst friend, keeping a secret from you. From myself. Everyone. I … Shit. I'm the worst person in the world."

"You could never," she says, shushing me, rubbing my arms.

"Oh, but I am. I've done something so horrible, so unforgivable, Scar. To make it all worse, I am so in love with Jace, but everything is so fucked up." I cry.

"I thought you had a wonderful time? What happened?" She looks around the room, trying to identify the problem so she can fix it.

But it's me that's the problem. I need fixing.

I shake my head. "We did. But that's the problem. We had a wonderful time, and now I'm about to fuck it all up. He's never going to forgive me."

"Why? What could you have possibly done?"

"Everything."

"Doubtful."

"Seriously, I have ..." I take a deep breath. Here goes nothing—or everything. I let the words pour out. I finally confess. "Okay, so you remember the day you made me open Sam's box?"

She nods waiting for me to continue.

"In the box, I found a bunch of letters to me, to Rhys, and to ... Nevermind. I'll get to that. Anyway, the thing I found last was a note that said,"—I use my fingers and air quote—"*Open First.* So I opened it. It was a note from Sam, explaining that he has letters written to Rhys that he would like me to give him on special occasions, like birthdays, graduation, and things like that. Also inside the envelope was a USB fob marked *Play This Next.* So I did, and that's when I figured it all out."

Bending over at the waist, I drop my head between my knees, taking deep ragged breaths.

"Figured *what* all out? Ry, you aren't making any sense. Also, why didn't you tell me what was in the box? I thought you hadn't opened it yet."

I shake my head again and shrug because I don't know what to say. I've never kept anything from her, but this time, it felt like I would be putting her in an impossible position. Hence keeping my shut mouth. Which I know was the wrong choice. I was too afraid to deal with the consequences. Instead, I buried my head in the sand. If I didn't say the words out loud, then I could justify it as protecting myself. I didn't want to feel the pain I felt seven years ago all over again.

"I don't know. A lot of reasons, I guess. But that's not the worst part," I whine. The tears have not stopped flowing.

Scarlett's eyebrows shoot up. "What was on the USB?"

With I sigh, I start at the beginning. Finally accepting that I can no longer keep Sam's secret.

My secret.

ONE MONTH AGO

I hit the play button. Sam's smile lights up his face, and I gasp. My heart sinks to my stomach.

"Rylann, if you are watching this video, it means ... Well, you know what it means. I know this might seem a little weird, but I got to thinking this might be the only way I can say what I need to. It's about 1:30 in the morning, and you and Rhys are sleeping down the hall. You two are the deepest sleepers I have ever had the pleasure to live with.

"I don't think you know this, but I wake up often and watch the two of you sleep. Total creeper, right? I have made so much noise in the house late at night, and neither of you have heard me. I like to think it's because the two of you feel safe with me.

"I even looked it up on the internet once. Turns out, it's not common and it means your brains are still working as you sleep. See, these are the things I do late at night or early in the morning while you two rocks sleep. I'm gonna miss these times."

Sam chuckles to himself, briefly looking off into the distance. He looks back into the camera and continues.

"Anyway, now to the serious stuff. Ry, before I get into why I made this video, I just want to tell you that you are the love of my life. The time we had together has been better than I ever could have imagined. You gave me everything and more. You gave me a family, you made me a husband and a father. Things I never dared to dream of. For this, I will forever be in your debt. I couldn't have asked for a better partner in life."

Sam puts his hand on his heart and takes a couple deep breaths.

"You are the most beautiful woman I ever laid eyes on. Add in your quick wit and those cute dimples, and I was a total goner from the start. I may not have shown you that in the beginning, but it's true. You are loving, loyal, a wonderful mother and best friend. You have the biggest heart. A heart that is capable of loving beyond what any average person can. A heart so loving, that I don't deserve to hold it, even when I cherish it every day.

"Thank you, Ry. Thank you for loving me, choosing me, and making my dreams come true. Thank you for all the wonderful memories we shared together."

Sam pauses again. Tears start pooling in my eyes, and I can feel my nose getting tingly. I hope I can get through this before I break down.

"Unfortunately, beautiful, there is one thing I kept from you for all these years. It has weighed heavy on my heart every day since I got you back. Even now, I'm too selfish to tell you in person. I'm not prepared to see anything other than love in your eyes. I am struggling to stay positive, but things just feel off this time around.

"So, instead of talking to you in-person like I should, I made this video. I would rather spend whatever days we have left in our little bubble. Because reality sucks, my love. Which brings me back to why I made this video. It is high time for you to learn some hard truths about me and our family. Truths that I am sure deep down you know and refuse to accept."

Sam points at the camera like he's pointing at me. I can feel his eyes boring into mine through the screen.

"But it's time. You have to learn to accept our truths and move forward, for yourself and especially for our son. Things are going to get hard, really hard, before they get better. But I believe with every fiber of my being that everything will work out in time.

"Let me start at the beginning. This all started when I was a dumbass and broke up with you before Hawaii."

Sam lets out a puff of air. I can see him mulling over his words before he speaks—he was good at that. He rubs two fingers to his forehead and looks back at the camera.

I can see in his eyes that I am not going to like what I hear.

I push pause again and move away from the desk. I know I have to finish this, but I think I need a drink first. I wish Scarlett or my mom were with me to watch the rest of this.

I head out of the office and down the hallway leading to the living room. I linger, slowing my steps to look at a couple of family photos hanging on the wall. I don't want Rhys to forget the good times we had with Sam.

I stop in front of our last family photo. It's a picture of us on our last ski trip. We had just finished our last run on the bunny hill, and Rhys was beyond tired from ski camp. Sam put him up on his shoulders. I was about to complain about Sam spoiling Rhys when he threw his arm over my shoulders and squeezed me tight, kissing my head. Scarlett called out, "Cheese," capturing the happy moment—us forever frozen, wearing our puffy ski jackets, goggles on our heads, and the biggest smiles on our faces.

I run my fingers over the cool glass and continue my way to the liquor cabinet in the dining room. Grabbing the bottle of tequila, I pour myself a shot and slam it down. The spiciness of the liquor hits my tongue before warming my stomach. I take a few deep breaths and decide to bring the bottle back with me to the office.

Sinking into Sam's plush office chair, I place my glass next to the laptop. I drop my head back, rubbing my hands up and down the arms rests where the leather is worn and soft. After a minute, the booze hits my system, calming me down enough to push play on the video once more.

"You have to understand ... I was not in a good headspace then. I was in agony. I had fallen hard and so fast for you. How could I not? You're an amazing woman.

"But when Scarlett and Levi got engaged, I felt like everything was happening too fast. I knew you were going to start thinking

about the future. Engagement, marriage, a family. I desperately wanted to have that stuff with you too.

"When I had that annual check-up right before our trip, I spiraled. We talked about this that night on the steps. I knew I couldn't give you everything you wanted. So, I decided that it would be best if I let you go. To push you away. I didn't want to burden you with the possibility that I might never be able to give you the life you wanted, so I ended us.

"As soon as I left your place, I knew without a shadow of a doubt I had just made the biggest mistake of my life. I didn't want to break up—I wanted to fight for us. Instead of jumping on a plane as I should have, I waited for you to come home from your trip. I never thought for a moment that you would meet someone else while you were there.

"Anyway, my plan was to tell you the truth about my battles with leukemia as a child and a teen. I was going to tell you about the side effects of the multiple sessions of chemo and what that meant for our future. And then, I would let you decide how you wanted to move forward.

"My need to confess flew out the window when you returned home, sad and heartbroken. I was devastated to learn that I had lost a piece of your heart to someone else. And it was all my fault.

"I made the decision right then and there that my only focus would be to take care of you and eventually win your heart back. I knew I had to fight for us. Lucky for me, you let me in and we slowly started to rebuild our relationship. When we found out you were pregnant with Rhys, I think that healed us the most.

"Learning we were having a baby was one of the happiest days of my life. I couldn't believe you were giving me such a precious gift. You had no doubt in us and our growing family. So, I proposed. Really, I jumped at the chance to make you my wife. I wasn't going to waste any of our time together.

"I know you love me something fierce, Ry. Just like I love you. But you love him too. I've accepted that. I know you're probably denying this right now, but it's true, Ry. When you went to Hawaii and met Jace, your heart made room for him and it never fully let him go.

"I'm not gonna lie, it hurt. In the back of my mind, I always worried I would lose you to him. I wanted to know who he was and what happened. I wanted to know if there was a chance he would come back and fight for you. I was curious enough that I asked Levi about him.

"Levi was quick to tell me that he didn't know exactly what happened, only that the two of you bonded. He was being kind, seeing as I knew the truth. Levi suggested I ask Scarlett, but I know Scar. She would never tell me a single thing. She's Team Rylann. Ride or die."

He chuckles to himself, and I find myself laughing at the screen too. Tears trickle down my cheeks as I remember the way he used to tease me and Scarlett about our friendship.

It feels good to laugh with him again. I miss him so much.

"Anyway, Levi didn't offer me any information, but he did offer me peace of mind. He made it very clear that Jace would never interfere in our life. Even after he lost his chance at fatherhood, Levi assured me he was devoted to making his marriage work.

"At first I wasn't sure, but as time went on, Levi turned out to be right. That didn't kill my curiosity about what kind of man he was, though. I got Levi to tell me about Jace. Little by little. What I learned was that he is a good man. A man who is a lot like you. Loyal to a fault. Loves his family, and he puts others first. After everything I've learned, I'm certain that both of you sacrificed your own happiness for the other. Like that old story, The Gift of the Magi. You know, the one where the couple sacrifices something they both value dearly for the other.

"But no more sacrificing. Please. I need you to find happiness again. I need you to move on. I don't want you to be sad. I want you to live. I want you to go on vacation adventures with Rhys. I want you to find love again."

What the … Rolling my eyes at my idiot husband, I wipe them with a tissue. I can't even fathom the thought of moving on.

"Right now, you're probably thinking, 'What the fuck, Sam? You're making me cry telling me you love me, and now you're trying to have me move on.' Don't roll your eyes at me, Ry."

I totally rolled my wet teary eyes at his ridiculousness.

"I'm not ridiculous. I'm trying to help you because I love you more than life itself. And I know your stubborn ass—you haven't clued in on what I am trying to say yet. Am I right?"

"You're right." I nod at the computer. Yep. I have officially lost it. I'm talking to my dead husband. Through a computer screen.

"Thought so. I'm not gonna sugar coat it anymore. Here is the point of the video and where I was trying to go with my story here … One of the side effects of all the chemo I had in my childhood was infertility …"

Sam pauses, taking a deep breath. His words swish around in my head but aren't clicking together just yet.

"There is no easy way to say this, so I'm going to be blunt. I can't have children. Rhys is my son, but he is not my biological son. I am not his real father. He belongs to you and Jace. It's the reason I came up with his name. Rylann and Jace together is Rhys. I know that's a lot of information to process. Maybe you should go get yourself a shot of tequila."

"What in the actual fuck?" I mutter to myself, slamming the screen to the laptop shut. Pressing the heel of my palms to my eyes, I start to panic.

My heart is flying a million miles an hour, and it's hard to breathe. This cannot be happening. *There is no way.* I would have known from the start. Rhys would have looked like Jace. Wouldn't he?

Although, how could anyone tell? Rhys looks like a mini version of me. Maybe his hair is a little lighter brown, but other than that he looks just like me. Same dimples and freckles on his cheek. Same tan skin. Same chocolate brown eyes.

Except ...

"Shit!" I pour and throw back a second shot, and jump up to pace the room.

Rhys has those crazy rings of gold around his pupils. A vision of green and gold eyes flashes before me.

I start going over everything, calculating. Rhys was born at the end of February. If he was Jace's, he would have been born in March. No, Sam is wrong. It can't be true. I rush over to the laptop and start the video again.

"I know you've taken that shot and have started to put the pieces together. I also know what you're doing. You're analyzing time, you're trying to rationalize everything. But I know you know due dates and birthdays are estimates, not guarantees. It's irrelevant, anyway. I am definitely unable to father children. I have been tested and was told repeatedly that it was impossible for me to father children. I triple-checked.

"This is the real reason why I broke it off back then. It wasn't just because of my annual scans and the possibility of my cancer coming back, like I said. I mean, I knew this is how it would always end for me. But I only gave you half of the truth. I really didn't want to tie you down, knowing that I wouldn't be able to give you the big family you always wanted. Shit, Ry. I am so ... so sorry."

Sam's voice cracks as he drops his chin to his chest. It feels like hours pass before he starts talking again, his voice thick with emotion. He's not even bothering to hold back his tears.

"I know I should have told you. It was wrong for me to keep this from you. I swear I was going to tell you, but things just kept happening that kept me from doing it. Like when Jace got engaged, or when Levi and Scarlett left for his wedding. You were so upset. You tried to hide it, but you did a shit job at it. Both times, you went to visit with your parents and couldn't be reached for days.

"I knew you were depressed and trying to protect my feelings at the same time. But you didn't need to. I was in, no matter what. I knew you loved him and always would. That's how you love, beautiful. With all that you are. Unconditionally."

Swiping away the tears streaming down my face, I push pause again, needing a moment to collect my thoughts. I know another shot isn't going to help me, so I get up and go check on Rhys.

He's sound asleep as usual. I sniffle through a chuckle because Sam's right—he does sleep like a log. After a minute, I head back to the office.

I don't know what I'm going to do next. Do I reach out to Jace? After all this time, would he even want to talk to me? Would he accept Rhys? So many thoughts bombard me. I can't think clearly right now.

"Ugh, this is a nightmare." My baby has lost the only father he has ever known. A father that adored him, comforted him when he was sick, and taught him how to ride his bike and play catch.

"Damn you, Sam! Why did you have to be so fucking wonderful? I can't even be mad at you." I slump in the leather chair. I can't go back and change course.

Would I even want to? Jace made his choice. There was no way I was going to break up his marriage. Baby or not, that is not something I would do. He chose his child. I know that, but he also chose *her.* I let him go for the sake of his unborn child. For him. To keep his heart from being torn apart.

I push play. I need to get this over with and figure out what the hell I am going to do next.

"I gave you your space during those times, even though I didn't want to. But I tend to always give you whatever you want. I'm a sucker for you like that. After a few weeks, we fell into a new normal and we were happy. We found out you were pregnant. Rhys was growing. I was falling more in love with you and him every day. You called him ours with so much conviction that I

took advantage. I got you to marry me. I made you and Rhys mine.

"The worst part in all this is that I would do it all over again. I would like to say that I regret what I did, but that's not true. I don't regret a single minute of my time with you and Rhys. I am that selfish.

"You two are my world. It pains me that I won't be here for you, to love and support you. I won't be able to see Rhys grow into the wonderful man I know he will be. The time we had together was truly amazing. The happiest years of my life."

Sam takes a deep breath, and I mimic him. He still finds a way to calm me.

"Now, we've arrived at the hard part. You need to face the truth, and you need to tell it to Jace. I am hoping that he is the man I think he is. I have faith that he will step in and fill the hole in Rhys's life. The one I left behind. He will be a good father. And along the way, should you and Jace find your way back to each other, embrace it. Life is short, my love. Spend it with the people you love.

"Take Rhys on adventures. Please, live for me, Ry. Be happy. Take care of our boy. I will always be with you. I love you with everything that I am. Oh, and if you need my help again, I left some stuff in the other envelopes for you. But only use it as a last resort. You will know when that is—just trust your gut. I love you forever, Rylann. Goodbye, beautiful."

"Oh. My. God," Scarlett says, stunned.

I don't blame her. It's a lot to take in.

"I know." I rub at my temples, trying to force the headache brewing from all my crying away. I feel hollowed out, broken.

I know, deep down to my bones, that I've ruined a chance at happiness with the love of my life. My soulmate.

"Your ring?" she asks, and I nod rubbing at the empty space. I'm surprised she hasn't brought that up sooner. "Why didn't you say anything? Levi and I could have helped you," she cries.

"I know." I groan, throwing my hands up in the air. "I was going to, then I walked into the kitchen through the patio and I heard Levi talking about Jace seeing someone, and I chickened the fuck out. After everything with Alina, I just wanted him to be happy."

"I get that but, babes, he might have gone on a few dates, but they've always meant nothing. Those women aren't you."

My chest tightens. I want that to be the truth, but I don't deserve it.

"It's true, Ry. After Sam ..." She shrugs, tilting her head side to side. "I hoped you two would—"

"Scarlett, don't." I can't allow myself to follow this line of thought right now.

"Fine." She puts her hands up in surrender.

I can't let myself go down that road. I royally fucked up. I let myself fall for him all over, but everything that we have shared on this trip—all of it—is meaningless now because I was a coward and couldn't tell him the truth.

"Fuck!" I shout, ripping at my hair.

Thankfully, Levi and Jace took the kids for a walk on the beach, so they can't hear me yelling obscenities at the fucked-upness that has become my life or hear the god-awful secrets that are coming out of my mouth.

"Fuck, fuck, fuck. What am I going to do, Scarlett? He is going to hate me. I should have told him as soon as I figured it all out. I should have known. I mean, Rhys—"

"His eyes," Scarlett gasps, covering her mouth with the palm of her hand, finally seeing it too.

I nod, tears spilling down my face.

He may look like me, but those eyes ... They are all Jace. The gleaming golden rims are the same color as his father's. The perfect mix of the both of us has been staring at me for the past seven years, waiting for me to see the truth.

"But, I thought you and Sam ..."

"Me too. But from before Hawaii. Before Jace. After would have been ... impossible."

"After, you and Sam never ..."

"Not for weeks. I-I couldn't."

She looks at me. I can see the sadness and sympathy written across her face. She was there. She remembers how sad I was. The depression, the half-smiles, the faraway looks, the sudden tears. My complete and utter heartbreak. She witnessed it all.

So did Sam.

Fuck, Sam. I feel guilty thinking back to when we started rebuilding our relationship. I was half a person. But he never gave up on me. He cared for me in a way no one ever had. He chose me, day in and day out. On my good days and on my bad. I wish he was here to help me through this now.

Ugh, he's part of the problem.

While that's the truth, I know deep down that Sam would've done anything to make things right for me. To make me and Rhys happy. We were always his priority.

The silence stretches between us, both lost in thought. Her trying to process the secret bomb I dropped on her and me coming to terms with the fact that I will more than likely be leaving paradise again, only to suffer through hell alone back home.

"So, what you're saying is that Jace is Rhys's biological father?" She's still attempting to wrap her head around everything.

"Yes." The word barely slips off my tongue before the door flies open, slamming against the wall and knocking pictures off it as a seething Jace steps through the door.

CHAPTER FIFTY-FOUR

Rylann

"He's my son?!" Jace roars.

"Jace!" I gasp.

How long has he been standing there, listening to me and Scarlett? Did he hear everything? He looks completely shocked. Devastated.

Oh, fuck. I think I'm going to throw up.

The last thing I wanted was for him to hear it this way. No, that's not right. The last thing I want to do is hurt him. I love and adore him with every fiber of my being. Hurting him is the last thing I ever want to do.

"Answer me. Is he my son?" Jace yells, face red and nostrils flaring.

"Yes," I say over the lump in my throat.

"How could you keep this from me?"

"It wasn't like that. Please, let me explain."

He shakes his head, backing away, "No. I don't want to hear it. You're not the person I thought you were."

Jace spins on his heel, almost running for the exit. I stand there frozen.

"Ry! Go after him!" Scarlett yells, breaking me from my trance.

Barefoot, I run after him. He's trying to escape this place like his ass is on fire. He's already at the driveway when I finally catch up to him.

I grab his wrist, but he shakes me off, pulling away like I burned him.

"Please, listen to me," I beg.

"I think I heard enough," he growls.

"No, you didn't. If you did, you wouldn't be walking away. Please, let me explain everything?"

"What's to explain? You lied to me. You kept my son a secret. You let another man raise him without a second thought. What the fuck, Rylann? How could you do that to me?"

"I ... I didn't mean to. I swear. I ..."

"You what?" he says with such vitriol, I'm taken aback.

The words are all jumbled in my brain, making it hard for me to articulate. He takes my hesitation as an admission of guilt.

"That's what I thought." He turns his back on me.

"Jace!" I yell at his back. He stops, so I try to continue, "I never meant to hurt you. I didn't even know myself. Sam, he ..." Jace whirls around so fast that I flinch when he comes toe to toe with me. I know he would never hurt me, but the rage in his eye is something I've never seen before. Like a knife to my heart, he cuts me deep with those hazels that only this morning shone with so much love and now hold contempt.

"Just don't! There is no excuse for keeping my son from me."

"It wasn't like that. I didn't know," I plead with him to hear me.

"You didn't know?" He laughs, his derisive tone cutting.

He's so angry. His chest is heaving, his fury palpable. I'm not going to get through to him. I don't blame him. This is a lot to take in. His anger is righteous.

I shake my head. I need him to believe me. There was no malice behind what I did. I was deeply heartbroken at the time. I think I was trying to protect myself.

"When we went our separate ways, I was broken, Jace. Broken. You have no idea. You walked away from me like I meant nothing to you. Like our time together meant nothing. You went back to her, and then I heard that you were marrying her. It fucking destroyed me. Okay? I couldn't even get out of bed."

"You let me walk away."

"I know!" I shriek, cutting him off. "But I had to. For the sake of your child. I had to let you go. You were having a baby with her, Jace! What was I supposed to do? You were so confused, I know that, but you had already decided. I saw it in your eyes. You had already given up on me. On us. So, yes. I let you go. I wanted you to fight. I wanted you to tell me we were going to figure it out. But that's not how our story ended. You didn't fight. You let me go too."

"I ..."

"No, don't. Please, let me finish. I only found out Rhys was yours last month. Sam kept things from me. I can explain more later. But I swear I went to Levi to help me. When I got to their house, I overheard him telling Scarlett that you were seeing someone. I assumed it was serious, that you were happy. That you were moving on. I thought, why would I want to blow up Jace's life again? He's been through so much. He deserves to be happy."

"Why? Why? How about because he's my son. My son!" he shouts, pointing to his chest, stabbing his finger to his heart.

He's too angry to listen to me, to listen to reason, and he's making me angry in return. Frustration boils beneath the surface, making me lash out.

"Rhys had a father!" I snap.

I regret the words the moment they pass my lips. He rears back like I just slapped him across the face.

"I'm sorry. That's not ... Ugh!" This is coming out all wrong. "Jace, I'm not trying to hurt you. I could never. I chickened out. I should have told you immediately. But I was scared. I even hoped you wouldn't be here so that I had time to come up with a way to fix everything. When I found out Rhys wasn't Sam's, I was devastated. So don't you ask me how could I. You don't understand how I felt back then. You *chose* to let me walk away from what we could have been together. But it was for the greater good. A baby. An innocent baby that needed all your love and attention. A precious life in need of their father. We would never have survived with you raising a child with another person. Your life was in California. Mine was in Oregon. The odds were stacked against us."

"What a cop-out. Besides, my life didn't pan out the way you're making it seem. You know this. I told you. I lost my child."

"You were still married! You married her! What are you not understanding?" I shout back, pulling my hair in frustration. He belonged to someone else, so how could I reach out to him without breaking my heart all over again?

"We could have made it work. Why didn't you even think it was a possibility for me to be his father? Did you go back to him as soon as you got home?" He looks at me in disgust.

"How dare you?! You do not get to look at me like that, and not that it's any of your business, but it took me weeks. Weeks! Before I even ..." I slam my mouth shut. I refuse to fill in those blanks. He's hurting, but he has no right to criticize my choices. For all I know, he fell into bed with Alina after leaving me. "You have no right to judge me. I have never judged you or your choices. I already told you how hurt I was when we ended. Honestly, I wasn't just broken, I was depressed. You ripped my fucking heart out when I found out you were getting married. My hope that you would come to me died that day. I cried myself to sleep for weeks. When I accepted that we were never going to happen, I finally gave Sam a second chance. I didn't even realize I was pregnant until I was well into my second trimester, and you ... you were already married. I just ... I can't explain it. It was like I wanted to block out any thoughts of you. I refused to let there be any room for doubt, and Sam let me."

I know this now. Looking back, I used Sam as a way to protect myself. I chose him because he was safe. I knew he would raise a child with me, no questions asked. It would be easy.

When I told Sam he was going to be a father, he was so happy. Elated, even. He was in my corner, protecting me, and I knew he would never change his mind about us again. I protected myself the only way I knew how to. Denial.

It was self-mother-fucking-preservation.

I couldn't go through any more rejection. Not only for me but for my baby too. The same rejection I see on Jace's face now.

"You ruined everything. I can never look at you the same. You're as bad as *her*. You're selfish and a liar. You don't give a shit about me or my feelings. Even if I could believe that you didn't think of me, it's un-fucking-fathomable to me. I never, not for one second, forgot about you. You were with me every day. I fucking loved you!" he yells in frustration, throwing his hand up in the air.

I gasp at the word "loved". Past tense. He purposely said that to hurt me.

Well, you win Jace. You broke me. A-fucking-gain.

He continues, ignoring the pain and shock he can so clearly see written across my face. "Not for a single day did I forget what we shared. It doesn't matter anymore. We'll be in touch. I won't let you keep him away from me," he sneers.

My heartbreak turns into anger. I can't believe he's doing this to me. Am I wrong? Of course. But I didn't do this out of spite. "Oh no! You don't get to come at me, calling me selfish, comparing me to her. I would never keep you from him. Your choices and your life with her are not my fault. It's not my fault you lost your child. I didn't do this to hurt you. Why would I do that when it hurts me too? When I love you so damn much it hurts? If you can't understand that I was protecting myself, then fine. Be an asshole. Go ahead, leave. Walk away ... again," I say with as much outrage as I can muster.

Please, don't go. Fight. Just do anything besides walking away.

"Just remember you didn't choose me. You. Chose. Her. You chose history over us. We were new, terrifyingly uncontrollable, an unknown factor. I get it. We were early days, but I felt it then and I know you did too. We were supposed to leave this island together. I felt it here." I slam my hand to my chest.

He wants to fire shots at me, then I'll fire them right back. I'm not the only one that made mistakes.

"I still do, Ace. I loved you then, and I love you now. I never stopped. Never will. I'm not the only one to blame for the shitstorm we're in now. You had a hand in this too. I will not be your scapegoat."

"I can't do this anymore," Jace says. He turns his back on me, again, ripping my heart from my chest.

This is it.

I can feel a piece of me leave with every step he takes away. I knew this was going to happen. He's hurt. Angry.

This is why I fought him when we arrived in this godforsaken paradise. Why I didn't want to go down this road with him. I knew it would end in heartbreak when I told him the truth.

But he pushed and pushed. Forcing me to give in to him. Spend time with him. Recreate our relationship. Fall madly and desperately in love with him all over again.

Now here I am, falling with no safety net. It's gonna fucking hurt when the dust settles and I'm left alone to pick up the pieces.

If he can't even fight for me now, for us, what chance do we have? There's no hope if he leaves without letting me explain further. Without giving me the benefit of the doubt.

I'm pissed now, and I yell at his back, "You want to be angry and blame me? Fine. But just know that Rhys and I don't need you. We will be just fine. Just like before. I have him, and he's got me."

He stops, not turning around. His fists are clenched tightly, his knuckles white with tension.

Turn back around and fight with me! Please!

Instead, his shoulders move up and down like he's taking deep ragged breaths, but then he continues walking down the driveway to his rental car.

He gets in and drives away without looking back.

Leaving me. Again.

I turn around to see Scarlett watching at the top of the driveway. I break into a sob, hot tears rolling down my face. Oh god, I hurt so bad.

My knees buckle, and I hit the ground.

"Ry!" Scarlett barrels down the driveway, trying to get to me.

After last night's promises, I thought he was capable of holding us both up. That we would be able to talk things out. I was wrong to assume Jace would be able to see past his pain and heartbreak.

Scarlett's arms wrap around me. I let the agony and loss take me.

"D-did y—?" I stutter, unable to finish my sentence.

"Yes, I heard it all. I'm so sorry, Ry." Scarlett rubs my back, tears in her eyes.

The comfort is warming, but lacking. I want it to be Jace. I want him to come back to me. I need him.

"It ... It's all my fault. He hates me. I've lost him forever." I can barely get the words out. I feel like my chest is caving in.

"No, babes. You didn't lose him. I don't believe for one second that it's over. Things got out of hand. This isn't your fault. I know that. Hell, Jace knows that. He just needs to wrap his head around being Rhys's father. He's hurt. That was a lot to take in."

I nod into her hair. I hope she's right.

The last thing I wanted to do was hurt him. I felt the same way when I got that video and let myself accept the truth.

Rhys comes running, yelling, from the beach, screeching to a halt in front of me. Panting. His eyes wild in fear.

"Why is my dad leaving?"

"What!?" Scarlett bellows at the same time as all the oxygen leaves my lungs at Rhys's words, choking me.

"Wh-what did you say?"

"My dad. Why is my dad leaving?" Rhys points down the road, fat tears streaming down his face.

I look back, hoping to see Jace's car. Instead, the driveway is empty, his car and himself long gone.

"Rhys, who told you Jace was your dad?" I reach out and grab Rhys's little hands in mine.

"Daddy did," he cries, his little body shaking.

"When did Daddy tell you this? I need you to help me understand. Please explain?" I can hear the panic in my voice.

I need to calm down; I don't want him to shut down. But how could he have known this the whole time and never uttered a word of it to me? We don't keep secrets from each other. He's only six, for crying out loud.

"Daddy told me the story of the surf king all the time."

"Okay. But what does that have to do with Jace?"

Rhys rolls his eyes at me like, *Get a clue, Mom.* After everything that just went down, I can't wrap my head around this new information.

"Daddy said the surf king's name was Jace."

I swallow the lump in my throat as I realize Sam wasn't making up fairy tales at all. He was telling our son about his father.

"How long have you known?"

"Since before Daddy died. He told me the surf king was real, and he was my dad. That we would find him in Hawaii, and he would take care of me. Daddy said he was sorry he was going to die and he loved me, but I didn't have to worry because I had two dads. And my other dad would take care of me and love me too."

Tears pour down my face.

My poor boy has known Jace was his dad this whole time and never said anything. I should have ripped the Band-Aid off the moment I found that video. Then maybe things wouldn't have blown up so spectacularly.

Rhys starts to sob uncontrollably, tearing my heart in two.

I fucked everything up for my baby. The one person I vowed never to hurt. Getting up off my knees, legs, shaking, I scoop him up into my arms. He tucks his face into my neck, wrapping his legs around my waist.

"M-ommy, why did m-y dad l-leave? Does h-he not want to be my d-ad? Does he not l-love me?" he asks between hiccups.

I squeeze him tight as he breaks down in my arms.

"Shh. No, baby. Your dad is just mad at me. Not you. Never you. He wants to be your dad so badly. He loves you so very much, my sweet boy. He's hurt and upset right now. He will come back for you. I promise. He will always come back for you."

Rhys nods his head against my chest, accepting my words as truth as his tears soak my dress.

My son shouldn't have to pay for my mistakes. Hell, I deserve all the anger Jace threw at me. He was right—I am selfish. By not telling him as soon as I found out, I became a liar too. I got so lost in my grief and guilt that I didn't think about his feelings until it was too late.

Jace has lost so much, and now I'm a part of the reason he's missed everything he's ever wanted. Being a father.

I don't deserve his forgiveness, let alone his love.

I'm not usually one for this kind of thing, but right now I am. I send out a prayer to any deity that is willing to listen that the man I love comes through for our son. I pray to Jace himself.

Please, for the love of our son, don't let him down, Jace. Come back to him.

Looking around, I find Scarlett long gone, leaving me alone to console my son. I rub circles over Rhys's back until his breathing evens out.

"Let's go celebrate Auntie Scar and Uncle Lee. Then, we can go home. I'm ready to leave this place. What do you think?"

"O-okay. Will my dad be able to find me if we go home?" he asks, his voice wobbly.

His words stab me in the heart like a knife would, shredding me.

"Bug, he'll find you anywhere," I promise.

I know in my gut that this is true. I have to believe it. I refuse to live a life in which Jace lets down our boy. He can hate me all he wants. But Rhys? No way. I know he will do right by him. He loves Rhys. I know it down to my soul. He just needs time.

He can hate me forever as long as he shows up for our son.

And if he doesn't?

He will.

I'll make damn sure Jace comes for Rhys.

CHAPTER FIFTY-FIVE

Rylann

Rolling out of bed, I stretch and twist side to side, rubbing my aching muscles. A nerve in my back pinches at the movement, and I hiss in pain. Pain. This small pain is a reminder of my mistakes and my son's heartbreak.

My heart stalls in my chest as my eyes cloud with unshed tears thinking about yesterday.

I groan, ruminating over how I messed up Scarlett and Levi's wedding, again. I spent the entire time consoling a tearful Rhys. He refused to stand on his own during both the ceremony and the dinner that followed, clinging to me while he cried off and on throughout the night.

Scarlett and Levi tried to help, but I assured them I had it and we were going to be okay. I wanted them to enjoy their night. I already felt horrible for ruining their day and sending Jace running.

Honestly, I didn't feel like I deserved any help from them. I made this mess, and now I need to suffer the consequences. I'm surprised Levi didn't ask me to leave, with the way I handled everything. Completely destroying Jace in the process.

I didn't miss the mixed looks of sympathy and shock from the Walkers as I held onto my son. I assume they heard everything. It's not like Jace and I had been quiet. Our argument could be heard from a mile away, with the way we'd yelled at each other.

I cringe at the thought of them knowing, but the truth had to come out at some point. I'm sure Julie will be calling Jace's mom soon to tell her all the sordid details if she hasn't already.

I can't think about that now. I'll deal with that later. The only person I need to worry about now is Rhys.

I look over my shoulder at his little sleeping body. He refused to sleep alone last night, and I wasn't about to let him down again, so I pulled him close and held him tight.

Once I'm safely under the spray of the hot water, I finally let my tears fall. After Rhys's breakdown, I pulled up my big-girl panties and kept my shit together. He needed my comfort more than I needed to break down. Rhys will always come first.

I haven't had much of a chance to process everything that's happened in the past twenty-four hours. Jace's anger. Rhys's knowledge about his dads. Yep, plural.

My life is officially an episode of Maury.

Picturing the look on Jace's face pierces my heart, but witnessing the fat tears that poured down Rhys's face, hurt me to my very soul. I don't think I'll ever be able to recover from the look of despair on my son's face when he thought Jace was leaving him because he didn't want to be his dad.

Alone in the water, I let myself wallow and drown in the pain of my mistakes. The pain of hurting the two men in my life that I love the most in the world.

Pulling myself together, I finish washing up and get out. After toweling off and drying my hair, I put on a pair of jeans and a shirt for our flight home. I'm packing my bags when Rhys finally wakes.

"Good morning, bug. Are you ready to go home?" I ask. He nods his little head, still tucked under the covers, curled in a ball. He hasn't said much since Jace left.

"Me too. Let's go get some breakfast, then Auntie Scarlett is going to take us to the airport, okay?" He nods again. His solemn face breaks my heart a little more. The shine in his eyes has dimmed, along with the gold in his irises. He looks as despondent as I feel on the inside.

Trying my best to keep my emotions in check and stay positive for him, I keep myself busy packing and tidying up the room.

Rhys quietly climbs out of bed and uses the restroom. When he returns, I hand him his clothes. After a little struggle on his part, I helped him dress. His little heart is too deflated to bother with the normal things. I get it. The only reason I feel capable of getting out of bed is because of him. He needs me to be strong. He's confused and sad.

He, like me, misses Jace.

As upset as Rhys is, I wonder if he truly understands what Sam meant. If he realizes what it means when we say Jace is his dad. I'll tackle that later.

First, I got to get us home.

After breakfast, Levi helps me wheel our suitcases to the rental sitting in the valet circle, where my bestie waits in the driver's seat.

Once Rhys is buckled in, I walk over to Levi, making sure we are out of earshot.

"Levi, I just want to thank you for everything that you've done for me and Rhys. Not just the trip, but every day. I don't think I'd have survived this last year without your and Scar's help. I-I'm really sorry I messed it all up with Jace and everything, how all that went down. I never ..." My throat swells, and my voice cracks.

He places his hands on my shoulders, consoling me. My eyes water, but I hold my tears at bay. "I know you didn't, sweetheart. I was there—I saw and heard everything. I wish it played out differently, but we are still family. Scarlett and I will always be there for you."

I throw my arms around him and give him a tight hug. "Thank you," I whisper into his chest.

He pulls back, his warm eyes reassuring me that he doesn't hold a grudge or even hate me in the slightest. "Have a safe flight. Call if you need anything."

"I will. Thank you. Again."

Levi leans in and says his goodbyes to a dejected Rhys.

Hopping in the passenger seat, I buckle in as Scarlett drives us away. Leaning my head back, I close my eyes.

I really messed everything up. Once again, I'm leaving this hotel alone, with half of my heart missing.

The car comes to a stop, and I open my eyes to see we're already at the airport. I'm surprised my bestie stayed quiet the entire ride. Although, what can be said at this point?

"Are you going to be okay, babes?" she finally asks.

No. Yes. I don't know.

I roll my head to the side, looking at her. She gives me a soft smile. I know she's sad and worried about me. She doesn't need to be this time around.

"Of course. I'm a big girl. Besides, I have,"—I throw a thumb to the dreary Rhys in the back seat before assuring her—"to take care of. We'll get through this."

She glances back at him in the mirror. Grabbing her hand, I squeeze, letting her know I can handle this. I'm not the same woman I used to be. I might be hurt, but I'm strong. I can get through this for my son. He's the reason I keep living, each and every day. And hopefully, I can figure out a way to fix this mess for him.

"We'll be okay, Scar. You go and have fun with Lee. Enjoy your alone time. I'll see you in a few days."

They are flying to Maui for three nights for a mini second honeymoon while the girls stay with their grandparents.

"Call me if you need anything," she says firmly.

"I will. Please tell Levi sorry again for me. I'm really grateful he doesn't hate me." I'm surprised he was so understanding. He listened to my entire story and then said it would all work out.

"Never. We love you guys. It will all work out."

"Maybe. Love you, Scarface." I appreciate her optimism.

"Love you, Rice Cakes."

I lean over and kiss my bestie's cheek before hopping out of the car. I gather the luggage and Rhys, and with a final wave and kiss goodbye, Scarlett drives off.

Rhys and I make our way through check-in, bag check, security, and boarding before he utters more than a yes or no to me.

"I'm sorry, Mommy," he mumbles while bucking his seatbelt.

I reach over and snap the buckle in for him, tightening the belt across his lap.

"Bug, why are you apologizing? You didn't do anything wrong," I say as convincingly as possible.

"I should have told you Jace was my dad. But Daddy made me promise to keep it a secret."

I take a deep breath. While I am super pissed at Sam for putting this on Rhys, I know Sam thought that if he broke the news to Rhys it would be easier for him to accept.

I appreciate Sam for trying to soften the blow, but the reality of the situation is much more nuanced than, "Hey, Rhys, you have two dads." It's more like, "So, buddy, your mom's a bit of a whore. She slept with me, then ran off to Hawaii, fell in love with another man, and slept with him too. Then he dumped her, so I decided to swoop in and steal you, even though I should have been honest. But it's all good, 'cause you'll have a new dad and I won't be here to deal with all the ramifications of my actions."

Thanks, Sam. Real cool of you. I still love you, though, you big jerk.

"Rhysie, you have nothing to apologize for. I'm proud of you for following your daddy's rules. But keeping secrets is ..."

Wrong, hurtful, pretty much lying. I can keep going if you want. Shut up, brain! I have enough guilt to deal with; I don't need the negative self-talk.

Sucking in a breath, I explain, "Keeping secrets is not good. Since Daddy is gone, we can't keep any more secrets from each other."

"Okay." His golden brown eyes find mine, and I swear, he never looked more like Jace's son.

My chest aches, and my breath hitches. How did it take me so long to see it?

"Baby boy, do you understand what it means for Jace to be your dad?"

He nods, growing quiet, and I'm not so sure.

I need him to tell me everything Sam said. I need to know the details, so I can figure out what the heck I'm going to do and say in order for us to fix this. Move forward.

"Can you please explain it to me like Daddy did?"

"Sure."

I sit there, tears blurring my vision as Rhys tells me the story Sam made up for him. My husband should have been a children's book author—he created a beautiful story for our son. Which is what I tell Rhys.

While it doesn't explain everything, the story has merit and a fuck-ton of truth to it. I don't know how Sam came up with this tale, but it only confirms how much he loved me.

"Do you really think my dad will come back for me?"

The plane takes off, and I clutch Rhys's hand tight, giving him the answer I know is certain. "Absolutely. He loves you, Rhys. Don't ever doubt that."

He smiles and pulls out a coloring book. I watch him color for the next hour before he falls asleep, propped up on my arm. I sit in my seat, holding onto my baby and thinking about everything that's happened.

It's interesting how my path has—and hasn't—intersected with Jace's.

Like Mexico. He was supposed to be there but backed out at the last minute. Both of us were with other people then, so life kept us apart. Then, there was Hawaii. We both arrived single, not anticipating the other. I knew the moment I met him that he was special. The jolt of electricity I felt the first time our hands touched confirmed that. Something in me attached itself to him instantly. Our path was destined to cross then. To meet. To fall in love. To create Rhys.

Unfortunately, fate can be a fickle bitch, and we had to go our separate ways. I moved on, knowing my heart belonged to Jace, and was still able to be loved by another amazing man. I won't deny it—Sam made mistakes, but I forgive him. I can't change the past any more than I could change the color of my eyes. It is what it is. Maybe if Sam and I didn't share a wonderfully happy life, I would feel wronged, but we didn't and I don't.

Sam was ... Sam. He was a wonderful husband and father. He loved me even when I loved another man. And for a small period of time, Sam had everything he desired. He deserved to be surrounded by people that loved him for his short life, and for that I'm grateful.

When we landed, my parents were there waiting for us. I had called my mom at the airport to let her know we were leaving Hawaii early. She knew something was wrong but didn't press for information. She said we'd speak later, and that was that. She knows me well enough to know that things didn't go well.

Sitting on the couch, I polish off the margarita in my hand. Rhys is asleep, and my parents are waiting for me to tell them what happened.

Today was rough, having to listen to Rhys tell them all about meeting his dad and how much fun he had. Rhys also told them about the fight and how he hasn't heard from him yet. Hearing him tell that story broke my heart.

I don't know how I'm going to fix this for Rhys. I'm scared Jace won't be able to forgive me and Rhys will suffer, which is what I tell my parents as I tell them what happened.

When I finish my story, my eyes feel dry and itchy from crying, and I've used up an entire box of tissues. My dad fills my glass with the pitcher he made for story time. He's been quietly listening the entire time.

"Go ahead, Momma, I'm ready. Tell me I told you so." She warned me this would happen if I didn't reach out to Jace immediately and figure this out. But I didn't listen. I was too chicken-shit to face the truth.

"Aye, *mija*, no."

"Why not? I would," I grumble, taking a big sip of the tangy drink.

Please, tequila, make my heart stop hurting.

"Because being right doesn't matter to me. You're hurting. Rhys is hurting. I didn't want to be right. I don't want my babies to be sad. I want you to be happy. After everything that's happened, you two deserve happiness."

Her words parrot Jace's, and I wish more than anything I believed that right now.

"Your mother is right, baby girl. You can't change what happened. All you can do now is try to fix it. If that's what you want. Are you willing to fight for him?"

"Yes. Of course. I love him, Dad."

"Okay. Now, you figure out a plan." He says it with such conviction, it's hard not to feel inspired. Then he finishes with, "To get your man." And it all goes out the window.

My mom laughs at my dad's joke, which makes me laugh too. They have *got* to stop watching reruns of Friends on TV.

"Thank you both for not judging me," I say between laughs.

"I wouldn't go that far." She pulls my hair, making me blush.

I know how it looks with Rhys's paternity in question. Since this all came out, my parents have been nothing but supportive. This is one of the many reasons why I love them and why we're so close. They have never judged or put unrealistic expectations on me. They've always been truthful, painfully so at times, and it's made me comfortable to be the same with them.

When I watched that video and my world crumbled, they were there for me, supporting me in any way they could. They were just as shocked to find out Sam lied. Sam was like a son to them. They were devastated when he passed. My dad especially. The two of them were close and spent time together with Rhys. The three of them would go on camping and fishing trips all the time.

"That's mean," I say around the lip of my cocktail before taking a gulp.

"Oh, I just love teasing you," she says playfully.

"I know, I know. But can we puh-lease not discuss my past slutty ways? I don't think I've drunk enough margaritas for that."

"Neither have I," my dad grumbles, making Mom and me burst out laughing.

Mom reaches out and clasps my hand in hers. I marvel at how both our hands are now the same size, when growing up I always thought she was so much larger than life itself.

"On a serious note." I pull my eyes away from our hands to her face, the same color as mine, only better because they shine with warmth. "I love you, baby. Keep your head up. Everything will work out the way it's supposed to." She gives a little shrug. "Who knows, maybe Sam is still out there looking out for you."

Her words are like a light switch turning on, and I jump up off the couch.

"Oh my god, Momma, you're a freaking genius! Thank you!"

"What did I say?" she asks.

Heading for the office down the hall, I look over my shoulder, and the heaviness in my chest eases. "You reminded me that Sam *is* looking out for me."

"What does that mean?" she whisper-hisses at me, trying to stay quiet for Rhys's sake.

I ignore her and make my way straight to Sam's box of letters. She'll see.

I pull out the last envelope labeled *Open In Case of Emergency*. If this doesn't qualify as an emergency, then I don't know what to do. Something tells me this is what Sam was referring to in that video.

When I walk back into the room, my parents stop whispering to each other. I'm sure they think I'm crazy. Maybe I am. But right now, for the first time since shit hit the fan, the letter in my hand has me feeling hopeful.

I hold up the evidence for my parents to see. Evidence that Sam is, in fact, still looking out for me. Even in death, he's giving me the support I need. His never-ending promise to take care of me and make sure I'm happy continues.

"When you said, 'Maybe Sam is still looking out for you,' I remembered that he left me an envelope in that box labeled *Open in case of an emergency*. For some reason, I think that's now."

My stomach flutters with nervous energy.

"Well, open it already," Mom says as I sit down on the sofa next to her.

We collectively take a deep breath as I break the seal on the envelope. I tilt it to the side, and a note and envelope come sliding out into my waiting palm. The envelope is labeled *For him,* and I gasp.

With shaking fingers I open the note and read it aloud.

Rylann,
    If you're opening this envelope, one of two things has happened. Or maybe even both.
    1. You finally told Jace about Rhys.
    2. You're back from Hawaii and things didn't go as planned.
    Stay hopeful, beautiful. You will get the happy life you deserve. As will our son. Please send this letter to Jace, and no snooping. I need you to let me keep this conversation, man to man. He deserves for me to explain a few things. I'm hoping this letter will help him heal and find his way back to you and Rhys.
    Love you with all my heart,
    Sam

My mom raps her arms around me in a hug as I grasp the letter to my chest, tears filling my eyes.

Thank you, Sammy. I knew you would always have my back. I love you.

"Okay, maybe I can forgive him after all," Dad chokes out. He's had a harder time with this than Mom, but hearing him say that makes me happy.

For what it's worth, I'm just ready to move forward.

Now, it's my turn. I'm going to do what Sam did for me—fight. I'm going to fight for Jace. This time, I won't give up on him and walk away. He might be angry and hurting right now, but I refuse to give up on him. On our family. I will love him enough for both of us. If he doesn't want to build a relationship with me, I'll accept it, but I know he wants one with his son. Jace loves Rhys, so I will focus on that first. I will support him any way he wants until I can earn his trust back. Maybe in time, he can open his heart to me again. But I'm not ready to lose him again. I love him.

He's my person.

The line rings in my ear as I wait for him to pick up. My parents went home an hour ago. I wanted to make this call alone.

His voice picks up on the other end of the line before it would click to voicemail. "Ry? What's going on? Are you and Rhys okay?"

"We're fine, Levi. I was actually hoping you could help me with something real quick, and I'll let you get back to Scar."

"Hey, babes!" Scarlett shouts in the background.

"You're on speaker, Ry. Is that okay?"

"Of course. No attorney-client privilege needed." My friends chuckle at my lame lawyer joke.

"Good to know. What can I help you with?"

"Well, I need Jace's address. I have a letter for him. I found it in the box Sam left behind for me. I think ... Well, I think it may say something he needs to hear."

"I see."

"I don't want to hurt him, Levi. I swear. But I need him to be there for Rhys."

"Give me a second." The line goes quiet until my phone beeps with a text. Levi forwarded me Jace's contact information. "Did you get my text?"

"Got it. Thank you, and I'm sorry. I should have come to you and Scar for help as soon as I found out. I just ... I don't even know. I was stupid to think keeping quiet would keep things from blowing up in my face. I hope you can forgive me."

"No apologies necessary. We all make mistakes, Ry. It's what you do next that matters."

"You're right."

"So, what are your next steps?"

"I'm going to fight for him. But ... I think I need to take it slow. Help him at least be here for Rhys at first. Then prove to him that he can trust me again. Prove that I love him more than anything."

"Awww." I hear Scarlett swoon in the background.

"Do you think he can forgive me?" I hold my breath.

"I've known Jace my whole life. I've only known him to act impulsively a handful of times. Two of those times, Ry, they were about you."

I wince at his response. Maybe this plan isn't so great after all. "I see." I can hear the hopelessness in my voice.

"No, you misunderstand me. Jace is always careful. Thoughtful. He never jumps without thinking, *except* with his feelings for you. Those, he's trusted from the beginning. I've never seen him look at anyone the way he looks at you. He's shocked and hurt right now. I think with time, he'll come around and see what we all do."

"What's that?" I ask nervously.

"That he loves you more than anything."

I release a breath and smile. "Thank you."

We say our goodbyes, and I promise to call if I need anything before they return in a few days.

The next morning, I write a short letter to Jace and attach it to Sam's letter before putting it in a new envelope. Without any hesitation, I address it to Jace and take it to the post office for speedy delivery.

Now, I wait and pray that Jace gets this and I hear from him soon. I'm tired of living without him. I've spent years without him, and I'm really tired of walking around with a part of my heart missing.

I want to hear his deep voice. I want to watch him hold our son. I want to hold him and tell him how sorry I am.

Most importantly, I want to tell him how much I love him. How much I need him in my life.

Always.

CHAPTER FIFTY-SIX

Jace

"Good morning fuck-face!" Eli rips open the curtains, letting in the morning sun, blinding me in the process.

Blinking the sleep from my eyes, I groan. They feel dry and gritty from lack of sleep and the excessive amount of alcohol I've been drinking. I haven't been sleeping since everything went down with Rylann.

It's been two weeks since I left her and her betrayal behind me in Hawaii. I'm not ready to leave the dark hole I've crawled into. I texted everyone what happened, called out of work, then powered off my phone to hide away.

I didn't want to answer questions, and I certainly didn't want my brothers coming over.

I've lost everything I have ever wanted. Twice.

I just want to be alone.

Something pokes my ear, and I pull the blankets over my head. I guess alone time is over.

"Ugh, leave me alone," I moan under the duvet.

"Nope. Mom called. Levi called. You're out of time. We let this go on too long. You're ignoring our texts and calls. You've hidden yourself away instead of manning the fuck up. Hawaii was a blow to the nuts, but what are you gonna do about it? Live like this forever?" Eli asks.

I can hear the annoyance in his voice. If he's here, my other brothers can't be too far. Throwing off the comforter, I sit up, a little too quickly, and my head spins. Feet dangling over the side of the bed, I rub my eyes.

Fucking hangover.

"You don't know shit," I grumble, my anger simmering below the surface.

"I know when I smell it, and you, Jay, smell like shit," another voice says.

I snap my pounding head up to find Cameron leaning against the door frame, eating an apple, arms crossed over his chest and legs crossed at his ankles.

"At least put on some fucking pants and eat breakfast with us. Mase brought breakfast sandwiches," Eli orders, walking out of the room.

Cameron continues to stare at me, taking a bite of his apple, crunching.

I return the stare, waiting for him to say something smart. He shakes his head at me in disappointment and pushes off the door jam, heading to the kitchen after Eli.

What the fuck does he have to be disappointed in me for? He didn't just find out the love of his life lied and didn't tell him they had a son together. I'm allowed to be angry and sad.

"Hurry up, asshole. We don't have all day!" Cameron shouts from the hallway.

Ugh, fuck.

The only way I'm getting rid of these dickbags is to get this over with. Then, I can go back to being alone.

Picking up a pair of sweatpants and a shirt off the floor, not even bothering to check if they're clean, I throw them on and head into the living room.

My stomach grumbles. I feel like garbage, but maybe some food will do me some good.

Entering my open-concept living room, I see Mason grabbing plates and utensils in the kitchen while Cameron and Eli carry over bags of food to the coffee table. The TV is on low, and there's a replay of last night's baseball game on.

Looks like they've made themselves at home. Maybe it won't be too bad to have them here for a while. I plop myself down onto the leather couch while Eli and Cameron take up residence in the matching armchairs.

Leaning my head back, I close my eyes. I'm still feeling the scotch. I'm hit in the chest by an egg sandwich, and I don't waste time ripping open the foil and taking a bite. The salty bacon and cheese hit the spot, and I find myself finishing the sandwich quickly. When I go to reach for another, Eli pulls the bag away.

"Nuh uh. You don't get another one until we talk."

The room falls silent. I have nothing to say. They know what happened between me and Rylann. The secrets and lies. How it all came to an end.

Mase walks over, putting a tray of coffees from the café down on the table in front of us, along with plates, napkins, and a pile of my mail before taking a seat next to me.

"I brought your mail in," he says, tapping it. "It's a big stack. Maybe you should look through it."

"Later. I'm not in the mood."

"Are you sure? Could be interesting," Eli says, acting weirder than usual.

"Yeah, you should check it. I hear credit card fraud is all the rage," Cameron adds, exchanging a look with Mason.

Those two and their secret conversations are already annoying the fuck out of me. I'm starting to regret their presence. Eli's too.

"Later. I doubt there is anything but junk. Just shut it already," I grumble, grabbing a coffee and taking a sip. The hot bitter liquid smooths my rough, hungover edges.

"For fuck's sake, check the mail, you idiot!" Eli yells at me.

"Jesus. What is wrong with you today?" It's too early for this shit.

I take another sip of coffee before putting it back on the table and wait for them to tell me what the hell is going on. I know they are here for a reason, and it's not because they want to check on me.

"Jay, Levi reached out to us last night. He made us come down here to check on you. Rylann sent you a letter. He said it was important for us to get you to read it," Mason explains.

I look over at Eli, his leg bouncing, looking equally annoyed and worried. Fuck it, I can't deal with his nervous energy. If it gets them out of my place sooner, fine.

Searching through the pile, I find mostly junk, until about halfway through when I come across a small manilla envelope addressed to me in soft feminine script. I run a finger over the address.

Rylann's address.

My heart races, and my stomach sinks. What could she possibly say to take away the pain she's caused?

Opening a letter from her is the last thing I want to do. I flip the envelope over in my hands, spinning it around, testing its weight. It feels like it weighs a hundred pounds.

Do I want to know what's written inside?

"Well, what the fuck are you waiting for? Open it," Eli snaps.

I ignore him and his shit attitude. "I don't know, E. It's not like whatever is in here can change anything. Rylann lied to me. I don't know if I can forgive her for that. I missed out on my son's life."

They all exchange a look, nonverbally coming to some sort of agreement before Eli continues like he's the one that drew the short stick and has the honor of delivering bad news.

"What would you have had her do, Jace? You made your choice. You married Alina. Yes, I understand you two lost the baby. But you still married her. Alina was your wife. You think Rylann should have come to you and said, 'Hey, Jace, I know you're married and you just lost your baby, but don't worry, I have another kid here for you.' Seriously, man? Do you think she deserved to be some baby mama? She has more self-respect than that." He throws his hands up, already exasperated with my excuses. "What about your son? Did he deserve to only have his father half the time? An evil stepmother in his life? Because, no doubt about it, he would have."

He has no right. He wasn't the one that was lied to and missed his son's life. "The fuck? You're taking her side?"

Eli grumbles something under his breath before saying, "I saw the devastation on her face that day. I saw this strong, beautiful woman crumble in defeat right in front of me. It was the saddest fucking thing I've ever witnessed. Do you think she wanted to raise a baby with a man that broke her heart and married another woman? Come on. Think about how she felt seeing you with that bitch—"

Mason puts a handout, stopping Eli from saying more.

"Jace, just listen. What Rylann did wasn't right, but see it from her side. Alina never would have made having a relationship with your son easy. She would have ruined any chance for you to see Rhys and any future chance with Rylann. You would have been doomed," Mason interjects calmly, piggybacking off Eli.

"Alina would have sunk her talons deeper into you out of spite," Eli continues.

"I agree with Eli and Mase. At least now, you might have a chance at something real. Alina would have tainted everything, and you know it," Cameron says. I'm pretty sure I hear a muttered, "Fucking bitch," under his breath.

I know they're right. Alina's vindictive. She'd have done anything to get her way and prevent me from having a relationship with Rhys. I see that. But I don't accept it. That doesn't excuse Rylann from keeping Rhys from me. From denying me my son.

"When did you idiots become so forgiving and insightful?" I grump, sinking into the couch.

"Fuck off!" All three of them respond, flipping me off.

"Stop being a bitch and open the envelope, you sad fuck," Eli says, smacking me upside the head.

"Hey, I might be a sad fuck, but I'll still kick your ass," I warn.

"Prove it," he says, taunting me, waving his hand at me to bring it.

I flop back in defeat. I don't have the heart to fight.

"That's what I thought. Now, open the fucking letter already. I'm tired of smelling you."

It's my turn to return the finger to Eli. Maybe having these guys around isn't so bad after all.

I flip the envelope over and break the seal. Inside is a smaller envelope, and clipped to it is a folded note. Rylann's loopy script jumps off the page at me as soon as I open it.

> Jace,
> I was told to give this to you in case of an emergency. I hope it helps. I'm sorry for hurting you. It was never my intention. I love you, and I always will. I hope with time, you can learn to forgive me and build a relationship with Rhys. I know he would like that very much. He knows everything and is waiting for you when you're ready.
> Love Always,
> Your Sunshine

My heart pounds in my chest as I flip the letter around. The attached envelope is addressed *For him* in bold letters, clearly a man's handwriting. My curiosity outweighs my anger at the moment.

I need to know what it says. Without further hesitation, I open the letter and read it.

Jace,

I know you probably hate my guts. I don't blame you. I would hate me too if I were you. But if you are reading this letter, then I'm guessing you need a little kick in the ass. And I'm here to give it to you.

Let's get the elephant in the room out of the way. You are angry. You've just found out you're a dad. You feel betrayed by the woman you love. You feel cheated out of time with your son. You have every right to feel this way.

But is your pride worth more than your family?

Please, let the anger go. It won't help you get the time back, and it certainly won't help you build a relationship with your family. If anything, it will keep you from living a happy life with them.

I want to start by saying that Rylann, myself included here, didn't keep Rhys a secret to hurt you. If anything, she did it to protect herself and if I know her, which I do, she did it to protect you and your happiness too.

When Rylann came home, she was hurting. I had never seen her so sad and broken. Her eyes had lost their sparkle. She confided in me and told me everything that happened between you. She explained how she fell in love with you and was planning on pursuing a relationship with you after the wedding, but it didn't work out. I was devastated, but I understood. She had no obligation to me when she met you and fell in love with you.

Rylann is easy to love. She's gorgeous, smart, funny, loving ... I could go on forever because Ry is everything good in this world. You know this. This is why you fell for her too and why you love her.

I don't know you or all the intricacies of the situation you were put in back in Hawaii all those years ago.

Who I do know is Rylann. She is the most giving and thoughtful person I have ever known. She is honest and good. Deep down, I know you know this.

What you don't know is that when she returned to me, she did not return as the same person. She was half a person.

I'm guessing that Ry chose to let you go so that you could build a life with the mother of your child. That's how she works. She gives the people she loves whatever she can. You wanted to work things out with the mother of your child for their well-being. In support of that,

Ry chose to never interfere with your life.

Which is why she never let herself believe that you could be Rhys's father. And I let her. She was not trying to be malicious. I'm the one that enabled her. If you want to hate anyone, let it be me. I'm the one that knowingly stole from you and lied to keep what wasn't mine.

I justified it by letting myself believe I was doing the right thing. That I was protecting Rylann and her child. Truth is, I wanted her for myself.

It was not easy to win her back, nor did I ever really win, but I fought for her. Every day. I did everything I could to make her happy and whole again. I loved her with every part of my being. I accepted that the love she held for you would never go away.

The day Rylann told me she was pregnant, I wanted to tell her the truth but I couldn't bring myself to do it. She was offering me the greatest gift. Fatherhood. It was a dream come true. I had known having children wasn't in the cards for me, but there it was, dangling there for me to take. So I did.

I know it was wrong, and I'm sorry that you were hurt in the process. I'm sorry for the part I played, for stealing your happiness and making it my own.

I hope that in time you can forgive me. I'm just a man, who knew his time was limited.

Being a father is a gift, one that I am grateful to you for. I know it came at your expense, but I want to thank you nonetheless.

Unfortunately, you weren't given the same opportunity to meet your other child all those years ago. I am very sorry for the child you lost and for the son you missed seeing grow. But Rhys is still here.

Please know, I never forgot that you are his true father. I named him Rhys for a reason. It's as close a combination of Rylann and Jace as I could make it.

I did my best to make sure you were still there, in his name and in the stories I told him about you. He knows who you are. It was important for me to tell him the truth in a way that would be safe and comforting for him after I was gone.

I love our son, Jace. He was my world. Please, make him yours too.

Now, for the kicker. Life has led you back to Rylann. To a life with a family that you deserve. A life owed to you. If you put aside everything else, all that should matter is them.

Go! Be with your family and don't look back.

You are a good man. I may not have known you, but I know Levi. If you are half the man he says you are, then you need to get off your ass and fight for your family. I know they love you and are waiting for you.

This is why you got this letter. There is still hope. They want you. Need you. Love you.

Go to them. I am counting on you to take care of them until your last breath. I'm their past, and you are their future.

So, go make our girl and our son happy. Love them with everything you have to give. Live a wonderful life together. I promise I won't haunt you. Instead, I'll be the ghost cheering you on.

I kept them safe and happy, waiting for you to find your way back to them. So go! Go get them, and never let them go.

-Sam

I fight the tears stinging my nose. I can't believe this guy had the foresight to write something so powerful.

"Well, shit. I can't hate this guy like I want to," I mutter under my breath.

My eyes focus on the last line of the page. *Go get them, and never let them go.* It's no wonder Rylann married this guy. He's not the complete dick I thought him to be.

I toss the letter onto the table. My head is spinning. Massaging my temples, I think about everything he said. Every word is a fucking blow to my damaged heart.

I know she was hurt when I left her. She tried to tell me, repeatedly. Looking back, there were moments when she was trying to elaborate and I'd cut her off.

Steamrolling her, her thoughts and emotions. I was so fixated making her fall for me, I couldn't see past my wants and needs.

I know Rylann would never want to hurt me. Us.

While I fucking hate this guy, on some level, I get it. Which makes hating him kind of impossible.

Asshole!

When I woke up this morning, the last thing I expected was to get my ass handed to me by a dead guy. I hate that he called me out on my shit.

Is he right, though? Are they waiting for me?

After the way I left Rylann in Hawaii, I'm not so sure she wants me back. I said some pretty cruel and unforgivable things.

Add in how long I waited to read this letter, Rylann's probably given up on me by now, and Rhys ... Fuck. I just left him without saying goodbye after blowing up at Rylann. How could he forgive me for walking away and disappearing for weeks?

I promised myself I wouldn't leave them, and when things got hard, that's exactly what I did.

I might lose them because I was too stubborn to listen. Instead of trying to understand why Rylann did what she did, I chose to lash out and then hide away, wallowing in takeout and booze. I didn't stop to think about how they were feeling.

Now, who's the selfish one?

"Let me read that." Eli grabs the letter from the table.

Flanked by Cameron and Mason, my three brothers read the letter. Taking advantage of the silence, I prop my head in my hands.

Ugh. What the fuck do I do now?

While Sam's letter brings some clarity, I don't know if I can move past this like nothing. If I can't move past the hurt, can I live without them in my life? Can I live without her?

My gut churns, and the breakfast sandwich I just ate doesn't settle so well with that thought. No. I can't.

There is still hope.

Sam's words flicker across my mind. Fuck, I hope so. I feel like half a man without them.

The thought of living without Rylann and Rhys sounds like the worst life imaginable. If our time in Hawaii showed me anything at all, it was that we felt right together. Because of them, I had the best damn vacation.

Without even realizing it, we were a family.

"Jace," Eli says.

"Yeah?"

"Get your head out of your ass, man. Go get your family. You love Rylann. You always have. You made a mistake back then. You chose wrong. This Sam guy is right. Let it go." Eli looks at me, and I think I can see tears in his eyes as he folds up the letter and hands it to me.

"Seriously, Jay. Listen to the dead guy. He's a smart fuckin' dude."

I scoff at Cameron. Only my baby brother can make me laugh at a time like this.

"It's not that simple," I admit.

"Yes, it is," Eli deadpans.

"I'm booking your flights. Where's your laptop and wallet? You have to get to fucking Portland, like, yesterday." Mason heads to my office and hurries back to the kitchen island with my laptop and gets to work.

"Guys ..."

"No. That's enough." Eli points at me, his brow arched in frustration. "Let it the fuck go. You *love* her man. Who the fuck cares about the past. What do you want? You want to keep living like this, like half a man?" He waves his hands around my dirty condo. "Or do you want the fairytale, bro? I know you—you are a good man. You are capable of moving past this and having a great life with the woman you love. Your soulmate. I've seen you two with my own eyes. She's it."

"But—"

"But nothing. Go be happy. I would give anything to have a chance with the one that got away. Mase, forward Jay's flight details to Levi, so he can pick him up from the airport when he lands."

Eli's confession throws me, and while I want to dig into that little piece of information, now's not the time.

"Well, what the fuck are you waiting for, Jay? Get off your fucking ass. Go shower because you smell like a fish's asshole. And pack. We'll drive you to the airport," Cameron booms, throwing a balled-up foil wrapper at my head.

I feel like I am in a haze until Eli claps his hands in my face, and I snap out of it.

"You're right. I love her. I love my son. I need them."

"Thank fuck, he's got a brain," Eli hoots.

Jumping off the couch, I hustle to my room to get my shit together.

She's it. I've always known that. I can't let her slip through my fingers again. I couldn't even get over her the first time I let her go. I don't think I will survive another. I have to take care of my family. I have to go to her, to him.

My son.

Damn, I never thought I would be able to say that. I'm a dad now. My son needs me, and so does Rylann.

My sunshine.

How could I be so foolish to think that she would do this on purpose to me?

She doesn't have a single dishonest bone in her body. I never should have let my anger get the best of me. I never should have walked away without hearing her out.

I hurt the woman I love all over again. I spewed misdirected anger at her. Anger at my ex, anger at myself, and my choices that led us here in the first place. I need to do what the author of this letter asks me to do.

Let it all go.

I'm gonna fight for my family. I'm gonna grovel at Rylann's feet until she forgives me for leaving her. Again.

Then, I'm gonna love her and Rhys with everything I have and never look back.

I spent the entire two-and-a-half-hour flight from L.A. to Portland riddled with anxiety while I nursed a glass of whiskey, stared at pictures of Rylann and Rhys on my phone, and rehearsed what I'm going to say.

I don't know what our next steps are going to be or how difficult it might be to get past the secrets and lies, but I want us to be together.

I wince, remembering the veiled threat I made about taking Rhys away from her. I would never do that. She's a wonderful mother and adores our son.

As promised, my brothers had Levi pick me up from the airport. He's been quiet during the drive to his place. The short conversation we did have was him telling me we needed to make a stop to pick up some ice cream for the kids. Seems he canceled his date with them after summer camp.

I listened to him call Scarlett, letting her know he was on his way home. I appreciated his discretion regarding my presence. I'd much rather Rylann learn I'm here herself. I want to talk to her and clear the air before I see Rhys.

There's so much I want to say. I'm not sure where to start.

Putting my hand in my pocket, I run my fingers over the letter.

"Go on then," Levi says, pulling me from my thoughts.

He points to the cute little house next door, and a smile pulls at my lips. Her home is a pale yellow raised ranch, with shaker siding, white trim, and a gray roof with a matching front door. Colorful flower pots decorate the porch.

It's my fucking sunshine personified.

Levi chuckles. "It's her to a T, isn't it?"

"It is. I shouldn't be surprised."

We sit quietly for a moment longer. My nerves are shot, and my hands are sweaty. I've practiced what I want to say, but right now, my mind is blanking out.

"So, did you fly all this way for us to sit in the car all day, or are you gonna grow a pair and knock on her door already?"

"I'm getting out. I just need a second."

"Fine. Take your time. It's only been seven years," he mocks.

I flip him off, and he laughs.

I look back at her house. I wish I knew what was waiting for me inside. Will she be happy to see me? I fucking hope so. When I wasn't drunk, I was missing her and Rhys.

"Lee?"

"Yeah?"

"Thanks, man ... For watching out for my family."

Levi tips his chin in acknowledgment. "Anytime. They're my family too. I'm glad you're here. I know everything has been hard to come to terms with. Hell, it was a shock to me too. But you both deserve to be happy. You were always supposed to be together."

"You think?"

"I know," he says with a sigh. "For what it's worth, Sam knew too. I know what he did was fucked up, but he was a good guy. He took care of them."

"He was a good friend, wasn't he?"

"He was. It was hard watching him get sick. Watching Ry struggle. Scarlett and I tried, but there wasn't anything we could do. We just sat with her. Watched her light fade to nothing. Rhys's too ..." He pauses, his eyes glossy. "If you tell anyone what I am about to tell you, I'll kill you. Understand?"

"Of course."

"I spent a lot of time with Sam those last few weeks. The last time we spoke, he made me promise to make Hawaii happen again. He said, 'You give her one year, Levi. Not a day more. If she's still sad, you take her back to that island and make sure he's there too. I don't care what excuse you use but make it happen. She deserves to be happy.' So I did what he asked. I brought us all back together."

I rub my mouth, throat swelling with emotion.

Memories of our call surface. It was so unexpected when Lee asked me to come on a vacation with them. Shaking my head to myself in disbelief, I get it now. Sam orchestrated all this.

For her.

Fuck, what is it with this guy? He keeps doing things that make me hate him less and less.

"Wow. I don't know what to say."

"Yeah. Like I said, he wasn't bad, Jay. He knew he'd never make it and wanted a slice of happiness before he went. It's greedy as hell. Wrong. But I get it. If I was in his place I'd give anything for one last day with my girls. To live the life I have, well ... You get it. Or at least, I hope you do."

Levi reaches for the shopping bags filled with ice cream sitting in the backseat and tosses one in my lap.

"Enough of that. Now, get the fuck out of my car and go get your family."

"Yes, sir." I chuckle.

Grabbing my duffle bag from the trunk, I say goodbye to my friend, giving him an extra tight hug. I think I might owe him my happiness.

Ice cream in hand, I walk up the path to Rylann's front door.

As I get closer, my heart starts to gallop and my palms start to sweat. I take the steps up her porch and approach her door. Placing my bag at my feet, I reach out and knock on the door.

CHAPTER FIFTY-SEVEN

Rylann

Dip, fill, roll.

Making enchiladas for dinner is messy and exactly what I need. The repetitive task is keeping both my hands and brain occupied.

I can't stop thinking about Jace. How he's doing, where he's at. If I'm not fussing over Rhys, Jace is occupying every thought in my brain. No one has heard from him, and it hurts knowing that it's all my fault he has hidden himself away.

It's been a hard couple of weeks being back home for me and Rhys. Work and Summer Camp have been my saving grace, keeping us busy and distracted.

Knock, knock.

I look over at my phone, noting the time. Who on earth could be knocking on the door around dinner time? Mom and Dad have plans tonight and would never knock. Levi is supposed to stop by with ice cream, but he'd come through the patio door.

Another double knock hits the door.

Geez, relax.

I finish up my last roll and wash my hands. Removing my apron, I double-check for food drops on my leggings and sweater before making my way to the door. On my way, I stop to check on Rhys. He hasn't moved, still sitting on the couch in the living room, absently watching TV.

I'm not surprised. He hasn't been himself since Hawaii. My sweet boy has been replaced by a sullen little thing. It hurts my heart to see him this way. He hasn't said it aloud, but not hearing from Jace is starting to get to him. I know Rhys blames me for his disappearance. He's trying not to show it, but this past week, he's been extra fresh with me and pushing my buttons. Testing boundaries. I'm trying not to hold it against him. As a mom, it's hard not to take his behavior personally. I understand. He's hurting. And if I'm being real, I'm hurting too.

Jace's disappearance adds to the pain and guilt I've been carrying. I figured sending the letter would help. If only to get him to be there for Rhys.

I stomp over to the door, my mood drastically taking a turn. Taking it out on the door, I whip it open without checking who's standing on the other side.

All the air is sucked from my lungs, and I do a double-take, blinking a few times to make sure what I am seeing is real and not a figment of my imagination.

Standing on my doorstep is the most wonderful sight I have ever seen. Shifting from foot to foot, in a pair of dark jeans and a hoodie, is Jace.

The butterflies in my stomach soar just looking at him. He's still as handsome as ever, even when he looks a little rough around the edges, which is to be expected. I did rip his beautiful heart out before stomping on it.

My arms ache to reach out and hug him. I missed him so much.

Rather than touch him, I hug myself, forcing my arms to stay at my side. I'm happy he's here for Rhys.

He could be here for you too.

Doubtful. I destroyed his trust, the way he sees me, our relationship—everything. I'm not sure he can forgive me, no matter what Levi says. I don't even forgive myself. All that matters is Rhys. As long as he has his father in his life, I'll be happy. Miserable, but happy.

"Hey," I croak out, finding my voice.

"Hey." Jace grabs at the back of his neck, and my heart plummets.

He's uncomfortable. This is all my fault. I broke us. Now, he doesn't even want to be near me.

I push back the tears stinging my eyes.

"Let me go get Rhys. He'll be so happy to see you. I'll give you guys some time alone." I turn to go back inside, but Jace stops me.

"No!" he shouts, and I freeze. I turn around and face him, his hazel eyes strained. He glances behind me before looking at me. "Don't. Not yet ... Do you think we can talk first?"

"Um, sure. Did you wanna ..." I shrug and thumb the door behind me, leaving it up to him to decide if he wants to come inside or not.

"Here is fine." He points to the porch steps that lead up to the house. "But first, maybe put this in the freezer. Levi said he promised to pick this up for Rhys." He hands me a plastic bag containing a few pints of ice cream.

Of course, Levi would come through to deliver Rhys's favorite flavor ice cream and his dad.

My heart swells. I love my friend so much. I peer over Jace's shoulder to find Levi standing at his front door, watching. He smirks, popping his chin at me before disappearing inside.

"Thanks. Uh, so you wait here,"—I point to the ground like a pathetic dork—"and I'll be back."

Jace nods, and I turn, rushing inside. I put the ice cream in the freezer and check on Rhys one more time. This time, the walk to the door is paved in quicksand.

Based on Jace's reaction to seeing me, I'm not looking forward to this conversation. I have a feeling he's here to let me down easy. I mean, he didn't want to come inside. That can't be good, right?

Then why did he have a duffle bag at his feet?

I ignore that piece of evidence, tamping down my hope that he could be here for me too. Before stepping outside, I take a deep cleansing breath.

It's fine. I'll be fine. I just need him to be there for Rhys. I can deal.

Pulling open the door, I step out and shut it behind me as quietly as I can and then proceed to take a seat on the step. He follows, sitting down next to me.

I can't bear to look him in the eyes, too scared to see what they might tell me. So I rush forth with my apology.

"I'm so sorry, Jace. For everything. I know there isn't a thing I can say that can prove just how sorry I am. I have no excuse for what I did, so I'm not going to sit here and justify my actions. I was sad and scared, and I don't know what I was thinking. I messed up. No. I fucked up. I hurt you. But thank you. I'm grateful that you're here for Rhys."

"Ry—" Jace goes to interrupt me, but I cut him off and power through the rest of my speech. It's easier if I push through and say what I need to say.

"I understand that you hate me. I hate me too. However, I hope we can work past it for Rhys. His happiness is my priority, and I will do everything in my power to keep him safe and happy. We can get a paternity test done and work out any kind of visitation or custody arrangements you see fit. Anything you want. Just, please don't take him away from me. I—"

"Geez, woman, will you please be quiet and let me talk?" he inserts, placing his finger over my mouth, shutting me up.

My eyes snap up to his. My lips tingle against the warmth of his long thick digit. His lips twist up in a small timid smile, and the tight cord around my chest loosens its grip at the sight.

"I need you to be quiet for a moment, Sunshine. Can you do that for me?"

He called me Sunshine. Is it possible that he doesn't hate me and might still want me?

My eyes never leave his as I nod.

"Good girl," he whispers, and I can't stop how my core tightens at his praise. He removes his finger and gently cups my jaw. "I got your letter. Took me a while, so I apologize if I worried you and Rhys. I needed a moment to get my head straight. To come to terms with the truth of it all. I—"

I go to interrupt him, to explain. I don't think he heard everything or understands why I did what I did. I want to tell him everything. He shakes his head at me. I close my mouth, biting my lips and letting him finish.

"This letter ..." He pulls the crumpled envelope out of his hoodie pocket to show me he has it before shoving it back in his sweatshirt. "It explains a lot, and it helped me see things differently. See things from your side. So, what I want to say is ... I forgive you. I'm not saying I completely understand, but I'm willing to listen to you and accept the things I can't change. It's not going to be easy. I'm still hurt. I'm sad. Angry that I missed out on so much. That *we* missed out on so much. But I want to move past it. I want to move forward. We have a lot to work on together and, like I said, it won't be easy. I made the mistake of letting you go once before, and I won't do that again. I don't want to go back to living a half-life. I want it all, with you. We were made for each other. It might have taken a long time and a lot of mistakes for us to find our way back, but here we are. Where we are supposed to be. Together. I know that deep inside here. You and Rhys are my whole heart." Jace places my hand on his chest over his heart. His strong steady heartbeat pounds under my palm.

Eyes locked on the other, we stare, refusing to break the spell we're under.

My eyes well with unshed tears. I don't know if I deserve his forgiveness, but I will do anything and everything I can to prove to him that I am worth it. We are worth it.

"I love you, Rylann. I always have, and I always will. It's us from now until forever."

Tears pour down my face at his earnest words of forgiveness and absolute unconditional love. Slowly, reverently, I run my hands up his strong chest and cup his scruffy jaw, cradling his face between the palms of my hands. My heart is flying in my chest. His words heal my aching soul. He's finally choosing me. This beautiful, one-of-a-kind man is mine. He forgives me.

He loves me.

Without a doubt, I love him too. He owns me. Body and soul. He's the love of my life. My soulmate.

"I love you. So much. I always have. It's you. It's always been you," I declare. I've never meant it more than I do now.

I bring his face towards mine and press my mouth to his in a slow deliberate kiss. Like always, the sparks crackle between our lips when they touch. Utter warmth and contentment fill my soul as he kisses me back.

Pulling away, he rests his forehead against mine. I drape my arms over his shoulders and hold him tight. I'm never letting him go again. Our breaths mingle as we take in the enormity of everything that's happened to bring us to this moment.

"I missed you so much, Ace."

He looks me in the eyes, hands resting on my hips. "I missed you too. Just ... promise me one thing?"

"Anything." Whatever he asks, I will gladly give him.

"From now on, we won't ever keep secrets from each other again. Nothing but honesty between us. From here on out. Can you promise me that?"

No promise has ever been so easy to keep. "You have my word."

"And you have mine," he promises, sealing our vow with a soft kiss on the lips.

"I have something else to tell you," I confess.

His smile drops and he rears back, but I don't let him get far. Grabbing his shoulders, I jump in his lap and straddle him.

"It's not bad," I say, my tone placating. He raises an eyebrow, placing his hands on my upper thighs, waiting for me to continue. "What I was going to say ... before you freaked out—which I understand with my track record and all ..." I pout, holding up my hands in surrender.

Jace's eyes light up, and he bites his lip holding back his smile before demanding, "Okay. Spill it, Sunny."

My tummy flutters at his use of my nickname. We're going to be okay. "Well, I ... Uh. I was going to say ... That kiss, while sweet, wasn't nearly enough."

The sexy smoldering grin I love seeing splits across Jace's face. He brushes the loose strands of my hair behind my ear, grazing my skin in the way I like. "Is that right?"

His smooth whiskey voice makes my panties flood with arousal. His voice alone could get me off. Especially when he's talking dirty to me.

My fingers curl into his hair, and I pull him closer. The smell of his clean citrus leather scent surrounds me.

For the first time in two weeks, my body relaxes. I missed him so much. His face, his smile, his scent, his strong body, his sexy voice, his gorgeous honest eyes. Every. Single. Thing.

"Yes. That's right," I hum, bringing my face closer to his.

"Well then, let's take care of that, shall we?" His breath fans across my lips.

"Please," I beg, swiping my tongue across my bottom lip, grazing his plump ones.

Jace crashes his mouth to mine in a searing kiss. Our tongues tangle in a sweet sensual dance. He tastes good, like mint, a hint of whiskey, and all him. His hands trail up my thighs, groping my ass. I cling to him as I groan, wrapping my arms around his neck, pulling him closer. Our kiss turns heated, and we match each other's intensity stroke for stroke, holding on tightly, afraid to let the other go.

Which I will never do again. Where he goes, I go. I will follow my heart, which beats in his chest, to the ends of the earth. In his arms, I feel like I'm home.

We stay in our embrace, sitting on the steps of my childhood home, making out for who knows how long. When I start to grind myself down on his growing erection, he breaks our connection, making me moan in dissatisfaction. Not wanting to stop, I chase his lips, wanting more.

"Love, you have to stop grinding your hot little pussy on me or I'm gonna come in pants right here on the street," he grunts crudely, making me giggle.

I never expected his mouth to be so filthy, but it is and it's hot as hell. I love when he talks dirty to me.

I kiss him again, continuing to rub myself all over him. I don't care who sees us. Including that awful Mrs. Haney across the street, who is for sure going to be reporting my indecency to my mother at some point. She can suck it.

I have the man of my dreams back in my arms, and if I want to straddle his lap, so help me god I will. The entire neighborhood can watch for all I care. This man is mine.

Jace breaks our kiss, resting his forehead against mine. I'm lost in his eyes, the glowing heat of amber in his irises warming me from the inside out. I squirm on his lap. I want him so badly. Right here, right now.

"I know what you're thinking, but no."

"Mmmm." I sulk, scrunching my nose at his willpower to stop.

He chuckles and gives my butt a playful swat. "Ry, as much as I love kissing these sweet soft lips,"—he plants a quick peck on my lips—"we have to go inside. Our son is probably going to come looking for you, and I'd kind of prefer that his first look at me in two weeks isn't with a raging boner."

"Shit! Rhys!" I jump off his lap like my ass is on fire. When his words register, I stop dead in my tracks. My heart expands in my chest, and I turn to him as my nose tingles with unshed tears. "You said *our* son."

An errant tear leaks out the corner of my eye, rolling down my cheek. I haven't heard him say that yet, at least not without it being laced with venom. My heart melts at the beauty of his simple testament.

Our son.

Jace stands, grabs my hips, and pulls me to his chest, whispering against my lips, "Our son."

I lock my arms around his waist, resting my cheek against his chest, squeezing him tight. I close my eyes to the sound of his heart beating, soaking in this moment.

This is real. He's here.

"I love the way that sounds," I whisper.

"Me too, Sunny."

He places a kiss on the crown of my head, and I breathe in his familiar and calming scent of citrus and leather.

"I love you, Ace," I tell him. I've held onto those words for too long and now that I've said them, I'll never stop saying them to him.

"I love you, Sunshine." He wraps his arms around me, hugging me tight. I'm finally safe in his arms. Before I start crying, I release him and step back.

"Let's go inside. There is so much I need to tell you and do to you, but mostly, I need you to go and take care of Rhys. He's missed you so much." I look up at my man and smile.

He looks so happy, a complete one-eighty from how he looked when I first opened the door. Grabbing his hands, I pull him inside our home. That's right—*our* home. Home is wherever we are together.

For now, that's here.

I'm standing in the hallway listening to Jace read Rhys a bedtime story.

Tonight has been amazing. Rhys was so happy to have Jace back, he didn't leave his side all night. Rhys's light is back, and that's all I could have hoped for, and yet, Jace has given me so much more than that.

Rhys spent dinner on his dad's lap, filling him in on everything that's happened since they'd been apart. I almost asked Rhys to sit in his own seat, but I decided against it. They needed this, and I loved watching the two of them reconnect. Father and son.

I was near tears watching them from across the table. Their easy affection and love for each other were a sight to behold. It was like they'd never known life apart from each other. I hope they never do again.

I know there still is so much for me and Jace to talk about—he said as much on the steps—but with every smile and wink he gave me across the table, he has begun to erase any doubt. He's here to stay.

"Jace?" Rhys murmurs, cutting though my thoughts.

"Yeah, buddy?"

"You're my dad too, right?"

I gasp at Rhys's question. I knew he was going to bring this up, and I was just hoping I could be there. To help navigate these strange waters we're wading into. We talked a little bit about Jace being his dad on the plane, but he hasn't brought it up since then.

I'm about to interrupt when Jace answers his question.

I stand back and let him do this. He needs to handle this his way. It's the only way for them both to figure out how to steer their relationship from here on out. I trust him to be honest with our boy. He'd move heaven and earth before he let anything hurt Rhys.

"I am. Is that okay with you?"

"Yeah."

"That's good. Do you have any questions for me?" Jace asks.

"No. My daddy told me I had two dads. He said when he was gone, you would come and take care of me. Does that mean that you're staying here to be my dad now?"

My heart stops, wondering how Jace is going to respond to that. We haven't talked about our next steps yet.

"Rhys, I ..." Jace briefly pauses before answering, "You know what? Yes, it does. I need to leave in a few days because I have grown-up things to take care of back where I live before I can be here full-time. But no matter what, I will always be here for you."

"Promise?"

"Promise, promise."

"Promise, promise," Rhys repeats, tasting the words on his tongue. I wish I could see his face.

"Now, get some sleep. We have a big day tomorrow. I'm going to need you to show me around town, so I know where to go when I move here."

"Okay." I can hear the excitement in Rhys's voice. The bed creaks, and a second later the light goes off before the night light clicks on.

"Good night, Rhys."

"Good night, J— Wait! Can I call you Dad?"

Jace clears his throat before answering, "Bud, you can call me whatever you're comfortable with. So Jace or Dad works for me."

"I like 'Dad'. Good night, Dad."

"Good night, son," Jace says, voice thick with emotion.

A moment later, Jace closes Rhys's door and notices me standing in the hall silently crying.

I'm a horrible voyeur, but I couldn't walk away if I wanted to. Listening to them restored a damaged part of my heart. I never meant to keep them apart, and I won't any more.

Jace wraps me up in his big strong arms, holding me tight to his chest. He rests his cheek on my head and takes a deep breath. "You heard all that, didn't you?"

I nod my head, unable to speak.

"I meant every word."

I know he did. But after everything, I owe it to him to take the risks.

"Jace, everything you said ... You don't have to move. I'll ... We'll move. I put you through enough. If you give me some time, I'll make it happen." I'm already trying to figure out what I need to do to prove to Jace that I'm all in.

He deserves someone to sacrifice for him. To love him un-conditionally. To give him everything. And that's me. I will do anything for him.

"Sunshine, while I love you even more for offering to move ... No. I don't belong in L.A. anymore. I belong here, with you and Rhys. I was already planning my move here that last night in Kona."

"But—"

He cuts me off with his finger, and I smile. He has a bad habit of interrupting me, but right now, I don't mind when he looks at me like he is now. Like I'm his whole world.

"No. I will not move Rhys away from the family he has grown up with. He belongs here. He's been through enough."

"Are you sure?"

"Absolutely."

"Why are you so perfect?" Because he is. After everything, he's still willing to sacrifice his life for me and Rhys.

"I'm not perfect, and neither are you. But together, we are per-fucking-fection."

I pull his face to mine, kissing him with everything I've got.

"You're really moving here?"

"Yes. I don't want to be anywhere you're not," he says, kissing my freckles. "Besides, I've always dreamed of living next door to my best friend again. But, I gotta know, does he still come over and eat all the leftovers?"

I cover my mouth, stifling my chuckle at his absurd question. I nod. "He does. So you better start locking the patio door."

We both laugh. He knows damn well Levi eats all the leftovers.

"So, we're doing this?" I ask into his chest.

Jace pushes me away, looking me dead on. "We're doing this. Now, stop asking."

He lifts me into his arms, spinning us around. It still feels surreal that he's here, kissing me and holding me outside our sleeping son's door.

"Okay, I think we need to move away from Rhys's door," he says, kissing my neck.

He places me back on my feet but not before pressing a soft kiss to my lips. I grab his hand, threading our fingers together.

After pouring each of us a glass of red, we sit on the couch in the living room. Side by side, we get everything left unsaid out in the open. No more secrets, just like he asked. I show Jace the video and tell him about the pain I felt losing him, our time apart, including my time with Sam. Everything.

We cling to each other and cry. Each word simultaneously sets us free from the past and brings us closer together, towards our future. Our hearts are healed and full. We plan our future, talking into the early hours of the morning, until we fall asleep on the couch in each other's arms. The only place I want to be.

When I wake up to the sun peeking through the curtains, I sit there and watch Jace sleep. His chest rises and falls in soft even breaths, the creases on his forehead and around his eyes gone. He looks at peace.

My thoughts drift to Sam and everything he's done for me. He made some mistakes, but in the end, he did right his wrongs. I look up to the sky and give him a final goodbye.

I will love you forever, Sammy. Thank you for taking care of me. I promise I won't let you down. From here on out, I will live, love, and be happy. Rhys and I are in good hands, just like you hoped.

Laying my head back on Jace's chest, I listen to his heartbeat, letting it lull me back to sleep, where I dream about our life together.

A long life, full of love and happiness.

CHAPTER FIFTY-EIGHT

Rylann

FOUR MONTHS LATER

I'm missing moving day, and I hate it.

I want to be home with my guys. I want to watch as Jace puts his surfboard in the garage, places his bulky recliner in the living room where I made space for him, and watch him finish putting the last of his clothes away.

I want to be there for it all.

For him.

This past summer has been a whirlwind. Equally amazing and chaotic.

After Jace and I got back together, we spent the summer traveling between states, trying to fit in as much time together as we could. We've had the most wonderful time being a family. We've taken Rhys to Los Angeles to spend time with Jace's family. We've gone to amusement parks, camping, baseball games, the beach, and so much more. In between all the fun, Jace and I have also worked hard on our relationship. From the start, Jace was adamant we attend therapy together, and I easily agreed. He had a lot of resentment and anger to work through, and I don't blame him one bit. After a few appointments, I learned that I did too.

In the beginning, our appointments with Rhys's family counselor, Dr. Frank, were hard. But after a few very intense sessions, we started to gain the tools we needed to communicate honestly and most importantly forgive. It wasn't easy, but we did it together. We still do weekly appointments, together and sometimes separately. We're a beautiful work in progress.

I hit Jace's number, and it rings through the car over Bluetooth.

"Sunshine," he answers on the second ring. He sounds prickly, and I smile.

"Don't take that tone with me. I should be home with you guys, helping," I pout.

"We talked about this, my love. I'm fine. I've got Rhys and Mason here to help. Levi too. Besides, I don't have much to unpack."

He's right. He'd been bringing his clothes and leaving them behind with every visit. It became official when he and Mason pulled up in a U-Haul early this morning.

He had been eager to leave his firm and move here. He said we had already spent too much time apart, and any more time away from each other was tantamount to living without his heart. I almost jumped him on the couch when he told me that. My man has such a swoony way with words.

Luckily, he started the ball rolling as soon as he returned to Los Angeles after his first trip to get us back. In an effort to expedite everything, Jace gave his notice at his firm, promising to see the last of his cases through, and then promptly sold his condo.

"I know. I just miss you, is all."

The end of summer left us both too busy to spend together. Between Rhys starting school, the move, and Jace leaving his firm, there's been little time to be alone.

"I've missed you too. Have a nice time with Scarlett, and we'll see you in a few hours," he says firmly, leaving me no room to bargain.

Not like I can race home, anyway. I'm sitting in the parking lot, pouting on the phone, while Scar grabs us a couple of ice teas from the café. We're headed to the spa for our reinstated monthly mom dates.

Unfortunately, this month, our appointment landed on the first full day Jace is home.

It makes me absolutely giddy knowing we now share the same address. With him officially moving in, I can finally breathe.

"Are you sure? I can be home in twenty minutes."

"We're fine, Sunny. Go and spend some time with Scarlett. Besides, Rhys and I are looking forward to some guy time with his uncle Mills before we have to take him to the airport."

I chuckle at Jace's use of Rhys's nickname for Mason. All his uncles have one. Mason's is the funniest, though. He didn't like calling him Uncle Mase because it sounds too much like Ace. Apparently, my nickname for his dad is gross because we kiss after I say it. We do a lot more than kiss, but he doesn't need to know that.

The family had a good laugh at that one, especially Rhys's uncles. Speaking of uncles, when Rhys learned that he had three of them, well ... I don't even think I saw him that excited on Christmas morning, surrounded by a room full of presents.

Rhys is probably over the moon having Mason around. I don't know how Jace convinced him to drive up here but he did, and they hit the road together, leaving Eli to work and Cameron traveling.

Mason leaves tonight for a tech conference in the Bay area, so I should leave the guys to themselves.

Rhys loves the attention his uncles give him. All of them. It's sweet how they each have a special relationship with him, and he eats it up every chance he gets. I even feel like I've gained three awesomely sweet jokester brothers overnight. I'm a huge softy for those crazy Miller boys. They have opened their hearts and lives to us without a backward glance and without judgment.

Same with Jace's parents, Karen and Mark. They have been incredibly welcoming and warm. Rhys has already had sleepovers at their house during our trips south, and they already spoil him rotten. Jace and I love seeing how much they adore Rhys. We also appreciate the time alone the grandparents offer us and take full advantage.

My life is pretty fantastic. Jace and I are as strong as ever, and we couldn't be happier.

"Fine, I'll go. But let it be noted that I don't like it. Drive safe, and have a good time. Not too much junk food, please. We don't need a crazy Rhys tonight," I warn.

Those two own my heart. I still get choked up when I see them together, but Rhys has Jace wrapped around his fingers and he can get carried away with spoiling his son.

Sometimes, I can't believe Jace forgave me and now he's here building a life with us. As a family. I'm the luckiest girl in the world.

"Noted, and no, can't do. We plan on pizza, ice cream, soda, the works. Now, stop worrying about us. Go have fun. I love you. I'll make sure to give you my undivided attention tonight."

See? Luckiest girl in the world.

"Promise?" I ask, biting my lip.

"Do I ever break my promises when it comes to sexy time with you?" His husky voice vibrates through the speakers and shoots right down to my core, making my thighs clench.

"Never," I answer, my voice thick.

"Damn straight. Now, go and be a good girl," he says, making me groan. I love it when he calls me "good girl". It's so wrong and hot.

"Yes, *sir*," I purr.

Calling him "sir" is a new little game we started to play. He snooped on me when I left my Kindle open on the bed one night while I was brushing my teeth. I came back to find him reading where I left off. The hero was in the middle of spanking the heroine for forgetting to call him "sir" in the bedroom.

At first, it was just a little joke I'd say on the phone when we were having sexy video call time. One night, I accidentally let it slip when I was going down on him. He growled, somehow grew harder in my mouth, and then proceeded to grab my hair while he fucked my face. Forcing me to take him faster and deeper with every thrust of his hips. It was fucking hot.

It was like this dominant switch got flipped, and my regular bossy bedroom lover turned into a kinky freak. The sex we had that night was explosive. I'm glad we had the foresight to send Rhys over to Scarlett's house for a sleepover because things got loud and out of hand. Spankings included.

I lick my lips just thinking about it.

Jace groans on the other end of the line. "You're a bad girl, Sunshine. You're gonna pay for that *later*. I'm hanging up now before my dick gets any harder in front of our son and my brother. Love you."

"I love you more, sir."

Jace disconnects the call with a growl before I drive us further down phone-sex lane.

I can't get enough of him lately. I've been extra horny for him the past two weeks. I've just missed him so much. We've been so busy, we haven't had a lot of time alone. We were barely able to pull off a quickie in the garage a couple of weeks ago.

My pussy clenches at the memory. Jace had me bent over the hood of the car in the garage while he drove into me from behind, his hand clamped over my mouth to keep me quiet.

"Ry, what are you thinking about?"

I squeak as the door flies open and Scarlett hops into the car, scaring the crap out of me. She hands me my drink, and I take a long sip, trying to cool off. Shaking my head at myself, I can't believe I was sitting here dreaming about getting off with my incredibly sexy baby daddy.

"Sorry, just thinking about all the things I need to do."

"You're such a bad liar. You were thinking about having sex with Jace, weren't you? You horn dog." She pokes me in the side with her finger, laughing at me.

I hate that she knows me so well. Pointing at her, I say, "I will cut you. Besides, if I'm not mistaken, I do remember a time in which you and Levi were attached at your genitals."

"Ha! Okay, fine. You got me there. Let's get out of here before we're late for our appointment."

Twenty minutes later, we are walking into our favorite spa in downtown Pine Hills.

It's amazing here. We've been coming since it opened a couple of years ago. It has a gorgeous living wall, and while it's bright and open, it also feels cozy and earthy at the same time.

When we walk through the door, I'm assaulted with the scent of eucalyptus, and saliva pools in my mouth as bile rises in my throat.

What the hell is that?

"Ry, you look green. Are you okay?" Scarlett rubs a hand down my arm.

I swallow down the bile and drag in deep, ragged breaths until the nausea subsides.

"Yeah, I'm okay. That was weird." I exhale.

We walk over to the receptionist's desk to check in for our appointments, and the young girl hands us a clipboard with our massage forms and releases. We've opted for the full-day experience, starting with a wax, then a massage, a facial, and then we'll finish with manis and pedis while sipping cucumber water.

I'm answering the questionnaire as usual when I pull up, stuck on one of the questions.

Are you pregnant or breastfeeding?

When was the last time I had a period? I start calculating. It was probably when Scarlett did. We always sync up.

"Pssst. Scar?" I hiss under my breath.

"Hmm?" She looks up at me from her forms.

"When was the last time you had a period?"

"Umm ... July," she drags out before biting her lip, looking away. Wait. What?

Nooo ...

"Scarlett Walker, are you *pregnant*?" I whisper-shout at my friend.

A sly smile spreads across her face. "Yes." She nods.

I jump out of my chair and scream, "My bestie is having a baby!"

"Umm, babies, actually," she says, cringing.

"Oh my god, Scarface! Twins again! I'm so happy for you guys!"

"Yay, twins." She raises her hands in the air, dryly cheering. "I'm sorry I didn't tell you sooner. I wanted to so badly. We only found out a couple of weeks ago. I had some spotting, so I wanted to wait until after the fourteen-week mark before I said anything. Besides, with everything going on with Jace and the move, I thought it would be best to wait until next weekend to let you know."

"I forgive you. This is amazing. How did I not see it?" I look her over, but I still can't tell. She's right, though—I've been preoccupied with everything going on.

"It's fall. Sweaters help." She giggles, lifting her sweater, where I see the small bump protruding from her stomach.

"Seriously, this is awesome. Congratulations, sis." I pull her to her feet and lock her in a tight hug.

"Thanks," she says, pulling back, hands on my shoulders, and pushes me to sit. "Can we circle back to the question you just asked me before, you know ..." She waves her hand around her stomach.

Oh, right.

"When was *your* last period, Ry?"

"Hmm."

I know I had one in August because it was right before my trip to visit Jace before school started. We haven't necessarily been careful. Like at all. Not even in Hawaii. Jace said if it happens, it happens. He can't wait to see my stomach round with his babies.

Think! Periods, remember?

Let's see ... Jace came up for Labor Day weekend, and we went at it like rabbits. After that ...

"Fuck."

"Rice Cakes?" Scarlett asks, knowingly.

"Not now. Let's enjoy our day, and then we can stop at the drugstore on the way home to confirm."

"Are you sure?" She's biting her lip, holding back a smile.

She knows what I know—I'm pregnant.

"I'm sure."

An hour in, and I regret my decision to wait.

I've added up all the other things out of the ordinary things I've been doing lately, like being tired and ready for a nap halfway through the day or being extra horny. My boobs freaking hurt. The disgusting smell of eucalyptus makes me want to puke. And my wax hurt like hell this time around, only further confirming what I already know.

I'm pregnant.

Sitting here with my cucumber water, trying not to anxiously bounce my legs while the poor nail technician paints my toes is impossible.

How did I not realize I missed my period? How did I not recognize the symptoms? I've been pregnant before.

I try thinking back, but nothing connects. With Rhys, I only remember the end. The beginning is all blurry.

I didn't realize I was pregnant until I was in my second trimester, and I missed a lot of clues.

"Ry, how are you feeling? Like, really feeling?" Scarlett asks. She's sitting in the massage chair next to me, in a matching fluffy mint green robe.

"I'm ..." I shrug and take stock of all the emotions floating around in my head.

My heart skips a beat, and my stomach flips like I'm on a rollercoaster. I look at my friend and smile. The worried look on her face disappears, and she smiles back.

I'm really happy.

"Congratulations, Ry."

"Congratulations, Scar."

We toast to motherhood and clink our glasses.

CHAPTER FIFTY-NINE

Rylann

I walk through the front door and toss my purse on the entry table.

It's been a day. Taking off my shoes, I make my way toward the living room looking for my guys. The TV is on, but the sound is off. It's too quiet, and all the lights are off.

"I'm home!" I call into the darkness. Nothing.

Where are they?

I head into the kitchen, and light from the backyard catches my eye. I walk to the patio door and pull it open.

My nose tingles as tears start to form in my eyes at the sight before me.

Standing outside on the deck, side by side, under what looks like a million twinkling lights, are my guys, surrounded by a thousand yellow flowers, wearing the biggest smiles I have ever seen. I want to snap a picture and capture this moment and those smiles forever while they wear matching outfits of blue jeans and white t-shirts.

They look so much alike. The golden rings around their pupils glow in the soft glow of the stream lights wrapped around and above the deck.

My ability to breathe disappears. It takes me another second to register that both their shirts have writing on them.

I gasp when the words written across Rhys's chest register.

Marry.

I look at Jace and then his shirt.

Me?

Jace drops to his knee, and Rhys does the same. Jace pulls out a small blue box and opens it for me, presenting me with the most beautiful ring I've ever seen.

Ohmigod. Is this really happening?

"Do you like it, Mom?" Rhys asks.

I nod. The words are lost in a squall of my emotions. I'm caught off guard, surprised by this beautiful scene, and the news I got before coming home is a lot to take in for a pregnant woman. My legs feel like lead weights as I stand, stock-still, watching the man I love with every ounce of my being down on one knee before me.

"Sunshine, you are the love of my life. I can't imagine spending it with anyone but you. We've had a rough go at things, but since you and Rhys have come back into my life, I've never been happier. You two make my life better. You make *me* better. You are everything I have ever dreamed about finding in a partner. You're strong, kind, funny, sassy, and goddamn, are you beautiful."

"You're not supposed to cuss, Dad." Rhys hisses, reprimanding his father in the middle of his sweet proposal.

"You're right. Sorry, bud," Jace says, then turns back to me, rolling his eyes.

I bite my lips as my tears cloud my eyes.

"You're forgiven," Rhys smarts smugly, his hands on his knee.

"Thanks. Think I can finish now?"

"Sure." Rhys shrugs, and I can't help but chuckle and cry at the same time while watching these two go back and forth with each other.

This is exactly what I want. Every day. For the rest of my life.

Jace clears his throat, bringing my attention back to him. "As I was saying, I love you, Sunshine. Will you please do me the honor of becoming my wife? Will you marry me?"

My body starts working again, and I rush to Jace, dropping to my knees in front of him. Before giving him his answer, I grab his face and kiss him hard on the mouth.

"Yes, Jace Miller. I will marry you. I love you so much."

"Yes!" Rhys yells as we kiss again.

Happy tears stream down my face as Jace slides a beautiful cushion-cut yellow diamond set in platinum down my finger. It fits me perfectly. Especially the color.

I stare down in wonder at the beauty that is this ring. It's way too big a diamond, but that's Jace. Always spoiling me.

"Do you like it?"

"Are you kidding? I love it. It's gorgeous and perfect, just like you."

I grab his face again and kiss the ever-loving crap out of him, right in front of our son, who mumbles, "Gross."

At the sound of whoops and hollers in the distance, we break our kiss. Scarlett, Levi, and the girls are watching from their patio, cheering us on.

"It's about time!" Levi yells, cupping his mouth.

Scarlett makes a cat-call whistle with her fingers, making us all laugh.

"Yeah, yeah," Jace yells.

Still, on our knees, he tilts my chin up with his thumb and forefinger, bringing my eyes to his. His green and gold depths are shining brightly, brimming with love and happiness.

"Sorry about the peanut gallery," he says, wrapping his arms around me and lifting me up. He places me on my feet and kisses my cheek. "Before we go pop some bottles with our friends, I want you to know why I chose yellow." He rubs his thumb over my finger and his ring—the ring that will never leave my hand. "Not only is yellow your favorite color, but a yellow diamond engagement ring also means everlasting love and hope. That's what we have together, Sun. Nothing can or will ever change that. I love you. Always have ..."

"Always will," I finish against his lips.

Jace presses his mouth to mine in a tender kiss. The tell-tale electrical current hums between us, letting me know I'm home.

I break us apart before we get distracted. I have news to deliver of my own.

"Jace, please don't get mad. But I have a secret."

I bite my lip and make bedroom eyes at him to soften the blow and let him know I'm playing around.

He hates secrets and with good reason. But this? Well ...

"Care to share, my love?" he asks, a hint of worry in his tone.

I lean up onto my toes and whisper into his ear, "I'm pregnant."

He grabs the tops of my arms and pushes me back, his eyes wide in shock.

"For real?"

"For real."

"Fuck yes!" he yells, picking me up and spinning us around, his arms squeezing me tight.

"Language, Dad!" Rhys yells.

Jace ignores him, focusing on me. "You've just made me the happiest man alive. Again."

He crashes his lips to mine, claiming my mouth like he has my heart, deeply. This kiss sends heat straight to my center, making my panties wet. If he keeps this up, I'll be climbing him like a tree without a care as to who sees us.

"Gross. Can you guys stop kissing already?" Rhys says.

We break apart to laugh.

"You know ... One day, kiddo, I'm going to hold this against you," Jace teases.

"Nope, never. Kissing is gross." Rhys makes a retching sound.

"We'll see," Jace says, winking at me, his face split in the biggest grin.

Rhys runs over to Levi as he, Scarlett, and—as Jace likes to call them—Double Trouble come walking across the backyard to join us on the patio.

"Let's not mention this to Rhys until we go to the doctor, okay?"

"Whatever you want, Sunshine," he whispers, wrapping me up in his arms.

"Scarlett knows, though."

"Of course she does," he says with a smile. He'd never expect anything different.

After a round of hugs with the Walkers, we call my mom and dad to share the news.

They decide to come over to join the celebration. My mom cries as much as I did when she sees the ring.

We video-chat with Jace's parents and brothers, who are all thrilled and promise to come up soon to visit.

We spend the rest of the evening celebrating with ice cream and pizza, and I wouldn't change a thing about it. The night is perfect. A dream come true.

Jace and me.

Madly in love.

Raising a big beautiful family together.

Epilogue

JACE

TWO+ YEARS LATER

"Yes, yes, yes," Rylann chants, roughly tugging my hair, as she chases her orgasm. "Right there. Oh, Ace."

Pulling my mouth away, I speak into her wet pussy, teasing her with my hot breath. "Shh, Sunny, or the kids will hear all the dirty things Daddy's doing to Mommy in the bathroom."

Shivers roll down her spine. She loves my filthy mouth.

"Sorry, I'll be quiet. Don't stop, please," she keens needily.

I have her panting, hips jutting forward searching for my mouth, begging for me to make her come.

Only moments ago, I surprised her in the hallway and dragged her into the bathroom. I was just planning on kissing and groping her a bit without the kids around before everyone shows up for the party.

I should have known that with Rylann, a kiss is never enough.

That's how I found myself falling to my knees, bunching her dress around her hips, pulling her panties down, and burying my face between her sexy thighs.

Using my thumbs, I spread her lips open and go back to licking my beautiful wife's needy wet pussy.

Wife.

I love how the word tastes on my tongue. Almost as much as the taste of her juices. And these days, she tastes extra sweet, making me insatiable for my sexy pregnant wife.

"Fuck, you taste so good, Sunny." She groans at my praise, her thighs contracting.

We're running out of time, so I focus on her clit and thoroughly lash at the tiny bud with the tip of my tongue before sucking it into my mouth. She chants my name again, and my cock turns to steel in my jeans. Swirling my tongue around the swollen nerves, she shutters, muscles quivering. I look up to see as she throws her head against the door, biting the back of her hand, muffling her cries of pleasure.

As much as I love to take my time, I really do need to be quick at making her come.

I shove two fingers deep inside her and tap her G-spot. Her body convulses instantly around my thick digits as her sweet honey floods my mouth. A feral growl rumbles deep in my chest as I lap at every last drop of her sweet cream.

She looks equally stunning and shattered as she comes down from her orgasm. Slowly removing my fingers from her center, I kiss her sensitive clit one last time. She sighs at my tender touch.

Before lowering her leg to the ground, I pepper her inner thighs and mound with kisses.

Sitting on my heels, I take in Rylann's swollen belly, running my hands over the firm bump. My chest puffs with pride as I stare at her stomach. She's six months along, and we couldn't be happier to be bringing baby number three into the world. Every time I see her carrying our child, I have to pinch myself to make sure I'm not dreaming. Watching her stomach round with my babies safely growing inside is the best gift I could ever ask for. She's made all my dreams come true with her big heart and beautiful soul.

Cradling her swollen belly in my hands, I place one last kiss on her taut skin before letting her dress fall over her hips. I stand, adjusting my uncomfortably hard dick in my boxer briefs when I catch Rylann staring at my cock, licking her lips.

"Don't look at me like that, Sun. We don't have time," I warn her. We've already been away from the kids long enough.

She reaches out and wraps her small hand around my shaft over my jeans, and gives it a light squeeze. "I think you can make it quick," she says, arching a mischievous brow at me.

Ry turns around and lifts her dress, exposing her ass. She places her hands on the door and looks over her shoulder at me before wiggling her bare ass. My cock grows harder, jumping at the idea of getting inside her hot wet center.

"Fuck it," I grunt, popping the button and unzipping my jeans.

The party can wait, but my woman can't. If she wants me to fuck her, than that's what I'm going to do. She could ask for anything, and I'd find a way to give it to her. She's my everything.

I pull my boxers and jeans down mid-thigh, releasing my stiff cock from its confines. Grabbing her hair, I twist her head to the side so I can claim her lips with mine. I notch my tip at her entrance and I pause, deepening our kiss, twining our tongues together. When she wiggles her ass again, the tip of my cock slips through her wet pussy.

I break our kiss with a grunt.

"Be a good girl and be quiet for me," I breathe into her ear before thrusting my hips forward, sheathing every one of my thick inches deep inside her.

We groan at our connection, and her pussy clenches around my dick. Her silky heat wrapped around my cock is the most incredible feeling. Her body was made for me to fill it.

"You feel so good. So wet. So tight." I pull out and push in with long hard strokes, moving slowly before taking her hard and fast. The way she likes it.

I reach around her waist and find her clit with my fingertips. Adding pressure to the bundle of nerves, I move my fingers in quick tight circles, bringing her to the edge as fast as I can. Her body responds as she pushes her ass into my dick, allowing me to take her harder.

"Fuck," I grunt, lost in the feel of her heat, the scent of her sweet skin.

I piston my hips faster, thrusting into her as deep as I can get. It's never deep enough with her. If I could bury myself inside her forever, I would.

"Yes, Ace. Just like that ... Give it to me," Ry whispers between moans.

She spreads her leg wider and lifts up onto her toes, urging me on. Her pussy muscles flutter as her orgasm builds with every hard stroke. Head to the side, I watch her eyes squeeze shut and her mouth part slightly as she whimpers in ecstasy. Releasing her hair, I lean back, hand on her hip, and watch her pussy swallow my cock. I love seeing our bodies connected, making us one.

Fuck, she looks good with my cock inside her.

My balls tingle, alerting me to my impending climax.

"I need you to come right fucking now. It's your turn to give it to me," I grunt out between clenched teeth.

Her legs tense. She's so close, but it's not enough. I give her ass a little swat while I furiously rubbing her clit, pushing her over the edge. She explodes around me, her pussy convulsing around my cock, taking me with her. I come so hard, my knees wobble as I release rope after rope of cum inside her. I drop my head to her back, trying to catch my breath. My hips shift, and I feel the aftershocks of her orgasm ripple through her, wringing my dick dry.

"Wow," she pants, chest heaving. "That was pretty amazing for a quickie."

"That wasn't quick, love. But it was mother-fucking fantastic." I chuckle, nipping at her shoulder.

I stand up, and I watch as my softening cock slips out of her channel, sending my cum dripping down her thighs.

Fuck, that's hot.

My cock perks up at the prospect of round two. I love filling her up with my cum and watching it trickle out of her pretty pussy. If she wasn't already pregnant, I'd probably shove it back inside her and fuck her with my fingers again to make sure it stays inside her.

"Stop looking at me like that, you caveman. I'm already knocked up." She scowls, turning around to face me, straightening her dress down.

I shove my dick back into my boxer briefs and zip up before grabbing her hips, pulling her to my chest. Locking my arms around her, I kiss the shit out of her.

"I can't help it." I peck her bee-stung lips again. "I love seeing you pregnant."

"I know, but this is the last one."

This has been a topic of conversation lately. It's also an argument she can't win. She might be done, but I'm not. My love will be giving me one more baby, even if I have to ply her with cheap margaritas and fuck her raw in the bathroom at her favorite restaurant. Again.

It wouldn't be the first time we used that bathroom as our own personal fuck spot. She doesn't believe me when I tell her that's where I knocked her up with our son the night of our rehearsal dinner. I can't wait to do it again.

What can I say? Bathrooms do it for me. Rylann does it for me.

She's right, though. I've turned into a caveman where she's concerned. She brings it out in me. I can't get enough of her, pregnant or not. But missing the pregnancy and birth of our first son, I have this primal urge in me to make up for the loss.

She cups my jaw in her warm palm, her eyes searching mine.

She sees my internal battle. "Ugh, fine." She sighs. "I know what you're thinking. You win. One more after this. But that's it, Ace. No more. I can't redo having Rhys for you. I'm sorry."

She looks down, and I feel like an asshole for making her feel guilty.

When we went to therapy the first year we were together, I made a promise to her and to me, that I would willingly let go of the resentment I held towards her and Sam. Over their choices. For missing so much of Rhys's life.

It wasn't easy, but once I accepted that if I didn't let it go I could lose her, it was a no-brainer. The thought of losing Rylann wasn't worth holding onto my anger. If I don't have a life with her, I don't have a life at all. I know. I lived that life. It was dark. I felt lost and incomplete. Lonely. I never want to be there again.

This is where I belong, with her and our children. With them, I'm whole. I love this gorgeous woman more than anything in the world.

Tilting her chin up, I look into her eyes. Worry and guilt swirl in her cocoa-brown depths instead of the love I've grown accustomed to. I need to see her eyes glow with love, not doubt.

"I know, Sunshine. I'm sorry if I implied that. I want a big family—you know this." She nods, so I continue. "But every time we have another baby, it feels like I get to wipe the slate clean. Like it somehow erases the fact that I missed all those years. I know it's stupid, and the last thing I want is for you to feel guilty. I promise, I let go of all that shit a long time ago. But in here,"—I place her hand on my chest, over my beating heart—"it's not enough to erase the need to see you have our children. You are a wonderful mother. I love watching you grow them, care for them, love them, dote on them. Everything. I love you so fucking much. You're my whole damn world. You and our babies. You mean everything to me. And well, that kind of love is addicting. I just want more of it. I'm not ready to give it up yet."

"How are you so dang sweet? You have got to be the swooniest husband alive. I love you so much, Jace Miller," she replies with her dimpled smile that makes my chest tighten every time I see it light up her face. "My soulmate, the love of my life, father to my children. You own me, heart and soul."

My beautiful wife tugs my face to hers in a loving kiss that's just like her heart, soft and sweet. I drown in the taste of her, cupping her perky ass cheeks and squeezing them in my hands. My fingers inch toward her bare center.

Catching me off guard, Rylan breaks our kiss and pushes my chest away, and I stumble back.

"No more. I need to clean up, and you need to go before the kids or Scarlett show up out of nowhere, looking for us."

"You've walked in on her and Levi. I say it's fair play." I scoff.

"While that's true,"—she shivers in mock disgust and continues shoving me out the door—"hard pass, husband. We are too old for that."

She opens the door and points to the hallway. I do as she asks and back out into the hallway, so she can clean up.

"We're not too old to fuck in the bathroom at Blue Cantina after margaritas, are we?" I ask because I know it's gonna rile her up.

She slams the door in my face, and yells, "You're a pig!"

"Sun?"

I wait for it ... Three, two, one.

"No! We're not. Now, go away, you dirty old man," she shouts at me through the closed door.

I walk away, laughing.

We will be fucking in that bathroom as soon as she's ready for baby number four, in about six to eight months.

The sooner the better.

Squeals of delight fill the air as I push Sariah—Riah for short—on the swing in our backyard.

Her sweet laugh brings me so much joy, my chest warms with a squall of love for my little girl.

"Dada, high. High!" my baby girl squeals.

"Yes, princess. High enough to touch the sky."

Her pudgy little hands reach up and her fingers claw at the air, making me chuckle.

She's the spitting image of her momma—dark brown hair, deep chocolatey eyes that shine, and dimples for days. She also has me wrapped around her little fingers, just like her brother and her momma. I'm going to be in major trouble when she becomes a teenager.

I don't know how my father-in-law, Ryan, managed to survive raising Rylann and Scarlett.

Glancing over to the windows in our kitchen, I catch a glimpse of my wife, laughing and dancing with Scarlett while they prep food. Rylann is wearing a soft yellow wrap dress and apron for the party, and she's never looked more stunning.

My heart skips a beat at the smile on her face. That smile still has the ability to make me feel as warm as the morning sun that shines down on me.

My sunshine.

Scarlett says something that has Rylann's head snapping back in laughter. Her dimples pop on her cheek, and I almost rush inside to kiss them. I refrain, only because I don't want to upset the princess on her special day.

I still hate being away from Rylann for long. We haven't spent a day apart since we got engaged, and I don't plan on ever being away from her again. It's been a little over two years since we found our way back to each other, and I'm still ravenous for her love and affection.

I can't get enough of her. I doubt I ever will. That woman owns me, and I wouldn't have it any other way.

I think back to our earlier tryst in the bathroom. My face between her legs. My cock buried deep inside her pussy. I adjust myself, grateful to have snuck her away for a little rendezvous before everyone arrives for Riah's Birthday Party.

My little princess is officially one today.

Along with my in-laws, the whole Miller gang will be here to help us celebrate. They never miss an opportunity to spoil the only girl in the Miller bunch. My poor daughter not only has a protective dad and older brother to put up with, but she also has three overbearing uncles to boot.

I look up at the clubhouse to find Rhys sitting up there, reading alone. He escaped to his hiding place as soon as I came outside to push Riah on the swing, no doubt counting down until his uncles get here to either throw or kick a ball around with him. He's avoiding the twin tornadoes that are currently throwing plastic balls at each other in the ballpit, and from the looks of it, he's avoiding Sadie and Lily too, who are in the small house Levi built.

I shake my head. Not even teenagers yet, and there's trouble in paradise.

I'm grateful for the littles. They might be exhausting, but they are definitely less drama. I look at the joint playhouse Levi and I expanded over the last year. We made it more toddler-friendly for Riah and Levi's boys, aka the twin tornadoes, Landyn and Sawyer. The three of them together are absolute terrors together. Since they all started walking, we grown-ups have had our hands full.

"Alright, princess, it's time for a break." I slow the swing to a stop and pull my girl out of the seat, placing her on my hip.

I prefer to carry her, even though she's officially a walker. The day she took her first steps, I cried. Not only because my baby girl is growing so fast, but because I know I will never miss another moment with my children again.

"Rhys!" I call out. He looks down at me through the mini window. "I'm going to go sit down with Uncle Lee. The rest of your uncles will be here soon."

"Okay, Dad." He gives me a quick salute and puts his nose back in his book.

If he's not playing soccer or baseball, he's either reading or taking pictures with the camera I bought him in Hawaii. He's grown so much this past year. He's embraced being a big brother with open arms. Watching him dote on his baby sister always brings a smile to my face. He's so patient with her, I have no doubt he will grow to be a wonderful man.

I glance up at him one more time, my chest tightening with love and adoration for my boy, before making my way to the deck with Riah. After placing her on the playmat with her toys, I glance around. The whole space is decorated with balloons, signs, cupcakes, and flowers in rainbow colors. Apparently, the theme is "sprinkles".

I don't get it, but my wife's enthusiasm for the decor brings a smile to my face. She loves celebrating birthdays. She likes them to be extra special. I think she makes every day special with her presence alone.

Honesty, she can do whatever she wants. She can decorate the entire house from top to bottom with streamers and balloons for all I care. As long as I get to have her in my arms every night from now until forever, I'll have everything I need.

Taking a deep breath, I take a seat next to Lee at the table.

"Tired of pushing the swing?" Levi reaches into the cooler at his side, pulling out a beer and handing it to me.

"You know it. I don't understand how they can sit in that thing for hours and never get bored." We laugh at how true that statement is.

Kids fucking love swings.

I crack open the beer and take a sip, leaning back in my chair with a sigh.

"For real, how are you doing today?" He tilts his head to the side, studying me.

The downside of having a lawyer as your best friend is that he can read you without having to dig deep.

"Good, good. Just ... feeling a little introspective today, I guess. Seeing as it's Sariah's birthday and all," I say, shrugging him off.

I won't mention how I made my wife feel like shit earlier. I plan on remedying that later tonight. Show her how much I love her.

"I get that. It's crazy how fast the days slip by when you have kids."

I nod, taking another sip of my beer. Levi and I sit and watch the kids play from across the yard.

"What are you two doing, sitting over here and leaving the twins unsupervised?" Scarlett asks.

"Oh, they're fine, Short Stack." Levi pulls Scar into his lap and kisses her. They're still as affectionate and sweet on each other as the day they met. "The plastic balls can't hurt them."

Nails run through my hair, scratching my scalp. Every hair on my body stands on end.

Fuck, I love it when she does that. It's always turned me the fuck on, and my cock agrees, twitching in my pants.

Standing behind me, Rylann runs her hands through my hair again, down my neck, and over my chest. She rests her chin on my shoulder before whispering, "Hey, hubs. You miss me?"

"Always," I answer. I place my hands over hers and pull her around and place her in my lap, where she belongs.

We watch Riah quietly play as I knead the small of Rylann's back. I run my palm over her hard stomach, feeling our son kick my hand. He's a feisty little guy.

"Aww, look how sweet you two are. But don't go trying to sneak off to the bathroom. I refuse to watch three babies," Scarlett sasses.

"Jesus, love, you told her," I groan, making Scarlett cackle.

"I did not! You just did," Rylann says, slapping my chest with a cackle like her best friend.

I shake my head at these two troublemakers.

"Oh, please. I knew as soon as I saw her. That glow was not a pregnancy glow. It was sex glow. Besides, her hair was all messed up. Dead giveaway."

"Why do we put up with her?" I gripe, ducking as Scarlett reaches out to smack me.

"She moved in next door, and I couldn't shake her," Rylann muses, lips puckered, holding back a laugh at Scarlett's crazy.

"I know what you mean." I nod, throwing a thumb at Levi. "Same."

"Hey now. Remember, I escaped you. You're the one that couldn't get enough of me and had to fall for my woman's best friend and move in next door. You're such a stalker."

"You're such a dick."

The four of us laugh, and this is par for the course with us. Laughing, messing with each other, having dinner, going on trips. We do everything together.

It's been awesome living next to my best friend like when we were kids. Only now, it's us raising and watching our children together as they become lifelong friends. It's pretty damn special. I love my life.

"So when are you two having the next one?" I ask.

Levi chokes on his beer while Scarlett gasps.

"How dare you say such a horrible thing, Jace Miller? I hope your balls shrivel up for even mentioning the word 'babies'. Just so you know, I will not be having more. In fact, this one is having a vasectomy." She points at Levi, who grunts and looks away.

Yeah, I doubt he's getting one of those.

"What's wrong with having more babies?" Rylann asks, puzzled by Scarlett's reaction.

Her question brings a smile to my face, considering our conversation in the bathroom. I squeeze my wife tight, kissing her shoulder. I'm definitely going to have to make it up to her tonight.

"Nothing. For you. You don't keep reproducing duplicates. Hell-to-the-no for me. I can't do it again," Scarlett complains, waving her hand around in the air, her head snapping side to side.

I'm not surprised—two sets of twins must be hard to manage.

"Can't do what anymore?" Mason's voice cuts in from the side of the house. Once again, he's bypassed the front door. Not that it matters. Since he's moved into the neighborhood, he's been here more often than not. Him and his wife.

"Have any more of Levi's devil twins," Scarlett retorts.

"Fuck, Scar. Seriously?"

She rolls her eyes, then grabs Levi's face and inappropriately kisses him.

My friend immediately melts, completely whipped by his wife. I guess he will be getting that vasectomy after all since Scarlett owns his balls.

Mason holds up both hands. "Sorry I asked." He takes a seat at the table with us.

"Beer?"

"If I have to listen to this, then yes. And keep them coming," he grumbles like the surly asshole he is. He nods, and Levi hands a beer. Mason cracks it open, taking a swig.

"Where's your better half?" Rylann asks Mason.

"She'll be here soon. She went to the event and to make sure everything was set up to their liking."

"I keep telling her she needs to fret less and let the interns manage without her," Scarlett adds in.

"From your lips to my wife's ears," he says, a smile playing on his lips. I love seeing him happy these days. It looks better on him than the grumpy mug he used to sport.

It's not long before my in-laws arrive. Followed by my parents, Cameron, and Eli with arms full of gifts.

The whole Miller crew arrives, ready to spoil the only girl in the bunch.

With the help of my budding photographer, Rhys and I snap picture after picture of our family throughout the day. We capture Riah as she smashes and eats her cake, tears the wrapping paper of her many gifts, and of her being carried around like the princess she is by everyone.

Riah's party is exactly what Rylann hoped it would be when she planned it—a day full of love and laughter, surrounded by our entire family.

I couldn't ask for a better way to celebrate my baby girl, my family, my life.

My life is full.

"Good night, Dad."

"Good night, kiddo. I love you."

"I love you too," Rhys says with a yawn.

Rylann and I split bedtime duties to speed up the process. She's taking care of a crabby Riah while I lucked out and got to hang with Rhys tonight.

We are working our way through the *Percy Jackson* books, and I've been enjoying our time together reading. I love spending time with him. We have regular guy-time activities. Sometimes, it's just a trip to the ice cream shop, and for others, it's trips to go fishing or attend soccer and baseball games. My hope is that, on some level, it makes up for some of the things we missed out on when he was little.

I rub at the center spot of my chest. It still aches with the loss of missing his early years. Not as much as it used to. Day by day, the pain lessens.

I was truthful when I told Ry that I put all that behind me. But sometimes, I can't help the ache. I love my son.

I watch Rhys curl up into a ball on his side. His breaths slowly even out as he falls asleep. I'm about to shut off the light when I catch a glimpse of the framed photo on Rhys's bookshelf.

Picking up the wood frame, I stare at the picture. It's a snapshot of a three-year-old Rhys, sporting a dimpled grin, on the shoulders of a tall blond-haired man. Sam.

Over the years, namely after watching Rylann carry Sariah and watching my daughter come into the world, have I come to understand him more. I would give anything in the world to feel that kind of joy. That raw, inexplicable happiness that comes with watching your child be born. I'm not saying what he did was right, but he did do right by Rylann and Rhys. That means something to me.

He took care of them when my choices lead me on a different path. He loved and supported the woman that owns my heart. He protected and healed her.

He made her whole so that when I found her again, she would be ready and waiting for me.

His sliver of happiness is nothing compared to what I've gained and will gain in the future. I have so much more. I have a long life ahead of me. I have air in my lungs. I have an abundance of love. I have my kids.

I have her.

I place the photo on the shelf and tell him the same thing I always do.

Thanks for watching out for them. I promise I have them now. Rest in peace, man.

I'm laying in bed, exhausted from the day, wishing my wife would hurry up in the bathroom already. The door swings open and the light clicks off.

Ry makes her way over to our king bed, wearing a sports bra and pregnancy panties. She hates them, but I think they're sexy as fuck.

She is by far the most beautiful woman I have ever seen.

I throw back the covers, patting the spot beside me. I hid her pregnancy pillow in the closet, so she's going to have to use me to get comfortable for now.

Or at least until after I have my way with her.

"Ace, where's my pillow?"

"Right here, Sunshine." I wave my hand over my body and wiggle my brows at her.

"Jay ..." She pouts, hands on her hips.

"Ry ..." I reply, matching her tone.

She growls in frustration. Giving in, she climbs into bed, entwines her legs with mine, and rests her head on my chest.

I take a deep breath, inhaling her sweet coconut scent, letting it sink in and soothe me like I do every night.

"You know, stealing a pregnant lady's pillow is hazardous to your health. In fact, it can lead to death."

I bark out a laugh at her snark. Pulling her closer to my side, I drop a kiss on her forehead. "You can have it back later."

I run my fingers over the smooth skin of her shoulder as she nuzzles into my side. She draws circles on my chest, and I almost purr like a damn cat.

When she grazes my dick with her inner thigh, making it perk up, I bite back a groan.

Before I make love to her and get lost in her body for the rest of the night, I need to clear the air. Our conversation in the bathroom has been bugging me all day. I feel like made her question my forgiveness and acceptance of the past earlier. She needs to know it has nothing to do with that.

She has more than proved to me with her honesty and vulnerability that she didn't maliciously set out to hurt me.

When we broke up all those years ago, I didn't understand the extent to which she grieved the loss of our relationship. Grieved me. She thought I was lost to her forever. So she did what she needed to do to keep moving forward. Better than I did, at least.

Looking back, I can see that I was drifting through life. Alone. Hurt. I was lost. Stuck in a dark place.

Not anymore.

"Sun?"

"Hmmm ..."

"I'm sorry for what I said in the bathroom earlier."

"Ace, it's fine."

"No. It's not fine. I hate hurting you. I want you to know that I will choose better words next time. Everything that happened back then is truly in the past for me. I swear it."

I roll my head to my side so we're face to face. Brushing her hair back behind her ear, I kiss her neck, sending goosebumps across her tan skin. She closes her eyes, and I press more kisses across her chest and jaw before kissing her mouth.

When she opens her big brown eyes, they shine with so much love. The warmth of their gaze heats me from the inside out.

"I believe you," she whispers before kissing my chest.

"You make me so unbelievably happy. I cannot fathom a life without you. Or our kids."

"You make me so happy too, Ace." She cups my jaw and runs her thumb across my bottom lip. "You and our babies."

"I love you so fucking much it hurts. Always have."

"Always will," she finishes.

She tips her lips up to mine and kisses me. It's not long before our kiss deepens, hands roam, hips grind, and I spend the rest of the night inside my wife.

Showing her over and over how much I love her.

When she's worn out like boiled spaghetti in my arms, I retrieve her pillow from the closet, spooning her until she finally falls asleep.

I stay up staring at the angel next to me, cocooned by the biggest pile of fluff I've ever seen.

I think back to the first time I met her. The electricity that zapped between us. Pulling us together. Our connection was so strong and intense.

In a moment of weakness, I ignored what my gut was telling me and I walked away. It was the biggest mistake of my life.

But I think I needed to make those mistakes so that we could have the life we do now. Free from past obstacles.

What we feel for each other, what we share, is one of a kind. Our love is a once-in-a-lifetime kind of love.

I know without a shadow of a doubt that I'm home when I'm with her. She is the other half of my soul.

Her love warms me from the inside out. She brightens my world, making everything vivid and sun-soaked.

My sunshine.

The light and love of my life.

Always has been and always will be.

THE END

Want to see how Jace and Rylann spent their engagement night? Curious who the next brother Miller brother is to find their girl?

Grab the Spicy Bonus Chapter & Sneak Peek at Chapter One of book two in the Miller Brothers series.
https://dl.bookfunnel.com/34sd3yx5gj

Please consider leaving a review on Amazon/Goodreads/Book-Bub.
They help indie authors like me SO MUCH!

Back of the Book Stuff

ACKNOWLEDGEMENTS

First, THANK YOU, my lovely reader, for taking a chance on this newbie author. This story is my book baby, and it means the world to me that you picked it and gave it a read. I hope it gave you all the feels and you got the HEA you wanted.

Super special thanks to my hubs. You have supported me through this entire process and I can't thank you enough for it. I'll never forget talking your ear off about my dream and your—not-so-subtle—suggestion to write it down. Well ... I did it. I hope I make you proud. I love you.

JKL, you guys own my heart. I love you so much. I know it got a little crazy at the end, but you three were champs. Thank you for supporting me throughout this journey and for all the times you tried not to bug me while I was writing. Yes. You can have a dessert now.

Big thanks to my family. I am so grateful for your endless support in my choice to write *sexy lady novels.*

Mommy, THANK YOU for being my number one fan, my rock, my soul mate, my everything. Yeah, I said it. 1, 2, 3 ... Mom.

I love you, doll face. You're the best mom there ever was. Xoxo88. Eleven more words.

Huge thanks to my writing bestie. My savior. C, without your unwavering love and support I don't know if I would have finished. Okay, you're right. I would have. It just would have taken me a lot longer. Love you, girl. I can't wait to return the favor. IOU big time.

To Swalls. eThank you for letting me use our friendship, your beautiful personality and heart as inspiration. I miss you and all our crazy hot fish adventures. Wish I could have kept you closer. Love you to pieces.

Special thanks to Pat and Danielle–your feedback made this story better. I hope you're ready for the next one.

To my stroller mom group; thank you for kind words—although sometimes inappropriate—your support, and love. I always look forward to our monthly dates.

To the team that brought this all together, THANK YOU. Life threw some wrenches at us but we all came out on the other side, and I couldn't be happier with the results. Nina, thanks for editing my book. Your kind notes literally brought me to tears when I needed them. Sarah, thank you for listening to me and creating the brand and website I envisioned. Echo, thank you for your tireless efforts to bring my book cover to life. I promise no more lei's.

And last but not least. Thank you Sam for visiting me in my dreams and begging me to give your girl the HEA she deserved. I hope I did it justice.

About Leslie Ann

LA resides in Westchester, NY with her husband, three sons, and wildly friendly dog, Pepper. This pink-haired, sneaker-wearing Cali girl is, and always will be, an avid reader of all things romance. She loves tea, summer, cooking, arts & crafts, and chilling at home with a glass of wine. When she's not reading or writing, she's watching her boys play soccer or watching their favorite team play. You can bet her stories will have that happily ever after you crave. Every. Time.

Stay Connected

Keep up with all things LA ...

Website lawritesromance.com
Instagram @la.writes.romance
Tiktok @la.writes.romance
Facebook @Leslie Ann
Pinterest @Leslie Ann Author
Amazon @lawritesromance
BookBub @LeslieAnnAuthor